Dear Reader—

Every author dreads the question, "Where do you get your ideas?" because the truth is, most of the time we just don't know. All we can do is hope and pray that they keep coming.

But sometimes we do actually know where those precious ideas come from, and *To Catch an Heiress* is one of those cases. I was struggling with the manuscript, thinking that it had to be the worst thing I'd ever written. (But of course I think that about every book while I'm writing it!) Most troubling, I wasn't sure I really knew Caroline, my heroine, and if there is one thing I need, it's to know my characters inside and out.

And then, right when I was just about ready to tear my hair out, my father did something *really* vexing. He subscribed me to the "A Word a Day" listserv. As if I weren't busy enough trying to finish a troublesome manuscript, now I was getting unsolicited vocabulary lessons via email!

But then it all fell into place. I knew who Caroline was, and I knew how to make the reader know, too. Caroline would keep a sort of diary—a personal dictionary, really, in which she jotted down new words and then used them in context. And every new entry would provide the reader (and me!) with a little more insight into her character. Flip to the first page of any chapter in this book, and you'll see what I mean. From that moment on, the-manuscript-that-wouldn't-behave became the-book-that-wrote-itself. I hope you enjoy it.

With my warmest wishes,

Julia Q.

Other Avon Romances by
Julia Quinn

ROMANCING MISTER BRIDGERTON
AN OFFER FROM A GENTLEMAN
THE VISCOUNT WHO LOVED ME
THE DUKE AND I
HOW TO MARRY A MARQUIS
BRIGHTER THAN THE SUN
EVERYTHING AND THE MOON
MINX
DANCING AT MIDNIGHT
SPLENDID

ATTENT[illegible]: ORGANIZATIONS AND CORPORATIONS
Most Avon [illegible]ks paperbacks are available at special quantity discounts for [illegible] purchases for sales promotions, premiums, or fund-raising. F[illegible]formation, please call or write:

Special Markets [illegible]artment, HarperCollins Publishers, Inc., 10 East 53rd Stre[illegible], New York, New York 10022-5299. Telephone: (212) 207-7528. Fax: (212) 207-7222.

Julia Quinn

To Catch An Heiress

AVON BOOKS
An Imprint of HarperCollins*Publishers*

This is a work of fiction. Names, characters, places, and incidents are products of the author's imagination or are used fictitiously and are not to be construed as real. Any resemblance to actual events, locales, organizations, or persons, living or dead, is entirely coincidental.

AVON BOOKS
An Imprint of HarperCollins*Publishers*
10 East 53rd Street
New York, New York 10022-5299

ISBN: 0-380-78935-3
www.avonromance.com

First Avon Books paperback printing: July 1998

Printed in the U.S.A.

10 9 8 7

For Mama Chiks, Sister Song, Freener, and Nosk
from Bools

And also for Paul, even though it's a miracle
I got this book finished at all since
he kept stealing my computer to play DOOM.

Chapter 1

con·tu·ber·nal *(noun). One who occupies the same tent; a tent-fellow, comrade.*

The thought of Percy Prewitt as my contubernal *causes me to break out in hives.*

—From the personal dictionary of Caroline Trent

Hampshire, England
July 3, 1814

Caroline Trent hadn't meant to shoot Percival Prewitt, but she had, and now he was dead.

Or at least she thought he was dead. There was certainly enough blood. It was dripping from the walls, it was splattered on the floor, and the bedclothes were stained quite beyond redemption. Caroline didn't know very much about medicine, but she was fairly certain a body couldn't lose that much blood and still live.

She was in big trouble now.

"Damn," she muttered. Although she was a gentlewoman, she hadn't always been raised in particularly gentle circumstances, and her language occasionally left a bit to be desired.

"You stupid man," she said to the body on the floor. "Why did you have to lunge at me like that? Why couldn't you have left well enough alone? I told your father I wasn't going to marry you. I told him I wouldn't marry you if you were the last idiot in Britain."

She nearly stamped her foot in frustration. Why was it her words never came out quite the way she intended them to? "What I meant to say was that you are an idiot," she said to Percy, who, not surprisingly, didn't respond, "and that I wouldn't marry you if you were the last man in Britain, and—Oh, blast. What am I doing talking to you, anyway? You're quite dead."

Caroline groaned. What the devil was she supposed to do now? Percy's father was due to return in just two short hours, and it didn't require an Oxford degree to deduce that Oliver Prewitt would not be pleased to find his son dead on the floor.

"Bother your father," she ground out. "This is all his fault, anyway. If he hadn't been so obsessed with catching you an heiress . . ."

Oliver Prewitt was Caroline's guardian, or at least he would be for the next six weeks, until she reached her twenty-first birthday. She had been counting down the days until August 14, 1814, ever since August 14, 1813, when she had turned twenty. Just forty-two days to go. Forty-two days and she would finally have control of her life and her fortune. She didn't even want to think about how much of her inheritance the Prewitts had already run through.

She tossed her gun onto the bed, planted her hands on her hips, and stared down at Percy.

And then . . . his eyes opened.

"Aaaaaaack!" Caroline let out a loud scream, jumped a foot, and grabbed her gun.

"You b—" Percy started.

"Don't say it," she warned. "I still have a gun."

"You wouldn't use it," he gasped, coughing and clutching at his bloody shoulder.

"I beg your pardon, but the evidence seems to indicate otherwise."

Percy's thin lips clamped into a straight line. He swore viciously, and then lifted his furious gaze to Caroline. "I told my father I didn't want to marry you," he hissed. "God! Can you imagine? Having to live with you for the rest of my life? I should go bloody insane. If you didn't kill me first, that is."

"If you didn't want to marry me you shouldn't have tried to force yourself upon me."

He shrugged, then howled when the movement sparked pain in his shoulder. He looked quite furious as he said, "You've quite a bit of money, but do you know, I don't think you're worth it."

"Kindly tell that to your father," Caroline snapped.

"He said he'd disinherit me if I didn't marry you."

"And you couldn't stand up to him for once in your pathetic life?"

Percy growled at being called pathetic, but in his weakened condition he couldn't do much about the insult. "I could go to America," he muttered. "Surely savages have to be a better option than *you*."

Caroline ignored him. She and Percy had been at odds since she had come to live with the Prewitts a year and a half earlier. Percy was quite under his father's thumb, and the only time he showed any spirit was when Oliver quit the house. Unfortunately, his spirit was usually mean and small and, in Caroline's opinion, rather dull.

"I suppose I'm going to have to save you now," she grumbled. "You're certainly not worth the gallows."

"You're too kind."

Caroline shook a pillow out of its case, wadded up the cloth—the highest quality linen, she noted, probably purchased with her money—and pressed it against Percy's wound. "We have to stop the bleeding," she said.

"It appears to have slowed down," Percy admitted.

"Did the bullet go straight through?"

"I don't know. Hurts like the devil, but I don't know if it's supposed to hurt more if it goes through or gets stuck in the muscle."

"I imagine they're both quite painful," Caroline said, lifting the wadded pillowcase and examining the wound. She turned him gently and looked at his back. "I think it went through. You've a hole in the back of your shoulder as well."

"Trust you to injure me twice."

"You lured me into your room under the pretense of needing a cup of tea for a head cold," she snapped, "and then you tried to rape me! What did you expect?"

"Why the hell did you bring a gun?"

"I always carry a gun," she replied. "I have since . . . well, never you mind."

"I wouldn't have gone through with it," he muttered.

"How was I to know that?"

"Well, you know I've never liked you."

Caroline pressed her makeshift bandage against Percy's bloody shoulder with perhaps a touch more force than was necessary. "What I *know*," she spat out, "is that you and your father have always quite liked my inheritance."

"I think I dislike you more than I like your inheritance," Percy grumbled. "You're too bossy by half, you're not even pretty, and you've the serpent's own tongue."

Caroline clamped her mouth into a grim line. If she had a sharp way of speaking, it wasn't her fault. She'd learned quickly that her wits were her only defense against the parade of horrible guardians she'd been forced to endure since her father's passing when she was ten. First there had been George Liggett, her father's first cousin. He hadn't been such a bad sort, but he certainly didn't know what to do with a small girl. So he'd smiled at her once—just once, mind you—told her he was happy to meet her, and then tossed her into a country home with a nurse and governess. And then he proceeded to ignore her.

But George had died, and her guardianship had passed on to *his* first cousin, who was no relation of hers or her father's. Niles Wickham was a mean old miser who'd seen a ward as a good substitute for a serving girl, and he'd immediately given her a list of chores longer than her arm. Caroline had cooked, cleaned, ironed, polished, scrubbed, and swept. The only thing she *hadn't* done was sleep.

Niles, however, had choked on a chicken bone, turned quite purple, and died. The courts were at a bit of a loss as to what to do with Caroline, who at fifteen seemed too well-bred and wealthy to toss into an orphanage, so they passed her guardianship on to Archibald Prewitt, Niles's second cousin. Archibald had been a lewd man who'd found Caroline entirely too attractive for her comfort, and it was then that she began her habit of keeping a weapon on her person at all times. Archibald had had a weak heart, however, and so Caroline had only had to live with him for six months before she attended his funeral and was packed off to live with his younger brother Albert.

Albert drank too much and used his fists, which resulted in Caroline's learning how to run fast and hide well. Archibald may have tried to grope her on every occasion, but Albert was a mean drunk, and when he struck her, it *hurt*. She also became quite adept at smelling spirits from across a room. Albert never raised a hand against her when he was sober.

But, unfortunately, Albert was rarely sober, and in one of his drunken rages he kicked his horse so hard that his horse kicked him back. Right in the head. By then Caroline was quite used to moving about, so as soon as the surgeon pulled the sheet over Albert's face, she packed her bag and waited for the courts to decide where to send her next.

She soon found herself residing with Albert's younger brother Oliver and his son, the currently bleeding Percy. At first Oliver had seemed the best of the bunch, but Caroline quickly realized that Oliver cared for nothing so much as money. Once he learned that his ward came with a rather large portion, he decided that Caroline—and her money—would not escape his grasp. Percy was only a few years older than Caroline, so Oliver announced that they would marry. Neither of the prospective couple was pleased by this plan, and they said so, but Oliver didn't care. He needled Percy until Percy agreed, and then he set about convincing Caroline that she ought to become a Prewitt.

"Convincing" entailed screaming at her, slapping her about, starving her, locking her in her room, and finally ordering Percy to get her with child so that she'd *have* to marry him.

"I'd rather bring it up a bastard than a Prewitt," Caroline muttered.

"What was that?" Percy asked.

"Nothing."

"You're going to have to leave, you know," he said, abruptly changing the subject.

"Believe me, that fact is quite clear."

"Father told me that if I don't get you with child, he'll take care of it himself."

Caroline very nearly threw up. "I beg your pardon?" she said, her voice uncharacteristically shaky. Even Percy was preferable to Oliver.

"I don't know where you can go, but you need to disappear until your twenty-first birthday, which is . . . when? . . . soon, I think."

"Six weeks," Caroline whispered. "Six weeks exactly."

"Can you do it?"

"Hide?"

Percy nodded.

"I'll have to, won't I? I'll need funds, though. I have a bit of pin money, but I don't have access to my inheritance until my birthday."

Percy winced as Caroline peeled the cloth away from his shoulder. "I can give you a little," he said.

"I'll pay you back. With interest."

"Good. You'll have to leave tonight."

Caroline looked around the room. "But the mess . . . We have to clean up the blood."

"No, leave it. Better I let you get away because you shot me than because I simply botched the plan."

"One of these days you're going to have to stand up to your father."

"It'll be easier with you gone. There is a perfectly nice girl two towns over I've a mind to court. She's quiet and biddable, and not nearly as skinny as you."

Caroline immediately pitied the poor girl. "I hope everything works out for you," she lied.

"No, you don't. But I don't care. Really doesn't matter what you think, as long as you're gone."

"Do you know, Percy, but that is precisely how I feel about you?"

Amazingly, Percy smiled, and for the first time in the eighteen months since Caroline had come to live with the youngest branch of the Prewitts, she felt a sense of kinship with this boy who was so nearly her age.

"Where will you go?" he asked.

"Better you don't know. That way your father can't badger it out of you."

"Good point."

"Besides, I haven't a clue. I haven't any relations, you know. That is how I ended up here with you. But after ten years of defending myself against my ever-so-caring guardians, I should think I should be able to manage in the outside world for six weeks."

"If any female can do it, it would be you."

Caroline raised her brows. "Why Percy, was that a compliment? I'm stunned."

"It wasn't even close to being a compliment. What kind of man would want a woman who could get along quite well without him?"

"The kind who could get along quite well without his *father*," Caroline retorted.

Percy scowled as he flicked his head toward his bureau. "Open up the top drawer . . . no, the one on the right . . ."

"Percy, these are your undergarments!" Caroline exclaimed, slamming the drawer shut in disgust.

"Do you want me to lend you money or not? That's where I hide it."

"Well, it stands to reason that no one would want to look in there," she murmured. "Perhaps if you bathed more often . . ."

"God!" he burst out. "I cannot wait until you leave. You, Caroline Trent, are the devil's own daughter. You are plague. You are pestilence. You are—"

"Oh, shut up!" She yanked the drawer back open, disgusted with how much his words stung. She didn't like Percy any better than he liked her, but who would enjoy being compared to locusts, gnats, and frogs; the Black Death; and rivers turning to blood? "Where is the money?" she demanded.

"In my stocking . . . no, the black one . . . no, not that black one . . . yes, over there, next to the . . . yes, that's it."

Caroline found the stocking in question and shook out some bills and coins. "Good heavens, Percy, you must have a hundred pounds here. Where did you get this much?"

"I've been saving for quite some time. And I nick a coin or two each month from Father's desk. As long as I don't take too much, he never notices."

Caroline found that hard to believe; Oliver Prewitt was so obsessed with money it was a wonder his skin hadn't turned the color of pound notes.

"You can take half of it," Percy said.

"Only half? Don't be stupid, Percy. I need to hide for six weeks. I may have unexpected expenses."

"*I* may have unexpected expenses."

"You have a roof over your head!" she burst out.

"I might not, once Father discovers I let you get away."

Caroline had to concede his point. Oliver Prewitt was *not* going to be pleased with his only son. She dumped half the money back into the stocking. "Very well," she said, stuffing her share into her pocket. "You have the bleeding under control?"

"You won't be charged with murder, if that's what you're worried about."

"It may be difficult for you to believe, Percy, but I don't want you to die. I don't want to marry you, and I certainly won't be sorry if I never clap eyes on you again, but I don't want you to die."

Percy looked at her oddly, and for a moment Caroline thought he was actually going to say something nice (or at least something as nice as she'd said) in return. But he just snorted. "You're right. I do find it hard to believe."

At that moment, Caroline decided to dispense with any last shred of sentimentality she might be feeling and stomped to the door. Hand on the knob, she said, "I'll see you in six weeks—when I come to collect my inheritance."

"And pay me back," he reminded her.

"And pay you back. With interest," she added before he could.

"Good."

"On the other hand," she said, mostly to herself, "there might be a way to conduct my affairs without meeting with the Prewitts again. I could do everything through a solicitor, and—"

"Even better," Percy interrupted.

Caroline let out a very loud, very irritated exhale and quit the room. Percy was never going to change. He was rude, he was selfish, and even if he was marginally nicer than his father—well, that still made him a boorish lout.

She scurried along the dark corridor and up a flight of stairs to her room. Funny how her guardians always gave her rooms in the attics. Oliver had been worse than most, relegating her to a dusty corner with low ceilings and deep eaves. But if he had meant to break her spirit he had failed. Caroline loved her cozy room. It was closer to the sky. She could hear the rain against the ceiling, and she could watch the tree branches bud in spring. Birds nested outside her window, and squirrels occasionally ran along her ledge.

As she threw her most prized belongings into a bag, she stopped to peer out the window. It had been a cloudless day and now the sky was remarkably clear. It somehow seemed fitting that this should be a starry night. Caroline had few memories of her mother, but she could recall sitting on her lap outside on summer nights, staring up at the stars. "Look at that one," Cassandra Trent would whisper. "I think it's the brightest one in the sky. And look over there. Can you see the bear?" Their outings had always ended with Cassandra saying, "Each star is special. Did you know that? I know that sometimes they all look the same, but each one is special and different, just like you. You are the most special little girl in the whole world. Don't ever forget that."

Caroline had been too young to realize that Cassandra was dying, but now she cherished her mother's final gift, for no matter how bleak or desolate she felt—and the last ten years of her life had given her many reasons to feel bleak and desolate—Caroline had only to look up at the sky to give her a measure of the peace. If a star twinkled, she felt safe and warm. Maybe not as safe and warm as that long-ago toddler on her mother's lap, but at least the stars gave her hope. They endured, and so could she.

She gave her room a final inspection to make certain she hadn't left anything behind, tossed a few tallow candles into her bag in case she needed them, and dashed out. The house was quiet; all the servants had been given the night off, presumably so there would be no witnesses when Percy attacked her. Trust Oliver to think ahead. Caroline was only surprised that he hadn't tried this tactic sooner. He must have originally thought that he could get her to marry Percy without resorting to rape. Now that her twenty-first birthday was approaching, he was growing desperate.

And so was Caroline. If she had to marry Percy, she'd die. She didn't care how melodramatic she sounded. The only thing worse than the thought of seeing him every day for the rest of her life was having to *listen* to him every day for the rest of her life.

She was making her way through the hall toward the front door when she noticed Oliver's new candelabra sitting majestically on the side table. He'd been crowing about the piece all week. Sterling silver, he'd said. The finest craftsmanship. Caroline growled. Oliver hadn't been able to afford sterling silver candelabras before he'd been appointed her guardian.

It was ironic, really. She'd have been happy to share her fortune—give it away, even—if she'd found a home with a family who loved her and cared for her. Someone who saw in her something more than a workhorse with a bank account.

Impulsively, Caroline yanked the beeswax candles out of the candelabra and replaced them with the tallow ones in her bag. If she needed to light a candle on her travels, she wanted the sweet-smelling beeswax Oliver reserved for himself.

She ran outside, mumbling a short thanks for the warm weather. "It's a bloody good thing Percy didn't decide to attack me in the winter," she muttered, striding down the drive. She would have preferred to ride—anything that would get her out of Hampshire faster—but Oliver kept only two horses, and they were currently attached to his carriage, which he'd taken with him to his weekly game of cards at the squire's house.

Caroline tried to look at the bright side and reminded herself that she could hide more easily on foot. She'd be slower, though, and if she ran into footpads . . .

She shuddered. A woman alone was very conspicuous. And her light brown hair seemed to catch all the moonlight, even with most of it stuffed into a bonnet. She'd have been smart to dress up like a boy, but she hadn't had enough time. Perhaps she should follow the coast to the nearest busy harbor. It wasn't that far. She'd be able to travel faster by sea, take herself far enough away so that Oliver couldn't find her within six weeks.

Yes, it would have to be the coast. But she couldn't travel via the main roads. Someone was bound to see her. She turned south and began to cut through a field. It was only fifteen miles to Portsmouth. If she walked quickly and through the night, she could be there by morning. Then she could book passage on a ship—something that would take her to another part of England. Caroline didn't want to leave the country, not when she needed to claim her inheritance in six short weeks.

But what was she supposed to do with herself during that time? She'd been cut off from society for so long she didn't even know if she was qualified for any type of gentle employment. She thought she might make a good governess, but it would probably take six weeks just to find a position. And then . . . Well, it just wasn't fair to take a position as a governess and then leave the post mere weeks later.

She did know how to cook, and her guardians had certainly made sure she knew how to clean. Maybe she could work for room and board at some little-known, *very* out-of-the-way inn.

She nodded to herself. Cleaning up after strangers wasn't terribly appealing, but it seemed to be her only hope of survival for the next few weeks. But no matter what, she had to get away from Hampshire and its neighboring counties. She could work at an inn, but it would have to be far away from Prewitt Hall.

And so she increased her pace toward Portsmouth. The grass under her shoes was soft and dry, and the trees shielded her from the view of the main road. There wasn't much traffic this time of night, but one couldn't be too careful. She moved swiftly, the only sound her footfall as her boots met the earth. Until . . .

What was that?

Caroline whirled around but saw nothing. Her heart raced. She could have sworn she'd heard something. "It was just a hedgehog," she whispered to herself. "Or perhaps a hare." But she didn't see any animals, and she didn't feel reassured.

"Just keep moving," she told herself. "You must get to Portsmouth by morning." She resumed her trek, walking so fast now that her breath began to come faster and faster. And then . . .

She whirled around again, her hand instinctively reaching for her gun. This time she'd definitely heard something. "I know you're out there," she said with a defiance she didn't quite feel. "Show your face or remain a coward."

There was a rustling noise, and then a man emerged from the trees. He was dressed completely in black, from his shirt to his boots—even his hair was black. He was tall, and his shoulders were broad, and he was quite the most dangerous-looking man Caroline had ever seen.

And he had a gun pointed straight at her heart.

Chapter 2

pug•na•cious *(adjective). Disposed to fight; given to fighting; quarrelsome.*

I can be pugnacious *when backed into a corner.*

—From the personal dictionary of Caroline Trent

Blake Ravenscroft wasn't certain what he thought the woman would look like, but this certainly wasn't it. He'd thought she'd look soft, coy, manipulative. Instead, she stood tall, held her shoulders square, and stared him in the eye.

And she had the most intriguing mouth he'd ever seen. He was at a complete loss to describe it, except that her upper lip arched in the most delightful way and—

"Do you think you could possibly point that gun elsewhere?"

Blake snapped out of his reverie, appalled by his lack of concentration. "You'd like that, wouldn't you?"

"Well, yes, actually, I would. I have this thing about guns, you see. I don't mind them, precisely. They're good for some purposes, I suppose—hunting and the like. But I don't particularly enjoy having them pointed at *me*, and—"

"Quiet!"

She shut her mouth.

Blake studied her for several moments. Something about her wasn't right. Carlotta De Leon was Spanish . . . well, half-Spanish at least, and this girl looked English through and through. Her hair couldn't be called blond, but it was definitely a light shade of brown, and even in the dark night he could see that her eyes were a clear bluish-green.

Not to mention her voice, which was tinged with the pommy accents of the British elite.

But he'd seen her sneaking out of Oliver Prewitt's house. In the dead of night. With all the servants dismissed. She had to be Carlotta De Leon. There was no other explanation.

Blake—and the War Office, which didn't precisely employ him but did give him orders and the occasional bank draft—had been after Oliver Prewitt for nearly six months now. The local authorities had known for some time that Prewitt was smuggling goods to and from France, but it was only recently that they had begun to suspect that he was allowing Napoleonic spies to use his small boat to carry secret diplomatic messages along with his usual cargo of brandy and silk. Since Prewitt's boat sailed from a little cove on the southern coast between Portsmouth and Bournemouth, the War Office hadn't originally paid much attention to him. Most spies made their crossings from Kent, which was much closer to France. Prewitt's seemingly inconvenient location had made for an excellent ruse, and the War Office feared that Napoleon's forces had been using him for their most delicate messages. One month ago they had discovered that Prewitt's contact was one Carlotta De Leon—half-Spanish, half-English, and one hundred percent deadly.

Blake had been on the alert all evening, as soon as he'd learned that all of the Prewitt servants had been given the night off—an uncommon gesture for a man as notoriously stingy as Oliver Prewitt. Clearly something was afoot, and Blake's suspicions were confirmed when he saw the girl slip out of the house under the cover of darkness. So she was a trifle younger than he'd supposed—he wasn't going to let her guise of innocence deter him. She probably cultivated that look of blooming youth. Who would suspect such a lovely young lady of high treason?

Her long hair was pulled back into a girlish braid, her cheeks had that pink, well-scrubbed look, and . . .

And her delicately boned hand was slowly reaching down toward her pocket.

Blake's finely tuned instincts took over. His left arm shot out with startling speed, knocking her hand off course as he lunged forward. He hit her with all his weight, and they tumbled to the ground.

She felt soft beneath him, except, of course, for the hard metal gun in her cloak pocket. If he'd had any doubts of her identity before, they were now gone. He grabbed the pistol, shoved it in his waistband, and stood back up, leaving her sprawled on the ground.

"Very amateur, my dear."

She blinked, then muttered, "Well, yes. That's to be expected as I'm hardly a professional at this sort of thing, although I do have some experience with . . ."

Her words trailed off into an unintelligible mumble, and he wasn't at all sure if she was speaking to him or herself. "I've been after you for nearly a year," he said sharply.

That got her attention. "You have?"

"Not that I knew who you were until last month. But now that I've got you, I'm not letting you go."

"You're not?"

Blake stared at her in irritated confusion. What was her game? "Do you think I'm an idiot?" he spat out.

"No," she said. "I've just escaped from a den of idiots, so I'm well familiar with the breed, and you're something else entirely. I *am*, however, hoping you're not a terribly good shot."

"I never miss."

She sighed. "Yes, I feared as much. You look the sort. I say, do you mind if I get back up?"

He moved the gun a fraction of an inch, just enough to remind her that he was aiming at her heart. "Actually, I find I prefer your position on the ground."

"I had a feeling you would," she muttered. "I don't suppose you're going to let me go on my way."

His answer was a bark of laughter. "I'm afraid not, my dear. Your spying days are over."

"My spying—my *what*?"

"The British government knows all about you and your treasonous plots, Miss Carlotta De Leon. I think you'll find we do not look kindly upon Spanish spies."

Her face was a perfect picture of disbelief. God, this woman was good. "The government knows about me?" she asked. "Wait a moment, about *who*?"

"Don't play dumb, Miss De Leon. Your intelligence is well-known both here and on the continent."

"That's a very nice compliment, to be sure, but I'm afraid there has been a mistake."

"No mistake. I saw you leaving Prewitt Hall."

"Yes, of course, but—"

"In the dark," he continued, "with all the servants dismissed. You didn't realize we'd been watching the hall, did you?"

"No, no, of course I didn't," Caroline replied, blinking furiously. Someone had been watching the house? How had she not noticed? "For how long?"

"Two weeks."

That explained it. She'd been in Bath for the past fortnight, attending to Oliver's sickly maiden aunt. She'd only returned this afternoon.

"But that was long enough," he continued, "to confirm our suspicions."

"Your suspicions?" she echoed. What the devil was this man talking about? If he was insane, she was in big trouble, because he was still pointing a gun at her midsection.

"We have enough to indict Prewitt. Your testimony will ensure that he hangs. And you, my dear, will learn to love Australia."

Caroline gasped, her eyes lighting up with delight. Oliver was involved in something illegal? Oh, this was wonderful! Perfect! She should have guessed he was nothing more than a lowly crook. Her mind raced. Despite what the man in black had said, she doubted Oliver had done anything bad enough to hang for it. But perhaps he'd be sent to jail. Or forced into indentured servitude. Or—

"Miss De Leon?" the man said sharply.

Caroline's voice was excited and breathy as she asked, "What has Oliver been doing?"

"For the love of God, woman, I've had enough of your playacting. You're coming with me." He stepped forward with a menacing growl and grabbed her by the wrists. "Now."

"But—"

"Not another word unless it's a confession."

"But—"

"That's it!" He stuffed a rag into her mouth. "You'll have plenty of time to talk later, Miss De Leon."

Caroline coughed and grunted furiously as he bound her wrists with a coarse piece of rope. Then, to her amazement, he put two fingers into his mouth, and let out a low whistle. A glorious black gelding pranced out of the trees, its steps high and graceful.

While she was gaping at the horse—who must have been the quietest and best-trained animal in the history of creation—the man hefted her up onto the saddle.

"Iiiii shrr . . ." she croaked, quite unable to speak with the grimy gag in her mouth.

"What?" He looked over at her and took in the way her skirts were cutting into her legs. "Oh, your skirts. I can cut them or you can dispense with propriety."

She glared at him.

"Propriety goes, then," he said, and hiked her skirts up so that she could straddle the horse with more comfort. "Sorry I didn't think to bring a side-saddle, Miss De Leon, but trust me when I tell you that you've far greater worries just now than my seeing your bare legs."

She kicked him in the chest.

His hand closed painfully around her ankle. "Never," he spat out, "kick a man who is pointing a gun at you."

Caroline stuck her nose in the air and looked away. This farce had gone on quite long enough. As soon as she got rid of this blasted gag she'd tell this brute she'd never even heard of his Miss Carlotta De Leon. She would bring the force of the law down on his head so fast he'd be begging for the hangman's noose.

But in the meantime, she would have to settle for making his life miserable. As soon as he mounted the horse and settled into the saddle behind her, she elbowed him in the ribs. Hard.

"What now?" he snapped.

She shrugged innocently.

"Another move like that and I'm stuffing a second rag in your mouth. And this one is considerably less clean than the first."

As if that were possible, Caroline thought angrily. She didn't even want to *think* about where her gag had resided before her mouth. All she could do was glare at him, and from the way he snorted at her she feared she didn't look fierce enough by half.

But then he set his horse into a canter, and Caroline realized that while they weren't riding toward Portsmouth, they also weren't heading anywhere near Prewitt Hall.

If her hands hadn't been bound she would have clapped them together with glee. She couldn't have escaped any faster if she'd arranged transport herself. This man might think she was someone else—a Spanish criminal to be precise—but she could straighten all that out once he'd taken her far, far away. In the meantime, she'd be quiet and still, and let him kick the horse into a full gallop.

Thirty minutes later a very suspicious Blake Ravenscroft dismounted in front of Seacrest Manor, near Bournemouth, Dorset. Carlotta De Leon, who had done everything short of hurl fire at his toenails when he'd cornered her in the meadow, hadn't put up even the tiniest resistance the entire ride to the coast. She hadn't struggled and she hadn't tried to escape. She'd been so quiet, in fact, that the gentlemanly side of him—which reared its polite head all too often for Blake's liking—was tempted to remove her gag.

But he resisted the impulse to be nice. The Marquis of Riverdale, his closest friend and frequent partner in crime prevention, had had previous dealings with Miss De Leon, and he had told Blake that she was deceptive and deadly. Her gag and bindings would not be removed until she was safely locked away.

He pulled her down off of the horse, holding her elbow firmly as he led her into his home. Blake employed only three houseservants—all of them discreet beyond compare—and they were used to strange visitors in the middle of the night. "Up the stairs," he grunted, pulling her through the hall.

She nodded cheerfully—cheerfully?!?—and picked up the pace. Blake led her up to the top floor and pushed her into a small but comfortably furnished bedchamber. "Just so you don't get any ideas about escaping," he said roughly, holding up two keys, "the door has two locks."

She looked over at the doorknob but other than that had no obvious reaction to his words.

"And," he added, "it's fifty feet down to the ground. So I wouldn't recommend trying the window."

She shrugged, as if she'd never for a moment considered the window a viable escape option.

Blake scowled at her, irritated by her nonchalance, and looped her wristcuffs over the bedpost. "I don't want you attempting anything while I'm busy."

She smiled at him—which was really quite a feat with the filthy gag in her mouth. "Bloody hell," he muttered. He was utterly confused by her, and he didn't like the feeling one bit. He checked to make certain that her bindings were secure and then began to inspect the room, making sure he'd left no objects lying about that she might turn into weapons. He'd heard Carlotta De Leon was resourceful, and he had no plans to be remembered as the fool who'd underestimated her.

He pocketed a quill and a paperweight before shoving a chair out into the hall. He didn't think she looked strong enough to break the chair, but if she somehow managed to snap off a leg, the splintered wood would be a dangerous weapon indeed.

She blinked with interest when he returned.

"If you want to sit down," he said curtly, "you can do it on the bed."

She cocked her head in an annoyingly friendly manner and sat on the bed. Not that she had much choice—he'd bound her hands to the bedpost, after all.

"Don't try to charm me by being cooperative," he warned. "I know all about you."

She shrugged.

Blake snorted with disgust and turned his back on her as he finished his inspection of the room. Finally, when he was satisfied that the chamber would make an acceptable prison, he faced her, his hands planted firmly on his hips. "If you have any more weapons on your person, you might as well give them up now, since I'm going to have to search you."

She lurched backward in maidenly horror, and Blake was pleased that he'd finally managed to offend her. Either that or she was a prodigiously good actress.

"Well, have you any weapons? I assure you that I will grow considerably less gentle if I discover that you have attempted to conceal something."

She shook her head frantically and strained against her bindings, as if trying to get as far away from him as possible.

"I'm not going to enjoy this either," he muttered. He tried not to feel like a complete cad as she shut her eyes tightly in fear and resignation. He knew that women could be just as evil and dangerous as men—seven years of work for the War Office had convinced him of that basic fact—but he'd never gotten used to this part of the job. He'd been brought up to treat women like ladies, and it went against everything in his moral fiber to inspect her against her will.

He cut one of her wrists free so that he could remove her cloak and proceeded to rifle through her pockets. They held nothing of interest, save for about fifty pounds in notes and coin, which seemed like a paltry sum for a notorious spy. He then moved his attention to her small satchel, dumping the contents onto the bed. Two beeswax candles—Lord only knew what she wanted those for, a silverbacked hairbrush, a small Bible, a leather-bound notebook, and some underthings that he could not bring himself to sully with his touch. He supposed everyone deserved some measure of privacy, even treasonous spies.

He picked up the Bible and flipped quickly through it, making certain there was nothing concealed between its pages. Satisfied that the book contained nothing untoward, he tossed it back onto the bed, noting with interest that she flinched as he did so.

He then picked up the notebook and looked inside. Only the first few pages contained any scribblings. "Contubernal," he read aloud. "Halcyon. Diacritical. Titivate. Umlaut." He raised his eyebrows and read on. Three pages full of the sort of words that earned one a first at Oxford or Cambridge. "What is this?"

She jerked her shoulder toward her mouth, motioning to the gag.

"Right," he said with a curt nod, setting the notebook next to the Bible."But before I remove that, I'll have to . . ." His words trailed off, and he let out an unhappy exhale. Both of them knew what he had to do. "If you don't struggle I'll be able to do this faster," he said grimly.

Her entire body was tense, but Blake tried to ignore her distress as he quickly patted her down. "There, we're done," he said, his voice gruff. "I must say I'm rather surprised you weren't carrying anything other than that pistol."

She glared at him in return.

"I'll remove the gag now, but one loud noise and it's going right back in."

She nodded curtly, coughing as he removed the rag.

Blake leaned insolently against the wall as he asked, "Well?"

"Nobody would hear me if I made a loud noise, anyway."

"That much is true," he conceded. His eyes fell back upon the leather-bound notebook, and he picked it up. "Now, suppose you tell me what this is all about."

She shrugged. "My father always encouraged me to expand my vocabulary."

Blake stared at her in disbelief, then flipped through the opening pages again. It was some kind of code. It had to be. But he was tired, and he knew that if she confessed to something that night, it wasn't going to be anything as destructive to her cause as the key to a secret code. So he tossed the book on the bed and said, "We'll talk more about this tomorrow."

She gave another one of those annoying shrugs.

He gritted his teeth. "Have you anything to say for yourself?"

Caroline rubbed her eyes, reminding herself that she had to remain on this man's good side. He looked dangerous, and despite his obvious discomfort at searching her, she had no doubt that he would hurt her if he deemed it necessary to his mission.

Whatever that was.

She was playing a dangerous game and she knew it. She wanted to remain here at this cushy estate as long as possible—it was certainly warmer and safer than any place she could afford on her own. To do that, however, she had to let him continue to believe that she was this Carlotta person. She had no idea how to do this; she didn't know Spanish and she certainly didn't know how a criminal was supposed to act when apprehended and tied to a bedpost.

She supposed Carlotta would try to deny everything. "You have the wrong person," she said, knowing he wouldn't believe her and taking a wicked delight in the fact that she was telling the truth.

"Ha!" he barked. "Surely you can come up with something a little more original."

She shrugged. "You can believe what you want."

"You seem to be acting very confidently for someone who is clearly at the disadvantage."

He had a point there, Caroline conceded. But if Carlotta truly was a spy, she'd be a master at bravado. "I don't appreciate being bound, gagged, dragged across the countryside, and tied to a bedpost. Not to mention," she bit off, "being forced to submit to your insulting touch."

He closed his eyes for a moment, and if Caroline hadn't known better she would have thought he was in some sort of pain. Then he opened them and once again looked at her with a hard and uncompromising gaze. He said, "I find it difficult to believe, Miss De Leon, that you have come so far in your chosen profession without having had yourself searched before."

Caroline didn't know what to say to that so she just glared at him.

"I'm still waiting for you to talk."

"I have nothing to say." That much, at least, was true.

"You might reverse your opinion after a few days without food or water."

"You plan to starve me, then?"

"It has broken stronger men than you."

She hadn't considered this. She'd known he would yell at her, she'd thought he might even hit her, but it had never occurred to her that he might withhold food and water.

"I see the prospect doesn't excite you," he drawled.

"Leave me alone," she snapped. She needed to develop a plan. She needed to figure out who the devil this man was. Most of all, she needed time.

She looked him in the eye and said, "I'm tired."

"I'm sure you are, but I'm not particularly inclined to let you sleep."

"You needn't worry about my comfort. I'm not likely to feel well-rested after spending an evening tied to the bedpost."

"Oh, that," he said, and with a quick step and flick of his wrist, he cut her free.

"Why did you do that?" she asked suspiciously.

"It pleased me to do so. Besides, you have no weapon, you can hardly overpower me, and you have no means of escape. Good night, Miss De Leon."

Her mouth fell open. "You're leaving?"

"I did bid you good night." Then he turned on his heel and left the room, leaving her gaping at the door. She heard two keys turn in two locks before she regained her composure. "My God, Caroline," she whispered to herself, "what have you gotten yourself into?"

Her stomach rumbled, and she wished she'd had something to eat before she'd run off that evening. Her captor appeared to be a man of his word, and if he said he wasn't going to give her food or water, she believed him.

She ran to the window and looked out. He hadn't been lying. It was at least fifty feet to the ground. But there was a ledge, and if she could find some sort of receptacle, she could put it out to collect rain and dew. She'd been hungry before; she knew she could handle that. But thirst was something else altogether.

She found a small, cylindrical container used to hold quills on the desk. The sky was still clear, but

English weather being what it was, Caroline figured there was a decent chance it'd rain before morning, so she set the container on the ledge just in case.

Then she crossed to her bed and put her belongings back in her satchel. Thank the heavens her captor hadn't noticed the writing inside the Bible. Her mother had left the book to her when she died, and surely he'd have wanted to know why the name Cassandra Trent was inscribed on the inside front cover. And his reaction to her little personal dictionary . . . good heavens, she was going to have trouble explaining *that*.

Then she had the strangest feeling . . .

She took off her shoes and slid off the bed, walking on silent, stockinged feet until she reached the wall that bordered the hall. She moved closely along the wall until she reached the door. Bending down, she peered through the keyhole.

Aha! Just as she'd thought. A wide gray eye was peering back at her.

"And good evening to you!" she said loudly. Then she took her bonnet and hung it over the doorknob so that it blocked the keyhole. She didn't want to sleep in her only dress, but she certainly wasn't about to disrobe with the chance that *he* might be watching.

She heard him curse once, then twice. Then his footsteps echoed as he strode down the hall. Caroline stripped down to her petticoat and crawled into bed. She stared up at the ceiling and started to think.

And then she started to cough.

Chapter 3

a·kim·bo *(adjective). Of the arms: In a position in which the hands rest on the hips and the elbows are turned outwards.*

I cannot begin to count the number of times he has stood before me, arms akimbo. *In fact, I shudder even to contemplate it.*

—From the personal dictionary of Caroline Trent

Caroline coughed through the night.

She coughed through the dawn.

She coughed as the sky turned bright blue, stopping only to check on her water-collector on the ledge. Blast. Nothing. She could have used a few drops of liquid. Her throat felt as if it were on fire.

But sore throat or no, her plan had worked like a charm. When she opened her mouth to test her voice, the sound that came out would have put a frog to shame.

Actually, she rather thought the frog itself would have been ashamed to have made a noise like that. No doubt about it, Caroline had rendered herself temporarily mute. That man could ask her all the questions he wanted; she wasn't going to be able to answer a thing.

Just to make certain her captor wouldn't think she was faking the affliction, she opened her mouth wide and looked in the mirror, angling her head so that the sunlight shone on her throat.

Bright red. Her throat looked positively monstrous. And the bags she'd developed under her eyes from staying up the entire night made her look even worse.

Caroline nearly jumped for joy. If only there were some way she could fake a fever to make her seem even more sickly. She supposed she could put her face next to a candle in the hope that her skin would grow unnaturally warm, but if *he* came in she'd have a devil of a time explaining why she had a candle lit on such a bright morning.

No, the mute throat would have to be enough. And even if it weren't, she didn't have any choice in the matter, because she could hear his footsteps sounding loudly down the hall.

She dashed across the room and scrambled into the bed, pulling the covers up to her chin. She coughed a couple of times, then pinched her cheeks to give them the appearance of being flushed, then coughed some more.

Cough cough cough.

The key turned in the lock.

Cough cough cough COUGH. It was murder on her throat, but Caroline wanted to give an especially good performance right as he was coming in.

Then another key started turning in another lock. Blast. She'd forgotten that there were two locks on the door.

Cough cough cough. Hack hack. Cough. GAG.

"Good God! What is that infernal noise?"

Caroline looked up, and if she weren't already mute she would have lost her voice. Her captor had looked dashing and dangerous in the dark, but by day he put Adonis to shame. He seemed somehow larger in the light. Stronger, too, as if his clothing only barely leashed the power of his body. His black hair was neatly trimmed, but an errant lock fell forward to his left eyebrow. And his eyes—they were clear and gray, but that was the only innocent thing about them. They looked like they had seen far too much in their lifetime.

The man grabbed her shoulder, his touch burning through her dress to her skin. She gasped, then covered it up with another cough.

"I believe I told you last night that I have grown weary of your playacting."

She shook her head quickly, grabbed her neck with her hands, then coughed again.

"If you for one moment think that I believe—"

She opened her mouth wide and pointed at her throat.

"I'm not going to look at your throat, you little—"

She pointed again, this time urgently jabbing her finger into her mouth.

"Oh, very well." His lips were clamped into a firm line as he turned on his heel, strode across the room, and wrenched a candle out of its holder. Caroline watched with undisguised interest as he lit the taper and crossed back to the bed. He sat down next to her, the weight of his body depressing his side of the mattress. She rolled a little toward him and put her hand out to stop her descent.

She connected with his thigh.

COUGH!

She very nearly flew to the other side of the bed.

"Oh, for the love of God, I've been touched by women more appealing and more interested than you," he snapped. "You needn't fear. I may starve the truth out of you, but I won't ravish you."

Oddly enough, Caroline believed him. His inclinations toward abduction aside, he didn't seem the type to take a woman against her will. In a rather strange sort of way she trusted this man. He could have hurt her—he could even have killed her—but he hadn't. She sensed he had a code of honor and morals that had been absent in her guardians.

"Well?" he demanded.

She inched back toward his end of the bed and placed her hands primly on her lap.

"Open up."

She cleared her throat—as if that were necessary—and opened her mouth. He brought the candle flame close to her face and peered in. After a moment he drew back, and she snapped her mouth closed, staring up at him expectantly.

His face was grim. "It looks as if someone took a razor to your throat, but I expect you know that."

She nodded.

"I suppose you were up all night coughing."

She nodded again.

He closed his eyes for a fraction of a second longer than was necessary before saying, "You have my reluctant admiration for this. Inflicting such pain upon yourself just to escape a few questions shows true dedication to the cause."

Caroline gave him her best expression of outrage.

"Unfortunately for you, you chose the wrong cause."

All she could manage this time was a blank stare, but it was an honest blank stare. She had no clue what cause he was talking about.

"I'm sure you can still speak."

She shook her head.

"Give it a try." He leaned forward and stared at her so hard she squirmed. "For me."

She shook her head again, this time quickly. Very quickly.

He leaned in even closer, until his nose was almost resting on hers. "Try."

No! She opened her mouth, and would have shouted it, but truly, not a sound emerged.

"You really can't speak," he said, sounding wholly surprised.

She tried to shoot him her best what-on-earth-do-you-think-I-would-have-been-trying-to-say-if-I-could-speak look, but she had a feeling that the sentiment was a bit too complex for a single facial expression.

He stood quite suddenly. "I'll return in a moment."

Caroline could do nothing but stare at his back as he left the room.

Blake sighed with irritation as he pushed open the door to his study. Damn, he was getting too old for this. Eight-and-twenty might still be relatively youthful, but seven years with the War Office was enough to leave anyone prematurely tired and weary. He'd seen friends die, his family was always wondering why he continually disappeared for long stretches of time, and his fiancée . . .

Blake closed his eyes in pain and remorse. Marabelle wasn't his fiancée any longer. She wasn't anyone's fiancée and wasn't likely to become one, buried as she was in her family plot in the Cotswolds.

She'd been so young, so beautiful, and so damned brilliant. It had been an amazing thing, really, to fall in love with a woman whose intellect surpassed one's own. Marabelle had been a prodigy of sorts, a genius at languages, and it was for that reason she'd been recruited at such an early age by the War Office.

And then she'd recruited Blake, her longtime neighbor, co-owner of England's best-furnished treehouse, and partner in dancing lessons. They'd grown up together, they'd fallen in love together, but Marabelle had died alone.

No, Blake thought. That wasn't really true. Marabelle had only died. He was the one who'd been left alone.

He'd continued to work for the War Office for several years. He told himself it was to avenge her death, but he often wondered if it wasn't just because he didn't know what else to do with himself. And his superiors didn't want to let him go. After Marabelle's death, he'd grown reckless. He hadn't much cared whether he lived or died, so he'd taken stupid risks in the name of his country, and those risks had paid off. He'd never failed in any of his missions.

Of course, he'd also been shot at, poisoned, and thrown over the side of a ship, but that didn't bother the War Office as much as the prospect of losing their star agent.

But now Blake was trying to put the anger behind him. There was no way he could bury his pain, but it seemed that he might have a chance to end this consuming hatred for the world that had stolen his true love and best friend. And the only way he could do this was to leave the War Office and at least attempt to lead a normal life.

But first he had to finish this one last case. It had been a traitor like Oliver Prewitt who had been responsible for Marabelle's demise. That traitor had been executed, and Blake was determined that Prewitt, too, would see the gallows.

To do that, however, he had to get some information out of Carlotta De Leon. Damn the woman. He didn't for one minute believe that she'd suddenly developed some strange, dreaded illness that had robbed her of speech. No, the chit had probably sat up half the night coughing her throat raw.

It had almost been worth it, though, just to see her expression of shock when she'd tried to yell,

"No!" at him. He had a feeling she'd expected some sort of sound to come out. He chuckled. He hoped her throat burned like the fires of Hades. She deserved no less.

Still, he had a job to do. This assignment would be his last for the War Office, and though he wanted nothing more than to retire permanently to the peace and quiet of Seacrest Manor, he had no intention of letting this mission meet with anything but success.

Carlotta De Leon *would* talk, and Oliver Prewitt *would* hang.

And then Blake Ravenscroft would become nothing but a boring landed gentleman, destined to live out his life in lonely tranquillity. Perhaps he would take up painting. Or breeding hounds. The possibilities were endless, and endlessly dull.

But for now, he had a job to do. With grim determination he gathered up three quills, a small bottle of ink, and several sheets of paper. If Carlotta De Leon couldn't tell him everything she knew, she could bloody well write it down.

Caroline was grinning from ear to ear. Thus far her morning had been a complete success. Her captor was now convinced that she couldn't speak, and Oliver—

Oh, that made her smile all the more, just thinking about what Oliver must be doing at that very moment. Screaming his foolish head off, most probably, and throwing the occasional vase at his son. Nothing precious, of course. Oliver was far too calculating in his rages to destroy anything of real monetary value.

Poor Percy. Caroline almost felt sorry for him—almost. It was hard to summon much sympathy for the thick-brained lout who had tried to force himself on her the night before. She shuddered to think how she'd feel if he'd actually succeeded.

Still, she had a feeling that if Percy ever managed to get out from under his father's thumb he might grow into a halfway decent human being. No one she would want to see on a regular basis, of course, but he certainly wouldn't go around attacking innocent women if his father didn't order him to do so.

Just then she heard her captor's footsteps in the hall. She quickly wiped her face free of its smile and placed one hand on her neck. When he reentered the room, she was coughing.

"I have a treat for you," he said, his voice suspiciously cheerful.

She cocked her head in reply.

"Look at this. Paper. Quills. Ink. Isn't it exciting?"

She blinked, pretending not to understand. Oh, blast, she hadn't considered this. There was no way she was going to convince him she didn't know how to write—she was clearly an educated woman. And it went without saying that she wasn't going to be able to manage to sprain her wrist in the next three seconds.

"Oh, of course," he said with exaggerated solicitude. "You require something upon which to lean. How inconsiderate of me not to consider your needs. Here, let me bring over this desk blotter. There you are, right on your lap. Are you comfortable?"

She glared at him, preferring his anger to his sarcasm.

"No? Here, let me fluff your pillows."

He leaned forward, and Caroline, who really had had enough of his sugary-sweet attitude, coughed onto his mouth and nose. By the time he drew back far enough to glare at her, her face was a picture of complete contrition.

"I'm going to forget you did that," he bit off, "for which you ought to be eternally thankful."

Caroline just stared down at the writing accouterments on her lap, desperately trying to devise a new plan.

"Now then, shall we begin?"

Her right temple itched, and she brought up her hand to scratch it. Her *right* hand. That was when it came to her. She had always favored her left hand. Her early teachers had scolded, screamed, and prodded, trying to get her to learn to write with her right hand. They'd called her bizarre, unnatural, and ungodly. One particularly religious tutor had even referred to her as the spawn of the devil. Caroline had tried to learn how to write with her right hand—oh Lord, how she had tried—but though she could grip the quill in a natural fashion, she'd never been able to master anything other than an unintelligible scrawl.

But everyone else wrote with their right hand, her teachers had insisted. Surely she didn't want to be different.

Caroline coughed to cover up her smile. Never before had she been more delighted to be "different." This fellow would expect her to write with her right hand, as he and the rest of his acquaintances undoubtedly did. Well, she'd be happy to give him what he wanted. She reached out with her right hand, picked up a quill, dipped it in the ink, and looked at him with bored expectation.

"I'm glad you've decided to cooperate," he said. "I'm sure you'll find it most beneficial to your health."

She snorted and rolled her eyes.

"Now then," he said, staring at her with shrewd intensity. "Do you know Oliver Prewitt?"

There was no use denying that one. He'd seen her leaving the house just the night before. Still, there was no point in wasting her secret weapon on such a simple question, so she nodded.

"How long have you known him?"

Caroline thought about that one. She had no idea how long Carlotta De Leon had been working with Oliver, if indeed that was the case, but she also suspected that the man standing in front of her with folded arms didn't know, either.

Best to tell the truth, her mother had always said, and Caroline didn't see any reason to depart from this policy now. It would be easier to keep her stories straight if they were as truthful as possible. Let's see, she had been living with Oliver and Percy for a year and a half, but she'd known them for some time longer than that. She held up four fingers, still wanting to save her handwriting for an answer that was nice and complex.

"Four months?"

She shook her head.

"Four *years*?"

She nodded.

"Good God," Blake breathed. They'd had no idea that Prewitt had been smuggling diplomatic information for so long. Two years, they'd thought, possibly two and a half. When he thought of all of the missions that had been compromised . . . Not to mention the lives that must have been lost as a result of Prewitt's treason. So many of his colleagues, gone. His own dearest . . .

Blake blazed with anger and guilt. "Tell me the exact nature of your relationship," he ordered, his voice clipped.

Tell you? she mouthed.

"Write it!" he roared.

She took a deep breath, as if preparing herself for some terrible chore, and laboriously began to write.

Blake blinked. Then he blinked again.

She looked up at him and smiled.

"What the devil language are you writing in?" he demanded.

She drew back, clearly affronted.

"For the record, I don't read Spanish, so kindly write the answer in English. Or, if you prefer, French or Latin."

She wagged her finger at him and made some sort of motion he wasn't able to interpret.

"I repeat," he bit off, "write down the exact nature of your relationship with Oliver Prewitt!"

She pointed to each collection of scribbles—he was hesitant to call them words—slowly and carefully, as if demonstrating something new to a small child.

"Miss De Leon!"

She sighed, and this time she mouthed something as she pointed to her scrawl.

"I don't read lips, woman."

She shrugged.

"Write it again."

Her eyes flared with irritation, but she did as he asked.

These results were even worse than before.

Blake balled his hands into fists to keep from wrapping them around her throat. "I refuse to believe that you do not know how to write."

Her mouth fell open in outrage and she jabbed furiously at the ink marks on the paper.

"To call that writing, madam, is an insult to quills and ink across the world."

She clapped her hand over her mouth and coughed. Or did she giggle? Blake narrowed his eyes, then got up and crossed the room to the vanity table. He picked up her little book—the one filled with the brainy words—and waved it in the air. "If you have such dreadful penmanship, then explain *this*!" he thundered.

She stared at him blankly, which infuriated him all the more. He marched back to her side and leaned in very close. "I'm waiting," he growled.

She drew back and mouthed something he couldn't decipher.

"I'm afraid I just don't understand." By now his voice had left the realm of angry and had ventured into the dangerous.

She began to make all sorts of odd motions, pointing to herself and shaking her head.

"Are you trying to tell me that you didn't write these words?"

She nodded vigorously.

"Then who did?"

She mouthed something he didn't understand—something he had a feeling he wasn't *meant* to understand.

He sighed wearily and walked back over to the window for a spot of fresh air. It just didn't make sense that she couldn't write legibly, and if she truly couldn't, then who had scribbled in the notebook and what did it mean? She had said—when she could still speak—that it was nothing more than a collection of vocabulary words, which was clearly a lie. Still . . .

He paused. He had an idea. "Write out the alphabet," he ordered.

She rolled her eyes.

"Now!" he roared.

She frowned with displeasure as she carried out her latest assignment.

"What's this?" he asked, holding up the cylindrical quill holder he found on the window ledge.

Water, she mouthed. Funny how she managed to make him understand her *some* of the time.

He scoffed and put it back on the ledge. "Any fool could see it isn't going to rain."

She shrugged, as if to say, *It could.*

"Are you done?"

She nodded, managing to look very irritated and very bored at the same time.

Blake walked back over to her side and looked down. The M, N, and O were barely legible, and C he supposed he could have picked out if his life were at stake over it, but beyond that . . .

He shuddered. Never again. Never would he risk his life, and in this case his very sanity, for the good of Mother England. He had sworn to the War Office that he was through, but they'd nagged and cajoled until he'd agreed to take care of this one last piece of business. It was because he lived so close to Bournemouth, his superiors had said. He could look into Prewitt's activities without arousing suspicion. It had to be Blake Ravenscroft, they'd insisted. No one else could do the job.

And so Blake had acquiesced. But he had never dreamed he'd end up nursing an oddly fetching half-Spanish spy with the worst handwriting in the history of the civilized world.

"I'd like to meet your governess," he muttered, "and then I'd like to shoot her."

Miss De Leon made another strange sound, and this time he was certain it was a giggle. For a treasonous spy, she had a rather decent sense of humor.

"You," he said, pointing at her, "don't move."

She planted her hands on her hips and gave him a silly look, as if to say, *Where would I go?*

"I'll be right back." He stalked out of the room, remembering only at the last minute to lock the door behind him. Damn. He was getting soft. It was because she didn't seem like a spy, he rationalized. There was something different about her. Most people in his line of work had a hollow look to them, as if they'd seen too much. But those blue-green eyes of hers—well, if one could get past the fact that they were a bit bloodshot from lack of sleep—they were . . . they were . . .

Blake stiffened and banished the thought from his mind. He had no business thinking about her eyes. He had no business thinking about any woman.

* * *

Four hours later he was ready to admit defeat. He had forced six pots of tea down her throat, which had resulted in nothing other than her making wild, crazed motions with her hands that he eventually interpreted as, "Leave the room so I can use the chamber pot."

But her voice didn't return, or if it did, she was rather skilled at hiding it.

He'd been foolish enough to try the quill and ink approach only one more time. Her hand had moved with grace and speed, but the marks she left on the paper resembled nothing so much as bird tracks.

And, blast the chit, she seemed to be trying to endear herself to him. Worse, she was succeeding. While he was grumbling at her lack of communicative skills, she'd folded one of the scribbled-on sheets of paper into an odd birdlike shape and then proceeded to shoot it straight at him. It glided smoothly through the air, and once Blake had dodged out of its way, it landed gently on the floor.

"Well done," Blake said, impressed despite himself. He'd always liked little gadgets like that.

She smiled proudly, folded up another paper bird, and sailed that one right out the window.

Blake knew he ought to berate her for wasting his time, but he wanted to see how well her little contraption did outside. He rose from the table and went to the window, catching sight of the paper bird just as it spiraled into a rosebush. "Brought down by the flora, I'm afraid," he said, turning to face her.

She shot him an irritated look and marched to the window.

"Do you see it?" Blake said.

She shook her head.

He leaned out next to her. "Right there," he said, pointing. "In the rosebush."

She pulled herself upright, planted her hands on her hips, and shot him a sarcastic look.

"You dare to mock my rosebushes?"

She made scissors-like motions with her fingers.

"You think they need pruning?"

She nodded emphatically.

"A spy who likes to garden," Blake said to himself. "Will wonders never cease?"

She cupped her hand next to her ear to let him know she hadn't heard him.

"I suppose you could do a better job?" he quipped.

She nodded again, moving back to the window to get another look at the bushes. But Blake hadn't seen her coming, and he stepped toward the window at the exact same moment. They crashed into each other, and he grabbed her upper arms to keep her from falling.

And then he made the mistake of looking into her eyes.

They were soft, and they were clear, and heaven help him, they weren't saying no.

Blake leaned down a fraction of an inch, wanting to kiss her more than he wanted to breathe. Her lips parted, and a small gasp of surprise escaped her mouth. He moved closer. He wanted her. He wanted Carlotta. He wanted—

Carlotta.

Damn, how could he have forgotten, even for a second? She was a spy. A traitor. Completely without morals or scruples. He shoved her away from him and strode to the door. "That won't happen again," he said, his voice clipped.

She looked too stunned to respond.

Blake swore under his breath and stalked out, slamming and locking the door behind him. What the hell was he going to do with her?

Even worse, what the hell was he going to do with himself? Blake shook his head as he bolted down the stairs. This was getting ridiculous. He had no interest in women for anything other than the most basic of reasons, and even for *that* Carlotta De Leon was monstrously inappropriate.

He had no wish to wake up with his throat slit, after all. Or not to wake up at all, as the case would probably be.

He had to remember who she was.

And he had to remember Marabelle.

Chapter 4

nos·trum *(noun). A medicine, or medical application, prepared by the person recommending it; a quack remedy.*

He doesn't seem to have much faith in his nostrums, *but still he forces them down my throat.*

—From the personal dictionary of Caroline Trent

Blake left her alone for the rest of the day. He was too enraged to trust himself near her. She and her bloody mute throat were infuriating, but the truth was, most of his anger was self-directed.

How could he have thought of kissing her? Even for a second? She might be half-Spanish, but she was also half-English, and that made her a traitor.

And it was a traitor who had killed Marabelle.

As if to mirror his mood, it started to rain as the sun went down, and all Blake could think about was the little quill-holder she'd left on the ledge to collect water.

He snorted. As if she were going to perish of thirst after all the tea he'd forced down her throat that afternoon. Still, as he ate his evening meal in silence, he couldn't help but think of her upstairs, locked in the tiny room. She had to be starving. She hadn't eaten all day.

"What is the matter with you?" he said aloud. Feeling sorry for the crafty little spy. Bah! Hadn't he told her he was going to starve her? He never made promises he didn't keep.

Still, she was a skinny little thing, and those eyes of hers . . . he kept seeing them in his mind. They were huge, so clear they practically glowed, and if he saw them right now, Blake thought with a mixture of irritation and remorse, they'd probably look hungry.

"Damn," he muttered, standing up so fast he knocked his chair backward. He might as well give her a dinner roll. There had to be better ways to get her to give him the information he needed than to starve her. Perhaps if he doled out the food in a miserly fashion, she'd grow so grateful for what he gave her, she'd start to feel beholden to him. He'd heard of situations where captives had begun to look upon their captors as heroes. He wouldn't mind seeing those blue-green eyes looking at him with a touch of hero worship.

Blake took a small roll from the tray on the table, then put it back in favor of a larger one. And maybe a little butter. It certainly couldn't hurt. And jam . . . no, he drew the line at jam. She *was* a spy, after all.

Caroline was sitting on her bed, going cross-eyed watching a candle flame, when she heard him at the door. One lock snapped open, then another, then he was there, filling the doorway.

How was it that every time she saw him he seemed even more handsome than before? It really wasn't fair. All that beauty wasted on a man. And a rather annoying one at that.

"I brought you a piece of bread," he said gruffly, holding something out to her.

Caroline's stomach let out a loud rumble as she took the roll from his hand. *Thank you,* she mouthed.

He perched at the end of the bed as she wolfed down the roll with little thought to manners or decorum. "You're welcome. Oh, I almost forgot," he said. "I brought you butter as well."

She looked ruefully at the scrap of bread left in her hand and sighed.

"Do you still want it?"

She nodded, took the little crock, and dunked her last bite in the butter. She popped it in her mouth and chewed slowly, savoring every morsel. Heaven!

I thought you were going to starve me, she mouthed.

He shook his head in incomprehension. "*Thank you,* I can manage, but that was quite beyond me. Unless you've your speaking voice back and would like to actually say that sentence aloud . . ."

She shook her head, which wasn't technically a lie. Caroline hadn't tested her voice since he'd left. She didn't want to know if it was back or not. It somehow seemed better to remain ignorant on the matter.

"Pity," he murmured.

She rolled her eyes in reply, then patted her stomach and looked hopefully at his hands.

"I only brought up one roll, I'm afraid."

Caroline looked down at her little pot of butter, shrugged, and stuck her finger in. Who knew when he'd choose to feed her next? She had to get her sustenance wherever she could, even if it meant eating plain butter.

"Oh, for goodness sake," he said. "Don't eat that. It can't be good for you."

Caroline shot him a sarcastic look.

"How are you faring?" he asked.

She waved her hands this way and that.

"Bored?"

She nodded.

"Good."

She scowled.

"I have no intention of entertaining you. You're not a houseguest."

She rolled her eyes and let out a little snort.

"Just so long as you don't start expecting seven-course meals."

Caroline wondered if bread and butter counted as two courses. If so, then he still owed her five.

"How long are you going to keep up this charade?"

She blinked and mouthed, *What?*

"Surely you have your voice back."

She shook her head, touched her throat, and made such a sorry face that he actually laughed.

"That painful, eh?"

She nodded.

Blake raked his hand through his black hair, a little bit peeved that this deceitful woman had made him laugh more in the past day than he had in the past year. "Do you know, if you weren't a traitor, you'd be rather entertaining."

She shrugged.

"Have you ever taken the time to consider your actions? What they cost? The people you hurt?" Blake stared at her intently. He didn't know why, but he was determined to find a conscience in this little spy. She could have been a good person, he was sure of it. She was smart, and she was funny, and—

Blake shook his head to cut off his wayward thoughts. Did he see himself as her savior? He hadn't brought her here for redemption; all he wanted was the information that would indict Oliver Prewitt. Then he would turn her over to the authorities.

Of course, she would probably see the gallows as well. It was a sobering thought, and one that somehow didn't sit well with him.

"What a waste," he muttered.

She raised her brows in question.

"Nothing."

Her shoulders rose and fell in a rather gallic motion.

"How old are you?" he asked abruptly.

She flashed all ten fingers twice.

"Only twenty?" he asked in disbelief. "Not that you look any older, but I thought—"

Quickly, she held up one hand again, all five fingers stretched out like a starfish.

"Twenty-five, then?"

She nodded, but she was looking out the window when she did so.

"You should be married with children clutching at your skirts, not running around betraying the crown."

She looked down, and her lips flattened into an expression that could only be called rueful. Then she twisted her hands in a questioning motion and pointed to him.

"Me?"

She nodded.

"What about me?"

She pointed to the fourth finger of her left hand.

"Why am I not married?"

She nodded, this time emphatically.

"Don't you know?"

She looked at him blankly, and then after several moments shook her head.

"I was almost married." Blake tried to sound flippant, but any fool could hear the sorrow in his voice.

What happened? she mouthed.

"She died."

Caroline swallowed and then placed her hand on his in a gesture of sympathy. *I'm sorry.*

He shook her away and closed his eyes for a second. When he opened them, they were devoid of emotion. "No, you're not," he said.

She put her hand back into her lap and waited for him to speak. Somehow it didn't seem right to intrude upon his grief. He didn't say anything, though.

Feeling awkward in the silence, Caroline got up and walked to the window. Rain pelted the glass, and she wondered how much water she'd been able to collect in her little receptacle. Probably not much, and she certainly didn't need the water after all the tea he'd fed her today, but she was still eager to see how well her plan had worked. She'd learned long ago how to entertain herself in the simplest of ways. A little project here and there, charting the way the night sky changed from month to month. Perhaps if he kept her here for a while she could do weekly measurements of rainfall. At the very least, it would help to keep her mind occupied.

"What are you doing?" he demanded.

She made no reply, verbal or otherwise, and grabbed the bottom of the window with her fingers.

"I asked you what you are doing." His footsteps accompanied his voice, and Caroline knew he was drawing near. Still she didn't turn around. The window eased up, and the drizzle blew into the room, dampening the front of her dress.

"You little fool," he said, clamping his hands over hers.

She whirled around in surprise. She hadn't expected him to touch her.

"You're going to be soaked through." With a slight shove, he pushed the window back down. "And then you'll truly be sick."

She shook her head and pointed to her little container on the ledge.

"Surely you can't be thirsty."

Just curious, she mouthed.

"What? I didn't catch that."

Jjuusstt ccuurriioouuss. She drew it out this time, hoping he'd be able to read her lips.

"If you spoke out loud," he drawled, "I might understand what you're saying."

Caroline stamped her foot in frustration, but when it landed, it landed on something considerably less flat than the floor.

"Owww!" he yelled.

Oh! His foot! *Sorry sorry sorry sorry sorry sorry,* she mouthed. *I didn't mean it.*

"If you think I can understand that," he growled, "you're crazier than I'd originally thought."

She chewed on her lower lip remorsefully, then placed her hand over her heart.

"I suppose you're trying to convince me that was an accident?"

She nodded earnestly.

"I don't believe you."

She frowned and sighed with impatience. This muteness was getting to be annoying, but she didn't see how else to proceed. Exasperated, she pointed her foot forward.

"What does that mean?"

She wiggled her foot, then set it down and stomped on it with her other foot.

He looked at her in utter confusion. "Are you trying to convince me you're some sort of masochist? I hate to disappoint you, but I've never gone in for that sort of thing."

She shook her fists in the air then pointed at him, then pointed at her foot.

"You want me to stomp on your foot?" he asked in disbelief.

She nodded.

"Why?"

I'm sorry, she mouthed.

"Are you really sorry?" he asked, his voice growing dangerously low.

She nodded.

He leaned closer. "Really and truly?"

She nodded again.

"And you're determined to prove it to me?"

She nodded yet again, but this time her movements lacked conviction.

"I'm not going to stomp on your foot," he whispered.

She blinked.

Blake touched her cheek, knowing he was insane, but unable to help himself. His fingers trailed down to her throat, reveling in the warmth of her skin. "You're going to have to make it up to me a different way."

She tried to take a step back, but his hand had snaked around to the back of her head, and he was holding her firmly.

"A kiss, I think," he murmured. "Just one. Just one kiss."

Her lips parted in surprise, and she looked so damned startled and innocent that he was able to delude himself, if only for this one moment, that she wasn't Carlotta De Leon. She wasn't a traitor or a spy. She was just a woman—a rather fetching woman—and she was here in his home, in his arms.

He closed the distance between them and brushed his mouth gently against hers. She didn't move, but he heard a soft gasp of surprise pass across her lips. The little noise—the first she'd made all day save for a cough—enchanted him, and he deepened the kiss, tracing the soft skin of her lips with his tongue.

She tasted sweet and salty and just like a woman ought, and Blake was so overcome that he didn't even realize that she wasn't kissing him back. But soon he noticed that she was completely still in his arms. For some reason, that infuriated him. He hated that he desired her this way, and he wanted her to be feeling the same torture.

"Kiss me back," he growled, the words hot against her mouth. "I know you want to. I saw it in your eyes."

For a second she made no response, but then he felt her small hand moving slowly along the length of his back. She pulled herself closer to him, and when Blake felt the heat of her body pressing gently against his he thought he might explode.

Her mouth wasn't moving with the same fervor as his, but her lips parted, tacitly encouraging him to deepen the kiss.

"Good Christ," he murmured, only speaking when he had to come up for air. "Carlotta."

She stiffened in his arms and tried to pull away.

"Not yet," Blake moaned. He knew he had to end this, knew he couldn't let it go where his body was begging it to, but he wasn't ready to release her. He still needed to feel her heat, to touch her skin, to use her warmth to remind himself that he was alive. And he—

She wrenched herself away and skidded several steps backward until she was pressed up against the wall.

Blake swore under his breath and planted his hands on his hips as he fought to regain his breath.

When he looked up at her, her eyes were almost frantic, and she was shaking her head urgently.

"I was that distasteful?" he bit out.

She shook her head again, the movement tiny but quick. *I can't*, she mouthed.

"Well, neither can I," he said, self-loathing evident in his voice. "But I did, anyway. So what the hell does that mean?"

Her eyes widened, but other than that, she made no response.

Blake stared at her for a long minute before saying, "I'll leave you alone then."

She nodded slowly.

He wondered why he was so reluctant to leave. Finally, with a few muttered epithets, he strode across the room to the door. "I'll see you in the morning."

The door slammed, and Caroline stared at the space where he'd been for several seconds before whispering, "Oh, my God."

The next morning Blake made his way downstairs before heading up to see his "guest." He was going to get her to talk today if it killed him. This nonsense had gone on long enough.

When he reached the kitchen Mrs. Mickle, his housekeeper and cook, was busy stirring something in a soup pot.

"Good morning, sir," she said.

"So that's what a female voice sounds like," Blake muttered. "I had nearly forgotten."

"I beg your pardon?"

"No matter. Would you please boil some water for tea?"

"More tea?" she questioned. "I thought you preferred coffee."

"I do. But today I want tea." Blake was fairly certain that Mrs. Mickle knew there was a woman upstairs, but she'd worked for him for several years, and they had a tacit agreement: he paid her well and treated her with the utmost of respect, and she in turn asked no questions and told no tales. It was the same with all his servants.

The housekeeper nodded and smiled. "Then you'll want another *large* pot?"

Blake smiled wryly back. Of course this silent understanding didn't mean that Mrs. Mickle didn't like to tease him when she could. "A very large pot," he replied.

While she was tending to the tea, Blake headed off in search of Perriwick, his butler. He found him polishing some silver that absolutely didn't need polishing.

"Perriwick," Blake called out. "I need a message sent to London. Immediately."

Perriwick nodded regally. "To the marquis?" he guessed.

Blake nodded. Most of his urgent messages were sent to James Sidwell, the Marquis of Riverdale. Perriwick knew exactly how to get them to London by the speediest route.

"If you'll just give it to me," Perriwick said, "I'll see that it leaves the district straightaways."

"I need to write it first," Blake said absently.

Perriwick frowned. "Might I suggest that you write your messages before asking me to have them delivered, sir? It would be an ever so much more efficient use of your time and mine."

Blake cracked a half-smile as he said, "You're damned insolent for a servant."

"I wish only to facilitate the smooth and graceful running of your household, sir."

Blake shook his head, marveling at Perriwick's ability to keep a straight face. "Just wait one moment, and I'll write it out now." He leaned over a desk, took out a paper, quill, and ink, and wrote:

J—

I have Miss De Leon and would appreciate your assistance with her immediately.

—B

James had had previous dealings with the half-Spanish spy. He might know how to get her to talk. In the meantime, Blake would just have to ply her with tea and hope she regained her voice. He really had no other option. It hurt his eyes too much to look at her handwriting.

When Blake reached the door to Carlotta's room he could hear her coughing.

"Damn," he muttered. Crazy woman. She must have begun to get her voice back and decided to cough it away again. He deftly balanced the tea service as he unlocked the door and pushed it open. "Still coughing, I hear," he drawled.

She was sitting on the bed, nodding, and her light brown hair looked a touch stringy. She didn't look well.

Blake groaned. "Don't tell me you're really sick now."

She nodded, looking for all the world as if she were about to cry.

"So you admit you faked your illness yesterday?"

She looked sheepish as she wiggled her hand in a manner that meant, *Sort of.*

"Either you did or you didn't."

She nodded ruefully, but pointed to her throat.

"Yes, I know you really couldn't speak yesterday, but we both know that was no accident, now was it?"

She looked down.

"I'll take that as a yes."

She pointed to the tray and mouthed, *Tea?*

"Yes." He set the service down and placed his hand against her forehead. "I thought to help you regain your voice. Damn, you've a fever."

She sighed.

"Serves you right."

I know, she mouthed, looking utterly contrite. In that moment he almost liked her.

"Here," he said, sitting down on the edge of the bed, "you'd better have some tea."

Thank you.

"Will you pour?"

She nodded.

"Good. I've always been clumsy with that sort of thing. Marabelle always said—" He cut himself off. How could he even think of talking about Marabelle with this spy?

Who is Marabelle? she mouthed.

"No one," he said sharply.

Your fiancée? she mouthed, her lips moving carefully to enunciate her silent words.

He didn't answer her, just stood up and strode to the door. "Drink you tea," he ordered. "And yank the bellpull if you start to feel ill."

He exited the room, slamming the door behind him before twisting the two locks shut with a vicious click.

Caroline stared at the door and blinked. What had that been all about? The man was as changeable as the wind. One minute she would swear he was actually growing fond of her, and the next . . .

Well, she thought, as she reached for the tea and poured herself a cup, he *did* think she was a traitorous spy. That ought to explain why he was so often brusque and insulting.

Although—she took a deep sip of the steaming tea and sighed with pleasure—it didn't explain why he'd kissed her. And it certainly didn't explain why she'd let him.

Let him? Hell, she'd enjoyed it. It had been like nothing else she'd ever experienced, more like the warmth and security she'd known when her parents were still alive than anything she'd felt since. But there had been a spark of something different and new, something exciting and dangerous, something so very beautiful and wild.

Caroline shuddered to think what would have happened if he hadn't called her Carlotta. It was the only thing that had jolted her back to her senses.

She reached out to pour herself another cup of tea, and in the process, brushed up against a cloth napkin covering a plate. What was this? She lifted the napkin.

Shortbread! It was heaven right here in a plate of biscuits.

She bit into a piece and let it melt in her mouth, wondering if he even knew he'd brought her food. She rather doubted he'd prepared the tea. Perhaps his housekeeper had put the shortbread on the tray without his instruction.

Better eat fast, she told herself. Who knew when he'd be back?

Caroline shoved another piece of shortbread into her mouth, giggling silently as the crumbs flew all over the bed.

Blake ignored her for the rest of the day and the next morning, only checking in on her to make certain she hadn't taken a turn for the worse and to bring her some more tea. She looked bored, hungry, and pleased to see him, but he did nothing other than silently leave the tea service on the table and check her forehead for signs of fever. Her skin was a little warm but by no means burning up, so he just told her again to ring the bellpull if she felt sick, and left the room.

He noticed that Mrs. Mickle had added a plate of small sandwiches to the tray, but he didn't have the heart to remove them. There was no use in starving her, he'd decided. The Marquis of Riverdale would surely arrive soon, and she wouldn't be able to keep silent with both of them questioning her.

There was nothing to do, really, but wait.

The marquis did arrive the next day, pulling his carriage to a halt in front of Seacrest Manor just before sundown. James Sidwell jumped down, elegantly dressed as always, his dark brown hair just a shade too long for fashion. He had a reputation that would make the devil blush, but he would give his life for Blake, and Blake knew it.

"You look terrible," James said bluntly.

Blake just shook his head. "After spending the past few days cooped up with Miss De Leon, I consider myself a worthy candidate for Bedlam."

"That bad, eh?"

"I vow, Riverdale," he said, "I could kiss you."

"I do hope it doesn't come to that."

"She's nearly driven me insane."

"Has she?" James replied with a sideways look. "How?"

Blake scowled at him. James's suggestive tone hit a little too close to the mark. "She can't talk."

"Since when?"

"Since she stayed up half the night coughing herself hoarse."

James chuckled. "I never said she wasn't resourceful."

"And she bloody well can't write."

"I find that difficult to believe. Her mother was the daughter of a baron. And her father is quite well-connected in Spain."

"Allow me to rephrase. She can write, but I defy you to decipher the marks she puts down on paper. Furthermore, she has a book full of the oddest words, and I vow I can't make any sense of them."

"Why don't you take me to see her? I may be able to convince her to locate her voice."

Blake shook his head and rolled his eyes. "She's all yours. In fact, you can take over the entire damned mission if you like. If I never laid eyes on the woman—"

"Now, now, Blake."

"I told them I wanted out of this," Blake muttered as he tromped up the stairs. "But did they listen? No. And what do I get? Not excitement. Not fame, not fortune. No, I get *her*."

James looked at him thoughtfully. "If I didn't know you better I'd think you were in love."

Blake snorted, turning away so that James couldn't see the light blush that stained his cheeks. "And if I didn't enjoy your company so well, I would call you out for that statement."

James laughed out loud and watched Blake as he stopped in front of a door and turned the keys in the locks.

Blake swung the door open and marched in, his hands on his hips as he turned to Miss De Leon with a belligerent expression. She was lounging on the bed, reading a book as if she hadn't a care in the world. "Riverdale's here," he barked, "so you'll see that your little game is over."

Blake turned to James, gleefully ready to watch him make mincemeat out of her. But James's expression, usually so controlled and urbane, was one of total and utter shock.

"I don't know what to tell you," James said, "except that this most definitely is not Carlotta De Leon."

Chapter 5

pule *(verb). 1. To cry in a thin or weak voice, as a child. 2. To pipe plaintively, as a chicken.*

Had I any voice left, I'm sure I should have puled.

—From the personal dictionary of Caroline Trent

"Oh dear," Caroline croaked, forgetting that she was supposed to be mute.

"And how the hell long have you had your damned voice back?" her captor demanded.

"I . . . ah . . . Not so long, really."

"Really, Blake," the second man said. "You might want to mind your language. There is a lady present."

"Bugger that!" Blake exploded. "Do you know how much time I've wasted with this woman? The real Carlotta De Leon is probably halfway to China by now."

Caroline swallowed nervously. So his name was Blake. It fit him somehow. Short and to the point. She wondered if it was his Christian name or his surname.

"And," he continued in a blaze of fury, "since you're obviously not the woman you said you are, who the devil are you?"

"I never said I was Carlotta De Leon," she insisted.

"The devil you didn't!"

"I just never said I wasn't."

"Who are you?"

Caroline pondered this question and decided that her only recourse was absolute honesty. "My name is Caroline Trent," she replied, her eyes meeting Blake's for the first time in their conversation. "Oliver Prewitt is my guardian."

There was a beat of dead silence as both men stared at her in surprise. Finally Blake turned to his friend and roared, "Why the hell didn't we know that Prewitt had a ward?"

The other man swore under his breath, then swore again, much louder the second time. "I'm damned if I know. Someone is going to answer for this."

Blake turned to Caroline and demanded, "If indeed you are Prewitt's ward, then where have you been the past fortnight? We've been surveying the house day and night, and you, my girl, were most definitely not in residence."

"I was in Bath. Oliver sent me to care for his elderly aunt. Her name is Marigold."

"I don't care what her name is."

"I didn't think you did," she mumbled. "I just thought I ought to say something."

Blake grabbed her shoulder and stared her down. "There is quite a bit you're going to have to say, Miss Trent."

"Let her go," Blake's friend said in a low voice. "Don't lose your temper."

"Don't lose my temper?!" Blake roared, sounding very much as if he'd already lost it. "Do you understand what—"

"Think," the other man said intently. "This makes sense. Prewitt had a large shipment arrive last week. He'd want her out of the way. She's obviously smart enough to sniff out what he's doing."

Caroline beamed at the compliment, but Blake didn't seem to care about her intellect one way or another. "That was the fourth time Oliver sent me off to visit his aunt," she added helpfully.

"See?" Blake's friend said.

Caroline smiled tentatively at Blake, hoping he'd accept the olive branch she'd just offered, but all he did was plant his hands on his hips in a most irritated manner and say, "What the hell do we do now?"

The other man didn't have an answer, and Caroline took advantage of their momentary silence by asking, "Who are you? Both of you."

The two men glanced at each other, as if trying to decide whether to reveal their identities, and then the one who had just recently arrived gave a nearly imperceptible nod before saying, "I am James Sidwell, Marquis of Riverdale, and this is Blake Ravenscroft, second son of Viscount Darnsby."

Caroline smiled wryly at such a barrage of titles. "How nice for you. My father was in trade."

The marquis let loose a loud hoot of laughter before turning to Blake and saying, "Why didn't you tell me she was so entertaining?"

Blake scowled and said, "How would I know? She hasn't spoken two words since the night I captured her."

"Now that isn't entirely true," Caroline protested.

"You mean to say you've been making speeches and I've gone deaf?" Blake returned.

"No, of course not. I merely meant that I have been quite entertaining."

The marquis clapped his hand over his mouth, presumably to stifle a laugh.

Caroline groaned. Another in a long list of sentences that came out absolutely wrong. Dear God, Mr. Ravenscroft must think she was referring to the kiss! "What I meant to say was . . . well, I have no idea what I meant to say, but you must admit you liked my little paper bird. At least until it crashed into the rosebush."

"Paper bird?" the marquis queried, looking confused.

"It— Oh, never you mind. Never both of you mind," Caroline said with a sigh and slow shake of her head. "I apologize for any frustration I might have caused."

Blake looked like he might cheerfully toss her out the window.

"It's just that—"

"It's just that *what*?" he snapped.

"Rein in your temper, Ravenscroft," the marquis said. "She might still be of use to us."

Caroline gulped. That sounded rather ominous. And the marquis, even though he was proving to be far more affable and friendly than Mr. Ravenscroft, looked as if he could be quite ruthless when the occasion warranted.

"What do you suggest, Riverdale?" Blake asked in a low voice.

The marquis shrugged. "We could ransom her. And then when Prewitt comes to collect—"

"No!" Caroline cried out, one hand moving to her throat at the burst of pain the shout caused. "I won't go back. I don't care what's at stake. I don't care if it means Napoleon takes over England. I don't care if it means both of you lose your jobs, or whatever it is you do for the government. I will never go back." And then, just in case they were hugely obtuse, she repeated, "Never."

Blake sat down at the foot of her bed, his expression hard. "Then I suggest you start talking, Miss Trent. Fast."

Caroline told them everything. She told them of her father's death and her five subsequent guardians. She told them of Oliver's plans to gain permanent control of her fortune, Percy's ill-fated attempt to rape her, and how she needed to spend the next six weeks in hiding. She told them so much that her voice gave out again and she had to write down the last third of her tale.

Blake noted grimly that when she used her *left* hand to write, her penmanship was exquisite.

"I thought you said she couldn't write," James said.

Blake stared at him with pure menace. "I don't want to talk about it. And you," he added, pointing at Caroline. "Stop smiling."

She glanced up at him, raising her eyebrows into a guileless expression.

"Surely you can allow the chit her pride at having outsmarted you," James said.

This time Caroline didn't even try to hide her smile.

"Get on with your story," Blake growled at her. She acquiesced, and he read each line of her history with grim anger, disgusted by the way Oliver Prewitt had treated her. She may have frustrated the hell out of him during the past few days, both intellectually and physically, but he couldn't deny a grudging measure of respect for this girl who had managed to thwart him at every turn. That the man who was supposed to be her guardian would treat her so abominably—it made him shake with fury.

"What do you suggest we do with you?" he asked when she finally stopped scribbling her life story.

"For the love of God, Ravenscroft," the marquis said. "Get the girl some tea. Can't you see she can't speak?"

"You get her some tea."

"I'm not leaving you alone with her. It wouldn't be proper."

"Oh, and I suppose it would be proper for *you* to remain with her?" Blake scoffed. "Your reputation is blacker than the Death."

"Of course, but—"

"Out!" Caroline croaked. "Both of you."

They turned to face her, seemingly having forgotten that the subject of their argument was still in the room.

"I beg your pardon," the marquis said.

I would like a few moments alone, she wrote down, shoving the paper in his face. Then she hastily scrawled, *my lord.*

"Call me James," he replied. "All of my friends do."

She shot him a wry look, clearly doubtful that their bizarre predicament qualified as friendship.

"And he is Blake," James added. "I gather the two of you are on a first name basis?"

I didn't even know his name until just now, she wrote.

"Shame on you, Blake," James said. "Such manners."

"I'm going to forget you said that," Blake growled, "because if I don't, I will have to kill you."

Caroline chuckled despite herself. Say what you will about the enigmatic man who'd abducted her, he did have a sense of humor to match her own. She glanced at him again, this time doubtfully. At least she hoped he was joking.

She shot him another worried glance. The glare he was sending the marquis would have felled Napoleon. Or at the very least delivered an extremely painful injury.

"Pay him no mind," James said cheerfully. "He has the devil's own temper. Always has."

"I beg your pardon," Blake replied, sounding very irritated.

"I've known him since we were twelve," James said. "We roomed together at Eton."

"Did you?" she said hoarsely, testing her voice out again. "How nice for you both."

James chuckled. "The unspoken portion of that sentence, of course, being that we deserve each other. Come along, Ravenscroft, let us leave the poor girl to her privacy. I'm sure she'll want to dress and wash and do all that stuff females like to do."

Blake took a step forward. "She's already dressed. And we'll need to ask her about—"

But James put up a hand. "We've all day to badger her into submission."

Caroline gulped. She didn't like the sound of that.

The two men left the room, and she jumped up, splashed some water on her face, and donned shoes. It felt heavenly to get up and stretch her muscles. She'd been stuck in bed for the past two days and was not used to such inactivity.

Caroline righted her appearance as best as she could, which wasn't saying much, as she'd been wearing the same clothes for four days. They were horribly wrinkled, but they looked clean enough, so she arranged her hair in a single thick braid, then tested the door. She was delighted to see that it was not locked. It wasn't difficult to find her way to the staircase, and she quickly ran down to the ground floor.

"Going somewhere?"

She looked up sharply. Blake was leaning insolently against the wall, his sleeves rolled up and his arms crossed. "Tea," she whispered. "You said I could have some."

"Did I?" he drawled.

"If you didn't, I'm sure you meant to."

His lips curved into an unwilling smile. "You do have a way with words."

She offered him a too-sweet grin. "I'm practicing. After all, I haven't used any for days."

"Don't push me, Miss Trent. My temper is hanging by a very slender thread."

"I rather thought it had already snapped," she retorted. "And beside that, if I'm to call you Blake, you might as well call me Caroline."

"Caroline. It suits you much better than Carlotta ever did."

"Amen to that. I haven't a drop of Spanish blood in me. A touch of French," she added, aware that she was babbling but too nervous in his presence to stop, "but no Spanish."

"You've quite compromised our mission, you realize."

"I can assure you it was not my intention."

"I'm sure it wasn't, but the fact remains that you're going to have to make amends."

"If my making amends will result in Oliver spending the rest of his life in prison, you can be assured of my complete cooperation."

"Prison would be unlikely. The gallows are a much more distinct probability."

Caroline swallowed and looked away, suddenly realizing that her involvement with these two men might send Oliver to his death. She detested the man, to be sure, but she couldn't like being the cause of anyone's demise.

"You'll need to discard your sentimentality," Blake said.

She looked up in shock. Was her face that easy to read? "How did you know what I was thinking?"

He shrugged. "Anyone with a conscience faces that dilemma when they first start in this business."

"Did you?"

"Of course. But I outgrew that quickly."

"What happened?"

He cocked a brow. "You ask a lot of questions."

"Not half as many as you did," she returned.

"I had a government-sanctioned reason to be asking so many questions."

"Was it because your fiancée died?"

He stared at her with such furious intensity that she had to look away. "Never mind," she mumbled.

"Don't bring her up again."

Caroline took an unintended step back at the harsh pain in his voice. "I'm sorry," she murmured.

"For what?"

"I don't know," she said, hesitant to mention his fiancée after the way he'd reacted the last time. "Whatever made you so unhappy."

Blake stared at her with interest. She seemed sincere, which surprised him. He'd been something considerably less than polite to her during the past few days. But before he could think of a reply, they heard the marquis enter the hall.

"I vow, Ravenscroft," James said, "can't you see your way to hiring a few more servants?"

Blake cracked a smile at the sight of the elegant Marquis of Riverdale balancing a tea service. "If I could find another I trust, I'd hire him in a minute. At any rate, as soon as I'm done with my duties at the War Office, the discretion of my servants will no longer be quite as paramount."

"Are you still determined to quit, then?"

"You have to ask?"

"I think he means yes," James said to Caroline. "Although with Ravenscroft, one never knows. He has an appalling habit of answering questions with questions."

"Yes, I'd noticed," she murmured.

Blake pushed himself off the wall. "James?"

"Blake?"

"Shut up."

James grinned. "Miss Trent, why don't we retire to the drawing room? The tea ought to restore your voice at least somewhat. Once we have you speaking without pain, we ought to be able to figure out what the devil to do with you."

Blake closed his eyes for a moment as Caroline trailed after James, listening to her raspy voice as she said, "You should call me Caroline. I've already given Mr. Ravenscroft leave to do so."

Blake waited for a minute or two before following, needing a moment of solitude to sort out his thoughts. Or at least to try. Nothing seemed clear where *she* was concerned. He'd felt such a rush of relief when he'd found out that Carlotta De Leon was not really Carlotta De Leon.

Caroline. Her name was Caroline. Caroline Trent. And he wasn't lusting after a traitor.

He shook his head in disgust. As if that were the only problem facing him just now. What the hell was he supposed to do with her? Caroline Trent was smart, very smart. That much was abundantly clear. And she hated Oliver Prewitt enough to help bring him to justice. It might take a little convincing to help her get past her distaste for espionage, but not much. Prewitt had, after all, ordered his son to rape her. Caroline wasn't likely to turn the other cheek after something like that.

The obvious solution was to keep her here at Seacrest Manor. She was surely full of information they could use against Prewitt. It was doubtful that she was privy to his illegal dealings, but with the proper questioning, he and James could unearth clues that she probably didn't even realize she knew. If nothing else, she'd be able to give them the layout of Prewitt Hall—invaluable information if he and James decided to break in.

So then, if she was such a good addition to their team, why was he so reluctant to ask her to stay?

He knew the answer. He just didn't want to look deep enough within his soul to admit it.

Cursing himself for seven different kinds of a coward, Blake turned on his heel and strode out the front door. He needed some air.

"What do you suppose is keeping our good friend Blake?"

Caroline looked up at the sound of James's voice as she poured his tea. "He certainly isn't my good friend," she replied.

"Well, I wouldn't call him your enemy."

"No, he isn't that. It's just that I don't think friends tie friends to the bedpost."

James choked on his tea. "Caroline, you have no idea."

"The point is moot, anyway," she said, glancing out the window. "He's walking away."

"What?" James shot up from the sofa and crossed the room. "Bloody coward."

"Surely he's not afraid of *me*," she joked.

James turned his head to look at her, his eyes boring into her face so sharply she grew uncomfortable. "Perhaps he is," he murmured, more to himself than to her.

"My lord?"

James shook his head, as if to clear his thoughts, but he didn't stop staring at her. "I told you to call me James." He grinned mischievously. "Or 'dear friend' if you think James is too familiar."

She let out a ladylike snort. "Both are too familiar, as you well know. Given my remarkable predicament, however, it seems silly to split hairs over such a matter."

"An eminently practical woman," he said with a smile. "The very best sort."

"Yes, well, my father was in trade," she quipped. "One must be practical to succeed in such endeavors."

"Ah, yes, of course. Trade. You keep reminding me. What sort of trade?"

"Shipbuilding."

"I see. You must have grown up near the coast, then."

"Yes. In Portsmouth until my— *Why* are you looking at me so oddly?"

"I'm sorry. Was I staring?"

"Yes," she said baldly.

"It's simply that you remind me of someone I once knew. Not in looks. Not even quite in mannerisms. It's more of a . . ." He cocked his head as he searched for the right word. "It's more of a resemblance of spirit, if there is such a thing."

"Oh," Caroline replied, for the lack of anything more intelligent to say. "I see. I do hope she was someone nice."

"Oh, yes. The very best. But never mind that." James walked back across the room and sat down in the chair adjacent to her. "I've been giving our situation a great deal of thought."

Caroline sipped at her tea. "Have you?"

"Yes. I think you should stay here."

"I have no problem with that."

"Not even for your reputation?"

Caroline shrugged. "As you said, I'm practical. Mr. Ravenscroft has already mentioned that his servants are discreet. And my other options are returning to Oliver—"

"Which really isn't an option at all," James interrupted, "unless you want to end up married to that lackwit son of his."

She nodded emphatically. "Or I can go back to my original plan."

"Which was?"

"I'd thought to find work at an inn."

"Not exactly the safest of prospects for a woman alone."

"I know," Caroline agreed, "but I really didn't have a choice."

James stroked his jaw thoughtfully. "You'll be safe here at Seacrest Manor. We're certainly not about to return you to Prewitt."

"Mr. Ravenscroft hasn't yet agreed to let me stay," she reminded him. "And this is his house."

"He will."

Caroline thought James was being a trifle overconfident. But then again he didn't know about the kiss she and Blake had shared. Blake had seemed rather disgusted by the entire affair.

James turned to face her suddenly. "We'll want you to help us bring your guardian to justice."

"Yes, Mr. Ravenscroft said as much."

"Didn't he tell you to call him Blake?"

"Yes, but somehow it seems too . . ."

Intimate. The word hung in her mind, as did the image of his face. Dark brows, elegantly molded cheekbones, a smile that rarely appeared . . . oh, but when it did . . .

It was really embarrassing, Caroline thought, how one of his smiles could make her feel so giddy.

And his kiss! Dear Lord, it had made her feel things that couldn't possibly be good for her sanity. He had leaned toward her, and she'd simply frozen, mesmerized by his heavy-lidded stare. If he hadn't upset the moment by calling her Carlotta, heaven only knew what she would have let him do.

The most amazing thing had been that he had seemed to enjoy the kiss as well. Percy had always said that she was the third-ugliest girl in all Hampshire, but then again Percy was a fool and his taste had always run toward buxom blonds . . .

"Caroline?"

She looked up sharply.

James's lips were curved into an amused smile. "You're woolgathering."

"Oh. Terribly sorry. I was just going to say that Mr. . . . er . . . I mean Blake already talked to me about helping you arrest Oliver. I must say, it's rather disconcerting to know that he may go to the gallows as a direct result of my involvement, but if, as you say, he has been conducting treasonous activities . . ."

"He has. I'm sure of it."

Caroline frowned. "He is a despicable man. It was beastly enough of him to order Percy to attack me, but to endanger thousands of British soldiers . . . I cannot fathom it."

James smiled slowly. "Practical and patriotic. You, Caroline Trent, are a prize."

If only Blake thought so.

Caroline let her teacup clatter into its saucer. She didn't like the direction her thoughts were taking regarding Blake Ravenscroft.

"Ah, look," James said, standing up rather suddenly. "Our errant host returns."

"I beg your pardon?"

James gestured toward the window. "He appears to have changed his mind. Perhaps he has decided our company is really not so bad as all that."

"Or it might just be the rain," Caroline retorted. "It has begun to drizzle."

"So it has. Mother Nature is clearly on our side."

A minute later Blake stalked into the drawing room, his dark hair damp. "Riverdale," he barked, "I've been thinking about her."

"*She* is in the room," Caroline said dryly.

If Blake heard her he ignored her. "She's got to go."

Before Caroline could protest, James had crossed his arms and said, "I disagree. Strongly."

"It's too dangerous. I won't have a female risking her life."

Caroline wasn't sure whether to be flattered or offended. She decided to side with "offended"—his views seemed to stem more from a poor opinion of the female gender as a whole than from any overwhelming concern for her well-being. "Don't you think that is my decision to make?" she put in.

"No," Blake said, finally acknowledging her presence.

"Blake can be rather protective of women," James said, almost as an aside.

Blake glared at him. "I won't have her getting killed."

"She won't get killed," James returned.

"And how do you know that?" Blake demanded.

James chuckled. "Because, my dear boy, I am confident that *you* won't allow it."

"Don't patronize me," Blake growled.

"My apologies for the 'dear boy' comment, but you know I speak the truth."

"Is there something going on here that I ought to know about?" Caroline asked, her head bobbing from man to man.

"No," Blake said succinctly, keeping his gaze a few inches above her head. What the hell was he supposed to do with her? It was far too dangerous for her to stay. He had to make sure she left before it was too late.

But she'd already woken up that part of him he liked to keep undisturbed. The part that cared. And the reason he didn't want her staying—it was simple. She frightened him. He had spent a great deal of his emotional energy keeping his distance from women who aroused anything other than disinterest or lust.

Caroline was smart. She was witty. She was damned appealing. And Blake didn't want her within ten miles of Seacrest Manor. He'd tried caring before. It had nearly destroyed him.

"Ah, bloody hell," he finally said. "She stays, then. But I want both of you to know that I completely disapprove."

"A fact which you have made abundantly clear," James drawled.

Blake ignored him and chanced a look over at Caroline. Bad idea. She smiled at him, really smiled, and it lit up her whole face, and she looked so damned *sweet*, and . . .

Blake swore under his breath. He knew this was a big mistake. The way she was smiling at him, as if she thought she could actually light the farthest corners of his heart . . .

God, she scared him.

Chapter 6

in•con•se•quen•ti•al•i•ty *(noun). The quality of not being consequential.*

There is little more unsettling than a perceived sense of inconsequentiality, *except, perhaps, for the embarrassment one feels when one tries to pronounce it.*

—From the personal dictionary of Caroline Trent

Caroline was so delighted about being allowed to remain at Seacrest Manor that it wasn't until the following morning that she realized a rather pertinent point: She had no information to share. She knew nothing about Oliver's illegal dealings.

In short, she was useless.

Oh, they hadn't figured that out yet. Blake and James probably thought she had all of Oliver's secrets stored neatly in her brain, but the truth was, she knew nothing. And her "hosts" were going to figure that out soon. And then she'd be right back where she'd started.

The only way to keep from being tossed into the cold was to make herself useful. Perhaps if she helped around the house and garden Blake would let her stay at Seacrest Manor even after he realized that she had nothing to offer the War Office. It wasn't as if she needed a permanent home—just a place to hide for six weeks.

"What to do, what to do," she mumbled to herself, walking aimlessly through the house as she looked for a suitable task. She needed to find a project that would take a long time to complete, something that would require her presence for at least several days, maybe a week. By then she should be able to convince Blake and James that she was a polite and entertaining houseguest.

She strolled into the music room and ran her hand along the smooth wood of the piano. It was a pity she didn't know how to play; her father had always intended to arrange for lessons, but he'd died before he could carry out his plans. And it went without saying that her guardians never bothered to have her meet with an instructor.

She lifted the lid and tapped her finger against one of the ivory keys, smiling at the sound it made. Music somehow brightened the whole morning. Not that her peckings could be called music without gravely insulting scores of great composers, but still, Caroline felt better for having made a little noise.

All she needed now to brighten the day in truth was to get a bit of light into the room. The music room had obviously not been occupied yet this morning, for the drapes were still pulled tightly shut. Or perhaps no one used this room on a regular basis, and they were kept closed to keep the sun off the piano. Never having owned a musical instrument, Caroline couldn't be sure whether too much sunlight could be damaging.

Whatever the case, she decided, one morning's worth of sun couldn't hurt too much, so she strode over to the window and pulled the damask drapes back. When she did, she was rewarded with the most perfectly splendid sight.

Roses. Hundreds of them.

"I didn't realize I was right below my little room," she murmured, opening the window and sticking her head out to look up. These must be the rosebushes she could see from her window.

Closer inspection proved her correct. The bushes were terribly neglected and overgrown, just as she remembered, and she saw a flash of white lodged just out of her reach that looked suspiciously like her little paper bird. She leaned out further to get a better look. Hmmm. She could probably reach it from the outside.

A few minutes later Caroline had her paper bird in her hand and was regarding the rosebushes from the other side. "You are in dire need of pruning," she said aloud. Someone had once told her that flowers responded well to conversation, and she had always taken the advice to heart. It wasn't difficult to talk to flowers when one had guardians like hers. The flowers inevitably compared quite favorably.

She planted her hands on her hips, cocked her head, and perused her surroundings. Mr. Ravenscroft wasn't the sort to boot her out while she was tidying his garden, was he? And Lord knew, the garden needed tidying. Aside from the rosebushes, there was honeysuckle that needed to be cut back, hedges that ought to be trimmed, and a lovely purple flowering bush she didn't know the name of that she was convinced would do better in full sun.

Clearly this garden needed her.

Her decision made, Caroline marched back into the house and introduced herself to the housekeeper, who, interestingly enough, didn't look the least bit surprised by her presence. Mrs. Mickle was quite enthusiastic about Caroline's plans for the garden, and she helped her to locate a pair of work gloves, shovel, and some long-handled shears.

She attacked the rosebushes with great enthusiasm and vigor, snipping here and trimming there, chattering to herself—and the flowers—all the while.

"Here you are. You will be much happier without"—*snip*—"this branch, and I'm sure you'll do better if you're thinned out"—*clip*—"right here."

After a while, however, the shears grew heavy, and Caroline decided to put them down on the grass while she dug up the purple flowering plant and moved it to a sunnier location. It seemed prudent to dig a new hole for the plant before moving it, so she surveyed the property and picked out a nice spot that would be visible from the windows.

But then she saw some other lovely flowering plants. These were dotted with pink and white blossoms, but they looked as if they ought to be producing more blooms. The garden could be a delightful riot of color if someone would only care for it properly. "Those should also get more sun," she said aloud. And so she dug up some more holes. And then some more, just for good measure.

"That ought to do it." With a satisfied exhale, she went over to the purple flowering bush that had initially captivated her and started to dig it up.

Blake had gone to bed in a bad mood and had woken up the next morning feeling even worse. This assignment—his *last* assignment, if he had anything to say about it—had turned into a fiasco. A nightmare. A walking disaster with blue-green eyes.

Why had Prewitt's stupid son chosen that night to attack Caroline Trent? *Why* did she have to go off running into the night the very evening he was expecting Carlotta De Leon? And worst of all, how the devil was he supposed to concentrate on bringing Oliver Prewitt to justice with her running about underfoot?

She was a constant temptation, and an aching reminder of all that had been stolen from him. Cheerful, innocent, and optimistic, she was everything that had been missing from his heart for so very long. Since Marabelle had been killed, to be precise. The entire bloody situation seemed to prove the existence of a higher power—one whose sole purpose was to drive Blake Ravenscroft absolutely and irrevocably insane.

Blake stomped out of his bedroom, his expression black.

"Ever cheerful, I see."

He looked up to see James standing at the end of the hall. "Do you lurk in dark corners, just waiting to bedevil me?" he growled.

James laughed. "I have far more important people to bedevil than you, Ravenscroft. I was just on my way down to breakfast."

"I've been thinking about *her*."

"I'm not surprised."

"What the hell is that supposed to mean?"

James shrugged, his expression beyond innocent.

Blake's hand descended heavily on his friend's shoulder. "Tell me," he ordered.

"Merely," James replied, removing Blake's hand and letting it drop, "that you look at her a certain way."

"Don't be stupid."

"I've many bad qualities, but stupidity has never been among them."

"You're insane."

James ignored his comment. "She seems like a nice girl. Perhaps you should get to know her better."

Blake turned on him in fury. "She isn't the sort one gets to know *better*," he roared, sneering the last word. "Miss Trent is a lady."

"I never said she wasn't. My my, what did you think I was implying?"

"Riverdale," Blake warned.

James just waved his hand in the air. "I was merely thinking that it has been quite some time since you've courted a female, and as she's conveniently right here at Seacrest Manor—"

"I have no romantic interest in Caroline," Blake bit out. "And even if I did, you know that I will never marry."

"*Never* is a very strong word. Even I don't go around saying I will never marry, and Lord knows I have more reason to avoid the institution than you do."

"Don't start, Riverdale," Blake warned.

James stared him hard in the eye. "Marabelle is dead."

"Do you think I don't know that? Do you think I don't remember that every single bloody day of my life?"

"Maybe it's time you *stopped* remembering that every single bloody day. It's been five years, Blake. Almost six. Stop doing penance for a crime you didn't commit."

"The hell I didn't! I should have stopped her. I knew it was dangerous. I knew she shouldn't—"

"Marabelle had a mind of her own," James said with surprising gentleness. "You couldn't have stopped her. She made her own decisions. She always did."

"I swore to protect her," Blake said in a low voice.

"When?" James asked flippantly. "I don't recall attending a wedding between the two of you."

In half a second Blake had him pinned up against the wall. "Marabelle was my affianced bride," he ground out. "I swore to *myself* that I would protect her, and in my view, that oath is more binding than anything sworn before God and England."

"Marabelle isn't here. Caroline is."

Blake abruptly let him go. "God help us."

"We have to keep her at Seacrest Manor until she's free of Prewitt's guardianship," James said, rubbing his shoulder where Blake had grabbed him. "It's the very least we can do after you abducted her and tied her to the bedpost. Tied her to the bedpost, eh? I should have liked to have seen that."

Blake glared at him with a ferocity that could have felled a tiger.

"And beside that," James added, "she may very well prove useful."

"I don't want to *use* a woman. Last time we did that in the name of the War Office she ended up dead."

"For the love of God, Ravenscroft, what will happen to her here at Seacrest Manor? No one knows she's in residence, and it's not as if we're going to send her out on missions. She'll be fine. Certainly safer than if we turned her out on her own."

"She'd do better if we packed her off to one of my relatives," Blake grumbled.

"Oh, and how are you going to explain that? Someone is going to wonder how you came to be in possession of Oliver Prewitt's ward, and then any hope we have of secrecy will be destroyed."

Blake grunted in irritation. James was right. He couldn't let his connection to Caroline Trent be made public. If he was going to protect her from Prewitt, he had to do it here at Seacrest Manor. It was either that or turn her out. He shuddered to think what would happen to her, alone on the streets of Portsmouth, which was where she'd been heading when he'd abducted her. It was a rough harbor town, filled with sailors—definitely not the safest place for a young woman.

"I see you concede my point," James said.

Blake nodded curtly.

"Very well, then. Shall we break our fast? I find myself salivating at the thought of one of Mrs. Mickle's omelettes. We can discuss what to do with our lovely houseguest over our meal."

Blake let James lead the way down the stairs, but when they reached the ground floor there was no sign of Caroline.

"Do you suppose she slept in?" James asked. "I imagine she must be quite tired after her ordeal."

"It wasn't an ordeal."

"For you, perhaps. The poor girl was kidnapped."

"The 'poor girl,' as you so sweetly put it, had me running around in circles for days. If anyone suffered an ordeal," Blake said rather firmly, "it was I."

While they were discussing Caroline's absence, Mrs. Mickle bustled into the room with a plate of scrambled eggs. She smiled and said, "Oh, there you are, Mr. Ravenscroft. I met your new houseguest."

"She was here?"

"What a lovely girl. So polite."

"Caroline?"

"It's so nice to meet a young person with such a sweet temperament. Clearly she was taught manners."

Blake just raised a brow. "Miss Trent was raised by wolves."

Mrs. Mickle dropped the eggs. "What?"

Blake closed his eyes—anything not to see the yellow eggs splattered on his perfectly polished boots. "What I meant, Mrs. Mickle, was that she might as well have been raised by wolves, given the pack of guardians to which she was subjected."

By then the housekeeper was on the floor with a cloth napkin, trying to clean up the mess. "Oh, but the poor dear," she said with obvious concern. "I had no idea she'd had a difficult childhood. I shall have to make her a special pudding this evening."

Blake's lips parted in consternation, as he tried to recall the last time Mrs. Mickle had done the same for him.

James, who'd been grinning to himself in the doorway, stepped forward and asked, "Do you have any idea where she went, Mrs. Mickle?"

"I believe she's working in the garden. She took with her quite a bit of equipment."

"Equipment? What kind of equipment?" Blake's mind was flashing with horrific images of mangled trees and hacked up plants. "Where did she find equipment?"

"I gave it to her."

Blake turned on his heel and strode out. "God help us."

He wasn't prepared for what he saw.

Holes.

Big, gaping holes, all over his formerly pristine lawn. Or at least he'd thought it had been pristine. In all truth, he had never paid much attention to it. But he did know that it had definitely not looked like *this*, with brown clumps of earth littered across the grass. He didn't see Caroline, but he knew she had to be there.

"What have you done?" he bellowed.

A head popped out from behind a tree. "Mr. Ravenscroft?"

"What are you doing? This is a disaster. And you," he said to James, who hadn't made a sound, "stop laughing."

Caroline emerged from behind the tree, her dress liberally streaked with dirt. "I'm fixing your garden."

"You're fixing my— You're *what?* This doesn't look the least bit fixed to me."

"It's not going to look so wonderful until I finish with my work, but when I do—"

"Your work? All I see is a dozen holes."

"Two dozen."

"I shouldn't have said that, were I you," James commented from a safe distance.

Caroline stuck the end of her shovel in the dirt and leaned on it as she spoke to Blake. "Once you hear my explanation, I'm sure you will understand—"

"I understand nothing!"

"Yes." She sighed, "men usually don't."

Blake started looking around the garden, his head whipping frantically from side to side as he tried to assess the damage. "I'm going to have to call in an expert from London to repair what you've done. Good God, woman, you're going to cost me a bloody fortune."

"Don't be silly," she replied. "These holes will all be filled up by evening. I'm merely moving your flowering plants into the sun. They'll do much better. Except for that impatiens, of course," she added, pointing to the lovely pink and white flowers planted right next to the house. "Those thrive in the shade."

"I say, Ravenscroft," James said, "perhaps you ought to let her continue."

"They were getting too much sun," Caroline explained. "The buds were burning off before they had a chance to bloom."

James turned to Blake and said, "It does sound as if she knows what she's doing."

"I don't care if she's earned a bloody doctorate in horticulture. She had no right to tear apart my garden."

Caroline planted her free hand on her hip. She was starting to get more than a little irritated with his attitude. "It's not as if you gave a care to the garden before I started my work here."

"And why would you think that?"

"Anyone with an ounce of gardening sense would have been appalled by the state of your rosebushes," she scoffed, "and the hedges are in dire need of trimming."

"You're not to touch my hedges," he warned.

"I wasn't planning on it. They've grown so high I couldn't possibly reach the top, anyway. I was going to ask *you* to do it."

Blake turned to James "Did I really agree to let her stay?"

James nodded.

"Damn."

"I was merely trying to be of help," she said, bristling at his insults.

He gaped at her, then gaped at the holes. "Help?"

"I thought it only polite to earn my keep."

"Earn your keep? It'd take you ten years to earn your keep after this damage!"

Caroline had been trying to keep her temper in check. In fact, she'd been mentally congratulating herself for remaining so level-headed and cheerful in the face of his anger.

No longer.

"You sir," she exploded, barely resisting the urge to swing the shovel at him, "are the rudest, most ill-mannered man in all creation!"

He raised a brow. "Surely you can do better than that."

"I can," she growled, "but I'm in polite company."

"You don't mean Riverdale?" Blake said with a laugh as he flicked his head toward his grinning friend. "He's about the least polite company I know."

"However," the marquis cut in, "I would have to agree with the lady on her assessment of your character, Ravenscroft." He turned to Caroline. "He's a brute."

"God save me from the two of you," Blake muttered.

"The least you could do," Caroline said with a little sniff, "is thank me."

"Thank you!?"

"You're welcome," she said quickly. "Now then, would you like to assist me in moving these plants to their new locations?"

"No."

James stepped forward. "I would be delighted."

"You're too kind, my lord," she said with a sunny smile.

Blake scowled at his friend. "We've work to do, Riverdale."

"We do?"

"Important work," Blake practically roared.

"What could be more important than assisting a lady while she's working in the hot sun?"

Caroline turned to Blake with a questioning smile and mischievous eyes. "Yes, Mr. Ravenscroft, what could possibly be more important?"

Blake stared at her in utter disbelief. She was a guest in his home—a guest!—and not only had she dug up his garden, she was also scolding him like some recalcitrant schoolboy. And Riverdale, who was supposed to be his best friend, was standing by her side, grinning like an idiot.

"I've gone mad," he murmured. "I've gone mad, or you've gone mad, or perhaps the whole world has gone mad."

"My vote's on you," James quipped. "I'm quite sane, and Miss Trent shows no signs of derangement."

"I don't believe this. I just don't believe this." Blake threw up his arms as he strode away. "Dig up the entire garden! Add a new wing to the house! What do I matter? I just own the place."

Caroline turned to James with concern as Blake disappeared around the corner. "How angry do you suppose he is?"

"On a scale of one to ten?"

"Er . . . if you think his mood would fit on such a scale."

"It wouldn't."

She chewed on her lower lip. "I was afraid of that."

"But I wouldn't worry," James said with a reassuring wave of his hand. "He'll come around. Ravenscroft isn't used to having his life disrupted. He's a bit grumpy, but he's not entirely unreasonable."

"Are you certain of that?"

James recognized her question as rhetorical and took the shovel from her hands. "Here now," he said, "tell me what you need me to do."

Caroline gave him instructions to dig under the purple flowering plant and knelt down to watch his work. "Mind that you don't break the roots," she said. Then a moment later: "Why do you suppose he is always so angry with me?"

James didn't reply for a few moments, and the shovel stilled in his hands as he obviously pondered how to answer her question. "He's not angry with you," he finally said.

She gave a little laugh. "We were obviously not watching the same person just now."

"I mean it. He's not angry with you." He stepped on the edge of the shovel and pushed it further down in the dirt. "He's afraid of you."

Caroline started coughing so hard James had to whack her on the back. When she caught her breath she said, "I beg your pardon."

There was another long moment of silence, and then James said, "He was engaged once."

"I know."

"Do you know what happened?"

She shook her head. "Just that she died."

"Blake loved her more than life itself."

Caroline swallowed, surprised by the squeezing pain in her heart elicited by James's statement.

"They'd known each other all their lives," he continued. "They worked together for the War Office."

"Oh, no," she said, her hand moving to her mouth.

"Marabelle was killed by a traitor. She'd gone out on a mission in Blake's place. He had a putrid throat or something of the sort." James paused to wipe a bit of sweat from his brow. "He forbade her to go, utterly forbade her, but she was never the sort to listen to ultimatums. She just laughed and told him she'd see him later in the evening."

Caroline swallowed, but the motion did little to ease the lump in her throat. "At least her family could take solace in the fact that she died for her country," she offered.

James shook his head. "They didn't know. They were told—everyone was told—that Marabelle had been killed in a hunting accident."

"I—I don't know what to say."

"There's really nothing to say. Or do. That's the problem." James looked away for a moment, his eyes focusing on some spot on the horizon, then asked, "Do you remember when I said you reminded me of someone?"

"Yes," Caroline said slowly, horror beginning to dawn in her eyes. "Oh, no . . . not her."

James nodded. "I'm not certain why, but you do."

She bit her lip and stared at her feet. Dear God, was that why Blake had kissed her? Because she somehow resembled his dead fiancée? She suddenly felt very small and very insignificant. And very undesirable.

"It's really nothing," James said, clearly concerned by her unhappy expression.

"I would never take a risk like that," Caroline said firmly. "Not if I had someone to love." She swallowed. "Not if I had someone who loved me."

James touched her hand. "It's been a lonely time for you these past few years, hasn't it?"

But Caroline wasn't ready for sympathetic comments. "What happened to Blake?" she asked sharply. "After she died."

"He was devastated. Drunk for three months. He blamed himself."

"Yes, I'm sure he would. He's the sort to take responsibility for everyone, isn't he?"

James nodded.

"But surely he realizes now that it wasn't his fault."

"In his head, perhaps, but not in his heart."

There was a long pause while they both stared at the ground. When Caroline finally spoke, her voice was soft and unnaturally tentative. "Do you really think he thinks I look like her?"

James shook his head. "No. And you don't look like her. Marabelle was quite blond, actually, with pale blue eyes and—"

"Then why did you say—"

"Because it's rare to meet a woman of such spirit." When Caroline didn't say anything, James grinned and added, "That was a compliment, by the way."

Caroline twisted her lips into something that was halfway between a grimace and a wry smile.

"Thank you, then. But I still don't see why he's being such a beast."

"Consider the situation from his view. First he thought you were a traitor, the very breed of vermin who'd killed Marabelle. Then he found himself in the position of your protector, which can only remind him of how he failed his fiancée."

"But he didn't fail her!"

"Of course he didn't," James replied. "But he doesn't know that. And furthermore, it's quite obvious he finds you rather fetching."

Caroline blushed and was immediately furious with herself for doing so.

"That, I think," James said, "is what scares him the most. What if, horror of horrors, he were to fall in love with you?"

Caroline didn't see that as the worst horror in the world, but she kept the thought to herself.

"Can you even count how many ways he'd think he was betraying Marabelle? He could never live with himself."

She didn't know what to say in reply, so she just pointed to a hole in the ground and said, "Put the plant there."

James nodded. "You won't tell him of our little chat?"

"Of course not."

"Good." Then he did as she asked.

Chapter 7

di·a·crit·i·cal *(adjective). Distinguishing, distinctive.*

One cannot deny that a complete lack of order is the diacritical *mark of Mr. Ravenscroft's garden.*

—From the personal dictionary of Caroline Trent

By the end of the day, Caroline had the garden looking the way she thought a garden ought. James agreed with her, complimenting her on her excellent sense of landscape design. Blake, on the other hand, couldn't be prodded into uttering even the most grudging words of praise. In fact, the only noise he'd made at all was a rather strangled groan that sounded a bit like: "My roses."

"Your roses had gone wild," she'd returned, thoroughly exasperated with this man.

"I liked them wild," he'd shot back.

And that had been that. But he'd surprised her by ordering two new dresses to replace the one she'd brought from Prewitt Hall. That poor rag had been through enough, what with being kidnapped, slept in for days, and dragged through the mud. Caroline wasn't sure when or where he'd managed to get two ready-to-wear dresses, but they seemed to fit her reasonably well, so she thanked him prettily and didn't complain that the hem dragged just a touch on the floor.

She took her supper in her room, not feeling up to another battle of wills with her somewhat cranky host. And besides, she'd obtained a needle and thread from Mrs. Mickle, and she wanted to get to work shortening her new dresses.

Since it was high summer, the sun hung in the sky well past the time she ate her evening meal, and when her fingers grew tired she put her sewing down and walked to the window. The hedges were neat and the roses were trimmed to perfection; she and James had clearly done an excellent job with the gardens. Caroline felt a sense of pride in herself that she hadn't experienced in a long time. It had been much too long since she had had the pleasure of starting and completing a task that interested her.

But she wasn't convinced that Blake had come to appreciate her worth as a helpful and courteous houseguest yet; in fact, she was rather certain he had not. So tomorrow she would have to find herself another task, preferably one that would take a bit more time.

He had told her that she could remain at Seacrest Manor until her twenty-first birthday, and she was damned if she was going to let him find a way to escape his promise.

The next morning found Caroline exploring Seacrest Manor on a full stomach. Mrs. Mickle, who was now her greatest champion, had met her in the breakfast room and fed her no end of delicacies and treats. Omelettes, sausages, kidney pie—Caroline didn't even recognize some of the dishes that graced the sideboard. Mrs. Mickle seemed to have prepared food for an entire army.

After breakfast she set about finding a new project to keep her busy while in residence. She peered into this room and that, finally ending up in the library. It wasn't as large as those in some of the grander estates, but it boasted several hundred volumes. The leather spines gleamed in the early morning light, and the room held the lemony smell of freshly cleaned wood. But a closer inspection of the shelves revealed that they had been filed in no order whatsoever.

Voilà!

"Clearly," Caroline said to the empty room, "he needs his books alphabetized."

She pulled down a stack of books, plunked them on the floor, and idly examined the titles. "I don't know how he has managed this long in such chaos."

More books found their way to the floor. "Of course," she said with an expansive wave of her hand, "there is no need for me to try to order these piles now. I'll have plenty of time to do that after I finish unloading all of the shelves. I'll be here for five more weeks, after all."

She paused to look at a random volume. It was a mathematical treatise. "Fascinating," she murmured, flipping through the pages so that she could glance at the incomprehensible prose. "My father always told me I should learn more arithmetic."

She giggled. It was amazing how slowly one could work when one really put one's mind to it.

When Blake came down for breakfast that morning he found a feast the likes of which he'd never seen since taking up residence at Seacrest Manor. His morning meal usually consisted of a platter of fried eggs, a slice or two of ham, and some cold toast. Those items were all in evidence, but they were accompanied by roast beef, Dover sole, and a variety of pastries and tarts that boggled the mind.

Mrs. Mickle had clearly found new culinary inspiration, and Blake had no doubt that her name was Caroline Trent.

He resolved not to let himself grow irritated at the way his housekeeper was playing favorites and instead decided simply to fill his plate and enjoy the bounty. He was munching on the most delicious strawberry tart when James strolled into the room.

"Good morning to you," the marquis said. "Where is Caroline?"

"Damned if I know, but half the ham is missing, so I imagine she's come and gone."

James whistled. "Mrs. Mickle certainly outdid herself this morning, didn't she? You should have had Caroline move in sooner."

Blake shot him an irritated glance.

"Well, you must admit that your housekeeper has never gone to such lengths to keep *you* so well-fed."

Blake liked to think that he would have responded with something utterly wry and cutting, but before he could think of anything the least bit witty, they heard a tremendous crash, followed by a feminine shriek of—was it surprise? Or was it pain? Whatever it was, it definitely came from Caroline, and Blake's heart pounded in his chest as he dashed toward the library and threw open the door.

He'd thought he'd been shocked by his dug-up garden the day before. This was worse.

"What the hell?" he whispered, too shocked to manage a normal speaking voice.

"What happened?" James demanded, skidding to a halt behind him. "Oh my good Lord. What on earth?"

Caroline was sitting in the center of the library, surrounded by books. Or perhaps it would have been more accurate to say that she was sprawled on the library floor, covered with books. An overturned stepstool lay next to her, and tall piles of books were stacked up on every table and a good portion of the rug.

In fact, not a single volume remained on the shelves. It looked as if Blake's houseguest had somehow managed to conjure a whirlwind for the sole purpose of tearing his library to pieces.

Caroline looked up at them and blinked. "I suppose you're both a bit curious."

"Er . . . yes," Blake replied, thinking that he ought to be yelling at her about something, but not sure what, and still a bit too surprised to come up with a good tirade.

"I thought to put your books in order."

"Yes," he said slowly, trying to take in the scope of the mess. "They look very well-ordered."

Behind him, James let out a snort of laughter, and Caroline planted her hands on her hips and said, "Don't tease!"

"Ravenscroft here wouldn't dream of teasing you," James said. "Would he?"

Blake shook his head. "Wouldn't dream of it."

Caroline scowled at them both. "One of you might offer to help me up."

Blake was about to move aside to let Riverdale pass, but the marquis shoved him forward until he had to lend the girl his hand or seem insufferably rude.

"Thank you," she said, awkwardly rising to her feet. "I'm sorry about the— Ow!" She pitched forward into Blake's arms, and for a moment he was able to forget who he was, and what he'd done, and simply savor the feel of her.

"Are you hurt?" he asked gruffly, oddly reluctant to let her go.

"My ankle. I must have twisted it when I fell."

He looked down at her with an amused expression. "This isn't another ill-conceived attempt to force us to let you remain here, now is it?"

"Of course not!" she replied, clearly offended. "As if I would deliberately injure myself to—" She looked up sheepishly. "Oh, yes, I did quite destroy my throat the other day, didn't I?"

He nodded, the corners of his mouth quivering toward a smile.

"Yes, well, I had a very good reason . . . Oh, you were teasing me, weren't you?"

He nodded again.

"It's hard to tell, you know."

"Hard to tell what?"

"When you're teasing," she replied. "You're very serious most of the time."

"You're going to have to stay off of that ankle," Blake said abruptly. "At least until the swelling subsides."

Her voice was soft when she said, "You didn't answer my question."

"You didn't ask a question."

"Didn't I? I suppose I didn't. But you did change the subject."

"A gentleman doesn't like to talk about how serious he is."

"Yes, I know." She sighed. "You like to talk of cards and hounds and horses and how much money you lost at the faro table the night before. I've yet to meet a truly responsible gentleman. Aside from my dear father, of course."

"We're not all so bad as that," he said, turning around to press James to help defend their gender. But James had disappeared.

"What happened to the marquis?" Caroline inquired, craning her neck.

"Damned if I know." His face colored as he remembered his manners. "Pardon my language."

"You didn't seem to have a problem cursing in front of Carlotta De Leon."

"The real Carlotta De Leon, I imagine, could teach *me* a thing or two about cursing."

"I'm not as delicate as I look," she said with a shrug. "My ears aren't going to burn up at the occasional use of the word *damn*. Lord knows my tongue hasn't fallen off for saying it."

His lips reluctantly curved into an honest smile. "Are you saying, Miss Caroline Trent, that you are not every inch a lady?"

"Not at all," she said archly. "I am very much a lady. Simply one who . . . ah . . . occasionally uses less than proper language."

He burst out in unexpected laughter.

"My guardians weren't always the most circumspect of men," she explained.

"I see."

She cocked her head and stared at him thoughtfully. "You should laugh more often."

"There are a lot of things I should do," he said simply.

Caroline didn't know what to make of that comment. "Er . . . should we try to find the marquis?"

"Clearly, he doesn't want to be found."

"Why not?"

"I haven't the slightest idea," he said, in a tone that said he had a very good idea. "Riverdale rather excels at disappearing when he's of a mind to do so."

"I suppose that comes in handy in your line of work."

Blake didn't reply. He had no wish to discuss his work for the War Office with her. Women tended to find his exploits dashing and glamorous, and he knew that they were anything but. There was nothing dashing or glamorous about death.

Caroline finally broke the long silence. "I'm sure you can let go of me now."

"Can you walk?"

"Of course I— Ow!"

She'd barely taken a step before she howled in pain again. Blake immediately swept her into his arms and said, "I'll carry you to the drawing room."

"But my books!" she protested.

"I believe they are *my* books," he said with a small smile, "and I'll have one of the servants come and put them back."

"No, no, please don't do that. I'll put them back myself."

"If you'll pardon my saying so, Miss Trent, you cannot even walk. How do you plan to rearrange a library?"

Caroline twisted her head to view the chaos she'd inflicted as he carried her out of the room. "Couldn't you leave them this way for a few days? I promise I'll take care of the mess once my ankle heals. I have grand plans for the library, you see."

"Do you?" he asked doubtfully.

"Yes, I thought to put all of your scientific treatises together, and to group the biographies onto one shelf, and, well, I'm sure you see my idea. It will be ever so much easier to find your books."

"It certainly has to be easier than it is now, with everything on the floor."

Caroline scowled at him. "I'm doing you a tremendous favor. If you cannot be grateful, at the very least you could contrive not to be quite so *un*grateful."

"Very well, I profess my undying and eternal gratitude."

"That didn't sound terribly sincere," she muttered.

"It wasn't," he admitted, "but it will have to do. Here we are." He set her down on a sofa. "Shall we elevate your leg?"

"I don't know. I've never twisted an ankle before. Is that what one is meant to do?"

He nodded and piled soft pillows under her leg. "It reduces the swelling."

"Bother the swelling. It's the pain I'd like to reduce."

"They go hand in hand."

"Oh. How long will I have to remain like this?"

"At least for the rest of the day, I should think. Perhaps tomorrow as well."

"Hmmph. That is perfectly dreadful. I don't suppose you could fetch me a spot of tea."

Blake drew himself back and looked at her. "Do I look like a nursemaid?"

"Not at all," she replied, clearly holding back a giggle. "It's just that Mrs. Mickle has gone to the village after preparing that lovely breakfast, heaven only knows where your butler is, and I don't think your valet fetches tea."

"If I can fetch it, he damned well can, too," Blake muttered.

"Oh, good!" she exclaimed, clapping her hands together. "Then you'll get some for me?"

"I suppose I must. And how the devil have you come to be on such good terms with my servants in only one day?"

She shrugged. "Actually, I've only met Mrs. Mickle. Did you know she has a nine-year-old granddaughter who lives in the village? She bought her the loveliest doll for her birthday. I should have loved a doll like that when I was a girl."

Blake shook his head in amazement. Mrs. Mickle had been working for him for nearly three years, and she'd never mentioned that she had a granddaughter. "I'll be right back with that tea," he said.

"Thank you. And don't forget to make enough for yourself as well."

He stopped in the doorway. "I won't be joining you."

Caroline's face fell. "You won't?"

"No, I . . ." He groaned. He'd done battle against some of the world's most devious criminals, but he was powerless in the face of her frown. "Very well, I'll join you, but only for a short while."

"Wonderful. I'm sure you'll have a lovely time. And you'll find that tea does wonders for your disposition."

"My disposition!"

"Forget I mentioned it," she mumbled.

Mrs. Mickle was nowhere to be found when Blake reached the kitchen. After hollering for the housekeeper for a minute or so, he remembered that Caroline had said she had gone to town.

"Dratted female," he muttered, not sure whether he was referring to Caroline or Mrs. Mickle.

Blake put some water on to boil and scrounged around in the cupboards for some tea. Unlike most men of his station, he knew his way around a kitchen. Soldiers and spies often had to learn how to cook if they wanted to eat, and Blake was no exception. Gourmet meals were quite beyond his repertoire, but he could certainly manage tea and biscuits. Especially since Mrs. Mickle had already baked the biscuits. All Blake had to do was set them on a plate.

It felt very strange to be doing this for Caroline Trent. It had been a long time since he'd taken care of anyone save for himself, and there was something comforting about listening to the teakettle squeak and howl as the water boiled. Comforting and yet at the same time unsettling. Preparing tea, tending to her twisted ankle—they weren't terribly intimate acts, and yet he could feel them pulling him closer to her.

He fought the urge to smack himself in the head. He was growing overly and stupidly philosophical. He wasn't becoming close to Caroline Trent, and he certainly had no desire to do so. They'd shared one kiss, and it had been an idiotic impulse on his part. As for her, she probably hadn't known any better. He'd bet his home and his fortune that she'd never been kissed before.

The water came to a boil, and Blake poured it into the china teapot, taking a sniff of the fragrant aroma as the tea began to steep. After placing a small pitcher of milk and a bowl of sugar on the tray, he picked up the service and headed back to the drawing room. He didn't really mind getting the tea; there was something rather soothing in performing the occasional mindless task. But Miss Trent was going to have to get it through her stubborn little skull that he wasn't going to play nursemaid and fetch her every whim and desire while she was living at Seacrest Manor.

He didn't want to act like some lovesick puppy, he didn't want Caroline to think he was acting like a lovesick puppy, and he certainly didn't want

James to see him acting like a lovesick puppy.

It didn't matter that he wasn't the least bit love-sick. James would never let him live it down.

Blake turned the last corner and headed into the drawing room, but when his eyes fell upon the sofa, there was an empty spot where Caroline should have been, and a rather large mess on the floor.

And then he heard a rather sheepish voice say, "It was an accident. I swear."

Chapter 8

***quaff** (verb). To drink deeply; to take a long draught.*

I have found that when a gentleman grows ill-tempered, oftentimes the best antidote is to invite him to quaff *a cup of tea.*

—From the personal dictionary of Caroline Trent

Freshly cut flowers were strewn on the floor, a priceless vase was overturned but thankfully not broken, and a wet stain was seeping across Blake's very new, very expensive Aubusson carpet.

"I just wanted to smell them," Caroline said from her position on the floor.

"You were supposed to stay still!" Blake yelled.

"Well, I know that but—"

"No 'buts'!" he roared, checking to see that her ankle wasn't twisted in some hideous fashion.

"There is no need to shout."

"I'LL SHOUT IF I—" He stopped, cleared his throat, and continued in a more normal tone. "I will shout if I damned well please, and I will speak like this if I damned well please. And if I want to whisper—"

"I'm sure I catch your meaning."

"May I remind you that this is *my* house, and I can do anything I want?"

"You don't need to remind me," she said agreeably.

Her friendly and accepting tone needled at him. "Miss Trent, if you are going to remain here—"

"I'm extensively grateful that you're going to let me stay," she interjected.

"I don't care about your gratitude—"

"Nonetheless, I'm happy to offer it."

He gritted his teeth. "We need to establish a few rules."

"Well, yes, of course, the world needs a few rules. Otherwise, chaos would ensue, and then—"

"Would you stop interrupting me!"

She drew her head back a fraction of an inch. "I believe *you* just interrupted *me*."

Blake counted to five before saying, "I'll ignore that."

Her lips twisted into something that an optimistic person might call a smile. "Do you think you might lend me a hand?"

He just stared at her, uncomprehending.

"I need to get up," Caroline explained. "My—" She broke off, not about to say to this man that her bum was getting wet. "It's damp down here," she finally mumbled.

Blake grunted something she doubted she was meant to understand and practically slammed the tea service, which he'd clearly forgotten he was still holding, down on a side table. Before Caroline had time to blink at the crash of the tray against the table, his right hand was thrust in front of her face.

"Thank you," she said with as much dignity as she could muster, which admittedly wasn't very much.

He helped her back to the sofa. "Don't get up again."

"No, sir." She gave him a jaunty salute, an act which didn't seem to have any sort of improving effect on his temper.

"Can't you ever be serious?"

"I beg your pardon?"

"Saluting me, knocking all of my books down, little paper birds—can't you take anything seriously?"

Caroline narrowed her eyes, watching him wave his arms wildly as he spoke. She'd only known him a few days, but that was more than enough to know that this burst of emotion was not characteristic. Still, she didn't much appreciate having her attempts at friendship and civility tossed back in her face like so much dirty bathwater.

"Do you want to know how I define *serious*?" she said in a low, angry voice. "*Serious* is a man who orders his son to rape his ward. *Serious* is a young woman with no place to go. *Serious* is *not* an overturned vase and a wet carpet."

He only scowled at her in response, so she added, "And as for my little salute—I was just trying to be friendly."

"I don't want to be friends," he bit off.

"Yes, I see that now."

"You are here for two reasons, and two reasons only, and you'd best not forget that."

"Perhaps you'd care to elucidate?"

"One: You are here to aid us in the capture of Oliver Prewitt. Two—" He cleared his throat and actually blushed before repeating the word. "Two: You are here because, after abducting you through no fault of your own, well, I owe you that much."

"Ah, so I am not supposed to try to help around the house and garden or in any way be friendly with the servants?"

He glared at her but did not reply. Caroline took that response as an affirmative, and she gave him a nod that would have done the queen proud. "I see. In that case, perhaps you'd best not join me for tea."

"I beg your pardon?"

"I have this terrible habit, you see."

"Just one?"

"Just one that would offend *you*, sir," she shot back, her tone not particularly nice. "When I take tea with other people, I tend to converse with them. And when I converse with people, I'm likely to do so in a polite and friendly manner. And when then happens—"

"Sarcasm doesn't become you."

"And when *that* happens," she continued in a louder voice, "the strangest thing occurs. Not all the time, mind you, and probably not with you, Mr.

Ravenscroft, but I'm sure you wouldn't like to chance it."

"Chance what?"

"Why, becoming friends with me."

"Oh, for the love of God," he muttered.

"Just push the tea service toward me, if you please."

Blake stared at her for a moment before doing as she asked.

"Would you like a cup to take with you?"

"No," he said perversely. "I'll stay."

"The consequences could be deadly."

"It seems to me that the consequences could be even deadlier to my furnishings if I leave you alone."

Caroline glared at him and slammed a teacup into a saucer. "Milk?"

"Yes. No sugar. And do try to be gentle with the china. It's a family heirloom. Now that I think of it . . ."

"Now that you think of what?" she snapped.

"I really should do something about the mess on the carpet."

"I'd clean it up myself," she said sweetly, "but you've ordered me not to help around the house."

Blake ignored her as he stood up and crossed to the open door. "Perriwick!" he bellowed.

Perriwick materialized as if Blake had conjured him. "Yes, Mr. Ravenscroft?"

"Our guest had a slight accident," Blake said, waving his hand toward the wet spot on the carpet.

"Our invisible guest, you mean?"

Caroline watched the butler with undisguised interest. All Blake did was say, "I beg your pardon?"

"If I might be so bold as to make a deduction based upon your behavior of the past few days, Mr. Ravenscroft—"

"Just get to the point, Perriwick."

"You clearly did not want it to be made public that Miss . . . ah . . . Miss . . . er . . . shall we call her Miss Invisible—"

"Miss Trent," Caroline supplied helpfully.

"—Miss Trent is here."

"Yes, well, she's here, and that's that," Blake said irritatedly. "You needn't pretend you don't see her."

"Oh, no, Mr. Ravenscroft, she is clearly visible now."

"Perriwick, one of these days I am going to strangle you."

"I do not doubt it, sir. But may I be so bold as to—"

"*What*, Perriwick?"

"I merely wanted to inquire as to whether Miss Trent's visit to Seacrest Manor is now meant to be made public."

"No!" Caroline answered, loudly. "That is, I would prefer you keep this information to yourself. At least for the next few weeks."

"Of course," Perriwick replied with a smart bow. "Now, if you will excuse me, I will see to the mishap."

"Thank you, Perriwick," Blake said.

"If I might be so bold, Mr. Ravenscroft—"

"What is it now, Perriwick?"

"I merely wished to suggest that you and Miss Trent might be more comfortable having your tea in another room while I tidy this one."

"Oh, he's not having tea with me," Caroline said.

"Yes, I am," Blake ground out.

"I don't see why. You yourself said you didn't want to have anything to do with me."

"That's not entirely true," Blake shot back. "I very much enjoy crossing you."

"Yes, *that* much is clear."

Perriwick's head bobbed back and forth like a spectator at a badminton match, and then the old man actually smiled.

"You!" Blake snapped, pointing at Perriwick. "Be quiet."

Perriwick's hand went to his heart in a dramatic gesture of dismay. "If I might be so—"

"Perriwick, you're the boldest damned butler in England, and you well know it."

"I merely intended," the butler replied, looking rather smug, "to ask if you would like me to remove the tea service to another room. I did suggest that you might be more comfortable elsewhere, if you recall."

"That is an excellent idea, Perriwick," Caroline said with a blinding smile.

"Miss Trent, you are clearly a woman of superior manners, good humor, and a fine mind."

"Oh, for the love of God," Blake muttered.

"Not to mention," Perriwick continued, "excellent taste and refinement. Were you responsible for the lovely rearrangement of our garden yesterday?"

"Yes, I was," she said, delighted. "Did you like the new layout?"

"Miss Trent, it clearly reflected the hand of one with a rare sense of the aesthetic, true brilliance, and just a touch of whimsy."

Blake looked as if he might happily boot his butler clear to London. "Perriwick, Miss Trent is *not* a candidate for sainthood."

"Sadly, no," Perriwick admitted. "Not, however, that I have ever considered the church to be of impeccable judgment. When I think of some of the people they've sainted, why, I—"

Caroline's laughter filled the room. "Perriwick, I think I love you. Where have you been all of my life?"

He smiled modestly. "Serving Mr. Ravenscroft, and his uncle before him."

"I do hope his uncle was a little more cheerful than he is."

"Oh, Mr. Ravenscroft wasn't always so ill-tempered. Why, when he was a young man—"

"Perriwick," Blake roared, "you are perilously close to being tossed out without a reference."

"Mr. Ravenscroft!" Caroline said reprovingly. "You cannot think to dis—"

"Oh, do not worry, Miss Trent," Perriwick interrupted. "He threatens to terminate my employment here nearly every day."

"This time I mean it," Blake ground out.

"He says that every day, too," Perriwick said to Caroline, who rewarded him with a giggle.

"I am not amused," Blake announced, but no one seemed to be listening to him.

"I'll just move this to the other room," Perriwick returned, piling the teacups back on the tray. "The service will be in the green room, should you desire to partake."

"I didn't even get a sip," Caroline murmured as she watched the butler disappear into the hall. "He is quite— Oh!"

Without a word, Blake scooped her up into his arms and thundered out of the room. "If you want tea," he growled, "then you'll get tea. Even if I have to follow that damned butler to Bournemouth."

"I had no idea you could be so agreeable," she said in a wry voice.

"Don't push me, Miss Trent. In case you hadn't noticed, my temper is hanging by a very fine thread."

"Oh, I noticed."

Blake stared at her in disbelief. "It's a wonder someone hasn't killed you before now." He strode across the hall, Caroline clutching his shoulders, and into the green room.

No sign of the tea service.

"Perriwick!" Blake bellowed.

"Oh, Mr. Ravenscroft!" came the butler's disembodied voice.

"Where is he?" Caroline could not help asking, twisting her head to look behind her.

"Lord only knows," Blake muttered, then yelled, "Where the devil— Oh, there you are, Perriwick."

"You do creep up on a soul," Caroline said with a smile.

"It's one of my most useful talents," Perriwick replied from the doorway. "I took the liberty of moving the tea service to the blue room. I thought Miss Trent might enjoy a view of the ocean."

"Oh, I should like that above all else," Caroline said with obvious delight. "Thank you, Perriwick. You are ever so thoughtful."

Perriwick beamed.

Blake scowled.

"Is there anything else I can do to see to your comfort, Miss Trent?" Perriwick inquired.

"She's fine," Blake growled.

"Clearly, she—"

"Perriwick, isn't the west wing on fire?"

Perriwick blinked, sniffed the air, and stared at his employer in dismay. "I do not understand, sir."

"If there is no fire that needs putting out," Blake said, "then surely you can find some other task to complete."

"Yes, of course, Mr. Ravenscroft." With a small bow, the butler left the room.

"You shouldn't be so mean to him," Caroline said.

"You shouldn't tell me how to run my household."

"I wasn't doing any such thing. I was merely telling you how to be a nicer person."

"That is even more impertinent."

She shrugged, trying to ignore the way she was jostled against him as he carried her through the house. "I'm often impertinent."

"One doesn't need to be in your company for very long to appreciate that fact."

Caroline remained silent. She probably should not be speaking so boldly to her host, but her mouth very often formed words with no direction whatsoever from her brain. Besides, she was fairly certain now that her place here at Seacrest Manor was secure for the next five weeks. Blake Ravenscroft might not want her here—he might not even like her—but he definitely felt guilty over having mistakenly abducted her, and his sense of honor required him to provide her with a place to stay until she was safe from Oliver Prewitt.

Caroline smiled to herself. A man with a sense of honor was a very good thing, indeed.

Several hours later Caroline was still in the blue room, but the blue room no longer bore anything more than a passing resemblance to the chamber she'd entered earlier that day.

Perriwick, in his desire to make "the lovely and gracious Miss Trent" as comfortable and happy as possible, had brought in several trays of food, a selection of books and newspapers, a set of watercolors, and a flute. When Caroline had pointed out that she did not know how to play the flute, Perriwick had offered to teach her.

Blake had finally lost his patience when Perriwick offered to move the piano into the room—or rather, offered to have Blake, who was quite a bit younger and stronger than he was—do it. That had been bad enough, but when Caroline asked if Perriwick was going to play for her, Perriwick had answered, "Goodness no, I don't know how to play, but I'm sure Mr. Ravenscroft would be happy to entertain you for the afternoon."

At that point, Blake had thrown up his arms and stalked out of the room, muttering something about how his butler had never been so courteous and concerned about *him*.

And that was the last Caroline had seen of him. She had managed to keep herself quite happy for the afternoon, however, munching on pastries and thumbing through the most recent copies of the *London Times*. Really, she could get used to such a life.

Even her ankle wasn't paining her so much any longer.

She was quite entranced by the society pages—not, mind you, that she had a clue who they were talking about, except, possibly, for the "Dashing and Dangerous Lord R—" who Caroline was beginning to suspect might be her new friend James, when the marquis himself walked into the room.

"You have been gone quite a while," she said. "Would you like a pastry?"

James looked around the room with undisguised curiosity. "Have we arranged for another feast without my knowledge?"

"Perriwick merely wanted to make certain I was comfortable," Caroline explained.

"Ah, yes. The servants do seem rather besotted with you."

"It is driving Blake mad."

"Good." James picked up a pastry off a plate and said, "Guess what I found?"

"I couldn't possibly."

He held up a sheet of paper. "You."

"I beg your pardon?"

"Your guardian appears to be looking for you."

"Well, I'm not surprised," she commented, taking the notice and looking down at it. "I'm worth quite a bit of money to him. Oh, this is funny."

"What?"

"This." Caroline pointed to the drawing of her, which was situated underneath a headline reading: MISSING GIRL. "Percy drew this."

"Percy?"

"Yes, I should have known Oliver would have Percy do it. He is far too tightfisted to spend money on a proper artist."

James cocked his head and looked at the drawing a bit more carefully. "It's not a very good likeness."

"No, it's not, but I expect Percy did that on purpose. He's actually quite handy with pen and paper. But remember, he doesn't want me to be found any more than I do."

"Silly boy," James murmured.

Caroline looked up in surprise, certain that she must have misheard. "I beg your pardon?"

"Percy. It's quite clear to me from what you've said that he isn't likely to do any better than you. If I were he, I would certainly not have complained about my father's choice of bride."

"If you were Percy," Caroline said wryly, "Percy would be a much finer man."

James chuckled.

"Besides," she continued. "Percy thinks I am highly unattractive, morbidly interested in books, and he never ceases to complain that I cannot sit still."

"Well, you can't."

"Sit still?"

"Yes. Just look at your ankle."

"That has nothing to do with—"

"It has everything to do with—"

"My, my," drawled a voice from the doorway. "Aren't we cozy?"

James looked up. "Oh, good day, Ravenscroft."

"And where did you disappear to this morning?"

James held up the posted bill he'd brought back from town. "I went out to investigate our Miss Trent."

"She isn't *our* Miss Tr—"

"Forgive me," James said with a wicked smile. "Your Miss Trent."

Caroline immediately took offense. "I'm not—"

"This is an exceedingly asinine conversation," Blake cut in.

"My thoughts exactly," Caroline muttered. Then she pointed to the notice about her and said, "Look what the marquis brought back."

"I thought I told you to call me James," James said.

"'The marquis' is just fine," Blake grumbled. "And what the hell is this?"

James handed him the paper.

Blake dismissed it immediately. "This looks nothing like her."

"You don't think so?" James asked, his expression positively angelic.

"No. Any fool could see that the artist put her eyes a bit too close together, and the mouth is all wrong. If the artist really wanted to capture her on paper, he should have shown her smiling."

"Do you think so?" Caroline asked, delighted.

Blake scowled, clearly irritated with himself. "I wouldn't worry that anyone is going to find you based on *this*. And besides, no one knows you're here, and I'm not expecting any guests."

"True," James murmured.

"And," Blake added, "why would anyone care? There is no mention of a reward."

"No reward?" Caroline exclaimed. "Why that cheap little—"

James laughed out loud, and even Blake, grumpy as he was, had to crack a smile.

"Well, I don't care," she announced. "I just don't care that he isn't offering a reward. In fact, I'm glad. I'm much happier here than I was with any of my guardians."

"I would be, too," Blake said wryly, "if Perriwick and Mrs. Mickle treated me this way."

Caroline turned to him with a wicked smile, the urge to tease him too strong to ignore. "Now, now, don't get snippy because your servants like me best."

Blake started to say something, then just laughed. Caroline felt an instant happy satisfaction spreading within her, as if her heart recognized that she had done something very good in making this man laugh. She needed Blake, and the shelter of his home, but she sensed that maybe he needed her just a little bit, too.

His was a wounded soul, far more so even than her own. She smiled up into his eyes and murmured, "I wish you'd laugh more often."

"Yes," he said gruffly, "you've said as much."

"I'm right about this." On impulse, she patted his hand. "I'll allow that I'm wrong about a great deal, but I'm sure that I'm right about this. A body can't go as long without laughing as you have."

"And how would you know?"

"That a body can't go without laughing, or that you haven't laughed in a long, long while?"

"Both."

She thought about that for a moment, then said, "As for you, well, all I can say is that I can just tell. You always look a bit surprised when you laugh, as if you don't expect to be happy."

Blake's eyes widened imperceptibly, and without thinking, he whispered, "I don't."

"And as for your other question . . ." Caroline said, a sad, wistful smile crossing her face. There was a long silence, as she tried to think of the right words. "I know what it's like not to laugh. I know how it hurts."

"Do you really?"

"And I know that you have to learn to find your laughter and your peace wherever you can. I find it in—" She blushed. "Never mind."

"No," he said urgently. "Tell me."

Caroline looked around. "What happened to the marquis? He seems to have disappeared again."

Blake ignored her question. James had a talent for disappearing when it was convenient. He would not put it past his friend to play matchmaker. "Tell me," he repeated.

Caroline stared at a spot just to the right of his face, not understanding why she felt so compelled to bare her soul to this man. "I find my peace in the night sky. It's something my mother taught me. Nothing more than a little trick, but—" She shifted her gaze to meet his eyes. "You probably think that is very silly."

"No," Blake said, feeling something very warm and very odd in the vicinity of his heart. "I think that might be the least silly thing I've heard in years."

Chapter 9

e·gre·gious *(adjective). Remarkable in a bad sense; gross, flagrant, outrageous.*

My mouth often displays an egregious *disregard for discretion, circumspection, and good sense of any kind.*

—From the personal dictionary of Caroline Trent

Caroline's ankle was much improved the following day, although she still required a cane to walk. Finishing her work in the library, however, was out of the question; she was clumsy enough without trying to move huge stacks of books while balancing on one foot. There was no telling what sort of mess she might make while still handicapped by a swollen ankle.

At supper the previous night, James had mentioned that she might draw a floor plan of Prewitt Hall. Blake, who had been most uncommunicative throughout the meal, had grunted in the affirmative when she had asked him if he thought that was a good idea. Eager to impress her hosts, she sat down at a desk in the blue room and began her sketch.

Mapping out the floor plan, however, proved to be more difficult than she had supposed, and soon the floor was littered with crumpled-up pieces of paper whose drawings she had deemed unacceptable. After thirty minutes of aborted attempts, she finally declared, out loud and to herself, "I have a new appreciation and respect for architects."

"I beg your pardon?"

Caroline looked up in mortification at having been caught talking to herself. Blake was standing in the doorway, but she couldn't quite tell if his expression was amused or irritated.

"I was just talking to myself," she stammered.

He smiled, and she decided with relief that he was amused. "Yes, that much is clear," he said. "Something about architects, I believe?"

"I am trying to draw a plan of Prewitt Hall for you and the marquis," she explained, "only I cannot get it right."

He walked to the desk and leaned over her shoulder to study her current drawing. "What seems to be the problem?"

"I can't seem to get the sizes of the rooms right. I—I—" She gulped. He was awfully close, and the scent of him brought back powerful memories of their stolen kiss. He smelled of sandalwood and mint and something else she couldn't identify.

"Yes?" he prodded.

"I . . . ah . . . well, you see, it's terribly difficult to get the shapes and the sizes of the rooms right at the same time." She pointed to her diagram. "I started by drawing all of the rooms on the west side of the main hall, and I had thought I'd gotten them right . . ."

He leaned in a little closer, which caused her to lose her train of thought. "Then what happened?" he murmured.

She swallowed. "Then I got to the last room before the south wall, and I realized I hadn't left enough space." She jabbed her ungloved finger at the tiny room at the rear. "It looks like nothing more than a closet here, but in actuality it's bigger than *this* room." She pointed at another square on her map.

"What is that room?"

"This one?" Caroline asked, her finger still occupying the larger square.

"No, the one you said should be larger."

"Oh, that is the south drawing room. I don't know very much about it other than that it ought to be bigger than I've shown. I wasn't allowed to go in there."

Blake's ears immediately perked up. "You don't say?"

She nodded. "Oliver called it his House of Treasures, which I always thought was rather silly, seeing as how it wasn't a house at all but just a room."

"What sort of treasures did he keep there?"

"That's the odd thing," Caroline replied. "I don't know. Whenever he bought something new—which he frequently did and I tend to think he was using my money—" She blinked, having completely lost track of what she was saying.

"When he bought something new," Blake prodded, with what he thought was remarkable patience.

"Oh, yes," she answered. "Well, when he bought something new, he liked to crow about it and admire it for weeks. And he always made certain that Percy and I admired it as well. So if he bought a new candelabra, one could be assured that it would be on display in the dining room. And if he bought a priceless vase, then—well, I'm sure you understand my meaning. It would be completely unlike him to purchase something rare and expensive and then hide it away from view."

Blake didn't say anything, so she added, "I've been rambling, haven't I?"

He stared at the map intently, then shifted his gaze to her eyes. "And you say he keeps this room locked?"

"All the time."

"And Percy isn't allowed to enter, either?"

She shook her head. "I don't think Oliver has very much respect for Percy."

Blake exhaled, feeling a familiar rush of excitement coursing through him. It was at times like these that he remembered why he had first gotten involved with the War Office, and why he had stayed with it for so many years, even though it had taken so much away from him.

He'd long ago realized that he liked to solve problems, to put little pieces of a puzzle together until the entire picture presented itself in his mind.

And Caroline Trent had just told him where Oliver Prewitt was hiding his secrets.

"Caroline," he said without thinking, "I could kiss you."

She looked up sharply. "You could?"

But Blake's mind had already jumped ahead, and not only did he not hear Caroline, he hadn't even noticed that he'd told her he could kiss her. He was already thinking of that little corner room at Prewitt Hall, and how he'd seen it from the outside when he'd been spying on the house, and what was the best way to get inside, and—

"Mr. Ravenscroft!"

He blinked and looked up at Caroline. "I thought I told you to call me Blake," he said absently.

"I did," she replied. "Three times."

"Oh. Terribly sorry." Then he looked back down at her map and ignored her again.

Caroline wrinkled her lips into a grimace that was half-irritated and half-amused, picked up her cane, and headed for the door. Blake was so engrossed in his thoughts he probably wouldn't notice that she was gone. But just when her hand touched the doorknob, she heard his voice.

"How many windows in this room?"

She turned around, confused. "I beg your pardon?"

"This secret room of Prewitt's. How many windows does it contain?"

"I'm not sure, precisely. I hardly ever went inside, but I certainly know the grounds well, and . . . Let me think." Caroline started pointing with her finger as she mentally counted the windows on the outside of Prewitt Hall. "Now then, that's three for the dining room," she murmured, "and two for the— One!" she exclaimed.

"Just one window? In a corner room?"

"No, I meant to say that there is only one window on the west wall, but on the south—" Her finger started to bob in the air again. "On the south wall there is also just one."

"Excellent," he said, mostly to himself.

"But you will have a devil of a time getting in, if that is your intention."

"Why?"

"Prewitt Hall wasn't built on level land," she explained. "It slopes down to the south and west. And so at that corner there is a good bit of the foundation showing. Since I was in charge of the gardens I planted some flowering bushes there to hide it, of course, but—"

"Caroline."

"Yes, of course," she said sheepishly, ending her digression. "What I meant to say is that the windows are quite high above the ground. They'd be very difficult to climb through."

He offered her a crooked smile. "Where there is a will, Miss Trent, there is a way."

"Do you really believe that?"

"What kind of question is that?"

She blushed and looked away. "A rather intrusive one, I suppose. Please forget I asked."

There was a long silence, during which he stared at her in a rather uncomfortable way, and then finally he asked, "How high above the ground?"

"What? Oh, the windows. About ten or twelve feet, I suppose."

"Ten feet? Or twelve?"

"I'm not really sure."

"Damn," he muttered.

He sounded so disappointed Caroline felt as if she had just lost a war for Britain. "I don't like being the weak link," she said to herself.

"What was that?"

She rapped her cane against the floor. "Come with me."

He waved her away as he resumed his perusal of her floor plan.

Caroline found she didn't much enjoy being ignored by this man. WHAM! She slammed her cane against the floor.

He looked up in surprise. "I beg your pardon?"

"When I said, 'Come with me,' I meant now."

Blake just stared at her for a moment, clearly perplexed by her newly autocratic attitude. Finally he crossed his arms, looked at her much as a parent might do to a child, and said, "Caroline, if you're going to be a part of this operation for the next week or so—"

"*Five* weeks," she reminded him.

"Yes, yes, of course, but you're going to have to learn that your desires can't always come first."

Caroline thought that was rather condescending, and she would have liked to have told him so, but instead, the following words erupted from her mouth: "Mr. Ravenscroft, you do not know the slightest thing about my desires."

He straightened to his full height, and a devilish gleam she'd never seen before appeared in his eye. "Well now," he said slowly, "that's not entirely true."

Her cheeks virtually erupted in flames. "Stupid, stupid mouth," she muttered, "always saying—"

"Are you speaking to me?" he inquired, not even bothering to hide his supercilious smile.

There was nothing to do but brazen it out. "I'm extremely embarrassed, Mr. Ravenscroft."

"Really? I hadn't noticed."

"And if you were any sort of a gentleman," she ground out, "you would—"

"But I'm not always a gentleman," he interrupted. "Only when it pleases me."

Clearly, it didn't please him now. She grumbled a few nonsense words under her breath and then said, "I thought we might go outside so that I could compare the height of these windows to those at Prewitt Hall."

He stood quite abruptly. "That is an excellent idea, Caroline." He held out his arm toward her. "Do you require assistance?"

After her shameful reaction to his kiss a few days earlier, Caroline was of the opinion that touching him was *always* a bad idea, but that seemed a rather embarrassing observation to make out loud, so she just shook her head and said, "No, I'm quite nimble with this cane."

"Ah, yes, the cane. It looks like the antique my uncle George brought back from the Orient. Where did you get it?"

"Perriwick gave it to me."

Blake shook his head as he held open the door for her. "I should have surmised as much. Perriwick would give you the deed to this house if he knew where to find it."

She tossed a mischievous smile over her shoulder as she limped into the hall. "And where did you say it was?"

"Sneaky wench. I've had it under lock and key since the day you arrived."

Caroline's mouth fell open in shock and laughter. "You trust me so little?"

"You, I trust. As for Perriwick . . ."

By the time they exited the rear door to the garden, Caroline was giggling so hard she had to sit down on the stone steps. "You must admit," she said with a magnanimous wave of her hand, "that the gardens look quite splendid."

"I suppose I must." His voice was part grumble and part laugh, and so Caroline knew he was not truly angry with her.

"I know that it has only been two days," she said, squinting at the plants, "but I am convinced that the flowers are healthier in their new locations." When she looked up at Blake, his face held an oddly tender expression. Her heart warmed, and she felt suddenly shy. "Let's examine the windows," she said hastily, standing back up. She hobbled onto the grass and stopped in front of the window to the study.

Blake watched her as she cocked her head to assess the window's height. Her face glowed healthy and pink in the morning air, and her hair was almost blond in the summer sun. She looked so damned earnest and innocent that it made his heart ache.

She'd told him he needed to laugh more. She was right, he realized. It had felt wonderful to laugh with her this morning. But that was nothing compared to the joy he'd felt when he'd made her laugh. It had been so long since he'd brought happiness into anyone else's life, he'd forgotten how nice it was.

There was a certain freedom in allowing oneself to be just plain silly every now and then. Blake resolved not to lose sight of that once he finally severed his ties with the War Office. Maybe it was time to stop being so damned serious all the time. Maybe it was time to allow himself a little joy. Maybe . . .

Maybe he was just being fanciful. Caroline might be rather entertaining, and she might be here at Seacrest Manor for the next five weeks, but she'd soon be gone. And she wasn't the sort of woman with whom one dallied; she was the sort one married.

Blake wasn't going to marry. Ever. So he was going to have to leave her alone. Still, he thought with typical male reasoning, there wasn't any harm in looking . . .

He stared shamelessly at her profile as she studied the window, her right arm moving up and down as she mentally measured its height. Turning quite suddenly to face him, she nearly lost her balance on the soft grass. She opened her mouth, then blinked, then closed it, then opened it again to say, "What were you looking at?"

"You."

"Me?" she squeaked. "Why?"

He shrugged. "There isn't much else to look at just now. We've already established that it's better for my temper not to pay too much attention to the garden."

"Blake!"

"Furthermore, I rather enjoy watching you work."

"I beg your— But I wasn't working. I was mentally measuring this window."

"That's work. Did you know you have a very expressive face?"

"No, I— What has that to do with anything?"

Blake smiled. She was rather fun to fluster. "Nothing," he replied. "Merely that I could practically follow the processes of your mind as you examined the window."

"Oh. Is that bad?"

"Not at all. Although I daresay you won't want to try to earn a living as a professional gambler."

She laughed at that. "Certainly not, but I—" Her eyes narrowed. "If you can tell so well what I am thinking, what precisely did you think I was thinking?"

Blake felt something young and carefree taking hold of him, something he hadn't felt in all the years since Marabelle's death, and even though he knew this couldn't possibly go anywhere, he was powerless to stop himself as he stepped forward and said, "You were thinking you'd like to kiss me again."

"I was not!"

He nodded slowly. "You were."

"Not even a little bit. Perhaps when we were in the study—" She bit her lip.

"Here, in the study. Does it really matter?"

She planted her free hand on her hip. "I am trying to be of assistance to your mission or operation or whatever you want to call it, and you're talking about *kissing* me!"

"Not precisely. I was actually talking about *you* kissing *me*."

Her mouth fell open. "You must be insane."

"Probably," he agreed, closing the distance between them. "I certainly haven't acted this way in a rather long while."

She looked up into his face, her mouth trembling as she whispered, "You haven't?"

He shook his head solemnly. "You have a very odd effect on me, Miss Caroline Trent."

"In a good way or a bad way?"

"Sometimes," he said with a crooked smile, "it's hard to tell. But I tend to think good."

He leaned down and brushed his lips against hers. "What were you going to tell me about the window?" he whispered.

She blinked. "I forgot."

"Good." And then he kissed her again, this time more deeply, and with more emotion than he thought he had left in his heart. She sighed and leaned into him, allowing his arms to wrap more fully around her.

Caroline dropped her cane, snaked her arms around his neck, and completely gave up trying to think. When his lips were on hers, and she was warm in his embrace, there didn't seem much sense in trying to figure out whether kissing him was such a good idea. Her brain, which had just seconds ago been trying to deduce whether he was likely to break her heart, was now thoroughly occupied with devising ways to keep this kiss going on and on and on . . .

She moved closer, standing on her tiptoes, and then—

"Owww!" She would have fallen if Blake weren't already holding her up.

"Caroline?" he asked, his expression dazed.

"My stupid stupid ankle," she muttered. "I forgot, and I tried to—"

He put a gentle finger to her lips. "It's better this way."

"I don't think so," she blurted out.

Blake carefully disentangled her arms from around his neck and stepped away. With one graceful swoop of his arm, he reached down and retrieved her forgotten cane from the ground. "I don't want to take advantage of you," he said gently, "and in my current frame of mind and body, I'm liable to do just that."

Caroline wanted to scream that she didn't care, but she held her tongue. They had reached a delicate balance, and she didn't want to do anything to jeopardize that. She felt something when she was near this man—something warm and kind and good, and if she lost it she knew she would never forgive herself. It had been so very long since she'd felt a sense of belonging, and heaven help her, she belonged in his arms.

He just didn't realize it yet.

She took a deep breath. She could be patient. Why, she even had a cousin named Patience. Surely that should count for something. Of course, Patience lived rather far away with her puritanical father in Massachusetts, but—

She nearly smacked herself on the side of the head. *What* was she doing thinking about Patience Merriwether?

"Caroline? Are you all right?"

She looked up and blinked. "Fine. Lovely. Never better. I was just . . . I was simply . . ."

"Simply what?" he asked.

"Thinking." She chewed on her lower lip. "I do that sometimes."

"A commendable pastime," he said, slowly nodding his head.

"I tend to wander off the subject on occasion."

"I noticed."

"You did? Oh. I'm sorry."

"Don't be. It's rather endearing."

"Do you really think so?"

"I rarely lie."

Her lips twisted into a vague grimace. " 'Rarely' isn't terribly reassuring."

"In my line of work one cannot last very long without the occasional fib."

"Hmmph. I suppose if the good of the country is at stake . . ."

"Oh, yes," he said with sincerity so absolute she couldn't possibly believe him.

She really couldn't think of anything else to say besides, "Men!" And she didn't say that with much grace or good humor.

Blake chuckled and took her arm to turn her face to the building. "Now then, you wanted to tell me something about the windows?"

"Oh yes, of course. I might be a bit off, but I would estimate that the bottom sill of the window in the south drawing room at Prewitt Hall is about as high as the third mullion on the study window."

"From the bottom or from the top?"

"The top."

"Hmmm." Blake examined the window with an expert eye. "That would make them about ten feet high. Not an impossible task, but still, a bit annoying."

"That seems an odd way to describe your job."

He turned to her with a somewhat weary expression. "Caroline, most of what I do is annoying."

"Really? I should have thought it rather dashing."

"It's not," he said harshly. "Trust me on this. And it isn't a job."

"It isn't?"

"No," he said, his voice a touch too forceful. "It's just something I do. It's something I won't be doing for very much longer."

"Oh."

After a moment of silence, Blake cleared his throat and asked, "How is that ankle?"

"It's fine."

"Are you certain?"

"Truly. I just shouldn't have stood on my tiptoes. It will most likely be completely healed by tomorrow."

Blake crouched down beside her and, to her great shock and surprise, took her ankle into his hands, gently palpating it before standing back up. "Tomorrow might be a bit optimistic. But the swelling has gone down considerably."

"Yes." She shut her mouth, suddenly at a complete loss for words. It was a most unusual state of affairs. What was one supposed to say in such a situation? *Thank you for the lovely kiss. Would it be possible to have another?*

Somehow, Caroline didn't think that sounded particularly appropriate, even if it would be most heartfelt. *Patience patience patience*, she told herself.

Blake looked at her oddly. "You look somewhat disturbed."

"I do?"

"Forgive me," he said immediately. "It was just that you looked so serious."

"I was thinking about my cousin," she blurted out, thinking that she sounded extensively foolish.

"Your cousin?"

She nodded vaguely. "Her name is Patience."

"I see."

Caroline was afraid he really did.

The corners of his mouth quivered. "She must be quite a role model for you."

"Not at all. Patience is quite a harridan," she lied. Actually, Patience Merriwether was an irritating combination of reserve, piety, and decorum. Caroline had never met her in person, but her letters were always preachy beyond measure—or, in Caroline's opinion, politeness. But Caroline had kept writing to her over the years, since anyone's letters were a welcome diversion from her awful guardians.

"Hmmm," he said noncommittally. "Rather cruel, I should think, saddling a child with a name like that."

Caroline thought about that for a moment. "Yes. It's hard enough living up to one's parents. Can you imagine having to live up to oneself? I suppose it might have been worse to have been named Faith, Hope, or Charity."

He shook his head. "No. For you, I think, Patience would have been the most difficult."

She punched him playfully in the shoulder. "Speaking of peculiar names, how did you come by yours?"

"Blake, you mean?"

She nodded.

"It was my mother's maiden name. It's a custom in my family to give the second son his mother's maiden name."

"The second son?"

Blake shrugged. "The firstborn usually gets something important from the father's side."

Trent Ravenscroft, Caroline thought. It didn't sound half-bad. She smiled.

"What are you grinning about?" he asked.

"Me?" she gulped. "Nothing. Just that, well—"

"Spit it out, Caroline."

She swallowed again, her brain whirring at triple-speed. There was no way she was going to admit to him that she was fantasizing about their offspring. "What I was thinking," she said slowly.

"Yes?"

Of course! "I was thinking," she repeated, her voice growing a bit more confident, "that you're very lucky your mother didn't have one of those hyphenated surnames. Can you imagine if your name were something like Fortescue-Hamilton Ravenscroft?"

Blake grinned. "Do you think I'd be called Fort or Ham for short?"

"Or," Caroline continued with a laugh, thoroughly enjoying herself now, "what if she were Welsh? You'd be completely without vowels."

"Aberystwyth Ravenscroft," he said, pulling the name from a famous castle. "It has a certain charm."

"Ah, but then everyone should call you Stwyth, and we'd all sound as if we were lisping."

Blake chuckled. "I had a mad crush on a girl named Sarah Wigglesworth once. But my brother convinced me that I must be a stoic and let her go."

"Yes," Caroline mused, "I can see where it might be difficult for a child to be named Wigglesworth Ravenscroft."

"I rather think David just wanted her for himself. Not six months later they were engaged."

"Oh, how perfect!" Caroline exclaimed with a hoot of laughter. "But now doesn't he have to name his child Wigglesworth?"

"No, only we second sons are obliged to follow the custom."

"But isn't your father a viscount? Why did he have to follow the custom?"

"My father was actually a second son himself. His older brother died at the age of five. By that time my father was already born and named."

Caroline grinned. "And what was his name?"

"I'm afraid Father wasn't nearly as lucky as I. My grandmother's maiden name was Petty."

She clapped her hand over her mouth. "Oh, dear. Oh, I shouldn't laugh."

"Yes, you should. We all do."

"What do you call him?"

"I call him Father. Everyone else simply calls him Darnsby, which is his title."

"What did he do before he gained the title?"

"I believe he instructed everyone to call him Richard."

"Is that one of his given names?"

"No," Blake said with a shrug, "but he much preferred it to Petty."

"Oh, that is funny," she said, wiping a tear of mirth from her eye. "What happens if a Ravenscroft doesn't have a second son?"

He leaned forward with a decidedly rakish glint in his eye. "We just keep trying and trying until we do."

Caroline's cheeks flamed. "Do you know," she said hastily, "but I suddenly feel extensively tired. I believe I shall go inside and have a short rest. You are, of course, welcome to join me."

She didn't wait for his reply, however, just turned on her heel and limped away—rather quickly, in fact, for one using a cane.

Blake watched her as she disappeared into the house, his cheeks unable to quit the smile that had graced his face for almost their entire interchange. It had been some time since he'd given thought to the family naming custom. Marabelle's surname had been George, and they had always joked that they should marry for this reason alone.

George Ravenscroft. He had almost been a real person in Blake's mind, with his raven curls and Marabelle's pale blue eyes.

But there would be no George Ravenscroft. "I'm sorry, Marabelle," he whispered. He had failed her in so many ways. He hadn't been able to protect her, and though he had tried to be faithful to her memory, he hadn't always managed that, either.

And today—today his indiscretion had moved beyond the mere needs of his body. He had enjoyed himself with Caroline, truly reveled in the sheer pleasure of her company. Guilt pierced his heart.

"I'm sorry, Marabelle," he whispered again.

But as he strolled back to the house, he heard himself say, "Trent Ravenscroft."

He shook his head, but the thought wouldn't go away.

Chapter 10

um·laut *(noun). 1. A change in the sound of a vowel produced by partial assimilation to an adjacent sound. 2. The diacritical sign (ex. ü) placed over a vowel to indicate such a change has taken place, esp. in German.*

Knowing what I now know about Mr. Ravenscroft, I really must thank my maker that I was not born German, with an umlaut *in my name.*

—From the personal dictionary of Caroline Trent

By mid-afternoon Caroline had come to two realizations. One, James had once again disappeared, presumably off somewhere to investigate Oliver and his treasonous activities. And two, she was in love with Blake Ravenscroft.

Well, that wasn't exactly true. To be more precise, she *thought* she *might* be in love with Blake Ravenscroft. She had a little trouble believing it herself, but there didn't seem to be any other explanation for the recent changes in her personality and demeanor.

Caroline was well used to her flaw of often speaking without first thinking about her words, but today she seemed to be blurting out utter nonsense. Furthermore, she had completely lost her usually hearty appetite. Not to mention the fact that she kept catching herself grinning like the veriest fool.

And if that weren't enough proof, she caught herself whispering, "Caroline Ravenscroft. Caroline Ravenscroft, mother of Trent Ravenscroft. Caroline Ravenscroft, wife of— Oh, stop!"

Even she could lose patience with herself.

But if Blake returned any of her feelings, he gave no indication. He certainly wasn't prancing about the house like a lovesick fool, shouting out odes to her beauty, grace, and wit. And she rather doubted he was sitting behind his desk in his study, idly doodling the words, "Mr. and Mrs. Blake Ravenscroft."

And if he were, there was really no reason to think that she might be the "Mrs. Blake Ravenscroft" in question. Heaven knew how many women back in London fancied themselves in love with him. And what if he fancied himself in love with one of *them*?

It was a sobering thought, that.

Of course, one couldn't entirely discount the kisses. He had definitely enjoyed their kisses. But men were different from women. Caroline had led a reasonably sheltered life, but that pertinent fact had made itself clear early on. A man might want to kiss a woman without an ounce of feeling behind it.

A woman, on the other hand— Well, Caroline wouldn't presume to speak for all women, but she knew that she couldn't possibly kiss a man the way she had kissed Blake that afternoon without a great deal of feeling behind it.

Which brought her back to her central hypothesis: that she was in love with Blake Ravenscroft.

While Caroline was busy delving into the rather circuitous depths of her heart, Blake was sitting on the edge of his desk, tossing darts at a dartboard in his office. The endeavor suited his mood perfectly.

"I won't"—*whoosh*—"kiss her again."

"I didn't"—*thunk*—"enjoy it."

"Well, all right, I did, but on a purely"—*whoosh*—"physical level."

He stood, his face determined. "She is a perfectly nice girl, but she means nothing to me."

He took aim, let fire, and watched with dismay as the dart sank a hole in his newly whitewashed wall.

"Damn damn damn," he muttered, striding over to pry the dart loose. How could he have missed? He never missed. He tossed these darts nearly every day and he never missed. "Damn."

"A little testy today, aren't we?"

Blake looked up and saw James standing in the doorway. "Where the hell have you been?"

"Furthering our investigation of Oliver Prewitt, which is more than I can say for you."

"I have had my hands more than full with his ward."

"Yes, I thought as much."

Blake yanked the dart free, sending little pieces of plaster to the floor. "You know what I meant."

"Absolutely," James said with a slow smile, "but I'm not entirely certain *you* know what you meant."

"Stop being so bloody annoying, Riverdale, and tell me what you found out."

James sprawled in a leather chair and loosened his cravat. "I did a bit more surveillance on Prewitt Hall."

"Why didn't you tell me you were going?"

"You would have wanted to come with me."

"You're damned right. I—"

"Someone," James interrupted, "had to remain here with our guest."

"Our *guest*," Blake replied sarcastically, "is a woman grown. She isn't going to expire from neglect if we leave her to her own devices for a few hours."

"True, but you might return to find another one of your rooms in shambles."

"Don't be an ass, Riverdale."

James made great pretense of studying his fingernails. "You're lucky I don't take offense at such comments."

"You're lucky I don't ram your bloody tongue down your throat."

"It's touching to see you so defensive of a woman," James said with a lazy smile.

"I'm not defensive. And stop trying to bait me."

James shrugged. "At any rate, one can spy with far more stealth than two. I didn't want to appear conspicuous."

"Riverdale, you live to be inconspicuous."

"Yes, it is rather jolly to blend into the woodwork on occasion, isn't it? It's quite amazing what people will say when they don't know who you are. Or," he added with a wicked smile, "when they don't even know you're there."

"Did you discover anything?"

"Nothing of import, although Prewitt is definitely living beyond his means. Or at least what his means ought to be."

Blake picked up another dart and took aim. "Step away."

James did so, watching without much interest as the dart sailed from Blake's hand to the bull's-eye.

"That's more like it," Blake murmured. He turned to James and said, "The problem is that we can't automatically assume his money is coming from treasonous activities. If he is indeed carrying messages for Carlotta De Leon, I'm certain he's been paid handsomely for it. However, we also know he smuggles brandy and silk; he's been making a living that way for years. And he certainly could be robbing Caroline's inheritance out from under her."

"I'd be damned surprised if he weren't."

"But as it happens," Blake said with a slightly smug smile, "I did a bit of investigating myself."

"Did you now?"

"It turns out Prewitt has an office he keeps locked at all times. Caroline wasn't allowed inside, and neither was his son."

James's face spread into a wide smile. "Bull's-eye."

"Exactly." Blake tossed the dart but his aim was wide. "Well, not always exactly."

"It might be time for a little clandestine visit to Prewitt Hall," James suggested.

Blake nodded. He wanted nothing more than to wrap up this case, retire from the War Office, and embark upon his new, respectable, and boring life. "I couldn't agree more."

They found Caroline in the library, sitting under a table.

"What the hell are you doing down there?" Blake demanded.

"What? Oh, good day." She crawled out. "Do your servants dust down here? I've been sneezing up quite a storm."

"You didn't answer my question."

"I was merely going through some of these piles. I'm trying to collect all of your history books."

"I thought you weren't going to proceed in here until your ankle was better," Blake said, rather accusingly in her opinion.

"I'm not putting the books back on the shelf yet," she replied. "I'm just grouping them by subject. I'm not using my ankle at all, which, by the way, is nearly healed. I haven't used my cane even once today, and it hasn't hurt me at all." She turned to James and beamed. "Oh, and it's lovely to see you again, my lord."

The marquis smiled and bowed in her direction. "Always a pleasure, my dear Caroline."

Blake scowled. "We are here for a purpose, Miss Trent."

"It never occurred to me that you weren't." She shifted her gaze back to James. "Have you noticed he likes to call me Miss Trent when he is irritated with me?"

"Caroline," Blake said, his voice clearly laced with warning.

"Of course," she added blithely, "when he is really angry he reverts to Caroline. He probably finds it too difficult to growl my full name."

James had his hand over his mouth, presumably to staunch his laughter.

"Caroline," Blake said in a louder voice, clearly ignoring her jests, "we need your assistance."

"You do?"

"It has come time for us to gather solid evidence against Prewitt."

"Good," Caroline replied. "I should like to see him pay for his crimes."

James chuckled and said, "Bloodthirsty wench."

She turned on him with a hurt expression. "That is a terrible thing to say. I'm not in the least bit bloodthirsty. It's merely that if Oliver has been doing all the terrible things you say he has been doing—"

"Caroline, I was just teasing," James said.

"Oh, well then I'm sorry for overreacting. I should have known you wouldn't be so mean—"

"If the two of you can move past your mutual admiration," Blake said acidly, "we have important business to discuss."

Caroline and James turned to him with equally irritated expressions.

"Riverdale and I are going to break into Prewitt Hall," Blake told her. "We will need you to give us every detail about the schedules of the family and of the servants so that we may avoid detection."

"You won't need every detail," she said with a matter-of-fact shrug. "You should simply go tonight."

Both gentlemen leaned forward and stared at her with questioning eyes.

"Oliver plays cards every Wednesday evening. He never misses a game. He always wins. I think he cheats."

James and Blake shared a look, and Caroline could practically see their brains springing into action, planning their mission. "If you recall," she continued, "it was a Wednesday night when I ran away. One week ago exactly. Oliver obviously chose his card night for Percy's attempted rape. No doubt he didn't want his ears bothered by my screams."

"Will Percy be at home?" James asked.

Caroline shook her head. "He almost always goes out and gets drunk. Oliver can't abide overindulgence of spirits. He says it makes a man weak. So Percy tipples on Wednesday nights when he can escape his father's watchful eye."

"What about the servants? How many are there?" This time, Blake asked the questions.

Caroline considered this for a moment. "Five, in total. Most are likely to be in residence. Last week Oliver gave everyone the night off, but I am certain he only did that so that none would rush to my assistance when Percy attacked me. He's terribly tightfisted when it comes to anyone other than himself, so I doubt he'd give them time off again without a very good reason."

"How nice to know that your rape qualified as a good reason," Blake muttered.

Caroline looked up and was astonished and just a touch delighted to see how angry he looked on her behalf. "But if you are careful," she added, "you should have no trouble avoiding them. It might be a bit confusing navigating your way around the hall, but since you'll be taking me along with—"

"We're not taking you," Blake bit off.

"But—"

"I said, we are *not* taking you."

"I'm sure if you just consid—"

"You will NOT be going," he roared, and even James blinked in surprise at the volume of his reply.

"Very well," Caroline said in an irritated voice. She was convinced that Blake was wrong, but it didn't seem either prudent or beneficial to her health to disagree any further.

"Don't forget that you have an injured ankle," James said gently. "You would not be able to move with your usual speed."

Caroline had a feeling that James agreed one hundred percent with Blake and was just trying to make her feel better—especially since she'd told them her ankle was quite healed—but she appreciated the effort nonetheless. "The housekeeper is quite deaf and retires early," she told them. "You won't have to worry about her."

"Excellent," Blake said. "And the rest?"

"There are two maids, but they live in the village and go home each night to sleep. They'll be long gone by the time Oliver leaves to play cards. The groom sleeps in the stables, so you're not likely to disturb him as long as you approach the house from the opposite side."

"A butler?" Blake prompted.

"Farnsworth will be the most difficult. He has very keen ears and he's dreadfully loyal to Oliver. His room is on the third floor."

"That shouldn't be too much of a problem, then," James said.

"Well, no, but . . ." Caroline's words trailed off, and she clamped her mouth into a grim line. Blake and James were talking intensely between themselves, and she might have been a piece of furniture for all the attention they were paying her.

And then, without so much as a farewell, they walked into Blake's study, and Caroline was left sitting among her books. "Of all the rude—"

"Oh, Caroline?"

She looked up hopefully. Blake had poked his head back into the library. Maybe he had decided that she could go with them to Prewitt Hall after all. "Yes?"

"Do you know, but I forgot to ask you about that odd little book you carry about."

"Excuse me?"

"The one with all the odd words. Does it have anything to do with Prewitt?"

"Oh. No. Actually, I told you the truth when you asked me about it the first time. It's a little personal dictionary. I like to jot down new words. The only problem is that I often forget what they mean after I write them down."

"You might try using them in context. It's the best way to remember the meaning." Then he turned on his heel and disappeared.

Caroline had to allow that his idea was a good one, but all that left her with was a burning desire to use *insufferable, arrogant,* and *irritating* all in one sentence.

Six hours later, Caroline was in an extremely grumpy mood. Blake and James had spent the entire afternoon closeted in Blake's study, planning their "attack" upon Prewitt Hall.

Without her.

And now they were gone, having ridden out under the cover of the moonless night. Even the stars had conveniently obscured themselves behind clouds.

Those blasted men. They thought they were invincible, but Caroline knew better. Anyone could bleed.

The worst part of it all was that they acted as if it was all so much bloody fun. They'd discussed their plans quite animatedly, arguing over times and transportation and the best approach. And to add insult to injury, they hadn't even bothered to shut the door to Blake's study. Caroline had heard every word from the library.

Right now they were probably nearing Prewitt Hall, preparing to break into the south drawing room . . .

Without her.

"Stupid, stupid men," she grumbled. She flexed her ankle. Not even the teeniest bit of pain. "Clearly, I could have accompanied them. I wouldn't have slowed them down."

Dressed entirely in black, they'd both looked heart-stoppingly handsome. As she'd watched them leave, Caroline had felt unbearably frumpy. She was wearing one of the new dresses Blake had purchased for her, but she still felt like a rather plain pigeon next to those two dashing ravens.

She sat down at a table in the library upon which she'd piled all the biographies. She had planned to spend the evening alphabetizing them by subject, a task which she was now completing with a bit more vigor than was probably necessary.

Plato before Socrates, Cromwell before Fawkes . . . Ravenscroft and Sidwell before Trent.

Caroline slammed Milton on top of Machiavelli. This wasn't right. They shouldn't have gone without her. She had diagrammed the floor plan of Prewitt Hall for them, but nothing could substitute for firsthand knowledge. Without her they were in danger of stepping into the wrong room, of waking a servant, of—she gulped with fear—getting themselves killed.

The thought of losing her newfound friends was like ice around her heart. She'd spent a lifetime on the fringes of families, and now that she'd finally found two people who needed her—even if it was purely on a level of national security—she didn't want to sit on her hands and watch them walk headfirst into danger.

The marquis himself had said that she was crucial to their investigation. And as for Blake— Well, Blake didn't much like to admit that she was in any way involved in their work for the War Office, but even he had said she'd done a good job briefing them about the Prewitt household and their habits.

She *knew* they would fare better with her on-scene assistance. Why, they didn't even know about—

Caroline clapped her hand to her mouth in horror. How could she have forgotten to tell them about Farnsworth's evening tea? It was a ritual for the butler. Every night, like clockwork, he took tea at ten. It was an odd custom, but one upon which Farnsworth insisted. Tea, steaming hot, with milk and sugar, butter shortbread and strawberry jam—he demanded his nightly snack, and woe to anyone who interrupted. Caroline had once borrowed the teapot and found herself without blankets for a week. In December.

Caroline's eyes flew to the grandfather clock. It was quarter past nine. Blake and James had left fifteen minutes ago. They would be arriving at Prewitt Hall at . . .

Oh dear Lord, they would be arriving right when Farnsworth was preparing his snack. The butler might be getting on in years, but he was certainly not frail, and he was rather handy with firearms. And he had to travel directly past the south drawing room on the way from his chambers to the kitchen.

Caroline stood, her eyes wide and her expression resolute. They needed her. Blake needed her. She could never live with herself if she didn't go to warn them.

Without a care to her ankle, she dashed from the room, heading directly toward the stables.

Caroline rode like the proverbial wind. She wasn't the finest rider; in all truth, most of her guardians hadn't given her much opportunity to practice, but she was competent and could hold her seat.

And she'd certainly never had such a good reason to carry on in full gallop.

By the time she reached the edge of Oliver's property, the pocket watch she'd snatched from Blake's desk gave the time as exactly ten o'clock. She tied the mare—which she'd also "borrowed" from Blake—to a tree and crept toward the house, keeping herself hidden behind the tall hedges that ran alongside the drive. When she reached Prewitt Hall, she dropped to her hands and knees. She doubted that anyone was still awake, save for Farnsworth in the kitchen, but it seemed prudent to keep her silhouette from passing by any windows.

"Blake had better appreciate this," she whispered to herself. Not only did she look utterly foolish, crawling on all fours, but it had just occurred to her that she was back at Prewitt Hall, the one place she absolutely didn't want to be for the next five weeks. And she'd come of her own volition! What an idiot. If Oliver got his hands on her . . .

"Oliver is playing cards. Oliver is cheating at cards. Oliver won't be back for several hours." It was easy to whisper such thoughts, but it didn't make her any less uneasy. In fact, her stomach felt as if she'd swallowed a brace of bloodhounds.

"Remind me not to mind being left out again," she said to herself. It had been rather irritating when Blake and James had gone off without her, but now that she was here, in the thick of the action, all she wanted was to be back at Seacrest Manor, with perhaps a cup of warm tea and maybe a thick piece of toast . . .

When it came right down to it, Caroline decided, she wasn't cut out for a life of espionage.

She reached the northwest corner of the house and peered around, her gaze sweeping down the length of the west wall. She didn't see Blake or James, which probably meant that they were accessing the room from the south window.

If they hadn't gotten in already.

Caroline bit her lip. If they were inside the south drawing room, Farnsworth was sure to hear them. And Oliver kept a loaded gun in one of the hall cabinets. If Farnsworth suspected intruders, he'd surely get the gun before investigating, and Caroline rather doubted the butler would ask questions before pulling the trigger.

Fresh panic rising within her, she scooted along the grass, moving faster than she'd ever thought one could do at a crawl.

And then she rounded the corner.

"Did you hear something?"

James looked down from his work on the window latch and shook his head. He was standing on Blake's shoulders so that he could reach the window.

As James continued with his ministrations, Blake looked right and left. And then he heard it again—a kind of scurrying noise. He tapped James on the foot and put his forefinger to his lips. James nodded and temporarily ceased his work, which had been causing the occasional clink and clank as he jabbed at the latch with his file. He hopped noiselessly to the ground as Blake crouched, instantly assuming a vigilant posture.

Blake pulled out his pistol as he inched his way to the corner, his back pressed flat against the wall. A slight shadow was approaching. It wouldn't have been discernible except that someone had left a candle burning in one of the windows on the west wall.

And that shadow was growing closer.

Blake's finger tightened on the trigger.

A hand appeared from around the corner.

Blake pounced.

Chapter 11

pleth•o•ra *(noun). Over-fullness in any respect, superabundance.*

Blake insists that there is a veritable plethora *of reasons not to put anything important in writing, but I cannot think of anything in my little dictionary one could find incriminating.*

—From the personal dictionary of Caroline Trent

One moment Caroline was crawling on all fours, and the next she was as flat as a crepe, with a large, heavy, and oddly warm weight on her back. That, however, wasn't nearly so disconcerting as the cold gun pressed up against her ribs.

"Don't move," a voice growled in her ear. A familiar voice.

"Blake?" she croaked.

"Caroline?" Then he uttered a word so foul she'd never heard of it before, and she thought she had heard them all from her various guardians.

"The very one," she replied with a gulp, "and I really couldn't move, anyway. You're rather heavy."

He rolled off her and pierced her with a stare that was one part disbelief and thirty-one parts unadulterated fury. Caroline found herself wishing it were the other way around. Blake Ravenscroft was definitely not a man to cross.

"I am going to kill you," he hissed.

She gulped. "Don't you want to lecture me first?"

He stared at her with a heavy dose of stupefaction. "I take that back," he said with precisely clipped words. "First I am going to strangle you, and then I am going to kill you."

"Here?" she asked doubtfully, looking around. "Won't my dead body look suspicious in the morning?"

"What the hell are you doing here? You had explicit instructions to stay—"

"I know," she whispered urgently, pressing her finger to her lips, "but I remembered something, and—"

"I don't care if you remembered the entire second book of the Bible. You were told—"

James put a hand on Blake's shoulder and said, "Hear her out, Ravenscroft."

"It's the butler," Caroline put in quickly, before Blake changed his mind and decided to strangle her after all. "Farnsworth. I forgot about his tea. He has a strange habit, you see. He takes tea at ten every night. And he walks right by . . ." Her voice trailed off as she saw a beam of light moving in the dining room. It had to be Farnsworth, holding a lantern as he walked through the hall. The dining room doors were usually left open, so if his lantern was rather bright, they would be able to see its glow through the window.

Unless he'd heard something and had actually gone into the dining room to investigate . . .

All three of them hit the ground with alacrity.

"He has very keen ears," Caroline whispered.

"Then shut up," Blake hissed back.

She did.

The traveling light disappeared for a moment, then reappeared in the south drawing room.

"I thought you said Prewitt keeps this room locked," Blake whispered.

"Farnsworth has a key," Caroline whispered back.

Blake motioned to her with his hands to move away from the south drawing room window, and so she slithered on her belly until she was next to the dining room. Blake was right behind her. She looked around for James, but he must have gone around the corner in the opposite direction.

Blake pointed to the building and mouthed, "Closer to the wall." Caroline followed his instructions until she was pressed up against the cool exterior stone of Prewitt Hall. Within seconds, however, her other side was pressed up against the warm body of Blake Ravenscroft.

Caroline gasped. The man was lying on top of her! She would have blistered his ears, except that she knew she had to keep her voice down. Not to mention the fact that she was lying facedown on the ground and had no desire to get a mouthful of grass.

"How old is the butler?"

She nearly gasped. His breath was warm against her cheek, and she could swear she felt the touch of his lips against her ear. "At—at least fifty," she whispered, "but he's a crack shot."

"The butler?"

"He served in the army," she explained. "In the Colonies. I believe he was awarded a medal for valor."

"Just my luck," Blake muttered. "I don't suppose he's handy with a bow and arrow."

"Why, no, but I did see him once hit a tree with a knife from twenty paces."

"What?" Blake swore under his breath—another one of those splendidly creative curses that so impressed her.

"I'm joking," she said quickly.

His entire body tensed with fury. "This is *not* the time or the place for—"

"Yes, I realize that now," she mumbled.

James appeared from around the corner, crawling on his hands and knees. He eyed them with interest. "I had no idea you were having such fun over here."

"We are not having fun," Blake and Caroline hissed in unison.

James shook his head with such solemnity that it was clear he was mocking them. "No, obviously you are not." He then focused his eyes on Blake, who was still lying on top of Caroline. "Let's get back to work. The butler's gone up to his room."

"Are you certain?"

"I saw the light leave the drawing room, then go upstairs."

"There's a window in the side stairwell," Caroline explained. "You can see it from the south."

"Good," Blake said, rolling off of her and moving into a crouch. "Let's get back to work opening those windows."

"Bad idea," Caroline said.

Both men turned to face her, and in the dark she couldn't be certain whether their expressions were interested or disdainful.

"Farnsworth will hear you from his room," she said. "It's only two stories up, and since it's warm out, he's most likely opened the windows. If he happens to look out, he will most certainly see you."

"You might have told us this before we attempted break in," Blake snapped.

"I can still get you in," she shot back.

"How?"

" 'Thank you, Caroline,' " she said sarcastically. " 'That is very thoughtful of you.' 'Why, you're welcome, Blake, it's no trouble at all to assist you.' "

He didn't look amused. "We don't have time for jokes, Caroline. Tell us what to do."

"Can you pick a lock?"

He looked affronted that she'd even asked. "Of course. Riverdale is faster, though."

"Fine. Follow me."

His hand landed heavily on her right shoulder. "*You* are not coming in."

"Am I supposed to remain out here by myself? Where anyone who passes by would recognize me and return me to Oliver? Not to mention thieves, brigands—"

"Begging your pardon, Caroline," James cut in, "but we are the thieves and brigands in this little tableau."

Caroline choked back laughter.

Blake fumed.

James looked back and forth between them with unconcealed interest. Finally he said, "She's right, Ravenscroft. We can't leave her alone out here. Lead on, Caroline."

Blake was cursing a streak so blue it might as well have been black, but he trudged behind James and Caroline without an otherwise negative comment.

She took them to a side door that was partially concealed by a tall English maple. Then she crouched down and put her finger to her lips, indicating that they should remain still. The two men looked at her with puzzlement and interest as she heaved upward, slamming her shoulder into the door. They heard a latch come undone, and Caroline swung the door open.

"Won't the butler have heard that?" James asked.

She shook her head. "His room is too far away. The only person who lives on this side of the Hall is the housekeeper, and she's quite deaf. I've sneaked in and out this way many times. No one has ever caught on."

"You might have told us this before," Blake said.

"You'd never have gotten it right. You have to hit the door just so. It took me weeks to learn."

"And what were you doing sneaking out at night?" he demanded.

"I fail to see how that is your business."

"You became my business when you took up residence in my house."

"Well, I wouldn't have moved in if you hadn't *kidnapped* me!"

"I wouldn't have kidnapped you if you hadn't been wandering about the countryside with no thought to your own safety."

"I was certainly safer in the countryside than I was at Prewitt Hall, and you well know it."

"You wouldn't be safe in a convent," he muttered.

Caroline rolled her eyes. "If that isn't the most ridiculous— Oh, never mind. If you're so upset that I didn't let you open the door, here, I'll close it again and you can have a go at it."

He took a menacing step forward. "Do you know, if I strangled you here and now there's not a jury in this country that wouldn't acquit—"

"If you two lovebirds can stop snapping at each other," James cut in, "I'd like to search the study before Prewitt returns home."

Blake glared at Caroline as if this entire delay were her fault, causing her to hiss, "Don't forget that if it weren't for me—"

"If it weren't for you," he shot back, "I would be a very happy man indeed."

"We are wasting time," James reminded them. "The both of you may remain here, if you cannot cease your squabbling, but I am going in to search the south drawing room."

"I'll go first," Caroline announced, "since I know the way."

"You'll go behind me," Blake contradicted, "and give me directions as we go along."

"Oh, for the love of Saint Peter," James finally burst out, exasperation showing in every line of his body. "*I'll* go first, if only to shut the two of you up. Caroline, you follow and give me directions. Blake, you guard her from the rear."

The trio made their way into the house, amazingly without another word except for Caroline's whispered instructions. Soon they found themselves in front of the door to the south drawing room. James pulled out an odd flat tool and inserted it in the lock.

"Will that thing really work?" Caroline whispered to Blake.

He nodded curtly. "Riverdale's the best. He can pick a lock faster than anyone. Here, watch. Three more seconds. One, two . . ."

Click. The door swung open.

"Three," James said with a slightly self-satisfied smile.

"Well done," Caroline said.

He smiled back at her. "I've never met a woman or a lock that didn't love me."

Blake muttered something under his breath and strode past them. "You," he said, turning around and pointing to Caroline, "don't touch anything."

"Would you like me to tell you what Oliver also did not want me to touch?" she asked, her smile patently false.

"I don't have time for games, Miss Trent."

"Oh, I wouldn't dream of wasting your time."

Blake turned to James. "I'm going to kill her."

"And I'm going to kill *you*," James returned. "Both of you." He stepped past them and made a beeline for the desk. "Blake, you inspect the shelves.

Caroline, you—well, I don't know what you should do, but try not to yell at Blake."

Blake smirked.

"He yelled at me first," Caroline muttered, well aware that she was acting juvenile.

James shook his head and went to work on the locked desk drawers. He carefully picked each lock, then examined the contents of each drawer, rearranging them afterward so that Oliver wouldn't notice they'd been tampered with.

After about a minute, however, Caroline took pity on him and said, "You might want to concentrate on the bottom left."

He looked back up at her with interest.

She shrugged, her head tilting to the side with the movement. "It's the one Oliver was always the most insane about. He once nearly took Farnsworth's head off just for polishing the lock."

"Couldn't you have told him this before he went through all of the other drawers?" Blake asked angrily.

"I tried," she retorted, "and you threatened to kill me."

James ignored their sniping and jimmied the lower left lock. The drawer slid open, revealing stacks of files, all of which were labeled with dates.

"What is it?" Blake asked.

James let out a low whistle. "Prewitt's ticket to the gallows."

Blake and Caroline crowded around, both eager for a look. There were perhaps three dozen files, each neatly labeled with a date. James had one of them open on the desk and was scanning the contents with great interest.

"What does it say?" Caroline asked.

"It documents Prewitt's illegal activities," Blake answered. "Damned stupid of him to have put it in writing."

"Oliver is terribly organized," she said. "Whenever he devises any sort of a plan he always puts it down on paper and then follows it without exception."

James pointed to a sentence beginning with the initials CDL. "That must be Carlotta," he whispered. "But who is this?"

Caroline's eyes followed his finger to MCD. "Miles Dudley," she said.

The two men turned to face her. "Who?" they both asked.

"Miles Dudley, I should think. I don't know his middle initial, but he is the only MD of whom I can think. He is one of Oliver's closest cronies. They've known each other for years."

Blake and James shared a glance.

"I find him detestable," Caroline continued. "He is always slobbering all over the housemaids. And me. I contrive to be absent when he comes to call."

Blake turned to the marquis. "Is there enough in that file to arrest Dudley?"

"There would be," James answered, "if we could be sure MCD truly is Miles Dudley. One can't go about imprisoning people on the basis of their initials."

"If you arrested Oliver," Caroline said, "I'm sure he would incriminate Mr. Dudley. They are rather good friends, but I doubt Oliver's loyalty would hold fast under such circumstances. When it comes right down to it, Oliver holds no true loyalty to anyone except himself."

"It's not a risk I'm prepared to take," Blake said grimly. "I will not rest until I see both of these traitors imprisoned or hanged. We need to catch both of them in action."

"Is there any way you can determine when Oliver plans his next smuggling run?" Caroline asked.

"Not," James replied, thumbing through the stack of file, "unless he's been really stupid."

Caroline leaned forward. "What about this one?" she asked, holding up a nearly empty file marked 31–7–14.

Blake grabbed it from her, leafed through the contents. "What an idiot!"

"I certainly shan't argue with you on the subject of Oliver's idiocy," Caroline put in, "but I must say I'm sure he wasn't expecting his office to be searched."

"One should never put this kind of information into writing," Blake said.

"Why, Ravenscroft," James said with a mischievous arch of his eyebrows, "with a thought process like that, you should make an excellent criminal."

Blake was so engrossed in the file he didn't even bother to glare at his friend. "Prewitt is planning something big. From the looks of it, bigger than anything he's done before. He mentions CDL and MCD and 'the rest.' He also names a rather large sum of money."

Caroline peered over his arm at the number written in the file. "Oh my good Lord," she breathed. "With money like that, what did he want with my inheritance?"

"There are some who feel they can never get enough," Blake replied caustically.

James cleared his throat. "I think we should wait, then, until the last of the month, and strike when we can nab them all. Eliminate the entire ring in one clean sweep."

"It sounds like a good plan," Caroline agreed. "Even if we do have to wait three weeks."

Blake turned on her with a furious expression. "*You* are not participating."

"The devil you say," she retorted, hands on her hips. "If it weren't for me, you wouldn't even know that he is planning something for that Wednesday." She blinked in thought. "I say, do you suppose he hasn't been spending all of those Wednesdays playing cards? I wonder if he's been smuggling on a regular basis. Every Wednesday and such."

She flipped through the files, checking the dates and mentally adding and subtracting sevens to each of them. "Look! All are for the same day of the week."

"I doubt he smuggles every Wednesday," James mused, "but it's an excellent cover for the times he does engage in illegal activities. With whom does he play cards?"

"Miles Dudley, for one."

Blake shook his head. "The entire damned game is probably involved. Who else?"

"Bernard Leeson. He's our local surgeon."

"It figures," Blake muttered. "I hate leeches."

"And Francis Badeley," she finished, "the magistrate."

"I suppose we shouldn't look to him, then, for assistance in our apprehension," James said.

"He'll probably be apprehended himself," Blake replied. "We'll have to call in men from London."

James nodded. "Moreton is going to want some evidence before deploying his men on such a grand scale. We're going to need to take these files."

"I shouldn't take them all, were I you," Caroline interjected. "Oliver comes into this room nearly every day. I'm sure he'll notice if his files have gone missing."

"You're getting quite good at this," James replied with a chuckle. "Are you certain you don't want to sign up?"

"She is not working for the War Office," Blake growled. Caroline had the feeling he would have roared the statement had they not been prowling in Oliver's study.

"We'll just take a couple," James replied, ignoring Blake's interjection. "But we can't take this one." He held up the file on the upcoming mission. "He'll be wanting to go over this sometime soon."

"Get Caroline a piece of paper," Blake drawled. "I'm sure she'll be happy to copy the information down. After all, she has exquisite penmanship."

"I don't know where Oliver keeps blank paper," she replied, ignoring his sarcasm. "He almost never allowed me into this room. I do, however, know where we can get some just down the hall. And a quill and ink, as well."

"Good idea," James said. "The less we ransack in here, the less chance there is Prewitt will notice someone's been through his things. Caroline, go get the paper and quill."

"Right." She gave him a jaunty salute and scurried out the door.

But Blake was fast on her heels. "You're not going alone," he hissed. "Slow down."

Caroline didn't slow her pace at all, having no doubt that he would follow her down the hall and into the east drawing room. It was the chamber she had used to entertain neighborhood ladies. Not that many had come to call, but still, Caroline had kept paper, quills, and ink there, in case anyone needed to jot down a note or correspondence.

But just as she was about to dart into the room, she heard a noise coming from the front door. A noise that sounded suspiciously like a key turning in a lock. She turned to Blake and hissed, "It's Oliver!"

He didn't even waste time on words. Before Caroline had any idea what was about, she'd been shoved into the east drawing room and was crouched behind a sofa. Her heart was beating so loudly she was surprised it didn't wake up the entire household. "What about James?" she whispered.

Blake put his finger to her lips. "He'll know what to do. Now hush, he's coming in."

Caroline clenched her teeth to keep herself from squeaking with fear as she listened to the sound of Oliver's shoes clicking down the hall. What if James hadn't heard him enter? What if James had heard him but wasn't able to hide in time? What if he was able to hide in time but forgot to close the door?

Her head ached with the myriad possibilities for disaster.

But Oliver's heels weren't clicking toward the south drawing room. They were clicking right toward her! Caroline stifled a gasp and nudged Blake in the ribs. He made no response save for the tightening of his already stiff posture.

Caroline glanced over to a side table, her eyes falling on a decanter of brandy. Oliver liked to take a glass up with him to bed. If he didn't turn around while pouring he wouldn't see them, but if he did . . .

Thoroughly panicked, she yanked on Blake's arm. Hard.

He didn't budge.

With frantic motions she poked at his chest and then pointed at the brandy decanter.

"What?" Blake mouthed.

"The brandy," she mouthed back, furiously jabbing her finger at the decanter.

Blake's eyes widened, and he looked quickly around the room, searching for another hiding place. The light was dim, though, and it was hard to see.

Caroline had the advantage, however, of knowing the room like the back of her hand. She jerked her head to the side, motioning for Blake to follow, and crawled behind another sofa, thanking her maker all the while that Oliver had chosen to lay down a carpet. A bare floor would have echoed her every movement, and then they would have been lost for sure.

At that moment Oliver entered the room and poured himself a brandy. A few seconds later she heard his glass thunk down on the table, followed by the sound of more brandy being poured. Caroline bit her lip in confusion. It was very unlike Oliver to drink more than one glass before bed.

But Oliver must have had a rough evening, for he sighed, "God, what a disaster."

And then, horror of horrors, he flopped his body directly onto the sofa behind which they were hiding and plopped his legs down on the table.

Caroline froze. Or she would have, she thought wildly, if she wasn't already paralyzed with fear. There could be no doubt about it.

They were trapped.

Chapter 12

pal·li·a·tive *(noun). That which gives superficial or temporary relief.*

A kiss, I am learning, is a weak palliative *when one's heart is breaking.*

—From the personal dictionary of Caroline Trent

Blake clamped his hand over Caroline's mouth. He knew how to be quiet; he'd had years of experience in the art of keeping oneself utterly silent. But God knew what Caroline would do. The crazy woman might sneeze at any moment. Or hiccough. Or fidget.

She glared at him over his hand. Yes, Blake thought, she would be a fidgeter. He moved his other hand to her upper arm and held firm, determined to keep her still. He didn't care if she had bruises for a week; there was no telling what Prewitt would do if he found his wayward ward hiding behind a sofa in the drawing room. After all, when Caroline had run away, she'd effectively taken her fortune with her.

Prewitt yawned and stood up, and for a moment Blake's heart raced with hope. But the blasted man just crossed to the side table and poured himself another brandy.

Blake looked at Caroline. Hadn't she once said Prewitt never overindulged in spirits? She shrugged, clearly at a loss as to what her guardian was doing.

Prewitt sat back down on the sofa with a loud grunt, then muttered, "Goddamn that girl."

Caroline's eyes widened.

Blake pointed to her and mouthed, *You?*

She lifted her shoulders and blinked.

Blake closed his eyes for a moment and tried to figure out who Prewitt meant. There was no way to be certain. It could be Caroline; it could be Carlotta De Leon.

"Where the hell could she be?" Prewitt said, followed by a swallowing sound that had to be more brandy.

Caroline pointed to herself and Blake felt her mouth form the word, *Me?* under his hand. He didn't respond, though. He was too busy focusing on Prewitt. If the traitorous bastard discovered them now the mission would be ruined. Well, not entirely. Blake was certain that he and James could easily apprehend Prewitt that night if the need arose, but that would mean that his co-conspirators might go free. Better to be patient and wait out the next three weeks. Then the espionage ring would be closed down for good.

Then, just when Blake felt his feet start to fall asleep under him, Prewitt plunked his glass down on a table and strode from the room. Blake counted to ten, then removed his hand from Caroline's mouth and heaved a sigh of relief.

She sighed, too, but it was a quick one, followed by the question, "Do you think he was talking about me?"

"I have no idea," Blake said honestly. "But I wouldn't be surprised if he was."

"Do you think he discovered James?"

He shook his head. "If he had, we would have heard some sort of commotion. That doesn't mean we're safe yet, though. For all we know, Prewitt is taking a leisurely stroll down the hall before entering the south drawing room."

"What do we do now?"

"We wait."

"For what?"

He turned sharply to face her. "You ask a lot of questions."

"It's the only way to learn anything useful."

"We wait," Blake said with an impatient exhale, "until we get a sign from Riverdale."

"What if he is waiting for a sign from us?"

"He's not."

"How can you be certain?"

"Riverdale and I have worked together for seven years. I know his methods."

"I really don't see how you could have prepared for this particular scenario."

He shot her a look of such irritation that she clamped her mouth shut. But not before rolling her eyes at him.

Blake ignored her for several minutes, which wasn't easy. The mere sound of her breathing excited him. His reaction was completely inappropriate under the circumstances, and one with which he had no experience, even with Marabelle. Unfortunately, there seemed to be nothing he could do about it, which pushed his temper even further into the vile.

Then she moved, and her arm accidentally brushed against his hip, and—

Blake absolutely refused to let that thought go any further. Abruptly he took her hand and stood. "Let's go."

Caroline looked around in confusion. "Did we receive some sort of sign from the marquis?"

"No, but it's been long enough."

"But I thought you said—"

"If you want to be a part of this operation," he hissed, "you need to learn to take orders. Without question."

She raised her brows. "I'm so glad you've decided to let me participate."

If Blake could have torn out her tongue at that moment, he would have done it. Or at least tried. "Follow me," he snapped.

Caroline saluted him and then did a little tiptoe march behind him to the door. Blake thought he deserved a medal for not picking her up by the collar and tossing her out the window. At the very least, he was going to demand some sort of hazard pay from the War Office. If they couldn't give him money, there had to be some small property somewhere that had been confiscated from a criminal.

Surely he deserved a little something extra for this mission. Caroline might be rather delightful to kiss, but on assignment she was bloody annoying.

He reached the open doorway and motioned for her to stay behind him. Hand on gun, he peered into the hall, ascertained that it was empty, and stepped out. Caroline followed without his verbal instruction, as he knew she would. That one certainly needed no prodding to step out into the face of danger.

She was too headstrong, too careless. It brought back memories.

Marabelle.

Blake squeezed his eyes shut for a split second, trying to drive his late fiancée from his mind. She might live in his heart, but she had no place here, this night, in Prewitt Hall. Not if Blake wanted to get the three of them out alive.

Marabelle's memory, however, was quickly put aside by Caroline's incessant poking at his upper arm. "What now?" he snapped.

"Shouldn't we at least get the paper and quills? Isn't that why we came here in the first place?"

Blake flexed his hands into tense starfishes and slowly said, "Yes. Yes, that would be a good idea."

She scurried across the room and gathered her supplies while he swore at himself under his breath. He was getting soft, growing weak. It wasn't like him to forget something as simple as a quill and ink. More than anything he wanted out of the War Office, away from all the danger and intrigue. He wanted to live a life where he didn't have to worry about seeing his friends get killed, where he could do nothing but read and raise lazy, spoiled hounds and—

"I've everything we need," Caroline said breathlessly, breaking into his thoughts.

He nodded, and they made their way into the hall. When they reached the door to the south drawing room, Blake tapped seven times on the wood, his fingers finding the familiar rhythm he and James had worked out years ago, when they were both schoolboys at Eton.

The door swung inward, just a fraction of an inch, and then Blake pushed it open far enough for him and Caroline to squeeze through. James had his back to the wall and his finger poised on the trigger of his gun. He breathed an audible sigh of relief when he saw that it was only Caroline and Blake entering the room.

"Didn't you recognize the knock?" Blake asked.

James gave a curt nod. "Can't be too careful."

"I'll say," Caroline agreed. All of this spywork was leaving her stomach rather queasy. It was exciting, to be sure, but nothing in which she'd wish to participate on a regular basis. She had no idea how the two of them had lasted this long without fraying their nerves completely.

She turned to James. "Did Oliver come in here?"

He shook his head. "But I heard him in the hall."

"He had us trapped for a few minutes in the east drawing room." She shuddered. "It was terrifying."

Blake shot her an oddly appraising look.

"I brought the paper, quills, and ink," Caroline continued, depositing the writing equipment on Oliver's desk. "Shall we copy the documents now? I should like to get going. I really had never intended to spend so much time at Prewitt Hall again."

There were only three pages in the folder, so they each took a page and hastily copied it down onto a new sheet of paper. The results weren't terribly neat, with more than one ink splotch marring the effort, but they were legible, and that was all that mattered.

James carefully replaced the file in the drawer and relocked it.

"Is the room in order?" Blake asked.

James nodded. "I straightened everything while you were gone."

"Excellent. Let's be off."

Caroline turned to the marquis. "Did you remember to take an older file as evidence?"

"I am certain he knows how to do his job," Blake said curtly. Then he turned to James and asked, "Did you?"

"Good God!" James said in a disgusted voice. "The two of you are worse than a pair of toddlers. Yes, of course I have the file, and if you don't stop arguing with one another, I'm going to lock the both of you in here and leave you to Prewitt and his sharpshooting butler."

Caroline's jaw dropped at the outburst from the normally even-tempered marquis. She stole a glance at Blake and noticed that he looked rather surprised as well—and perhaps a touch embarrassed.

James scowled at both of them before pinning his stare on Caroline and asking, "How the hell do we get out of here?"

"We can't go out the window for the same reason we couldn't go in that way. If Farnsworth is still awake he would certainly hear us. But we can leave the way we came."

"Won't someone be suspicious tomorrow when the door isn't locked?" Blake asked.

Caroline shook her head. "I know how to shut the door so that the latch fastens itself. No one will ever know."

"Good," James said. "Let's be off."

The trio moved silently through the house, pausing outside the south drawing room so that James could relock the door, and then exited into the side yard. A few minutes later they reached the men's horses.

"My mount is over there," Caroline said, pointing to a small collection of trees across the garden.

"I suppose you mean *my* mount," Blake snapped, "which you conveniently borrowed."

She snorted. "Pray forgive my use of imprecise English, Mr. Ravenscroft. I—"

But whatever she was going to say—and Caroline wasn't even certain herself what that would be—was lost under the sound of James's cursing. Before she or Blake could say another word, he'd called them both baconbrains, idiots, and something else entirely, which Caroline didn't quite understand. She was fairly certain, however, that it was an insult. And then, before either one of them had a chance to respond, James had hopped onto his horse and ridden off over the hill.

Caroline blinked and turned to Blake. "He's rather irritated with us, isn't he?"

Blake's response was to heave her up onto his horse and hop up behind her. They rode the perimeter of Prewitt Hall's property until they reached the tree where she'd tied her horse. Soon Caroline was atop her own mount.

"Follow me," Blake instructed, and he took off at a canter.

An hour or so later Caroline followed Blake through the front door of Seacrest Manor. She was tired and sore and wanted nothing more than to crawl into bed, but before she could dash up the stairs he took her by the elbow and steered her into his study.

Or perhaps *propelled* would be a more accurate term.

"Can't this wait until morning?" Caroline asked, yawning.

"No."

"I'm terribly sleepy."

No response.

Caroline decided to try a different tactic. "What do you suppose happened to the marquis?"

"I don't particularly care."

She blinked. How odd. Then she yawned again, unable to help herself. "Is it your intention to scold me?" she asked. "Because if it is, I might as well warn you that I'm really not up to it, and—"

"You're not *up* to it?!" he fairly roared.

She shook her head and headed for the door. There was no use trying to reason with him when he was in such a mood. "I'll see you in the morning. I'm certain whatever it is that has you so upset will keep until then."

Blake caught a handful of the fabric of her skirt and hauled her back to the center of the room. "You are not going anywhere," he growled.

"I beg your pardon."

"Just what the hell did you think you were doing tonight?"

"Saving your life?" she quipped.

"Don't make jokes."

"I wasn't. I did save your life. And I don't recall hearing one word of thanks for it."

He muttered something under his breath, followed by, "You didn't save my life. All you did was endanger your own."

"I won't quibble with the latter sentence, but I certainly did save your life this evening. If I hadn't rushed out to Prewitt Hall to warn you about Farnsworth and his ten o'clock tea, he would surely have shot you."

"That's a moot point, Caroline."

"Of course it is," she replied with a disdainful sniff. "I saved your miserable life, and Farnsworth was never given the opportunity to shoot at you."

He stared at her long and hard. "I am going to say this only once. You are not to get involved with our work bringing your former guardian to justice."

Caroline remained silent.

After a moment Blake clearly lost patience with her lack of response, so he demanded, "Well? Don't you have a reply?"

"I do, but you wouldn't like it."

"Goddamn it, Caroline!" he exploded. "Don't you give even a thought to your own safety?"

"Of course I do. Do you think I had *fun* risking my neck for you this evening? I could have been killed. Or worse, you could have been killed. Or Oliver could have captured me and forced me to marry Percy." She shuddered. "Good God, I'll probably have nightmares about that last scenario for weeks."

"You certainly seemed to be enjoying yourself."

"Well, I wasn't. I felt sick the entire time, knowing that we were in danger."

"If you were so petrified, why weren't you crying and carrying on like a normal woman?"

"A *normal* woman? Sir, you insult me. You insult my entire gender."

"You must admit that most women would have needed smelling salts tonight."

She glared at him, her entire body shaking with fury. "Am I expected to apologize because I didn't fall apart and simper and cry and ruin the entire operation? I was scared—no, I was petrified, but what good would I have been if I hadn't kept up a brave front? Besides," she added, her expression growing sullen, "I was so angry with you most of the time I forgot how scared I was."

Blake looked away. Hearing her admit her fear made him feel even worse. If anything had happened to her that night it would have been his fault. "Caroline," he said in a low voice, "I won't have you endangering yourself. I forbid it."

"You have no right to forbid me anything."

A muscle started to twitch in his neck. "As long as you are living in my house—"

"Oh, for goodness sake, you sound like one of my guardians."

"Now *you* insult *me*."

She let out a frustrated exhale. "I don't know how you bear it, living constantly in such danger. I don't know how your family bears it. They must worry terribly about you."

"My family doesn't know."

"What?" she screeched. "How is that possible?"

"I've never told them."

"That is abominable," she said with great feeling. "Truly abominable. If I had a family I should never treat them with such disrespect."

"We are not here to discuss my family," he ground out. "We are here to discuss your foolhardy behavior."

"I refuse to acknowledge my behavior as foolhardy. You would have done the exact same thing were you in my shoes."

"But I wasn't in your shoes, as you so delicately put it, and furthermore, I have nearly a decade of experience with these matters. You do not."

"What do you want from me? Do you want me to promise I shall never interfere again?"

"That would be an excellent beginning."

Caroline planted her hands on her hips and jutted her chin forward. "Well, I won't. I should like nothing more than to keep myself out of peril for the rest of my life, but if you are in danger, and I can do something to help, I certainly will not remain idle. How could I have lived with myself if you'd been hurt?"

"You are the most muleheaded woman I have ever had the misfortune to meet." He raked his hand through his hair and muttered something under his breath before saying, "Can't you see I'm trying to protect you?"

Caroline felt something rather warm tickling within her, and tears formed in her eyes. "Yes," she said, "but can't you see I'm trying to do the same?"

"Don't." His word was cold, clipped, and hard, so hard that Caroline actually took a step back.

"Why are you being so cruel?" she whispered.

"The last time a woman thought to protect me . . ."

His voice faded away, but Caroline needed no words to understand the stark grief etched on his face. "Blake," she said softly, "I don't want to argue about this."

"Then promise me something."

She swallowed, knowing that he was going to ask something to which she couldn't agree.

"Don't put yourself in danger again. If something happened to you, I—I couldn't bear it, Caroline."

She turned away. Her eyes were growing teary, and she didn't want him to see her emotional response to his plea. There was something in his voice that touched her heart, something about the way his lips moved for a moment before he spoke, as if he were searching in vain for the right words.

But then he said, "I can't let another woman die," and she knew this wasn't about her. It was about him, and the overwhelming guilt he felt over the death of his fiancée. She didn't know all of the details surrounding Marabelle's demise, but James had said enough for her to know that Blake still blamed himself for her death.

Caroline choked down a sob. How could she compete with a dead woman?

Without looking at him, she stumbled toward the door. "I'm going upstairs. If you have anything more to say to me you can say it in the morning."

But before she could wrap her hand around the doorknob she heard him say, "Wait."

Just one word and she was helpless to resist. Slowly, she turned around.

Blake stared at her, unable to take his eyes from her face. He wanted to say something; a thousand words crashed through his mind, but he couldn't think of a single sentence. And then, without realizing what he was doing, he took a step toward her, and then another, and then another, and then she was in his arms.

"Don't scare me again," he murmured into her hair.

She didn't reply, but he felt her body growing warm and softening against him. Then he heard her sigh. It was a soft sound, barely audible, but it was sweet and it told him she wanted him. Maybe not the way he wanted her—hell, he doubted that was possible; he couldn't remember ever wanting a woman with this white-hot brand of need. But still, she wanted him. He was sure of it.

His lips found hers and he devoured her with all the fear and desire he'd been feeling all evening. She tasted like his every dream and felt like pure heaven.

And Blake knew he was damned.

He could never have her, never love her in the ways she deserved to be loved, but he was too selfish to let her go. Just for this moment he could—and would—pretend that he was hers, and she was his, and that his heart was whole.

They tumbled onto the sofa, Caroline landing softly on top of him, and he wasted no time in exchanging positions with her. He wanted to feel her squirming beneath him, writhing with the same force of desire that was consuming him. He wanted to watch her eyes as they darkened and smoldered with need.

His hands stole under the hem of her skirt, daringly squeezing her supple calf before sliding up to her soft thigh. She moaned beneath him, a delectable sound that might have been his name, or it might have just been a moan, but Blake didn't care. All he wanted was her.

All of her.

"God help me, Caroline," he said, barely recognizing the sound of his own voice. "I need you. Tonight. Right now. I need you."

His hand went to the fastening of his breeches, moving frantically to free himself. He had to sit up to get them undone, though, and that was just enough time for her to look at him, to really look at him. And in that split second her haze of passion cleared and she lurched up off the sofa.

"No," she gasped. "Not like this. Not without— No."

Blake just watched her go, hating himself for coming at her like such an animal. But she surprised him by pausing at the door.

"Go," he said hoarsely. If she didn't leave the room that instant, he knew he would go after her, and then there would be no escape.

"Will you be all right?"

He stared at her in shock. He had very nearly dishonored her. He would have taken her virginity without a backward glance. "Why are you asking?"

"Will you be all right?"

She wasn't going to leave without a response, so he nodded.

"Good. I'll see you tomorrow."

And then she was gone.

Chapter 13

dith•er *(noun). A state of tremulous excitement or apprehension; also, vacillation; a state of confusion.*

Just a word from him sets me in a dither, *and I vow I do not like it one bit.*

—From the personal dictionary of Caroline Trent

It was Caroline's fiercest desire to avoid Blake for the next fifteen years, but as luck would have it, she quite literally bumped into him the following morning. Unfortunately for the sake of her dignity, this "bump" involved her spilling about a half-dozen rather thick books onto the floor, several of which hit Blake's legs and feet on the way down.

He howled in pain, and she wanted nothing more than to howl in embarrassment, but instead she just mumbled her apologies and dropped to the carpet so that she could gather her books. At least that way he wouldn't see the bright blush that had stained her cheeks the moment she'd collided with him.

"I thought you were limiting your redecorating endeavors to the library," he said. "What the devil are you doing with those books out here in the hall?"

She looked straight up into his clear gray eyes. Drat. If she *had* to see him this morning, why did she have to be on her hands and knees? "I'm not redecorating," she said in her haughtiest voice, "I'm bringing these books back to my room to read."

"Six of them?" he asked doubtfully.

"I'm quite literate."

"I never doubted that."

She pursed her lips, wanting to say that she was electing to read so that she might remain in her chamber and never have to see him again, but she had a feeling that would lead to a long, drawn-out argument, which was the last thing she wanted. "Was there anything else you desired, Mr. Ravenscroft?"

Then she blushed, really blushed. He'd made it quite clear the night before what he desired.

He waved his hand expansively—a motion she found annoyingly condescending. "Nothing," he said. "Nothing at all. If you want to read, be my guest. Read the whole bloody library if it suits you. If nothing else, it will keep you out of trouble."

She bit back another retort, but it was growing difficult to maintain such a circumspect mouth. Hugging her books to her chest, she asked, "Has the marquis risen yet this morning?"

Blake's expression darkened before he said, "He's gone."

"Gone?"

"Gone." And then, as if she couldn't grasp the meaning of the word, he added, "Quite gone."

"But where would he go?"

"I imagine he would go just about anywhere that would remove him from our company. But as it happens, he went to London."

Her lips parted in shock. "But that leaves us alone."

"Quite alone," he agreed, holding out a sheet of paper. "Would you like to read his note?"

She nodded, took the note into her hands, and read:

Ravenscroft—

I have gone to London for the purpose of alerting Moreton to our plans. I have brought with me the copy of Prewitt's file. I realize this leaves you alone with Caroline, but truly, that is no more improper than her residing at Seacrest Manor with the both of us.

Besides which, the two of you were driving me mad.

—Riverdale

Caroline looked up at him with a wary expression. "You can't like this situation."

Blake pondered her statement. No, he didn't "like" this situation. He didn't "like" having her under his roof, just an arm's reach away. He didn't "like" knowing that the object of his desire was his for the taking. James hadn't been much of a chaperone—certainly no one who could have salvaged her reputation should word of their uncommon living arrangements get out—but he'd at least created a buffer between Blake and Caroline. All that was now standing between him and the end of this damned frustration and lust was his own conscience.

And his body was starting to get rather frustrated with his conscience.

He knew that should he make a concerted effort to seduce Caroline, she would be helpless to stop him. The little innocent had never even been kissed; she'd never know what hit her if Blake used all the sensual weapons in his arsenal.

Of course one couldn't discount the presence of Perriwick and Mrs. Mickle. The pair of servants had taken to Caroline like clotted cream to scones, and Blake had no doubt that they would guard her virtue with their very lives.

He looked back at Caroline, who also appeared lost in her thoughts. Then suddenly her chin lifted and she said, "We were acting rather juvenile, weren't we?"

Before Blake even had a chance to nod, she added, "Of course, it was nothing that should require the marquis to feel the need to put a hundred miles between us, or however long it is to London. I say, how far is it to London?"

He stared at her in amazement. She had the most remarkable talent of making the most serious topics rather mundane. "Actually, a hundred miles is about right," he answered.

"Is it? I've never been to London. I've been shuttled about between Kent and Hampshire, with a brief spell in Gloucestershire, but never London."

"Caroline, *what* are you talking about?"

"I am *trying* to be polite," she replied, using much the same condescending tone he had. "You, however, are making it extremely difficult."

He let out a frustrated sigh. "Caroline, we are going to be living in the same house together for the next five weeks."

"I am well aware of that, Mr. Ravenscroft."

"We are going to have to make the best of a rather uncomfortable situation."

"I see no reason why it should be uncomfortable."

Blake disagreed. In fact his body was disagreeing rather strongly that very second. He was *quite* uncomfortable, and he could only give thanks to the current fashions for hiding it from her so well. But he wasn't about to go into all that, so he just flayed her with his most supercilious stare and said, "Don't you?"

"Not at all," she replied, clearly unintimidated. "There is no reason why we should be uncomfortable if we simply take pains to avoid one another's company."

"You really think we can avoid one another for three weeks?"

"Is that how long the marquis plans to be gone?"

"From the tone of his letter, I'd venture to guess that he plans to stay away as long as possible."

"Well, I suppose we can do it. It's a big enough house."

Blake closed his eyes. The entire county of Dorset wasn't big enough.

"Blake? Blake? Are you feeling quite all right? You look a bit flushed."

"I'm fine," he said.

"It's really quite remarkable how well you can enunciate even when you talk through your teeth. But still, you don't look at all the thing. Perhaps I ought to put you to bed."

The room suddenly felt stiflingly hot, and Blake blurted out, "That is a very bad idea, Caroline."

"I know, I know. Men make the worst patients. Can you imagine if you had to deliver babies? The human race should never have made it so far."

He turned on his heel. "I'm going to my room."

"Oh, good. You should. You'll feel much better, I'm sure, if you get some rest."

Blake didn't answer her, just strode toward the stairs. When he reached the first step, however, he realized that she was still right behind him. "What are you doing here?" he snapped.

"I'm following you to your room."

"Are you doing this for any particular reason?"

"I'm seeing to your welfare."

"See to it elsewhere."

"That," she said firmly, "is quite impossible."

"Caroline," he ground out, thinking his jaw was going to snap in two at any moment, "you are trying my nerves. Severely."

"Of course I am. Anyone would in your condition. You are clearly suffering from some sort of illness."

He stomped up two steps. "I am not ill."

She stomped up one step. "Of course you are. You could have a fever, or perhaps a putrid throat."

He whirled around. "I repeat: I am not ill."

"Don't make me repeat my statement as well. We're starting to sound rather childish. And if you don't allow me to tend to you, you'll only grow sicker."

Blake felt a pressure rising within him—something he was quite powerless to contain. "I am *not* ill."

She let out a frustrated sigh. "Blake, I—"

He grabbed her under her arms and hauled her up until they were nose to nose, her feet dangling helplessly in the air. "I am not ill, Caroline," he said, his words clipped and even. "I don't have a fever, I don't have a putrid throat, and I damned well don't need you to take care of me. Do you understand?"

She nodded. "Could you possibly put me down?"

"Good." He set her down on the floor with surprising gentleness, then turned and marched back up the stairs.

Caroline, however, was right behind him.

"I thought you wanted to avoid me," he snapped, whirling around to face her once he reached the landing.

"I did. I mean, I do. But you're ill, and—"

"I'm not ill!" he thundered.

She didn't say anything, and it was quite clear she didn't believe him.

He planted his hands on his hips and leaned forward until their noses were scant inches apart. "I will say this slowly so that you will understand me. I am going to my room now. Don't follow."

She didn't listen.

"My God, woman!" he burst out, not two seconds later when she collided with him rounding the corner, "what does it take to get a command through your skull? You are like the plague, you— Oh, Christ, now what is the matter?"

Caroline's face, which had been so militant and determined in her efforts to nurse him, had positively crumpled. "It's nothing," she said with a sniffle.

"Obviously it's something."

Her shoulders rose and fell in a self-deprecating shrug. "Percy said the same thing to me. He's a fool, and I know that, but it still hurt. It was just that I thought . . ."

Blake felt like the worst sort of brute. "What did you think, Caroline?" he asked gently.

She shook her head and started to walk away.

He watched her for just a moment, tempted to let her go. After all, she'd been a thorn in his side—not to mention other parts of his anatomy—all morning. The only way he was going to get any peace was to keep her out of his sight.

But her lower lip had quivered, and her eyes had looked a little wet, and—

"Damn," he muttered. "Caroline, come back here."

She didn't listen, so he strode down the hall, catching up with her just as she was heading down the stairs. With quick steps he positioned himself between her and the staircase. "Stop, Caroline. Now."

He heard her sniffle, and then she turned around. "What is it, Blake? I really should go. I'm sure you can take care of yourself. You said so, and you certainly don't need me to—"

"Why do you suddenly look as if you're going to cry?"

She swallowed. "I'm not going to cry."

He crossed his arms and gave her a look that said he didn't believe her for one second.

"I said it was nothing," she mumbled.

"I'm not going to let you go down these stairs until you tell me what is wrong."

"Fine. Then I'll go up to my room." She turned around and took one step away, but he caught a handful of the fabric of her skirt and pulled her back to him. "I suppose that now you're going to say you're not going to let me go until I tell you," she growled.

"You're growing perceptive in your old age."

She crossed her arms mutinously. "Oh, for goodness sake. You're being quite ridiculous."

"I told you once that you are my responsibility, Caroline. And I don't take my responsibilities lightly."

"Meaning?"

"Meaning that if you're crying, I want to put a stop to it."

"I'm not crying," she muttered.

"You were about to."

"Oh!" she burst out, throwing her arms up in exasperation. "Has anyone ever told you that you're as stubborn as . . . as . . ."

"As you?" he said helpfully.

Her lips clamped into a firm and slightly twisted line as she glared daggers at him.

"Spit it out, Caroline. I'm not letting you pass until you do."

"Fine! Do you want to know why I was upset? Fine. I'll tell you." She swallowed, summoning courage she didn't feel. "Did you happen to notice that you compared me to the plague?"

"Oh, for the love of—" He bit his lip, presumably to keep himself from cursing in her presence.

Not, Caroline thought caustically, that that had ever stopped him before.

"You must know," he said, "that I did not mean that literally."

"It still hurt my feelings."

He stared at her intently. "I will allow that that wasn't the nicest comment I have ever made, and I do apologize for it, but I know you well enough to know that that alone wouldn't make you cry."

"I wasn't crying," she said, quite automatically.

"Almost cry," he corrected, "and I would like you to tell me the full story."

"Oh very well. Percy used to call me pestilence and plague all the time. It was his very favorite insult."

"You mentioned that. And I will take that as yet another sign that I spoke stupidly."

She swallowed and looked away. "I never put any stock into his words. It was Percy, after all, and he is a dozen different kinds of fool. But then you said it, and—"

Blake closed his eyes for a long second, knowing what was coming next and dreading it.

A slightly choked sound emerged from Caroline's throat before she said, "And then I thought it might possibly be true."

"Caroline, I—"

"Because you're not a fool, and I know that even better than I knew Percy was one."

"Caroline," he said firmly, "I *am* a fool. A bloody, stupid fool for referring to you with anything but the highest of praise."

"You needn't lie to make me feel better."

He scowled at her. Or rather, at the top of her head, since she was looking at her feet. "I told you I never lie."

She looked up suspiciously. "You told me you *rarely* lie."

"I lie when the security of Great Britain is at stake, not your feelings."

"I'm not certain if that is an insult or not."

"It is definitely *not* an insult, Caroline. And why would you think I was lying?"

She rolled her eyes at him. "You were less than cordial to me last evening."

"Last evening I bloody well wanted to strangle you," he admitted. "You put your life in danger for no good reason."

"I thought saving your life was a rather good reason myself," she shot back.

"I don't want to argue about that right now. Do you accept my apology?"

"For what?"

He raised a brow. "Is that meant to imply that I have more than one transgression for which I must apologize?"

"Mr. Ravenscroft, I cannot count high enough . . ."

He grinned. "Now I know you've forgiven me, if you're making jokes."

This time she raised a brow, and he noted that she managed to look every bit as arrogant as he did. She said, "And what makes you think that was a joke?" But then she laughed, which quite broke the effect.

"I am forgiven?"

She nodded. "Percy never apologized."

"Percy is clearly an idiot."

She smiled then—a small, wistful smile that very nearly melted his heart. "Caroline," he said, barely recognizing his voice.

"Yes?"

"Oh, hell." He leaned down and brushed his lips against hers in the most feathery light of kisses. It wasn't that he wanted to kiss her. He *needed* to kiss her. He needed it the way he needed air, and water, and the afternoon sunshine on his face. The kiss was almost spiritual; his entire body trembled just from the barest touch of their lips.

"Oh, Blake," she sighed, sounding as bewildered as he felt.

"Caroline," he murmured, trailing his lips along the elegant line of her neck. "I don't know why . . . I don't understand it, but—"

"I don't care," she said, sounding quite determined for one whose breathing had gone way past erratic. She threw her arms around his neck and returned his kiss with artless abandon.

The warm press of her body against his was more than Blake could bear, and he swept her into his arms and carried her through the upstairs hall to his room. He kicked the door shut, and they tumbled onto the bed, his body covering hers with a possessiveness he'd never dreamed he could feel again.

"I want you," he murmured. "I want you now, in every way." Her soft heat beckoned him, and his fingers flew along the buttons of her frock, slipping them through their buttonholes with ease and haste.

"Tell me what you want," he whispered.

But she just shook her head. "I don't know. I don't know what I want."

"Yes," he said, pushing her dress down to bare one silky shoulder, "you do."

Instantly, her eyes flew to his face. "You know I've never—"

He put a gentle finger to her lips. "I know. But it doesn't matter. You still know what feels right."

"Blake, I—"

"Hush." He closed her lips with a searing kiss, then opened them again with a hot flick of his tongue. "For example," he said against her mouth, "do you want more of this?"

She didn't move for a moment, and then he felt her lips move up and down as she nodded.

"Then you shall have it." He kissed her fiercely, savoring the subtle minty taste of her.

She moaned beneath him, and tentatively placed her hand on his cheek. "Do you like that?" she asked shyly.

He growled as he tore off his cravat. "You may touch me anywhere. You may kiss me anywhere. I burn just for the sight of you. Can you imagine what your touch does?"

With sweet hesitation she slid down and kissed his smooth-shaven jaw. Then she moved to his ear, then his neck, and Blake thought he would surely die in her arms if his passion remained unfulfilled. He pushed her dress even lower, revealing one small but, in his opinion, perfectly shaped breast.

He bent his head to her and took the nipple in his mouth, the rosy bud tightening between his lips. She was moaning beneath him, calling out his name, and he knew she wanted him.

And the knowledge thrilled him.

"Oh Blake oh Blake oh Blake," she groaned. "Can you *do* that?"

"I assure you I can," he said with a low chuckle.

She gasped as he sucked a touch harder. "No, but is it allowed?"

His chuckle turned into a throaty laugh. "Anything is allowed, my sweet."

"Yes, but I— ooooooohhhhhh."

Blake grinned with a very masculine smugness as her words lost their coherence. "And now," he said with a wicked leer, "I can do it to the other one."

His hands went to work pushing her dress off her other shoulder, but just before he revealed his prize, he heard the most awful sound.

Perriwick.

"Sir? Sir? Sir!!!" This, accompanied by the most annoyingly persistent knocking.

"Blake!" Caroline gasped.

"Shhh." He clamped his hand over her mouth. "He'll go away."

"Mr. Ravenscroft! It's most urgent!"

"I don't think he's going to go away," she whispered, her words getting muffled under his palm.

"Perriwick!" Blake bellowed. "I'm busy. Go away. *Now!*"

"Yes, I thought as much," the butler said through the door. "It's what I most feared."

"He knows I'm here," Caroline hissed. Then, quite suddenly, she turned red as a raspberry. "Oh, dear Lord, he knows I'm here. What have I done?"

Blake cursed under his breath. Caroline had clearly just regained her senses and remembered that no lady of her consequence did the sort of things she'd been doing. And, damn it, that made him remember as well, and he was quite unable to take advantage of her while his conscience was in full working order.

"I can't let Perriwick see me," she said frantically.

"He's just the butler," Blake replied, knowing that wasn't the point but a little too frustrated to care.

"He's my friend. And his opinion of me matters."

"To whom?"

"To me, you nodcock." She was trying to right her appearance with such haste that her fingers kept slipping over the buttons of her dress.

"Here," Blake said, giving her a shove. "Into the washing room."

Caroline dashed into the smaller chamber with alacrity, grabbing her slippers at the very last minute. As soon as the door clicked behind her, she heard Blake yank open the door to his room and say, rather nastily, "What do you want, Perriwick?"

"If I may be so bold, sir—"

"Perriwick." Blake's voice was laced with heavy warning. Caroline feared for the butler's safety if he didn't get to the point with all possible haste. At this rate, Blake was likely to boot him right out the window.

"Right, sir. It's Miss Trent. I can't find her anywhere."

"I wasn't aware that Miss Trent was required to apprise you of her whereabouts at every given moment."

"No, of course not, Mr. Ravenscroft, but I found this at the top of the stairs, and—"

Caroline instinctively leaned closer to the door, wondering what "this" was.

"I'm sure she just dropped it," Blake said. "Ribbons fall from ladies' hair all the time."

Her hand flew up to her head. When had she lost her ribbon? Had Blake run his hands through her hair when he was kissing her in the hall?

"I realize that," Perriwick replied, "but I am worried nonetheless. If I knew where she was, I am certain I could allay my fears."

"As it happens," came Blake's voice, "I know exactly where Miss Trent is."

Caroline gasped. Surely he wouldn't give her away.

Blake said, "She decided to take advantage of the fine weather and has gone for a stroll in the countryside."

"But I thought you said her presence here at Seacrest Manor was a secret."

"It is, but there is no reason she can't go outside as long as she doesn't wander too far from the grounds. There are very few conveyances traveling this road. No one is likely to see her."

"I see. I shall keep an eye out for her, then. Perhaps she would like something to eat when she returns."

"I'm sure she would like that above all else."

Caroline touched her stomach. She was a little hungry. And to be completely truthful, the thought of a walk along the beach sounded quite nice. Just the sort of thing to clear her head, which the Lord certainly knew needed clearing.

She took a step away from the door, and Blake's and Perriwick's voices faded. Then she noticed another door on the opposite side of the washing room. She tested the doorknob gingerly, and was pleasantly surprised to note that it let her out in the side stairwell—the one usually used by servants. She looked over her shoulder, toward Blake, even though she couldn't see him.

He'd said she could go for a walk, even if it had been part of an elaborate fabrication designed to fool poor Perriwick. Caroline couldn't see any reason not to go ahead and do just that.

Within a few seconds she had dashed down the stairs and was outside. A minute later she was out of sight of the house and striding along the edge of the cliff that overlooked the blue-gray English Channel. The sea air was invigorating, but not nearly as much as the knowledge that Blake was going to be completely confused when he peered into the washing room and found her missing.

Bother the man, anyway. He could use some confusion in his life.

Chapter 14

nic·tate *(verb). To wink.*

I have found that nervous situations often cause me to nictate *or stutter.*

—From the personal dictionary of
Caroline Trent

An hour later Caroline was feeling quite refreshed—at least in the physical sense. The crisp salty air held remarkable restorative properties for the lungs. Unfortunately, it wasn't quite as effective with the heart and the head.

Did she love Blake Ravenscroft? She certainly hoped so. She'd like to think that she wouldn't have behaved in such a wanton manner with a man for whom she didn't feel a deep and abiding affection.

She smiled wryly. What she *ought* to be considering was whether Blake cared for *her*. She thought he did, at least a little bit. His concern for her welfare the night before had been obvious, and when he kissed her . . . well, she didn't know very much about kissing, but she could sense a hunger in him, and she instinctively knew that that hunger was reserved solely for her.

And she could make him laugh. That had to count for something.

Then, just as she was beginning to rationalize her entire situation, she heard a tremendous crash, followed by the sound of splintering wood, followed by some decidedly feminine shrieking.

Caroline's eyebrows shot up. What had happened? She wanted to investigate, but she wasn't supposed to make her presence here in Bournemouth known. It wasn't likely that one of Oliver's friends would be traveling this little-used road, but if she were recognized it would be nothing short of disaster. Still, someone might be in trouble . . .

Curiosity won out over prudence, and she trotted toward the sound of the crash, slowing her pace as she drew close just in case she changed her mind and wanted to remain hidden.

Concealing herself behind a tree, she peered out at the road. A splendid carriage lay drunkenly in the dirt, one wheel completely splintered. Three men and two ladies were milling about. No one seemed injured, so Caroline decided to remain behind the tree until she could assess the situation.

The scenario quickly became a fascinating puzzle. Who were these people and what had happened? Caroline quickly figured out who was in charge—it was the better dressed of the two ladies. She was quite lovely, with black curls that spilled out from under her bonnet, and was giving orders in a manner that revealed that she had been dealing with servants her entire life. Caroline judged her age to be about thirty, perhaps a bit older.

The other lady was probably her maid, and the gentlemen—Caroline guessed that one was the driver and two were outriders. All three men were dressed in matching dark blue livery. Whoever these people were, they came from an extremely wealthy household.

After a minute of discussion, the lady in charge sent the driver and one of the outriders off to the north, presumably to fetch some help. Then she looked at the trunks which had fallen off the carriage and said, "We might as well use them as seats," and the three remaining travelers plopped down to wait.

After about a minute of sitting around and doing nothing, the lady turned to her maid and said, "I don't suppose my embroidery is packed anywhere accessible?"

The maid shook her head. "It's in the middle of the largest trunk, my lady."

"Ah, that would be the one that is miraculously still fastened to the top of the carriage."

"Yes, my lady."

The lady let out a long breath. "I suppose we ought to be thankful that it isn't overly hot."

"Or raining," the outrider put in.

"Or snowing," said the maid.

The lady speared her with an annoyed glance. "Really, Sally, that's hardly likely at this time of year."

The maid shrugged. "Stranger things have happened. After all, who would have thought we'd have lost a wheel the way we did. And this being the most expensive carriage money can buy."

Caroline smiled and edged away. Clearly these people were unhurt, and the rest of their traveling party would be back soon with help. Better to keep her presence a secret. The fewer people who knew she was here in Bournemouth the better. After all, what if this lady was a friend of Oliver's? It wasn't likely, of course. The lady seemed to have a sense of humor and a modicum of taste, which would immediately eliminate Oliver Prewitt from her circle of friends. Still, one couldn't be too careful.

Ironically, that was exactly what Caroline was saying to herself—*still, one couldn't be too careful*—when she took a false step, landed on a rather dried-up twig, and broke it in half with an extremely loud snap.

"Who's there?" the lady immediately demanded.

Caroline froze.

"Show yourself immediately."

Could she outrun the outrider? Unlikely. The man was already walking purposefully in her direction, his hand on a bulge in his pocket that Caroline had a sneaking suspicion was a gun.

"It's only me," she said quickly, stepping out into the clearing.

The lady cocked her head, her gray eyes narrowing slightly. "Good day, 'me.' Who are you?"

"Who are you?" Caroline countered.

"I asked you first."

"Ah, but I am alone, and you are safely among your traveling companions. Therefore, common courtesy would deem that you reveal yourself first."

The woman drew her head back in a combination of admiration and surprise. "My dear girl, you are speaking the utmost nonsense. I know all there is to know about common courtesy."

"Hmmm. I was afraid you would."

"Not to mention," the lady continued, "that of the two of us, I am the only one accompanied by an armed servant. So perhaps you ought to be the first to reveal her identity."

"You do have a point," Caroline conceded, eyeing the gun with a wary grimace.

"I rarely speak just for the sake of hearing my own voice."

Caroline sighed. "I wish I could say the same. I often speak without first considering my words. It's a dreadful habit." She bit her lip, realizing that she was telling a total stranger about her faults. "Like right now," she added sheepishly.

But the lady just laughed. It was a happy, friendly sort of laugh, and it put Caroline right at ease. Enough so that she said, "My name is Miss . . . Dent."

"Dent? I'm not familiar with that name."

Caroline shrugged. "It's not terribly common."

"I see. I am the Countess of Fairwich."

A countess? Good gracious, there seemed to be quite a few aristocrats in this little corner of England of late. First James, now this countess. And Blake, although not titled, was the second son of the Viscount Darnsby. Caroline glanced up toward heaven and mentally thanked her mother for making sure that she taught her daughter the rules of etiquette before she died. With a smile and a curtsy, Caroline said, "I'm quite pleased to meet you, Lady Fairwich."

"And I you, Miss Dent. Do you reside in the area?"

Oh dear, how to answer that one? "Not too terribly far away," she hedged. "I often take long walks when the weather is fine. Are you also from this area?"

Caroline immediately bit her lip. What a stupid question. If the countess was indeed from the Bournemouth area, it would stand to reason that everyone would know about it. And Caroline would immediately be revealed as an impostor.

Luck, however, was on her side, and the countess said, "Fairwich is in Somerset. But I am coming from London today."

"Are you? I have never been to our capital. I should like to go someday."

The countess shrugged. "It grows a bit hot in the summer with all the crowds. There is nothing like the fresh sea air to make one feel whole again."

Caroline smiled at her. "Indeed. Alas, if it could only mend a broken heart . . ."

Oh, stupid stupid mouth. Why had she said that? She had meant it as a joke, but now the countess was grinning and looking at her in that maternal sort of way that meant she was going to ask an extremely personal question.

"Oh, dear. Is your heart broken, then?"

"Let's just say it's a bit bruised," she said, thinking that she was getting far too good at the art of lying. "It's just a boy I've known all my life. Our fathers were hoping for a match, but . . ." She shrugged, letting the countess draw her own conclusions.

"Pity. You are a darling girl. I should introduce you to my brother. He lives quite nearby."

"Your brother?" Caroline croaked, suddenly taking in the countess's coloring. Black hair. Gray eyes.

Oh, *no.*

"Yes. He is Mr. Blake Ravenscroft of Seacrest Manor. Do you know him?"

Caroline practically choked on her tongue, then managed to say, "We have been introduced."

"I am on my way to visit him right now. Are we very far from his home? I have never been."

"No. No, it's—it's just over the hill there." She pointed in the general direction of Seacrest Manor, then quickly brought her hand down when she realized it was shaking. What was she going to do? She couldn't remain at Seacrest Manor with Blake's sister in residence. Oh, damn and blast that man to hell and back! Why hadn't he told her his sister would be paying a visit?

Unless he didn't know. Oh, no. Blake was going to be furious. Caroline swallowed nervously and said, "I didn't realize Mr. Ravenscroft had a sister."

The countess waved her hand in a manner that reminded Caroline instantly of Blake. "He's a wretch, always ignoring us. Our older brother just had a daughter. I've come to tell him the news."

"Oh. I'm—I'm—I'm certain he'll be delighted."

"Then you're the only one. I am quite certain he'll be beyond annoyed."

Caroline blinked furiously, not understanding this woman one bit. "I—I—I beg your pardon?"

"David and Sarah had a daughter. Their fourth daughter, which means that Blake is still second in line for the viscountcy."

"I . . . see." Actually, she didn't, but she was so happy she hadn't stuttered she didn't much care.

The countess sighed. "If Blake is to be Viscount Darnsby, which is not entirely unlikely, then he'll have to marry and produce an heir. If you live in this area, then I'm sure you are aware he is a confirmed bachelor."

"Actually, I don't really know him very well at all." Caroline wondered if she sounded just a bit too determined to make that point, so she added, "Just at—at local functions and all that. You know, county dances and the like."

"Really?" the countess asked with undisguised interest. "My brother has attended a provincial county dance? The mind boggles. I suppose that next you're going to try to tell me that the moon recently crashed into the channel."

"Well," Caroline added, swallowing rather painfully, "he only attended once. It's a . . . small community here near Bournemouth, and so naturally I know who he is. Everyone knows who he is."

The countess was silent for a moment, and then she abruptly said, "You say my brother's house isn't very far?"

"Why no, my lady. It shouldn't take more than a quarter of an hour to walk there." Caroline eyed the trunks. "You'll have to leave your things behind, of course."

The countess waved her hand in the air in what Caroline was now terming the Ravenscroft wave. "I shall simply have my brother send his men to fetch them later."

"Oh, but he—" Caroline started coughing wildly, trying to cover up the fact that she'd been about to blurt out that Blake employed only three servants, and of them, only the valet was strong enough to do any heavy lifting.

The countess whacked her on the back. "Are you quite all right, Miss Dent?"

"Just—just swallowed a bit of dust, that's all."

"You sounded quite like a thunderstorm."

"Yes, well, I am occasionally given to fits of coughing."

"Really?"

"Once I was even rendered mute."

"Mute? I can't imagine."

"Neither could I," Caroline said quite honestly, "until it happened."

"Well, I'm certain your throat must be terribly sore. You must accompany us to my brother's home. A spot of tea will be just the thing to restore you."

Caroline coughed again—this time for real. "No no no no no no," she said, rather more quickly than she'd have liked. "That is really not necessary. I would hate to impose."

"Oh, but you wouldn't be imposing. After all, I need you to direct us to Seacrest Manor. Offering you tea and a bit of sustenance is the very least I can do to repay your kindness."

"It's really not necessary," Caroline made haste to say. "And the directions to Seacrest Manor are quite simple. All you have to do is follow the—"

"I have a terrible sense of direction," the countess interrupted. "Last week I got lost in my own home."

"I find that difficult to believe, Lady Fairwich."

The countess shrugged. "It's a large building. I've been married to the earl for ten years now and I still haven't set foot in the east wing."

Caroline just swallowed and smiled weakly, having no idea how to respond to that.

"I insist that you accompany us," the countess said, linking her arm through Caroline's. "And I might as well warn you that there is no use arguing. I always get my way."

"That, Lady Fairwich, I don't find difficult to believe at all."

The countess trilled with laughter. "Miss Dent, I think you and I are going to get along famously."

Caroline gulped. "Then you plan to stay here in Bournemouth for some time?"

"Oh, just a week or so. It seemed foolish to travel all the way down here and then turn right back again."

"All the way? Isn't it just a hundred miles?" Caroline frowned. Wasn't that what Blake had said that morning?

"A hundred miles, two hundred miles, five hundred miles . . ." The countess did the Ravenscroft wave. "If I have to pack, what difference does it make?"

"I—I—I'm sure I don't know," Caroline replied, feeling as if she'd just been leveled by a whirlwind.

"Sally!" the countess called out, turning to her maid. "Miss Dent is going to show me to my brother's house. Why don't you remain here with

Felix and guard our bags? We shall send someone for you with all possible haste."

Then the countess took a step in the direction of Seacrest Manor, practically dragging Caroline along with her. "I daresay my brother will be surprised to see me!" she chirped.

Caroline moved forward on wobbly legs. "I daresay you're right."

Blake was not in a good mood.

He had obviously misplaced every shred of good sense he had ever possessed. There was no other explanation for his carrying Caroline off to his room and nearly ravishing her in broad daylight. And if that weren't bad enough, now he was aching with unfulfilled need thanks to his meddling butler.

But the worst—the absolute *worst*—part of all was that now Caroline had up and gone missing. He'd searched the house from top to bottom, front to back, and she was nowhere to be found. He didn't think she'd run away; she had far too much sense for that. She was probably out wandering the countryside, trying to clear her head.

Which would have been a perfectly understandable and indeed commendable pursuit if her likeness weren't depicted on bills plastered all over the county. It was a bad likeness, to be sure—Blake still thought the artist should have drawn her smiling—but still, if someone found her and returned her to Prewitt . . .

He swallowed uncomfortably. He didn't like the hollow feeling he felt at the thought of her leaving.

Blast that woman! He didn't have time for a complication like this, and he certainly didn't have room in his heart for another woman.

Blake swore under his breath as he pushed aside a gauzy piece of curtain and scanned the side garden. Caroline must have left via the servants' stairs; that was the only exit she'd have had access to from the washing room. He'd searched the grounds completely, but he'd been checking the side the most often; for some reason he thought she'd come back the way she had gone. He didn't know why. She just seemed the sort who would do that.

There was no sign of her, however, so Blake just cursed again and let the curtain drop. It was then that he heard a loud, rather strident knock at the front door.

Blake cursed for a third time, unaccountably irritated that he'd incorrectly anticipated her behavior. He made his way to the door in long, quick strides, his brain filled to the brim with all the lectures he was going to pelt at her. By the time he was through with her, she'd never dare pull this sort of stunt again.

His hand touched the doorknob and he yanked it open, his voice an angry growl as he said, "Where the hell have you—"

His mouth fell open.

Then he blinked.

Then he snapped his mouth shut again.

"Penelope?"

Chapter 15

so•ror•i•cide *(noun). The action of killing one's sister.*

I feared sororicide. *I truly did.*

—From the personal dictionary of Caroline Trent

Penelope smiled breezily at him and strode into the hall. "It is so lovely to see you, Blake. I'm sure you're surprised."

"Yes, yes, you could say that."

"I would have been here earlier—"

Earlier?

"—but I had a slight carriage accident and if it weren't for dear Miss Dent here—"

Blake looked back out the door and saw Caroline.

Caroline?

"—I should have been completely stranded. Of course I had no idea we were so close to Seacrest Manor, and as I was saying, if it weren't for dear Miss Dent—"

He looked back at Caroline, who was frantically shaking her head at him.

Miss Dent?

"—who knows how long I would have remained sitting on my trunk by the side of the road, mere minutes from my destination." Penelope paused for breath and beamed at him. "Doesn't the irony just kill you?"

"That's not the only thing," Blake muttered.

Penelope stood on her toes and kissed him on the cheek. "You're the same as ever, dear brother. No sense of humor."

"I have a perfectly fine sense of humor," he said, a touch defensively. "It's simply that I'm not used to being surprised—completely surprised I might add—by an unexpected guest. And you've dragged along Miss—" Ah, damn. What the hell had Penelope called her?

"Dent," Caroline supplied helpfully. "Miss Dent."

"Ah. And have we been introduced?"

His sister sent an angry look his way, which didn't surprise him in the least. A gentleman was not supposed to forget a lady, and Penelope took great stock in good manners. "Don't you recall?" she said loudly. "It was at the county dance last autumn. Miss Dent told me all about it."

The bloody county dance? What sort of tales had Caroline been spinning about him? "Of course," he said in a smooth voice. "I don't recall who introduced us, though. Was it your cousin?"

"No," Caroline replied in a voice so sweet it might as well have been dripping honey, "it was my great aunt. Mrs. Mumblethorpe. Surely you remember her?"

"Ah, yes!" he said expansively, motioning for her to enter the hall. "The magnificent Mrs. Mumblethorpe. How could I have possibly forgotten? She is a singular lady. Last time we dined together she was showing off her new yodeling skills."

Caroline tripped on the step. "Yes," she said through her teeth, bracing her arm against the doorjamb to keep from falling, "she had such a brilliant time on her trip to Switzerland."

"Mmmm, yes. She said as much. As a matter of fact, by the time she finished her demonstration, I think the entire county knew how much she enjoyed her travels."

Penelope listened to the exchange with interest. "You shall have to introduce me to your aunt, Miss Dent. She sounds most interesting. I would so like to meet her while I am in Bournemouth."

"Exactly how long do you plan to stay?" Blake cut in.

"I'm afraid I can't introduce you to Aunt Hortense," Caroline said to Penelope. "She so enjoyed her travels to Switzerland that she has decided to embark upon another journey."

"Where to?" Penelope asked.

"Yes, where to?" Blake echoed, enjoying the momentary look of panic on Caroline's face as she groped for a suitable country.

"Iceland," she blurted out.

"Iceland?" said Penelope. "How odd. I've never known anyone to visit Iceland before."

Caroline smiled tightly and explained, "She has always had a great fascination with islands."

"Which would explain," Blake said in a perfectly dry voice, "her recent jaunt to Switzerland."

Caroline turned her back to him and said to Penelope, "We should see about sending someone to fetch your belongings, my lady."

"Yes, yes," Penelope murmured, "in a moment. But first, Blake, before I forget to answer your rather rude question, I will tell you that I anticipate staying approximately a week, perhaps a bit longer. Provided that suits you, of course."

Blake glanced down at her with amused disbelief. "And when has my agreement ever determined your actions?"

"Never," Penelope replied with a carefree shrug, "but I must be polite and pretend, mustn't I?"

Caroline watched as brother and sister sparred, a lump of wistful envy building in her throat. Blake was obviously irritated by his sister's unheralded arrival, but it was equally clear that he loved her beyond measure. Caroline had never known the affectionate camaraderie of siblings; indeed, she had never even *seen* it before that day.

Her heart ached with longing as she listened to their interaction. She wanted someone who would tease her; she wanted someone who would hold her hand when times grew scary and unsure.

Most of all, she wanted someone who would love her.

Caroline caught her breath as she realized how perilously close she was to tears. "I really need to be off," she blurted out, making a beeline for the door. Escape was foremost in her mind. The last thing she wanted was to find herself sobbing in Seacrest Manor's front hall, right in front of Blake and Penelope.

"But you haven't had tea!" Penelope protested.

"I'm really not thirsty. I—I—I must go home. I'm expected there."

"Yes, I'm sure you are," Blake drawled.

Caroline paused on the front steps, wondering where on earth she was going to go. "I don't want anyone to worry over me."

"No, I'm sure you wouldn't," Blake murmured.

"Blake, darling," Penelope said, "I insist that you see Miss Dent home."

"A fine idea," he agreed.

Caroline nodded gratefully. She didn't much feel like facing his questions just now, but the alternative was wandering the countryside with no place to go. "Yes, I would appreciate that."

"Excellent. It's not far, you say?" His lips curved ever so slightly, and Caroline wished she could tell whether his smile was one of irony or supreme irritation.

"No," she replied. "Not far at all."

"Then I propose that we walk."

"Yes, that would probably be most convenient."

"I will wait here, then," Penelope put in. "I'm sorry I cannot accompany you home, but I'm most weary from my travels. It has been lovely meeting you, Miss Dent. Oh! But I do not even know your given name."

"You must call me Caroline."

Blake shot her a sideways glance, looking a bit surprised and intrigued that she had not used an alias.

"If you are Caroline," Penelope replied, "then I am Penelope." She grasped her hands and squeezed affectionately. "I have a feeling we are going to be splendid friends."

Caroline wasn't certain, but she thought she heard Blake mutter, "God help me," under his breath. And then they both smiled at Penelope and exited the house.

"Where are we going?" Caroline whispered.

"To hell with that," he hissed back, glancing over his shoulder to make certain they were out of earshot of the house, even though he knew that he'd shut the front door behind him. "Would you care to tell me what the hell is going on?"

"It wasn't my fault," she said quickly, following his steps away from the house.

"Why, I wonder, do I have trouble accepting that statement?"

"Blake!" she burst out, yanking on his arm and grinding him to a halt. "What do you think, that I sent your sister a note and asked her to pay you a visit? I had no idea who she was. I didn't even know you *had* a sister! And she wouldn't have even seen me if I hadn't stepped on that bloody twig."

Blake sighed, beginning to realize what had happened. It was an accident—a great, big, huge, monstrously inconvenient and annoying accident. His life seemed littered with those these days. "What the hell am I going to do with you?"

"I have no idea. I certainly can't remain in the house while your sister is visiting. You yourself told me that your family doesn't know about your work for the War Office. I assume that includes Penelope?"

At Blakes's curt nod, she added, "If she discovers that I have been staying at Seacrest Manor, she will undoubtedly learn of your clandestine activities."

Blake swore under his breath.

"I don't approve of your secretiveness with regard to your family," Caroline said, "but I will respect your wishes. Penelope is a dear lady. I shouldn't want her to worry over you. That would upset her, and it would upset you."

Blake stared at her, unable to speak. Of all the reasons that Caroline shouldn't let his sister know she'd been staying at Seacrest Manor, she had to pick the only one that was completely unselfish. She could have said that she worried for her reputation. She could have said that she was afraid that Penelope would turn her over to Oliver. But no, she wasn't worried about all that; she was worried that her actions might hurt *him*.

He swallowed, suddenly feeling awkward in her presence. Caroline was watching his face, clearly waiting for a reply, and he had no idea what to say. Finally, after she prodded him with a questioning, "Blake?" he managed to get out, "That is most thoughtful of you, Caroline."

She blinked in surprise. "Oh."

"Oh?" he echoed, jutting his chin out slightly toward her in a questioning manner.

"Oh. Oh . . . Oh." She smiled weakly at him. "I guess I thought you were going to scold me further."

"I thought I was, too," he said, sounding just as surprised as she did.

"Oh." Then she caught herself and said, "Sorry."

" 'Ohs' aside, we're going to have to figure out what to do with you."

"I don't suppose you've a hunting lodge somewhere nearby?"

He shook his head. "I've no place in the region where you can hide. I suppose I could put you in a carriage to London."

"No!" Caroline replied. She grimaced, a bit embarrassed by the forcefulness of her reply. "I really cannot go to London."

"Why not?"

She frowned. That was a good question, but she wasn't about to tell him that she'd miss him. Finally she said, "Your sister is going to expect to see me. I'm sure she'll ask me to call."

"A tricky maneuver indeed, considering that you have no home to which she may send an invitation."

"Yes, but she doesn't know that. She will certainly ask you for my direction. And then what will you say?"

"I could always say you've gone to London. In general, the truth is always the best option."

"Wouldn't that be lovely?" she said, sarcasm more than evident in her voice. "With my luck she'll turn around and head back to London and look for me there."

Blake let out an irritated exhale. "Yes, my sister is obstinate enough to do just that."

"I suppose it runs in the family."

He only laughed. "That it does, my dear, but we Ravenscrofts cannot hold a candle to the Trents when it comes to sheer muleheadedness."

Caroline grumbled, but she didn't contradict him because she knew it was true. Finally, thoroughly irritated with his rather smug smile, she said, "We can argue about our respective bad traits all we want, but that doesn't solve the problem at hand. Where am I to go?"

"I think you'll have to go back to Seacrest Manor. I know I cannot think of a suitable alternative. Can you?"

"But Penelope is there!"

"We shall have to hide you. There is nothing else for it."

"Oh, dear Lord," she muttered. "This is a disaster. A bloody disaster."

"On that point, Caroline, we are in complete agreement."

"Will the servants be in on the ruse?"

"I should think they would have to be. They already know about you. It's a good thing there are only three of— *Good God!*"

"What?"

"The servants. They don't know not to mention you to Penelope."

Caroline paled.

"Don't move. Don't move an inch. I'll be right back."

Blake took off at a run, but he'd barely covered ten yards, when another potential disaster found its way to Caroline's mind. "Blake!" she yelled. "Wait!"

He skidded to a halt and turned around.

"You can't go through the front door. If Penelope sees you she'll wonder how you managed to see me home so quickly."

He swore under his breath. "I'll have to use the side entrance. I assume you're familiar with it."

Caroline shot him an annoyed look. He knew very well she'd used the side entrance to make her escape earlier that day.

"You might as well come with me now," Blake said. "We'll sneak you up through the side and figure out what to do with you later."

"In other words, you mean for me to wait in your washing room indefinitely?"

He grinned. "I hadn't gotten that far in my plans, but now that you mention it, yes, that's an excellent idea."

At that point, Caroline decided that her mouth was altogether too big. Luckily, before she could offer up any more bad ideas, Blake grabbed her hand and took off at a run, practically dragging her behind him. They skirted the perimeter of the property until they were hidden among the trees facing the side entrance.

"We're going to have to make a run for it through the clearing," Blake said.

"What do you think are the chances she's on this side of the house?"

"Very small. We left her in the front sitting room, and if anything, she's likely to go upstairs and find a bedchamber."

Caroline gasped. "What if she finds mine? My clothes are there. I've only three dresses, but they clearly don't belong to *you*."

Blake swore again.

She raised her brows. "Do you know, but I've started to find your cursing rather comforting. If you weren't cursing, life would seem almost abnormal."

"You're a strange woman."

Blake tugged on her hand, and before Caroline realized what was happening, she was tripping across the lawn, her mind echoing with a stream of prayers that Penelope wouldn't see them. She had never been a particularly religious sort, but it seemed as good a time as any to develop a pious nature.

They barreled through the side door, both heaving with exertion as they collapsed on the stairs.

"You," Blake said. "Up to the washroom. I'll find the servants."

Caroline nodded and dashed up the stairs, slipping silently into his washing room. She looked around with a good dose of chagrin. The Lord only knew how long she was going to be stranded there.

"Well," she said aloud, "it could be worse."

Three hours later Caroline had discovered that the only way to stave off boredom in the washing room was to entertain herself by listing all of the situations that would be worse than her current one.

It wasn't easy.

She immediately dismissed all sorts of fanciful scenarios, like being trampled by a two-headed cow, and instead concentrated on more realistic possibilities.

"He could have a small washing room," she said to her reflection in the mirror. "Or it could be very dirty. Or . . . or or or . . . or he could forget to feed me."

Her lips twisted into a peevish line. The bloody man *had* forgotten to feed her!

"The room could have no windows," she tried, glancing up at the aperture. She grimaced. One would have to possess an extraordinarily optimistic nature to call that little sliver of glass a window.

"He could have a pet hedgehog," she said, "which he keeps in the basin."

"It's unlikely," came a male voice, "but possible."

Caroline looked up to see Blake in the doorway. "Where have you been?" she hissed. "I'm starving."

He tossed her a scone.

"You're too kind," she muttered, wolfing it down. "Was that my main course or merely an appetizer?"

"You'll be fed, don't worry. I thought Perriwick was going to have palpitations when he heard where you were hiding. I imagine he and Mrs. Mickle are preparing a feast even as we speak."

"Perriwick is clearly a nicer man than *you*."

He shrugged. "No doubt."

"Did you manage to intercept all the servants before they mentioned me to Penelope?"

"Yes. We're safe, have no fear. And I have your things. I moved them to my room."

"I'm not staying in your room!" she said, rather huffily.

"I never said you were. You're certainly free to remain here in the washing room. I'll find some blankets and a pillow for you. With a little ingenuity, we can make this place quite comfortable."

Her eyes narrowed dangerously. "You're enjoying this, aren't you?"

"Only a touch, I assure you."

"Did Penelope ask after me?"

"Indeed. She has already written you a letter asking you to pay a call tomorrow afternoon." He reached into his pocket, pulled out a small envelope, and gave it to her.

"Well, that is certainly a boon," Caroline grumbled.

"I shouldn't complain, were I you. At least it means you can escape the washing room."

Caroline stared at him, really annoyed by his smile. She stood and planted her hands on her hips.

"My, my, we're looking militant this afternoon, aren't we?"

"Don't condescend to me."

"But it's so much fun."

She hurled a chamber pot at him. "You can use *this* in your own room!"

Blake ducked and then laughed despite himself when the pot broke into pieces against the wall. "Well, I suppose one can take some comfort in the fact that it wasn't full."

"If it had been full," she hissed, "I would have aimed at your head."

"Caroline, this situation isn't my fault."

"I know, but you don't have to be so bloody jolly about it."

"Now, you're being just a bit unreasonable."

"I don't care." She whipped a bar of soap at him. It stuck against the wall. "I have every right to be unreasonable."

"Oh?" He ducked as his shaving kit sailed through the air.

She glowered at him. "For your information, in the past week, I have been, oh let's see, nearly raped, kidnapped, tied to a bedpost, forced to cough my voice into nothingness—"

"That was your own fault."

"Not to mention the fact that I embarked upon a life of crime by breaking and entering into my former home, was nearly trapped by my odious guardian—"

"Don't forget your sprained ankle," he supplied.

"Ooooohhhh! I could kill you!" Another bar of soap flew by his head, grazing his ear.

"Madam, you are certainly doing an able job of trying."

"And now!" she fairly yelled. "And now, as if all of that weren't undignified enough, I am forced to live for a week in a bloody bathroom!"

Put that way, Blake pondered, it was damned funny. He bit his lip, trying to hold back his laughter. He wasn't successful.

"Stop laughing at me!" she wailed.

"Blake?"

He went utterly sober in under a second. "It's Penelope!" he whispered.

"Blake? What is all that yelling about?"

"Quick!" he hissed, shoving her back toward the side stairwell. "Hide!"

Caroline scurried away, and just in time, too, for Penelope pushed open the door to the washing room just as she closed the one to the stairwell.

"Blake?" Penelope queried for the third time. "What is all the commotion?"

"It was nothing, Penny. I—"

"What happened here?" she screeched.

Blake looked around and gulped. He'd forgotten about the mess on the floor. Chamber pot shards, his shaving kit, a towel or two . . .

"I . . . ah . . ." It seemed to him that it was far easier to lie for the sake of national security than it was to his older sister.

"Is that a bar of soap stuck to the wall?" Penelope asked.

"Um . . . yes, it appears to be."

She pointed down. "And is this another bar of soap on the floor?"

"Er . . . yes, I must have been rather clumsy this morning."

"Blake, is there something you're keeping from me?"

"There are quite a few things I keep from you," he said with absolute honesty, trying not to think about Caroline sitting out in the stairwell, presumably laughing her bloody head off at his predicament.

"What's this on the floor?" Penelope bent down and picked up something white. "Why, it's the note I wrote to Miss Dent! What is it doing here?"

"I haven't had a chance to send it yet." Thank God Caroline had forgotten to open it.

"Well, for heaven's sake, don't leave it here on the floor." She narrowed her eyes and looked up at him. "I say, Blake, are you feeling quite the thing?"

"Actually, no," he replied, seizing the opportunity she'd offered him. "I've been a touch dizzy for the last hour or so. That's how I knocked over the chamber pot."

She touched his forehead. "You don't have the fever."

"I'm sure it's nothing a good night's sleep won't cure."

"I suppose." Penelope pursed her lips. "But if you're not feeling better by tomorrow I'm summoning a doctor."

"Fine."

"Perhaps you ought to lie down right now."

"Yes," he said, practically pushing her out of the bathroom. "That is an excellent idea."

"Right, then. Here, I'll turn down your sheets."

Blake let out a huge sigh as he shut the bathroom door behind him. He certainly wasn't happy about the latest turn of events; the last thing he wanted was his older sister fussing over him. But it was certainly preferable to her discovering Caroline amid the chamber pot shards and soap slivers.

"Mr. Ravenscroft?"

He looked up. Perriwick was standing in the doorway, balancing a silver tray laden with a veritable feast. Blake started shaking his head frantically, but it was too late. Penelope had already turned around.

"Oh, Perriwick," she said, "what is that?"

"Food," he blurted out, clearly confused by her presence. He glanced around.

Blake frowned. The damned butler was obviously looking for Caroline. Perriwick may have been discreet, but he was damned clumsy when it came to out-and-out subterfuge.

Penelope looked to her brother with questioning eyes. "Are you hungry?"

"Er . . . yes, I thought to have a bit of an afternoon snack."

She lifted the lid off of one of the platters, revealing an enormous roast ham. "This is quite a snack."

Perriwick's lips stretched into a sickly sweet smile. "We thought to give you something substantial now, since you requested such light fare for supper."

"How thoughtful," Blake growled. He'd bet his front teeth that that ham had originally been intended for supper. Perriwick and Mrs. Mickle were probably planning on sending up all the good food to Caroline and feeding gruel to the "real" occupants of Seacrest Manor. They certainly had made no secret of their disapproval when Blake had informed them of Caroline's new domicile.

Perriwick turned to Penelope as he set the tray down on a table. "If I might be so bold, my lady—"

"Perriwick!" Blake roared. "If I hear the phrase 'if I might be so bold' one more time, as God is my witness, I'm going to toss you into the channel!"

"Oh dear," Penelope said. "Perhaps he does have the fever, after all. Perriwick, what do you think?"

The butler reached for Blake's forehead, only to have his hand nearly bitten off. "Touch me and die," Blake snarled.

"A bit cranky this afternoon, eh?" Perriwick said, grinning.

"I was perfectly fine until *you* came along."

Penelope said to the butler, "He's been acting rather strangely all afternoon."

Perriwick nodded regally. "Perhaps we ought to leave him be. A bit of rest might be just the thing."

"Very well." Penelope followed the butler to the door. "We shall leave you alone. But if I find out you haven't taken a nap, I'm going to be very angry with you."

"Yes, yes," Blake said hurriedly, trying to usher them out of the room. "I promise I'll rest. Just don't disturb me. I'm a very light sleeper."

Perriwick let out a loud snort that was definitely not in keeping with his usual dignified mien.

Blake shut the door behind them and leaned against the wall with a huge sigh of relief. "Good Christ," he said to himself, "at this rate I'll be a doddering fool before my thirtieth birthday."

"Hmmph," came a voice from the washing room. "I'd say you're well on your way already."

He looked up to see Caroline standing in the doorway, an annoyingly huge grin on her face. "What do you want?" he bit off.

"Oh, nothing," she said innocently. "I just wanted to tell you that you were right."

His eyes narrowed suspiciously. "What do you mean?"

"Let's just say I've discovered the humor in our situation."

He growled at her and took a menacing step forward.

But she appeared unintimidated. "I can't really remember the last time I laughed so hard," she said, grabbing the tray of food.

"Caroline, do you value your neck?"

"Yes, I'm rather fond of it. Why?"

"Because if you don't shut up, I'm going to wring it."

She darted back into the washing room. "Point taken." Then she shut the door, leaving him fuming in his bedroom.

And if that weren't bad enough, the next sound he heard was a loud click.

The damned woman had locked him out. She'd taken all the food and locked him out.

"You'll pay for this!" he yelled at the door.

"Do be quiet," came the muffled reply. "I'm eating."

Chapter 16

ti•ti•vate *(verb). To make small alterations or additions to one's toilet.*

Stranded as I am in a washing room, at least I have time for titivation*—I vow my hair has never looked so smart!*

—From the personal dictionary of Caroline Trent

It occurred to Blake as he was eating supper later that night that he would very much like to kill Miss Caroline Trent. It also occurred to him that this was not a new emotion. She hadn't just turned his life upside down; she'd flipped it sideways, pulled it inside out, and, at certain unmentionable times, lit a fire under it.

Still, he thought generously, perhaps *kill* might be slightly too strong a word. He wasn't so proud that he couldn't admit that she'd grown on him just a bit. But he definitely wanted to muzzle her.

Yes, a muzzle would be ideal. Then she couldn't talk.

Or eat.

"I say, Blake," Penelope said with an apprehensive look on her face, "is this soup?"

He nodded.

She looked at the nearly transparent broth in her bowl. "Truly?"

"It tastes like salty water," he drawled, "but Mrs. Mickle assures me it's soup."

Penelope downed a hesitant spoonful, then took a rather long sip of red wine. "I don't suppose you have any of that ham left over from your snack?"

"I can assure you that it would be most impossible for us to partake of that ham."

If his sister found his wording a trifle odd, she didn't say so. Instead, she put down her spoon and asked, "Did Perriwick bring anything else? A crust of bread, perhaps."

Blake shook his head.

"Do you always eat so . . . lightly in the evening?"

Again, he shook his head.

"Oh. So then this is a special occasion?"

He had no idea how to answer that, so he just took another spoonful of the atrocious soup. Surely there had to be some sort of nutritional value in it somewhere.

But then, much to his surprise, Penelope clapped her hand over her mouth, turned beet red, and said, "Oh, I'm so sorry!"

He set his spoon down slowly. "I beg your pardon?"

"Of course this is a special occasion. I had completely forgotten. I'm so sorry."

"Penelope, what the devil are you talking about?"

"Marabelle."

Blake felt an odd sort of clutching feeling in his chest. Why would Penelope bring up his dead fiancée now? "What about Marabelle?" he asked, his voice completely even.

She blinked. "Oh. Oh, then you don't remember. Never mind. Please forget I said anything."

Blake watched his sister in disbelief as she attacked the bowl of soup as if it were manna from heaven. "For God's sake, Penelope, whatever it was you were thinking about, just say it."

She bit her lip in indecision. "It's the eleventh of July, Blake." Her voice was very soft and filled with pity.

He stared at her in one blessed moment of incomprehension until he remembered.

The eleventh of July.

The anniversary of Marabelle's death.

He stood so abruptly that his chair toppled over. "I will see you tomorrow," he said, his voice clipped.

"Wait, Blake! Don't go!" She rose to her feet and hurried after him as he strode out of the room. "You shouldn't be alone right now."

He stopped in his tracks but he didn't turn around to face her as he said, "You don't understand, Penelope. I will always be alone."

Two hours later Blake was good and drunk. He knew it wouldn't make him feel any better, but he'd kept thinking that one more drink might make him feel *less*.

It didn't work, though.

How had he forgotten? Every year he'd marked her passing with a special token, something to honor her in death the way he had tried and failed to honor her in life. The first year it had been flowers on her grave. Banal, he knew, but his grief was still raw, and he was still young, and he hadn't known what else to do.

The following year he'd planted a tree in her honor at the place she'd been slain. It had somehow seemed fitting; as a young girl Marabelle had been able to climb a tree faster than any boy in the district.

Subsequent years had been marked with a donation to a home for foundlings, a gift of books to her old school, and an anonymous bank draft to her parents, who were always struggling to make ends meet.

But this year . . . nothing.

He stumbled down the path to the beach, using one arm for balance while the other clutched his bottle of whiskey. When he reached the end of the trail, he plopped inelegantly onto the ground. There was a grassy spot before the hard ground gave way to the delicate sand for which Bournemouth was famous. He sat there, staring out at the Channel, wondering what the hell he was meant to do with himself.

He'd come outside for fresh air and escape. He didn't want Penelope or her well-meaning questions intruding upon his grief. But the salty air did little to ease his guilt. All it did was remind him of

Caroline. She'd come home that afternoon with the smell of the sea in her hair and the touch of the sun on her skin.

Caroline. He closed his eyes in anguish. He knew that Caroline was the reason he'd forgotten Marabelle.

He poured more whiskey down his throat, drinking straight from the bottle. It burned a ragged path to his stomach, but Blake welcomed the pain. It felt raw and undignified, and somehow that seemed appropriate. Tonight he didn't feel like much of a gentleman.

He lay back on the grass and gazed up at the sky. The moon was out, but it wasn't bright enough to diminish the light of the stars. They looked almost happy up there, twinkling as if they hadn't a care in the world. He almost felt as if they were mocking him.

He swore. He was growing fanciful. That, or maudlin. Or maybe it was just the drink. He sat up and took another swig.

The liquor dulled his senses and muddled his mind, which was probably why he didn't hear footsteps until they were nearly on top of him. "Whosh there?" he slurred, awkwardly raising himself up onto his elbows. "Who is it?"

Caroline stepped forward, the starlight glinting off her light brown hair. "It's only me."

"What are you doing here?"

"I saw you from my window." She smiled wryly. "Excuse me, *your* window."

"You should go back up."

"Probably."

"I'm not fit company."

"No," she agreed, "you're quite drunk. It's not good to drink on an empty stomach."

He let out a short burst of hollow laughter. "And whose fault is my empty stomach?"

"You do know how to hold a grudge, don't you?"

"Madam, I assure you I have an excruciatingly long memory." He winced at his words. His memory had always served him well—until this night.

She frowned. "I brought you some food."

He didn't say anything for a long moment, then said, in a very low voice, "Go back inside."

"Why are you so upset?"

He didn't say anything, just wiped his mouth with his sleeve after taking another drink of whiskey.

"I've never seen you drunk before."

"There are a lot of things you don't know about me."

She took another step forward, her eyes daring him to look away. "I know more than you think I do."

That got his attention. His eyes flared with momentary anger, then went blank as he said, "Pity for you, then."

"Here, you should eat something." She held out something wrapped in a cloth napkin. "It'll soak up the whiskey."

"That's the last thing I want to do."

She sat beside him. "This isn't like you, Blake."

He turned on her, his gray eyes glowing fiercely. "Don't you tell me what is or isn't like me," he hissed. "You have no right."

"As your friend," she said softly, "I have every right."

"Today," Blake announced with an off-balance flourish of his arm, "is the eleventh of July."

Caroline didn't say anything; she didn't know what to say to such an obvious announcement.

"The eleventh of July," he repeated. "It shall go down in infamy in the saga of Blake Ravenscroft as the day he . . . as the day I . . ."

She leaned forward, shocked and moved by the choking sound in his voice. "As what day, Blake?" she whispered.

"As the day I let a woman die."

She blanched at the pain in his voice. "No. It wasn't your fault."

"What the hell do you know about it?"

"James told me about Marabelle."

"Bloody interfering bastard."

"I'm glad he did. It tells me so much more about you."

"Why the hell would you want to know more?" he asked caustically.

"Because I lo—" Caroline stopped, horrified by what she'd almost said. "Because I like you. Because you're my friend. I haven't had many in my life, so perhaps I recognize how special friendship is."

"I can't be your friend," he said, his voice unbearably harsh.

"Can't you?" She held her breath, waiting for his reply.

"You don't want me to be your friend."

"Don't you think that's for me to decide?"

"For the love of God, woman, what does it take to get you to listen? For the last time, I cannot be your friend. I could never be your friend."

"Why not?"

"Because I want you."

She forced herself not to pull away. He'd been so blunt, so bare with his need—it almost frightened her. "That's the whiskey talking," she said hastily.

"Do you think so? You know very little about men, my sweet."

"I know about *you.*"

He laughed. "Not half as much as I know about you, my dear Miss Trent."

"Don't mock me," she whispered.

"Ah, but I've been watching you. Shall I prove it? All the things I know, all the little things I've noticed. I could fill one of those books you're so fond of."

"Blake, I think you should—"

But he cut her off with a finger to her lips. "I'll start here," he whispered, "with your mouth."

"My m—"

"Shhh. It's my turn." His finger traced the delicate arch of her upper lip. "So full. So pink. You've never painted them, have you?"

She shook her head, but the motion brought on the sensual torture of his finger rubbing along her skin.

"No," he murmured, "you wouldn't have to. I've never seen lips like yours before. Did I ever mention that they were the first thing I noticed about you?"

She sat utterly still, too nervous to shake her head again.

"Your lower lip is lovely, but this one"—he traced her upper lip again—"is exquisite. It begs to be kissed. When I thought you were Carlotta . . .

even then I wanted to cover your lips with mine. God, how I hated myself for that."

"But I'm not Carlotta," she whispered.

"I know. It's worse this way. Because now I can almost justify wanting you. I can—"

"Blake?" Her voice was soft, but it was urgent, and she thought she'd die if he didn't complete his thought.

But he just shook his head. "I digress." He moved his fingers to her eyes, skimming the tips over her eyelids as she closed them. "Here is another thing I know about you."

She felt her lips part, and her breathing grew ragged.

"Your eyes—such heavenly lashes. Just a touch darker than your hair." He moved his fingers to her temples. "But I think I like them open better than closed."

Her eyes flew open.

"Ah, that's better. The most exquisite color in the world. Have you ever been out to sea?"

"Not since I was a very little girl."

"Here by the coast the water is gray and murky, but once you get away from the taint of the land, it is clear and pure. Do you know what I'm talking about?"

"I—I think so."

He shrugged rather suddenly and dropped his hand. "It still doesn't hold a candle to your eyes. I've heard the water is even more breathtaking in the tropics. Your eyes must be the exact color of the ocean as it skims along the equator."

She smiled hesitantly. "I should like to see the equator."

"My dear girl, don't you think you should at least try to see London first?"

"Now you're being cruel, and you don't really mean it."

"Don't I?"

"No," she said, reaching within herself to find the courage she needed to speak to him so plainly. "You're not angry with me. You're angry with yourself, and I'm convenient."

His head tilted slightly in her direction. "You think you're very observant, don't you?"

"How am I supposed to answer that?"

"You're observant, but not, I think, enough to save yourself from me." He leaned forward, his smile dangerous. "Do you know how much I want you?"

Her voice lost to her, she shook her head.

"I want you so much I lie awake every night, my body hard and aching with need."

Her throat went dry.

"I want you so much the scent of you makes my skin tingle with desire."

Her lips parted.

"I want you so much—" The night air filled with his angry laughter. "I want you so damned much I forgot about Marabelle."

"Oh, Blake. I'm sorry."

"Spare me your pity."

She started to stand up. "I'll go. It's what you want, and you're clearly in no state for conversation."

But he grabbed her and pulled her back down. "Didn't you hear me?"

"I heard every word," she whispered.

"I don't want you to go."

She said nothing.

"I want *you*."

"Blake, don't."

"Don't what? Don't kiss you?" He swooped down and kissed her hard on the mouth. "Too late."

She stared at him, not certain if she should be scared or elated. She loved him; she was sure of that now. But he wasn't acting like himself.

"Don't touch you?" His hand snaked over her midriff and along her hip. "I'm far too gone for that."

His lips found her jaw, then her neck, then nibbled on her ear. She tasted sweet and clean, and smelled vaguely like the lather he used to shave. He wondered what she'd been doing with herself up in his bathroom, then decided he didn't much care. There was something wildly satisfying about smelling his scent on her.

"Blake," she said, her voice lacking conviction, "I'm not certain this is what you really want."

"Oh, I'm certain," he said with a masculine laugh. "I'm very certain." He pressed his hips against her as he worked her hair free of its fastenings. "Can't you feel how certain I am?"

He moved his mouth to hers and devoured her, his tongue skimming first along the line of her teeth, then moving to the soft skin of her inner cheek.

"I want to touch you," he said, his words a soft breath against her mouth. "Everywhere."

Her dress was flimsy, with few buttons and bows, and it took mere seconds for him to push it over her head, leaving her clad only in a thin chemise.

His body tightened yet again as he hooked his fingers under the thin straps that held up the soft slip of silk.

"Did I buy this for you?" he asked, his voice hoarse beyond recognition.

She nodded, gasping as one of his large hands closed over her breast. "When you got me the dresses. It was in one of the boxes you brought back from town."

"Good," he said, then pushed the strap over her shoulder. His lips found the elegantly stitched lace that edged her bodice, and he followed it as he pushed it down, stopping only when he reached the pinkened edge of her nipple.

She whispered his name as he kissed the dusky aureole, then nearly shouted it when he closed his mouth around her nipple and began to suck.

Caroline had never felt anything as wonderfully primitive as the sensations curling in her belly. Pleasure and need were unfolding within her, spreading from the very center of her being to every inch of her skin. She'd thought she'd felt desire when he'd kissed her that morning, but it was nothing compared to what was devouring her now.

She looked down at his head at her breast. Good Lord, *he* was devouring her.

She was hot, so hot, and she thought she must be burning up wherever he touched her. One of his hands was now creeping up her calf, and his trouser-clad knee was using gentle pressure to open her legs. He settled his weight between them, and the hard proof of his arousal pressed up against her intimately.

His hand moved ever higher, past her knee, along the smooth skin of her inner thigh, and then it paused for a moment, as if giving her one last chance to refuse.

But Caroline was too far gone. She could refuse him nothing, for she wanted everything. Perhaps she was wanton, perhaps she was shameful, but she wanted every wicked touch of his hands and mouth. She wanted the weight of him pressing her into the ground. She wanted the rapid beat of his heart and ragged rasp of his breath.

She wanted his heart, and she wanted his soul. But most of all, she wanted to give herself to him, to heal whatever wounds lay beneath the surface of his skin. She'd finally found a place of belonging—with him—and she wanted to show him the same joy.

And so, when his fingers found the core of her femininity, no words of refusal or protest passed her lips. She gave herself into the pleasure of the moment, moaned his name, and clutched at his shoulders as he teased her desire into a merciless vortex.

She clung to him as she spun out of control, the pressures within her building to a fever pitch. She felt taut, stretched to the limit, and then he slipped one finger inside her as his thumb continued its sensual torture on her hot skin.

Her world exploded in an instant.

She bucked beneath him, her hips rising off the ground and actually lifting him in the air. She shouted his name and then reached frantically from him as he rolled off her.

"No," she gasped, "come back."

"Shhh." He stroked her hair, then her cheek. "I'm right here."

"Come back."

"I'm too heavy for you."

"No. I want to feel you. I want—" She gulped. "I want to please you."

His face grew taut. "No, Caroline."

"But—"

"I won't take that away from you." His voice was firm. "I shouldn't have done what I did, but I'm damned if I take your virginity."

"But I want to give it to you," she whispered.

He turned on her with unexpected ferocity. "No," he bit out. "You will save that for your husband. You are too fine to waste it on another."

"I—" She broke her words off, not willing to mortify herself by saying she'd hoped he would be that husband.

But he could obviously read her thoughts, for he turned away from her and said, "I won't marry you. I *can't* marry you."

She scrambled for her clothing, begging a prayer to God that she wouldn't start to cry. "I never said you had to."

He turned around. "Do you understand me?"

"I'm quite proficient in English." Her voice caught. "I know all the big words, remember?"

He gazed upon her face, which wasn't nearly as stoic as she'd hoped. "Christ, I never meant to hurt you."

"It's a little late for that."

"You don't understand. I can never marry. My heart belongs to another."

"Your heart belongs to a dead woman," she spat out. She immediately clapped her hand to her mouth, horrified by her venomous tone. "Forgive me."

He shrugged fatalistically as he handed her one of her slippers. "There is nothing to forgive. I took advantage of you. For that I apologize. I am only glad I had the presence of mind to stop when I did."

"Oh, Blake," she said sadly. "Eventually, you're going to have to allow yourself to stop hurting. Marabelle is gone. You're still here, and there are people who love you."

It was as close to a declaration as she was willing to make. She held her breath, waiting for his reply, but he just handed her her other slipper.

"Thank you," she murmured. "I'll go inside now."

"Yes." But when she didn't immediately move he said. "Do you plan to sleep in the washing room?"

"I hadn't really thought about it."

"I'd give you my bed but I don't trust Penelope not to come in and check on me in the night. She occasionally forgets her younger brother has grown up."

"It must be nice to have a sister."

He looked away. "Take the pillows and blankets off my bed. I'm sure you can fashion something comfortable."

She nodded and started to walk away.

"Caroline?"

She whirled around, hope flaring in her eyes.

"Lock the door behind you."

Chapter 17

es•cu•lent *(adjective). Suitable for food, eatable.*

I have often heard that even the nastiest of food seems virtuous and esculent ***when one is hungry, but I disagree. Gruel is gruel, no matter how loud one's stomach rumbles.***

—From the personal dictionary of Caroline Trent

Caroline awoke the following morning to a knock on the bathroom door. At Blake's order, she'd turned the key in the lock the night before—not because she thought he would try to ravish her in the night, but because she wouldn't put it past him to check the door just to see if she'd followed orders. And she certainly didn't want to give him the satisfaction of scolding her.

She'd slept in her chemise, and she wrapped herself in a blanket before opening the door a crack and peeking out. One of Blake's gray eyes was peering back at her.

"May I come in?"

"That depends."

"On what?"

"Do you have breakfast?"

"Madam, I haven't had access to decent food for nearly twenty-four hours. I was hoping Perriwick had brought you something to eat."

She opened the door. "It isn't fair for the servants to punish your sister. She must be starving."

"I imagine she'll eat well enough at teatime. You're expected to pay a visit, remember?"

"Oh yes. How are we meant to manage that?"

He leaned against a marble washbasin. "Penelope has already ordered me to send for you in my finest carriage."

"I thought you only had one carriage."

"I do. That's beside the point. I'm to send a carriage to your . . . ah . . . *home* to pick you up."

Caroline rolled her eyes. "I should like to see that. A carriage rolling up to the washing room. Tell me, would you bring it by way of your bedroom or the servant's stairs?"

He shot her a look that said he wasn't amused. "I'm to have you back here in time for a four o'clock visit."

"What am I supposed to do before then?"

He looked around the room. "Wash?"

"That isn't funny, Blake."

There was a moment of silence, then he said quietly, "I'm sorry about what happened last night."

"*Don't* apologize."

"But I must. I took advantage of you. I took advantage of a situation that can go nowhere."

Caroline gritted her teeth. Her experience the previous night was the closest she'd felt to being loved in years. To have him say he was sorry it had happened was unbearable. "If you apologize again I shall scream."

"Caroline, don't be—"

"I mean it!"

He nodded. "Very well. I'll leave you alone then."

"Ah yes," she said with a wave of her arm, "my oh-so-fascinating life. There is so much to do here, I really don't know where to start. I thought I might wash my hands, and after that my toes, and if I'm really ambitious I might attempt my back."

He frowned. "Would you like me to bring you a book?"

Her demeanor changed instantly. "Oh, would you please? I don't know where I left that pile I was planning to bring up yesterday."

"I'll find them."

"Thank you. When should I . . . ah . . . expect your carriage?"

"I suppose I shall have to order the carriage a bit before half three, so why don't you be ready on the hour for me to spirit you to the stables?"

"I can make it to the stables on my own. You'd do better to make certain that Penelope is occupied on the other side of the house."

He nodded. "You're right. I will tell the groom to expect you on the hour."

"Is everyone aware of our deception, then?"

"I thought I might be able to limit it to the three house servants, but now it appears as if the stable staff will have to be in on the secret, as well." He took a step to leave, then turned around and told her, "Remember, be on time."

She glanced around with a dubious expression. "I don't suppose you've any clocks here."

He handed her his pocket watch. "Use this. It will need to be wound in a few hours, though."

"You'll bring those books?"

He nodded. "Never let it be said that I'm not the most gracious of hosts."

"Even when you relegate the occasional guest to the washing room?"

"Even then."

At precisely four o'clock that afternoon, Caroline knocked on the front door of Seacrest Manor. Her journey to that spot had been rather bizarre, to say the least. She'd sneaked out of the washing room, down the servants' stairs, dashed across the lawn at precisely three o'clock, hopped up into the carriage, and proceeded to ride about aimlessly until the groom returned to the house at four.

It certainly would have been more direct to have exited through Blake's bedroom and gone down the main stairs, but after spending all day with no company save for a washbasin and a tub, Caroline didn't mind a bit of excitement and scenery.

Perriwick answered the door in record time, winked at her, and said, "It's a delight to see you again, Miss Trent."

"Miss *Dent*," she hissed.

"Right," he said, saluting her.

"Perriwick! Someone might see."

He looked furtively about. "Right."

Caroline groaned. Perriwick had developed a bit too much of a taste for subterfuge.

The butler cleared his throat and said very loudly, "Allow me to show you to the drawing room, Miss *Dent*."

"Thank you . . . er . . . what did you say your name was?"

He grinned at her approvingly. "It's Perri*stick*, Miss Dent."

This time Caroline couldn't help herself. She smacked him in the shoulder. "This isn't a game," she whispered.

"Of course not." He opened the door to the drawing room, the same one where he'd plied her with feasts while her ankle was mending. "I'll tell Lady Fairwich that you're here."

She shook her head at his enthusiasm and walked over to the window. It looked as if it might rain later that evening, which was just as well to Caroline, seeing as how she'd most likely be stuck in Blake's washing room all night.

"Miss Dent—Caroline! How lovely to see you again."

Caroline turned to see Blake's sister gliding into the room. "Lady Fairwich, you have been too kind to invite me."

"Nonsense, and I believe that yesterday I insisted you call me Penelope."

"Very well . . . Penelope," Caroline said, then motioned to her surroundings with her hand. "This is a lovely room."

"Yes, isn't the view breathtaking? I am ever jealous of Blake, living out here by the sea. And now I suppose I must be jealous of you as well." She smiled. "Would you care for some tea?"

If food had been sent up to Caroline's erstwhile room, Blake had somehow managed to intercept it, and her stomach had been screaming at her all day. "Yes," she said, "I would adore some tea."

"Excellent." I would ask for biscuits as well, but"—Penelope leaned in as if to tell a secret—"Blake's cook is really dreadful. I think we had better just stick with tea, to be on the safe side."

While Caroline was busy trying to think of a polite way to tell the countess that she would perish from hunger if she didn't let Mrs. Mickle send up some biscuits, Blake entered the room.

"Ah, Miss Dent," he said, "welcome. I trust your drive here was comfortable."

"Indeed it was, Mr. Ravenscroft. Your carriage is exceptionally well-sprung."

He nodded at her distractedly and glanced around the room.

"I say, Blake," Penelope said, "are you looking for something?"

"I was just wondering if perhaps Mrs. Mickle had sent up some tea. And," he added forcefully, "biscuits."

"I was just about to ring for some, although I'm not certain about the biscuits. After last night's meal . . ."

"Mrs. Mickle makes *excellent* biscuits," Blake said. "I shall have her send up a double batch."

Caroline sighed in relief.

"I suppose," Penelope conceded. "After all, I did have a lovely breakfast this morning."

"You had breakfast?" Blake and Caroline said in unison.

If Penelope thought it was strange that her guest was questioning her about her eating habits she did not say so, or perhaps she just didn't hear. She shrugged and said, "Yes, it was the oddest thing, actually. I found it on a tray near my room this morning."

"Really?" Caroline said, trying to sound like she was asking just out of polite interest. She'd bet her life that food had been meant for her.

"Well, to be truthful it wasn't exactly near my room. It was actually closer to your room, Blake, except I knew that you were already up and about. I thought the servants must have not wanted to come so close to my door for fear of waking me up."

Blake shot her a look of such disbelief that Penelope was forced to lift her hands in an accommodating gesture and say, "I didn't know what else to think."

"*I* think that perhaps my breakfast was on that tray, as well," he said.

"Oh. Yes, that would make sense. I thought there was rather a lot of food there, but I was so hungry after last night's meal, I truly didn't stop to think."

"No harm done," Blake said. Then his stomach proved him a liar by grumbling quite loudly. He winced. "I'll just see to that tea. And . . . ah . . . the extra biscuits."

Caroline coughed.

Blake halted in his tracks and turned around. "Miss Dent, are you also hungry?"

She smiled prettily. "Famished. We had a bit of a mishap in our kitchen at home and I have had nothing at all today."

"Oh dear!" Penelope cried out, clasping her hands over Caroline's. "How awful for you. Blake, why don't you see if your cook can prepare something a bit more substantial than biscuits? If you think she's up to it, that is."

Caroline thought she ought to say something polite like, "You shouldn't go to the trouble," but she was terrified that Penelope might actually take her seriously.

"Oh, and Blake!" Penelope called out.

He halted in the doorway and turned around slowly, clearly irritated that he'd been detained yet again.

"No soup."

He didn't even dignify that with an answer.

"My brother can be a bit grumpy," Penelope said, once he'd disappeared from view.

"Brothers can," Caroline agreed.

"Oh, then you have a brother?"

"No," she said wistfully, "but I know people who do."

"Blake really isn't a bad sort," Penelope continued, motioning for Caroline to sit down as she herself did so, "and even I must admit he's quite devilishly handsome."

Caroline's lips parted in surprise. Was Penelope trying to play matchmaker? Oh, dear. How impossibly ironic.

"Don't you think?"

Caroline blinked and sat. "I beg your pardon?"

"Don't you think that Blake is handsome?"

"Well, yes, of course. Anyone would."

Penelope frowned, clearly not satisfied with that answer.

Caroline was saved from having to say anything more by a small commotion in the hall. She and Penelope looked up to see Mrs. Mickle in the doorway, joined by a scowling Blake.

"Are you satisfied now?" he grumbled.

Mrs. Mickle looked straight at Caroline before saying, "I just wanted to be sure."

Penelope turned to Caroline and whispered, "My brother has the oddest servants."

The housekeeper scurried away, and Blake said, "She wanted to be certain that we have guests."

Penelope shrugged and said, "Do you see what I mean?"

Blake came back into the drawing room and sat down, saying, "Don't let my appearance put a halt to your conversation."

"Nonsense," Penelope said, "it's only that . . . hmmm."

"Why don't I like the sound of this?" Blake muttered.

Penelope jumped to her feet. "I have something I simply must show to Caroline. Blake, will you keep her company while I fetch it from my room?"

In a flash, she was gone, and Blake asked, "What was that about?"

"I'm afraid your sister might have taken it into her head to play matchmaker."

"With you?"

"I'm not *that* bad," she snapped. "Some might even consider me a matrimonial prize."

"I beg your pardon," he said quickly. "I didn't mean to offend. It's just that this must mean she's getting quite desperate."

She gaped at him. "Could you possibly be unaware of how rude that sounded?"

He had the grace to color slightly. "Once again, I must apologize. It is only that Penelope has been trying to find me a wife for years, but she usually limits her search to ladies whose families she can trace back to the Norman invasion. Not," he said hastily, "that there is anything wrong with your family. Just that Penelope cannot know your background."

"I'm sure if she did, she would find it unsuitable," Caroline said peevishly. "I may be an heiress, but my father was in trade."

"Yes, so you keep saying. None of this should have ever come to pass if Prewitt hadn't so determined to catch an heiress for his son."

"I don't think I enjoy the comparison to a fish."

Blake looked at her sympathetically. "You must know that that is how people view heiresses—as prey to be caught." When she didn't reply, he added, "It really doesn't signify, however. I will never marry."

"I know."

"Still, you should feel flattered. It means Penny must like you very much."

Caroline just gave him a stony stare. "Blake," she finally said, "I believe you are choking on your foot."

There was an awkward silence, and then Blake attempted to patch things up by saying, "Mrs. Mickle refused to prepare any food unless she knew you were here."

"Yes, I surmised as much. She's very sweet."

"That is not quite the adjective I would use to describe her, but I can see where you might think so."

There was yet another uncomfortable silence, and this time Caroline broke it. "I understand your brother had a daughter recently."

"Yes, his fourth."

"You must be delighted."

He looked at her sharply. "Why would you say that?"

"I should think it would be lovely to have a niece. Of course, as an only child I shall never be an aunt." Her gaze grew wistful. "I adore little babies."

"Perhaps you will have one of your own."

"I doubt it." Caroline had always hoped to marry for love, but since the man she loved intended to go to the grave a bachelor, it seemed she would remain unwed as well.

"Don't be silly. You can't possibly know what the future holds for you."

"Why not?" she countered. "You seem to think you do."

"Touché." He regarded her for a moment, then his eyes filled with something that looked suspiciously like regret, and he said, "I do rather enjoy my nieces."

"Then why were you so upset about the new one?"

"Why should you think that?"

She scoffed. "Oh, please, Blake. It's quite obvious."

"I am not in the least displeased with my new niece. I'm sure I shall adore her." He cleared his throat and smiled wryly. "I just wish she had been a boy."

"Most men would be thrilled at the prospect of being next in line for a viscountcy."

"*I* am not most men."

"Yes, that much is clear."

Blake narrowed his eyes and regarded her intently. "What is that supposed to mean?"

She just shrugged.

"Caroline . . ." he warned.

"It's quite obvious that you adore children, and yet you're determined not to have any of your own. That particular line of reasoning shows even less logic than usually demonstrated by the males of our species."

"Now you're beginning to sound like my sister."

"I shall take that as a compliment. I quite like your sister."

"So do I, but that doesn't mean I always do what she says."

"I'm back!" Penelope sailed into the room. "What are you talking about?"

"Babies," Caroline bluntly replied.

Penelope started, then her eyes filled with unconcealed glee. "Really? How intriguing!"

"Penelope," Blake drawled, "what was it you wanted to show Caroline?"

"Oh, that," she said distractedly. "Couldn't find it. I shall have to look later and invite Caroline to return tomorrow."

Blake wanted to protest, but he knew that tea with Caroline was the only way he was going to get a decent meal.

Caroline smiled and turned to Penelope. "Have your brother and his wife named their new daughter?"

"Oh, you were talking about *their* baby," Penelope said, sounding more than vaguely disappointed. "Yes, they did. Daphne Georgiana Elizabeth."

"All those names?"

"Oh, that is nothing. The older girls have even more names—the oldest is called Sophie Charlotte Sybilla Aurelia Nathanaele—but David and Sarah are quite running out."

"If they have another daughter," Caroline said with a smile, "they will have to simply call her Mary and leave it at that."

Penelope laughed. "Oh no, that would be quite impossible. They've already used Mary. Their second daughter is Katharine Mary Claire Evelina."

"I don't dare guess what their third child is called."

"Alexandra Lucy Caroline Vivette."

"A Caroline! How lovely."

"I'm amazed," Blake said, "that you can remember all those names. It's all I can do to recall Sophie, Katharine, Alexandra, and now Daphne."

"If you had children of your own—"

"I know, I know, dear sister. You needn't repeat yourself."

"I was merely going to say that if you had children of your own you shouldn't have any trouble remembering names."

"I know what you were going to say."

"Do you have children, Lady Fairwich?" Caroline asked.

A look of pain crossed Penelope's features before she replied softly, "No. No, I don't."

"I'm so sorry," Caroline stammered. "I shouldn't have asked."

"It is nothing," Penelope said with a shaky smile. "The earl and I have not yet been blessed with children. Perhaps that is why I so dote on my nieces."

Caroline swallowed uncomfortably, well aware that she'd inadvertently brought up a painful topic. "Mr. Ravenscroft says that he, too, dotes on your nieces."

"Yes, he does. He's quite a wonderful uncle. He should make an ex—"

"Don't say it, Penelope," Blake interrupted.

Further conversation on the topic was thankfully prevented by the entrance of Perriwick, who was staggering under the weight of an overcrowded tea service.

"Oh my!" Penelope exclaimed.

"Yes," Blake drawled, "it is quite a feast for high tea, isn't it?"

Caroline just smiled and didn't even bother to feel embarrassed by the way her stomach was roaring.

Over the next few days it became apparent that Caroline was in possession of a crucial bargaining chip: The servants refused to prepare a decent meal unless they could be certain she would be partaking of it.

And so she found herself "invited" to Seacrest Manor with increasing regularity. Penelope had even gone so far as to suggest that Caroline spend the night once when it was raining.

In all truth, it wasn't raining that hard, but Penelope was no fool. She'd noticed the servants' peculiar habits, and she liked breakfast as well as anybody.

Caroline soon became fast friends with Blake's sister, although it was becoming difficult to keep putting her off whenever she suggested a jaunt into Bournemouth. There were too many people who might recognize Caroline in the small city.

Not to mention the fact that Oliver had apparently plastered her likeness in every public place, and Blake reported that the last time he'd gone into town, he'd noticed that a reward was now being offered for Caroline's safe return.

Caroline didn't particularly relish the thought of trying to explain *that* to Penelope.

She didn't see so much of Blake, however. He never missed teatime; it was the only opportunity for a decent meal, after all. But other than that, he avoided Caroline's company save for the occasional visit to the bathroom to give her a new book.

And so life ambled on in this bizarre yet oddly comfortable routine—until one day, nearly a week after Penelope's arrival. The threesome were all hungrily wolfing down sandwiches in the drawing room, each hoping the others wouldn't notice his deplorable lack of manners.

Caroline was reaching for her third sandwich, Penelope munching her second, and Blake slipping his sixth into his pocket when they heard booted footsteps in the hall.

"Who could that be, I wonder?" Penelope asked, blushing slightly when a crumb blew out of her mouth.

Her question was answered moments later, as the Marquis of Riverdale strode into the room. He took in the scene, blinked in surprise, and then said, "Penelope, it's good to see you. I had no idea you were acquainted with Caroline."

Chapter 18

ar·is·tol·o·gy *(noun). The art or "science" of dining.*

As a field of research and study, aristology is *highly underrated.*

—From the personal dictionary of Caroline Trent

Utter silence ensued, followed by a burst of nervous chatter so loud and forceful that Perriwick actually poked his head into the room to see what was going on. He did so under the guise of coming in to clear away the rest of the tea and biscuits, which caused nothing short of mutiny, and Blake practically yanked the tray from his hands before pushing him back out the door.

If Penelope had noticed that the Marquis of Riverdale had been so forward as to call Miss Dent by her given name, she made no remark, commenting instead upon how overwhelmingly surprised she was that they were acquainted.

Caroline was talking very loudly about how the Sidwells had long been friends with the *Dents*, and James was agreeing profusely with everything she said.

The only person not adding to the din was Blake, although he did emit a rather loud groan. He didn't know which was worse: the fact that James had arrived and nearly blown Caroline's cover, or the newly fierce matchmaking gleam in his sister's eye. Now that she'd discovered that Caroline's family was in some way—however tenuous—connected to the marquis's, she'd obviously decided that Caroline would make an excellent Ravenscroft wife.

Either that, he thought grimly, or she'd decided to concentrate her prodigious matchmaking skills toward Caroline and *James*.

All in all, Blake decided, this had the makings of a truly colossal disaster. His eyes made a slow sweep of the room, watching Penelope, James, and Caroline, and he decided that the only thing keeping him from violence was that he couldn't decide which of them to strangle first.

"Oh, but it's been an age, Caroline," James was saying, clearly enjoying himself now. "Almost five years, I should think. You are very changed since we last met."

"Really?" Penelope queried. "How?"

Put on the spot, James stammered for a moment, then said, "Well, her hair is quite longer, and—"

"Really?" Penelope said again. "How interesting. You must have had quite a crop, Caroline, because it isn't so very long now."

"There was an accident," Caroline improvised, "and we had to cut it quite short."

Blake bit his lip to keep from asking her to tell them about the "accident."

"Oh, yes, I remember that," James said with great enthusiasm. "Something involving honey and your brother's pet bird."

Caroline coughed into her tea, then grabbed a cloth napkin to keep from spraying it all over Blake.

"I thought you didn't have any brothers or sisters," Penelope said, furrowing her brow.

Caroline wiped her mouth, suppressed an urge toward nervous laughter, and said, "It was my cousin's bird, actually."

"Right," James said, slapping his forehead. "How silly of me. What was his name?"

"Percy."

"Good ol' Percy. How is he these days?"

She smiled peevishly. "Much the same, I'm afraid. I do my best to avoid him."

"That is probably a wise course of action," James agreed. "I remember him as a mean-hearted sort of fellow, always yanking on people's hair and the like."

"Riverdale!" Penelope said in a disapproving voice. "You are speaking of Miss Dent's relation."

"Oh, I don't mind," Caroline assured her. "I'd be quite pleased to disown Percy."

Penelope shook her head in confusion and looked up at her brother with a faintly accusing expression. "I cannot believe that you did not tell me that our dear Caroline is friends with Riverdale."

Blake shrugged and forced himself to unclench his fists. "I didn't know."

Perriwick entered the room with uncharacteristic unobtrusiveness and began to clear away the half-eaten remnants of high tea.

"NO!" Blake, Penelope, and Caroline yelled in unison.

James looked at them with interest and confusion. "Is something amiss?"

"We're just—" Penelope said.

"—a little—" Caroline interjected.

"—hungry," Blake finished emphatically.

James blinked. "Apparently so."

Penelope filled the ensuing lull by turning to James and asking, "Will you be staying with us, my lord?"

"I had thought to, yes, but only if there is an extra room for me." He glanced over at Caroline. "I hadn't realized that Miss Dent was here."

Penelope scrunched her brow. "But surely you realize that Caroline is only visiting for the day. She lives barely a mile away."

"Father bought a summer house near Bournemouth just last autumn," Caroline blurted out. "I'm afraid we haven't yet gotten around to informing everyone of the move."

"Hmmm," Penelope mused, her eyes growing narrower by the second, "I was under the impression that you had resided in Bournemouth for some time."

Caroline smiled weakly. "We visited quite often."

"Yes," Blake said, thinking that he ought to do something to save the situation, even though he was quite furious with both Caroline and James, "didn't you say that your father leased the house for a number of seasons before he bought it?"

Caroline nodded. "That's exactly it."

Blake shot her the most arrogant of smiles. "I am in possession of a remarkable memory."

"Of that I have no doubt."

There was an immeasurably awkward silence, and then Caroline stood. "I had best be getting home. It's growing late, and . . . ah . . . I think Cook is preparing something special for supper."

"Lucky you," Penelope muttered.

"I'm sorry?"

"It was nothing," Penelope said quickly, glancing between Blake and James. "But I am sure one of our two gentlemen will be happy to accompany you."

"That's not necessary. Truly, it's not a long way."

James jumped to his feet. "Nonsense. I should love to walk with you. I am certain we have a great deal of catching up to do."

"Yes," Caroline agreed. "Probably much more than you would have ever imagined."

The moment the front door closed behind them, Caroline turned to James and said, "Have you anything edible in your carriage?"

"A bit of cheese and bread I brought with me from an inn, why?"

But Caroline was already scrambling into the conveyance. "Where is it?" she asked, poking her head back out.

"Good God, woman, haven't they been feeding you?"

"Not really, and it's been worse for Penelope and Blake, although I have little sympathy for the latter."

James climbed in and pulled a hunk of bread from a satchel on the seat. "What the devil is going on?"

"Mmmble nnn munchke."

"I beg your pardon?"

She swallowed. "I'll tell you in a minute. Have you anything to drink?"

He removed a small flask from his pocket. "Just a spot of brandy, but I don't think that's what you—"

But she'd already grabbed it and taken a gulp. James waited patiently while she coughed, sputtered, and gagged, then said, "I was going to say that I didn't think brandy was precisely what you wanted."

"Nonsense," she said hoarsely. "Any liquid would have done."

He took the flask back, screwed the top on, and said, "Suppose you tell me why the three of you look gaunt and starved. And why the hell is Penelope here? She'll ruin the entire operation."

"Then you got permission from London to go ahead with your plans?"

"I'm not answering a single one of your questions until you answer mine."

She shrugged. "We should pretend to walk, then. I'm afraid this might take a great deal of time."

"*Pretend* to walk?"

"It certainly isn't going to take us an hour to walk me back to Blake's bathroom."

James's mouth fell open. "*What?*"

She sighed. "Would you like the long version or the short version?"

"Since it appears I must somehow use up an hour

accompanying you to Ravenscroft's bathroom, I'll opt for the long version. It's bound to be more interesting, anyway."

She hopped out of the carriage, clutching the chunk of cheese she'd found with the bread. "You have no idea."

Two hours later, Blake was feeling very irritable. Downright mean, as a matter of fact.

James and Caroline had been gone a long time—much longer than it should have taken for them to go to the bathroom.

Blake swore at himself. Even his thoughts were beginning to sound inane.

Still, James only needed to be gone an hour to perpetuate the ruse that he'd walked Caroline home. Not that anyone, Caroline included, had any idea just how far away her "home" was supposed to be, but Blake had never taken longer than an hour to pretend to fetch her for tea.

He had spent so much time pacing back and forth in his washing room that Penelope undoubtedly thought he had some sort of vile stomach ailment.

Finally, as he perched on the edge of the washbasin, he heard laughter and footsteps coming up the side stairs. He hopped down onto the ground, settled his mouth into a grim line, and crossed his arms.

A second later, the door flew open, and Caroline and James practically fell in, both laughing so hard they could hardly stand.

"Where the hell have you been?" Blake demanded.

They looked like they were trying to answer him, but he couldn't understand what they were saying through their laughter.

"And what the devil are you laughing about?"

"Ravenscroft, you've done some truly bizarre things," James gasped, "but this—" He waved his arm at the washing room. "This is without compare."

Blake just scowled at him.

"Although," James said, turning to Caroline, "you've done quite a nice job turning this place into home. The bed is a nice touch."

Caroline looked down at the neat pile of blankets and pillows she'd arranged on the floor. "Thank you. I do my best with what I have to work with." She giggled again.

"Where have you *been*?" Blake repeated.

"I could do with a few more candles," Caroline said to James.

"Yes, I can see where it would grow quite dark in here," he replied. "That window is abysmally small."

"Where have you *BEEN*?" Blake roared.

Caroline and James looked at him with identically blank expressions.

"Were you talking to us?" James asked.

"I'm sorry?" Caroline said at the very same time.

"Where," Blake said through clenched teeth, "have you been?"

They looked at each other and shrugged.

"I don't know," James said.

"Oh, out and about," Caroline added.

"For two hours?"

"I had to fill him in on all of the details," she said. "After all, you wouldn't want him to say something wrong to Penelope."

"I could have told him all the pertinent facts in under fifteen minutes," Blake grumbled.

"I'm sure you could have done," James replied, "but it wouldn't have been nearly as entertaining."

"Well, Penelope wants to know where you've been," Blake said testily. "She wants to throw a fête in your honor, Riverdale."

"But I thought she was planning on leaving in two days," Caroline said.

"She *was*," he snapped, "but now that our dear friend James is here she's decided to extend her stay. Says it isn't every day we've a marquis in residence."

"She's married to a bloody earl," James said. "What does she care?"

"She doesn't," Blake replied. "She just wants to marry the lot of us off."

"To whom?"

"Preferably to each other."

"All three of us?" Caroline looked from man to man. "Isn't that illegal?"

James laughed. Blake just shot her the most contemptuous of stares. Then he said, "We've got to get rid of her."

Caroline crossed her arms. "I refuse to do anything mean to your sister. She is a kind and gentle person."

"Ha!" Blake barked. "Gentle, my foot. She is the most determined, interfering woman of my acquaintance, except, perhaps, for you."

Caroline stuck out her tongue.

Blake ignored her. "We need to find a way to get her to go back to London."

"It should be easy to fake a message from her husband," James said.

Blake shook his head. "Not nearly as easy as you'd think. He's in the Caribbean."

Caroline felt a pang of heartsickness. He'd once described her eyes as the color of water in the tropics. It was a memory she'd have to carry with her the rest of her days, as it was becoming increasingly obvious that she wouldn't have the man.

"Well, then," James said, "what about a note from her housekeeper or butler? Something saying the house burned down."

"That is too cruel," Caroline said. "She would be beside herself with worry."

"That's the point," Blake put in. "We want her worried enough to leave."

"Couldn't you allude to a flood?" she asked. "It's ever so much less worrisome than a fire."

"While we're at it," James said, "why not throw in a rodent infestation?"

"Then she'll never leave!" Caroline exclaimed. "Who'd want to go home to a rat?"

"Many women of my acquaintance do," Blake said dryly.

"That's a terrible thing to say!"

"But true," James agreed.

Nobody said anything for a few moments, and then Caroline suggested, "I suppose we could just go on as we have been. It hasn't been so bad here in the bathroom now that Blake has taken to bringing me reading material. Although I would appreciate it if we could work out new arrangements regarding our meals."

"May I remind you," Blake said, "that in two weeks Riverdale and I will be launching our attack on Prewitt?"

"Attack?" Caroline exclaimed, clearly horrified.

"Attack, arrest," James said with a wave of his hand, "it all amounts to the same thing."

"Whatever the case," Blake said loudly, trying to regain their attention, "the last thing we need is the presence of my sister." He turned to Caroline. "I couldn't care less if you spend the next two weeks chained to my washbasin, but—"

"How hospitable of you," she muttered.

He ignored her. "I'll be damned if Prewitt slips through my fingers due to my sister's misplaced desire to see me married."

"I don't like the idea of playing a cruel prank on Penelope," Caroline said, "but I'm sure if the three of us put our heads together we can devise some sort of acceptable plan."

"I have a feeling that your definition of 'acceptable' and mine are vastly different," Blake commented.

Caroline scowled at him, then turned to James and smiled. "What do you think, James?"

He shrugged, looking more interested in the way Blake was glaring at the both of them than he was in her words.

But that was before they heard someone banging at the door.

They froze.

"Blake! Blake! Who are you talking to?"

Penelope.

Blake started motioning frantically toward the door to the side stairs while James pushed Caroline out. As soon as the door clicked behind her, Blake opened the bathroom door, and, with an utterly bland expression on his face, said, "Yes?"

Penelope peered in, her eyes darting from corner to corner. "What's going on?"

Blake blinked. "I beg your pardon?"

"Who were you talking to?"

James stepped out from behind a dressing screen. "Me."

Penelope's lips parted in surprise. "What are you doing here? I didn't realize you were back."

He leaned against the wall as if it were the most natural thing in the world for him to be in Blake's bathroom. "I returned about ten minutes ago."

"We had a few matters to discuss," Blake added.

"In the washing room?"

"Brings back memories of Eton and all that," James said with a devastating smile.

"Really?" Penelope did not sound convinced.

"No one had any privacy there, you know," Blake said. "It was really quite barbaric."

Penelope pointed to the pile of blankets on the floor. "What are those doing here?"

"What?" Blake asked, stalling for time.

"The blankets."

He blinked. "Those? I have no idea."

"You have a pile of blankets and pillows on the floor of your washing room and you don't know why?"

"I suppose Perriwick might have left them there. Maybe he meant to have them cleaned."

Penelope scowled. "Blake, you're an abominable liar."

"Actually, I'm a rather good liar. I'm just a touch out of practice."

"Then you do admit you're lying to me?"

"I don't think I admitted any such thing." He turned to James with a guileless expression. "Did I, Riverdale?"

"I don't think so. What do you think, Penelope?"

"I think," Penelope growled, "that neither of you is leaving this room until you tell me what is going on."

Caroline listened to the conversation through the door, holding her breath as Penelope grilled the two gentlemen with the skill of an executioner.

Caroline let out a silent sigh and sat down. The way things sounded in the bathroom, she might be stuck in the stairwell for hours. Penelope certainly exhibited no signs of giving up her interrogation.

Time to look on the bright side, she decided, dismissing the fact that it was dark as pitch in the stairwell. She might be trapped in the most bizarre of situations, but it was still heads and tails above being stuck with the Prewitts. Good heavens, if she hadn't run off, she'd probably be a Prewitt herself by now.

What a hideous thought.

But not nearly as hideous as what happened next. Maybe she'd stirred up some dust when she sat down, maybe the gods were simply aligned against her, but her nose began to tickle.

Then it began to itch.

She jammed the side of her index finger up against her nostrils, but it was to no avail.

Tickle, itch, tickle, itch.

Ah . . . Ah . . . Ah . . .

AH-CHOO!

"What was that?" Penelope demanded.

"What was what?" Blake replied at the very same moment James began to sneeze uncontrollably.

"Stop that ridiculous act," Penelope snapped at James. "I heard a female sneeze, and I heard it distinctly."

James started sneezing at a higher pitch.

"Cease!" Penelope ordered, striding toward the door to the stairs.

Blake and James made a mad dash toward her, but they were too late. Penelope had already wrenched the door open.

And there, on the landing, sat Caroline, hunched over, her entire body wracked by sneezes.

Chapter 19

lat·i·tu·di·nar·i·an *(adjective). Allowing, favoring, or characterized by latitude in opinion or action; not insisting on strict adherence to conformity with an established code.*

In Bournemouth—as opposed to London—one can act in a more latitudinarian *manner, but still, even when in the country, there are certain rules of conduct to which one must subscribe.*

—From the personal dictionary of Caroline Trent

"You!" Penelope accused. "What are you doing here?"

But her voice was drowned out by that of Blake, who was yelling at Caroline, "Why the hell didn't you run down the stairs when you heard us coming?"

His only answer was a sneeze.

James, who was rarely ruffled by anything, raised a brow and said, "It appears she's a bit incapacitated."

Caroline sneezed again.

Penelope turned to James, her expression furious. "I suppose you're in some way connected to this subterfuge as well."

He shrugged. "In some way."

Caroline sneezed.

"For heaven's sake," Penelope said testily, "get her out of the stairwell. Clearly there is something putrid amid the dust that is sending her into convulsions."

"She isn't having a bloody convulsive fit," Blake said. "She's sneezing."

Caroline sneezed.

"Well, whatever the case, move her into your bedroom. *No!* Not your bedroom. Move her into my bedroom." Penelope planted her hands on her hips and glared at everyone in turn. "And what the devil is going on here? I want to be apprised of the situation this very minute. If someone doesn't—"

"If I might be so bold," James interrupted.

"Shut up, Riverdale," Blake snapped as he picked up Caroline. "You sound like my damned butler."

"I'm sure Perriwick would be most flattered by the comparison," James said. "However, I was merely going to point out to Penelope that there is very little untoward about Caroline being in your bedroom, seeing as how she and I are also in attendance."

"Very well," Penelope conceded. "Set her down in your bedroom, Blake. Then I want to know what is going on. And no more nonsense about honey and pet birds."

Caroline sneezed.

Blake turned to his sister and suggested, "Maybe you could get her some tea?"

"Ha! If you think I'm going to leave her alone in here with the two of you—"

"*I'll* get some tea," James interrupted.

As soon as he left, Penelope narrowed her eyes at Blake and Caroline and demanded, "Are you having an affair?"

"No!" Caroline managed to exclaim between sneezes.

"Then you had best start explaining your presence. I had judged you to be a lady of stern moral character, and it is requiring all of my tolerance and broad-mindedness not to alter that opinion."

Caroline looked to Blake. She wasn't about to give away his secrets without his permission. But he just groaned, rolled his eyes, and said, "We might as well tell her the truth. Lord knows she's going to ferret it out eventually."

The entire tale took twenty minutes. It probably would have only required fifteen, except that James returned with the tea—thankfully accompanied by fresh scones—and the narrative naturally slowed while they all partook of it.

Penelope asked no questions during the telling except for "Milk?" and "Sugar?" which really didn't signify as she was pouring the tea.

Blake, James, and Caroline, however, interrupted one another to an astonishing degree. Still, after a quarter of an hour, they managed to relate the events of the past few weeks to everyone's satisfaction.

When they were through, Caroline watched Penelope's impassive face with a mixture of curiosity and dread. She had grown quite fond of Blake's sister, and it tore her heart in two to think that the countess would cut her off completely.

But Penelope surprised them all by murmuring a quiet, "I see," followed by an even quieter, "Hmmm."

Caroline leaned forward.

James leaned forward.

Blake started to lean forward, then caught himself and snorted in disgust. He was well used to his sister's tactics.

Finally Penelope took a deep breath, turned to Blake, and said, "You are a beast not to have informed the family of your governmental activities, but I will not address that insult now."

"How kind of you," he murmured.

"It is indeed lucky for you," she continued, "that the thoughtlessness of your secrecy has been eclipsed by a matter of even graver concern."

"Indeed."

Penelope glared at him as she jabbed her finger first at the marquis, then back at her brother. "One of you," she announced, "is going to have to marry her."

Caroline, who had been studiously examining the tips of her shoes so as not to give Blake an I-told-you-so smirk when Penelope scolded him about his secrecy, jerked her head up. The sight that awaited her was not reassuring.

Penelope was pointing her long index finger directly at her, and Blake and James had gone utterly white.

That evening found Blake having an exceedingly unpleasant conversation with his sister. She was trying to convince him to marry Caroline with all possible haste, and he was doing his best to ignore her.

He wasn't terribly worried about the outcome of this latest debacle. He had sworn never to marry; Penelope knew it, Caroline knew it, James knew it. Hell, the entire world knew it. And James wasn't the sort to let his best friend's sister goad him into doing anything he didn't want to do. In fact, the only way that Penelope could ensure that Caroline would be swiftly married would be to tell tales and create a huge scandal.

That, Blake was sure, was not a danger. Penelope might be willing to create a little gossip, but she wasn't about to ruin the woman she was now calling "my dearest, closest friend."

Penelope, could, however, endeavor to make a general nuisance of herself and annoy the hell out of everyone at Seacrest Manor. And in Blake's case, she was succeeding handily.

"Blake," she said, "you know you need a wife."

"I know no such thing."

"Caroline has been irrevocably compromised."

"Only if you decide to tell tales in London."

"That is beside the point."

"That is exactly the point," Blake growled. "She has been living here to safeguard national security."

"Oh please," Penelope said disdainfully. "She is staying here to escape the clutches of that guardian of hers."

"A guardian who is a threat to national security," Blake shot back. "And Caroline has been assisting us in his apprehension. A most noble endeavor if you ask me."

"I didn't ask you," Penelope said with a sniff.

"You should have," he snapped. "Caroline's presence here is vital to the security of England, and only the worst sort of unpatriotic buffoon would use that to ruin her reputation." So he was exaggerating a bit about the national security. Desperate times did occasionally call for desperate measures.

James chose that moment to wander in. "I suppose you're still talking circles around Caroline's future," he said.

They both leveled annoyed stares in his direction.

"Well," James said, stretching his arms like a cat and yawning as he sank onto a sofa, "I've been thinking about marrying her."

"Oh, how lovely!" Penelope exclaimed, clapping her hands together, but her comment was drowned out by Blake's yell of, "*WHAT?*"

James shrugged. "Why not? I have to get married eventually."

"Caroline deserves someone who will love her," Blake bit off.

"I certainly *like* her. That is more than most marriages can claim."

"That is true," Penelope said.

"You," Blake snapped, pointing at his sister. "Be quiet. And you—" He turned his furious visage toward the marquis, but intelligent discourse escaped him, so he just blurted out, "You be quiet, too."

"Well said." James chuckled.

Blake glared at him, feeling quite capable of murder.

"Tell me more," Penelope begged. "I think that Caroline will make a lovely marchioness."

"Indeed she would," James replied. "And it would be a rather convenient match. I do need to marry at some point, and it appears that Caroline needs to marry quite soon."

"There is no reason for her to marry," Blake growled, "as long as my sister keeps her mouth shut."

"Penelope is certainly discreet," James continued in a voice that Blake was beginning to find irritatingly jovial, "but that cannot be a guarantee that no one will find out about our peculiar living arrangements. Caroline might not be a member of the *ton*, but that does not mean that she deserves to have her name dragged through the mud."

Blake jumped to his feet and roared, "Don't you dare accuse me of wanting to sully her good name. Everything I have done—"

"The problem," Penelope smoothly interrupted, "is that you have done nothing."

"I refuse to sit here and—"

"You're standing," Penelope pointed out.

"James," Blake said in a dangerously low voice, "if you don't restrain me, I shall surely commit a great many crimes in the next ten seconds, the least regretful of which shall involve the painful death of my sister."

"Er . . . Penelope," James said, "I'd move out of his reach were I you. I think he might be serious."

"Bah!" was Penelope's response. "He's just out of sorts because he knows I'm right."

A muscle started twitching in Blake's jaw and he didn't even bother to look at James when he said, "You don't have a sister, do you, Riverdale?"

"No."

"Consider yourself blessed." Then he turned on his heel and stalked away.

James and Penelope stared at the doorway through which Blake had just exited until Penelope finally blinked a few times, turned to James and said, "I don't think he's very pleased with us just now."

"No."

"Were you serious?"

"About marrying Caroline?"

Penelope nodded.

"I would hardly make a statement like that if I weren't prepared to see it through."

"But you don't *want* to marry her," Penelope said, her eyes narrowing.

"Certainly not the way Blake does."

"Hmmm." She crossed the room and sat down. "You're quite clever, Riverdale, but your plan may very well backfire. Blake can be very stubborn."

James sat down across from her. "A fact of which I am well aware."

"I'm sure you are." She curved her lips, but it wasn't really a smile. "And are you also aware that I share the same trait?"

"Stubbornness, you mean? My dear Penelope, I would run unclothed across England in the dead of winter just to escape a battle of wills with the likes of you."

"Nicely put, but if your little declaration fails to produce the desired results, you *will* marry Caroline."

"I have no doubt that you will hold a pistol to my back until I do."

Penelope's voice rose. "This is not a joke, Riverdale."

"I know. But I meant what I said earlier. I need to marry eventually, and Caroline is a damned sight better than I'm likely to do if I go hunting for a wife in London."

"Riverdale!"

He shrugged. "It's true. I quite like Caroline, and if I have to marry her because Blake is too cowardly to do it himself—well, then, so be it. Frankly, I can think of worse fates."

"What a coil." Penelope sighed.

"Don't worry. Blake will propose," James said with a confident wave of his hand. "It'd kill him to see me married to her."

"I hope you're right. Lord knows he needs a little happiness." And then Penelope sighed and sagged back against the back of her chair. "I just want him to be happy. Is that so very much to ask?"

Outside the doorway, Caroline stood with her hand over her open mouth. She'd thought her humiliation was complete when Penelope had demanded that someone—anyone!—marry her. But this—

She choked back a sob. This went beyond humiliation. Humiliation was something she could live through, something she could endure and eventually put behind her.

But this was different. Something inside her was dying, and Caroline wasn't sure whether it was her heart or her soul.

It didn't matter which, she realized as she ran back up to her room. All that mattered was that she was hurting, and the pain was going to last the rest of her lifetime.

It took two hours, but eventually Caroline was able to compose herself. A bit of cold water reduced the puffiness around her eyes, and several minutes of deep breaths had managed to remove the quaver from her voice. Unfortunately, there wasn't much she could do to take her heart out of her eyes.

She made her way down the stairs and wasn't surprised to find James and Penelope still sitting in the drawing room. Their conversation drifted down the hall, and Caroline was thankful to hear that they had moved on to more ordinary topics.

They were discussing the theatre when she reached the doorway, and she knocked softly against the doorframe. James stood up instantly when he saw her.

"May I come in?" she asked.

"Of course," Penelope said. "Here, sit by me."

Caroline shook her head. "I'd rather stand, thank you.

"As you wish."

"Do you know where Blake is?" Caroline asked, her posture as regal as a queen's. "I wish to say this only once."

"I'm right here."

Caroline whipped her head around. Blake was standing in the doorway, his body somehow rigid and weary at the same time. His cheeks were touched with color, and she wondered if he'd been walking in the chill night air.

"Good. I would like to say something if I may."

"Please do," Blake said.

Caroline gave each of the room's three other occupants an assessing glance and then finally said, "I do not require a husband. I certainly do not require a husband who does not require a wife. All I wish is to be allowed to remain here, in hiding, until my twenty-first birthday."

"But Caroline!" Penelope protested. "These gentlemen have compromised you. You must allow one of them to make it right."

Caroline swallowed. She didn't have much in life, but she did have her pride, and she wasn't about to let Blake Ravenscroft humiliate her any more than he had already. She looked straight at him even as she addressed her words to his sister. "Lady Fairwich, these gentlemen have done nothing to compromise me."

"Nothing?" Blake asked.

Caroline glared at him, wondering what devil had prompted him to speak when he was so vocal about avoiding marriage. "Nothing which meant anything," she said in a scathing voice.

Their eyes met, and both knew she was talking about their encounter on the beach. The difference was that only Caroline knew she was lying.

Her time with Blake had meant everything to her.

Every minute of every encounter was held close to her heart.

She blinked back tears. Soon she'd be gone, and all she'd have to keep her warm inside were memories. There would be no man to hold her, no friends to tease her, no seaside manor that had, in just a few short weeks, become home.

But of all the things she would miss, the absence that would hurt the most was that of Blake's smile. It was so rare, but when his lips turned up at the edges . . . And then when he actually laughed, the pure joy of the sound made her want to sing.

But he wasn't smiling now. His face was hard, and he was glaring at her as if she were some sort of antidote, and she knew that if she didn't get out of the room that instant she was going to make an utter fool of herself. "Excuse me," she said quickly, rushing toward the door.

"You can't go now!" Penelope exclaimed, jumping to her feet.

Caroline didn't turn around as she said, "I've said what I came here to say."

"But where are you going?"

"Out."

"Caroline."

It was Blake's voice, and just the sound of it made her eyes tear up. "What?" she managed to say. Perhaps it was a rude reply, but it was the best she could do.

"It's dark out. Or hadn't you noticed?"

"I'm going out to look at the stars."

She heard his footsteps and then felt his hand on her shoulder, slowly drawing her away from the door.

"The night is cloudy," he said, his voice surprisingly gentle. "You won't be able to see the stars."

She didn't even turn around as she said, "I know they're there. And that's all that matters."

Blake closed his eyes as she ran from the room, for some reason not wanting to see her retreating form.

"Now look what you've done," he heard his sister say. "You've broken that poor girl's heart."

He didn't answer, not knowing—hell, not *wanting* to know if his sister's words were true. If he had broken her heart, then he was a bastard of the worst sort. And if it wasn't true, it meant that Caroline didn't care about him, that their one night of passion hadn't meant anything to her.

And that was almost too painful to bear.

He didn't want to think about what he felt for her. He didn't want to analyze it, to pick it to pieces, or to try to put a label on it. Because he was terrified that if he did, the only word he'd be able to come up with was *love,* and that would have to be the cruelest joke of all.

Blake opened his eyes just in time to see the expression of disgust on Riverdale's face as he said, "You're an ass, Ravenscroft."

Blake said nothing.

"Marabelle is dead," James hissed.

Blake turned on his friend with such violence that Penelope flinched. "Don't mention her," he said in a threatening voice. "She has no place in this conversation."

"Exactly," James replied. "She's dead, and you can't go on mourning her forever."

"You don't know," Blake said, shaking his head. "You don't know what it's like to love."

"And you know all too well," James murmured. "In fact, you've known twice."

"Blake," Penelope said softly, putting her hand on his arm. "I know you loved her. We all loved her. But Marabelle wouldn't have wanted you to go on like this. You're just a shell. You buried your soul along with hers."

Blake swallowed convulsively, wanting more than anything to flee the room, yet somehow he remained rooted to the spot.

"Let her go," Penelope whispered. "It's time, Blake. And Caroline loves you."

His head whipped around. "She said that?"

Penelope wanted to lie. He could see it in her eyes. But finally she shook her head. "No, but it's easy to see."

"I won't hurt her," he vowed. "She deserves better."

"Then marry her," Penelope implored.

He shook his head. "If I marry her . . . God, I'd hurt her in more ways than you could imagine."

"Bloody hell!" James burst out. "Stop being so damned afraid. You're afraid of loving, you're afraid of living. The only bloody thing you're not afraid of is death. I'll give you one night. One night only."

Blake narrowed his eyes. "For what?"

"To make up your mind. But I promise you this: I *will* marry Caroline if you don't. So ask yourself if you'll be able to bear *that* for a lifetime."

James turned on his heel and stalked from the room.

"He's not making an idle threat," Penelope said. "He's quite fond of her."

"I know that," Blake snapped.

Penelope gave him a brief nod, then walked to the door. "I'll leave you to your thoughts."

That, Blake thought bitterly, was the last thing he wanted.

Chapter 20

hal·cy·on *(adjective). Calm, quiet, peaceful, undisturbed.*

I shan't look back upon these as halcyon *days.*

—From the personal dictionary of Caroline Trent

Caroline was sitting on the sandy portion of the beach, gazing up at the sky. Just as Blake had pointed out, it was cloudy, so all she could see was the pale, blurry glow of the moon. She wrapped her arms around her bent knees and huddled against the cool breeze, her shoes lying next to her.

"It doesn't matter," she told herself, wiggling her toes in the coarse sand. "It just doesn't matter."

"What doesn't matter?"

Her head jerked up. Blake.

"How did you get here without my hearing you?"

He motioned behind him. "There is another path about fifty yards back."

"Oh. Well, if you have come to check up on me, you'll see that I am perfectly fine, and you can go back to the house."

"Caroline." He cleared his throat. "There are a few things I need to tell you."

She looked away. "You don't owe me any explanations."

He sat down beside her, unconsciously adopting the same position. He rested his chin on his knees and said, "There were reasons I swore never to marry."

"I don't want to hear it."

"Nonetheless, I need to say it."

She didn't say anything, so he continued. "When Marabelle died . . ." His voice caught.

"You don't have to do this," she said quickly. "Please."

He ignored her. "When she died, I thought—I felt—God, it's so hard to put into words." He exhaled, a world of heartbreak in that rush of air. "I was dead inside. That's the only way to describe it."

Caroline swallowed, barely able to resist the impulse to offer him the comfort of her hand on his arm.

"I can't be what you need."

"I know," she said bitterly. "I can't compete with a dead woman, after all."

He flinched at her words. "I swore I'd never marry. I—"

"I never asked that of you. I may have— Never mind."

"You may have what?"

Caroline just shook her head, unwilling to tell him that she may have wished for it. "Please continue," she said in a distracted voice.

He nodded, although it was clear that he was still curious about what she'd almost said. "I always told myself that I could not marry out of respect for Marabelle, that I didn't want to be disloyal to her memory. And I think I really believed it. But tonight I realized that was no longer true."

She turned to face him, a thousand questions in her eyes.

"Marabelle's dead," he said in a hollow voice. "And I know that. I can't bring her back. I never thought I could. It's just . . ."

"It's just what, Blake?" she prompted in a low, urgent voice. "Please tell me. Make me understand."

"I felt I couldn't fail her in death as I had in life."

"Oh, Blake. You've never failed anyone." She touched his arm. "Someday you'll have to realize that."

"I know." He closed his eyes for a moment. "I've always known that, deep down. She was so headstrong. I couldn't have stopped her."

"Then why are you so determined to be unhappy?"

"It isn't about Marabelle any longer. It's me."

"I don't understand."

"Somewhere along the way I lost something inside. I don't know whether it was the grief or the bitterness, but I just stopped caring."

"That's not true. I know you better than you think."

"Caroline, I feel nothing!" he burst out. "Nothing deep and meaningful, at least. Don't you see that I'm dead inside?"

She shook her head. "Don't say that. It's not true."

He grasped her shoulder with startling urgency. "It *is* true. And you deserve more than I can give you."

She stared at his hand. "You don't know what you're saying," she whispered.

"The hell I don't." He wrenched himself away from her and stood, his posture bleak as he stared at the surf. After a moment of silence he said, "James has said he will marry you."

"I see."

"Is that all you have to say?"

She let out an impatient exhale. "What do you want me to say, Blake? Tell me, and I'll say it. But I don't know what you want. I don't even know what I want anymore." She buried her face in her knees. That was a lie. She knew exactly what she wanted, and he was standing next to her, telling her to marry another man.

She wasn't surprised, but she hadn't expected it to hurt so much.

"He'll take care of you," Blake said in a low voice.

"I'm sure he will."

"Will you accept?"

She looked up sharply. "Do you care?"

"How can you ask that?"

"I thought you didn't feel. I thought you didn't care about anything."

"Caroline, I do care about your future. I just can't be what you need in a husband."

"That's an excuse." She stood, her posture militant. "You're nothing but a coward, Blake Ravenscroft."

She started to walk away, but her feet sank in the sand, and he was able to catch up with her quickly. "Don't touch me!" she yelled when his hand closed around her arm. "Leave me alone."

He didn't let go. "I want you to accept Riverdale's proposal."

"You have no right to tell me what to do."

"I know that. But I'm asking nonetheless."

Caroline let her head fall back. Her breath came in short, shallow pants, and she squeezed her eyes shut for a moment against the emotions colliding in her mind. "Go away," she finally managed to say.

"Not until I have your word that you will marry Riverdale."

"No!" she cried out. "No! I won't marry him. I don't love him and he doesn't love me, and that's not what I want."

His grip tightened around her arm. "Caroline, you must listen to me. Riverdale will—"

"No!" With strength that was born of fury and heartbreak, she yanked her arm away and started to run down the beach. She ran until her lungs burned, until her eyes were so filled with tears that she couldn't see. She ran until the pain in her body finally eclipsed that in her heart.

She stumbled along the sand, trying to ignore the sound of Blake's footsteps drawing closer. Then his body slammed into hers with stunning force, knocking them both to the ground. Caroline landed on her back, with Blake's body covering hers intimately.

"Caroline," he said, his breath coming in hard pants.

She stared up at him, her eyes wildly searching his face for some sign that he loved her. And then she reached out, grabbed the back of his head, and pulled his mouth down to hers, kissing him with all the love and desperation in her heart.

Blake tried to resist. He couldn't have her; he knew that. She was going to marry his best friend. But her lips were sweet and demanding, and the press of her body against his turned his blood to flame.

He murmured her name over and over, like a mantra. He'd tried to be noble, he'd tried to push her away, but he wasn't strong enough to say no when her tongue was on his lips and her bare feet were rubbing along his calves.

His hands were nimble and quick, and he had her dress off in under ten seconds. He laid it down beneath her to protect her from the sand, but that was his last rational thought before his entire being was overtaken by the need to possess her.

"I will have you," he vowed, rubbing his fingertips past her calves to her thighs.

"I will have you," he pledged, yanking off her chemise and placing his hand over her heart.

"I will have you," he groaned, just before his mouth closed over her nipple.

All she said was, "Yes."

And Blake's heart soared.

Caroline arched her back as high-pitched sounds of desire escaped her mouth. It seemed that for every longing he fulfilled, he created two more, whipping her body into a frenzy of need.

She wasn't certain what to do, but she knew she wanted to feel his skin against hers, so she moved her hands to the buttons of his shirt. Her movements were rough and clumsy, however, and she soon found herself pushed aside by Blake, who tore the garment off with a savage cry.

A second later, he was back on top of her, the heat of his bare chest against hers. His mouth slanted over hers, and he devoured her from the inside out.

She moaned into him, clutching at his back, then skimming her hands down to the waistband of his breeches. She paused, gathered her courage, then hooked one finger underneath., touching the smooth skin of his buttocks.

Blake's lips slid across her cheek to her ear, murmuring, "I want to feel you," against her skin. His breath was hot and moist, and so very erotic. She could feel each of his words even more than she could hear them.

"I want to feel you, too," she whispered.

"Oh, you shall. You shall." He rolled off her just long enough to divest himself of the rest of his clothing, and then he was on top of her again, the hot, naked length of him burning into her skin.

The surf was rising, and the cold water tickled her bare toes. Caroline shivered, but the movement only rubbed her more intimately against Blake, and she heard him groan with desire.

"I'm going to touch you," he whispered, his voice hot against her cheek.

She knew what he meant, but it was still a shock when he brushed his fingers against her most intimate place. She stiffened, then relaxed as his lips pressed up against her ear with a soft, "Shhh."

One finger slipped inside her, and she gasped with pleasure. "I want to touch you, too," she said.

He let out a ragged breath. "It would probably kill me if you did."

Her eyes flew to his face.

"I want you so much," he tried to explain. "I'm damned near bursting with it, and I can't—"

"Shhh." It was her turn now to comfort him, and she placed a gentle finger on his lips. "Just show me. Show me everything. I want to please you."

A hoarse sound came from deep in Blake's throat as he nudged her legs apart. He touched her with the very tip of his manhood and nearly flinched at the pleasure of the contact. She was so hot and willing, and he knew she wanted *him*, damaged soul and all.

"Oh, Caroline, I'll make this good for you," he vowed. "I'll bring you such joy. I promise."

"You already have," she said softly, then gasped as he began to penetrate her.

He took her slowly, giving her body time to adjust to his size and strength. It was so difficult to hold back when every fiber of his being ached to pound into her, branding her as his own. Something very primitive had been awakened inside him, and he didn't just want to make love to her; he wanted to devour her, possess her, bring her such pleasure that she couldn't even dream of giving herself to another.

But he held back, straining to maintain a gentle touch. She wasn't ready for the ferocity of his desire. She wouldn't understand it. And he cared too much to frighten her.

He cared.

It was a stunning revelation, and his entire body froze.

"Blake?"

He'd known he liked her, he'd known he desired her. But it had taken this moment of intimacy to realize that his emotions were far more intense. He, who had thought that he'd lost the power to feel anything deeply, had been touched by this woman, and—

"Blake?"

He looked down.

"Is something wrong?"

"No," he said, a touch of wonder in his voice. "No. As a matter of fact, I think that everything might actually be just right."

A hint of a smile graced her lips. "What do you mean?"

"I'll tell you later," he said, worried that this magical feeling might disappear if he examined it too closely. "But for now . . ."

He pushed forward. Caroline gasped.

"Did I hurt you?" he asked.

"No. It's just that—I feel so, well, *full* somehow."

Blake let out a shout of laughter. "I'm not even halfway there," he said with an amused smile.

Her mouth fell open. "You're not?"

"Not yet," he said solemnly. "Although this"—he pressed forward, the motion bringing exquisite friction to them both—"does bring me a little closer."

She gulped. "Only closer? Not all the way there?"

He smiled slowly and shook his head. "Of course if I did this"—he gave his hips a tiny thrust—"I'd be almost there."

"But did you— Am I still—"

"—a virgin?" he completed for her. "Technically, I suppose, yes, but as far as I'm concerned, you're mine."

Caroline swallowed and blinked back tears, barely able to contain her emotions. It was amazing what a simple sentence could do to her. *You're mine.* Oh, how she wanted that to be true. Forever.

"Make me yours," she whispered. "In every way."

She could see in his face how much his restraint was costing him. The night air was chilly, but Blake's brow was beaded with sweat, and the muscular cords of his throat stood out prominently.

"I don't want to hurt you," he said, his voice straining against itself.

"You won't."

And then, as if the last bit of his reserve had been used up, he let out a hoarse cry and plunged forward, sheathing himself within her completely. "Sweet Lord," he gasped. "Caroline."

She couldn't fight off a crazy urge to laugh. "Oh, Blake," she gasped. "I see the difference now."

"Do you?"

"There's more?"

He nodded. "Just wait and see."

And then he began to move.

* * *

Later Caroline couldn't decide which part she'd liked best. Was it the feeling of completeness she felt when they were joined as one? Was it the primitive rhythm of his body as he claimed her as his own? Certainly she couldn't discount the explosive climax she'd felt, immediately followed by Blake's shout of passion as he left his seed in her.

But now, as she lay in his arms, the ocean breeze caressing their bodies, she thought that *this* might be the best of all. He was so warm and close, and she could hear his heartbeat as it slowed to its normal, sedate pace. She could smell the salt on his skin and the passion in the air. And there was something so *right* about it all, as if she'd waited her whole life just for this moment.

But mixed in with her happiness was an uneasy fear. What happened now? Did this mean he wanted to marry her? And if he did, was that only because he now felt it was the right thing to do? And if that were the case, did she care?

Well, of course she *cared*. She wanted him to love her with the intensity of emotion she felt for him. But maybe he would learn to love her if they were married. She *might* be miserable if she married a man who didn't love her, but she *knew* she'd be miserable without him. Maybe she should just close her eyes, jump in, and hope for the best.

Or maybe, she thought with a frown, she ought to remember that he hadn't said more than two words to her since they'd made love, and certainly nothing about marriage.

"Why the long face?" Blake asked, idly stroking her hair with his fingers.

She shook her head. "Nothing. Just woolgathering."

"About me, I imagine," he said quietly. "And my intentions."

She drew back in horror. "I would never dream of manipulating you into—"

"Shush," he said with soft authority. "I know."

"You do?"

"We will be married as soon as I can obtain a special license."

Her heart leaped. "Are you sure?"

"What kind of question is that?"

"A stupid one," she mumbled. Hadn't she just decided that she didn't care if he wanted to marry her just because it was the right thing to do?

No, that wasn't right. She did care. She was just going to marry him anyway.

"Caroline?" Amusement was evident in his voice.

"Yes?"

"Are you going to answer my question?"

She blinked. "Did you ask me one?"

"I asked you if you would . . ." He paused. "No, actually I didn't ask."

Before Caroline realized what he was about, he rolled over and got up on one knee. "Caroline Trent, soon to be Ravenscroft," he said, "will you do me the honor of becoming my wife?"

If her eyes hadn't filled with so many tears, she might have actually chuckled at the sight of him proposing to her stark naked. "Yes," she said, nodding furiously. "Yes, yes, yes."

He lifted her hand to his lips and kissed it. "Good."

Caroline closed her eyes for a few seconds. She wanted to close off all her senses so that she might savor the moment in her mind. No sight, no touch, no smell—nothing to distract her from the exquisite joy in her heart.

"Caroline?"

"Shhh." She waved her hand at him and then, a few seconds later, opened her eyes and said, "There. What were you going to say?"

His expression was curious. "What was that all about?"

"Nothing, I— Oh look!" She pointed up at the sky.

"What?" he asked, his eyes following her finger.

"The sky must have cleared up. The stars are out."

"So they are," he murmured, a ghost of a smile touching his lips. "But then again, you were the one who said they were there all along."

Caroline squeezed his hand in hers. "Yes," she agreed. "They were."

A half hour later they were dressed—albeit rather disheveled—and trying to slip into the house as quietly as possible.

James, however, was waiting in the front hall.

"I told you we should have used the back stairs," Caroline muttered.

"I assume you're back for the night?" James said mildly. "Perriwick wanted to lock the door, but I wasn't sure you'd brought a key."

"We've decided to be married," Blake blurted out.

James merely lifted one eyebrow and murmured, "I thought you might."

Chapter 21

prov•e•nance *(noun). Origin, derivation.*

I cannot claim to know or understand the provenance *of romantic love, but I'm not sure that it is something that needs to be understood, just appreciated and revered.*

—From the personal dictionary of Caroline Ravenscroft

They were married one week later, much to the delight of Penelope, who insisted upon purchasing a trousseau for the bride. Caroline had thought that the two ready-made dresses Blake had purchased for her were a luxury, but nothing could compare to Penelope's idea of a suitable wardrobe. Caroline let her soon-to-be sister choose everything—with one exception. The dressmaker owned a bolt of blue-green silk the exact color of her eyes, and Caroline insisted upon having an evening gown fashioned out of it. She had never given much thought to her eyes before, but after Blake had skimmed his fingers across her eyelids and declared her eyes the exact color of the ocean at the equator . . . Well, she really couldn't help becoming a little bit proud of them.

The wedding ceremony was small and private, with only Penelope, James, and Seacrest Manor's servants in attendance. Blake's older brother had wanted to come, but one of his daughters had taken ill, and he didn't want to leave her. Caroline thought that was as it should be and penned him a note expressing her desire to meet him at a more convenient time.

Perriwick gave the bride away. Mrs. Mickle was so jealous she insisted upon playing the part of mother of the bride, even though that role didn't entail her actually taking part in the ceremony.

Penelope was matron of honor, and James was best man, and a lovely time was had by all.

Caroline smiled her way through the next few days. She couldn't ever remember being as happy as she was as Caroline Ravenscroft of Seacrest Manor. She had a husband and a home, and her life was as near to perfect as she could imagine. Blake hadn't professed his love to her, but she supposed that was too much to expect from a man who had until recently been in so much emotional pain.

In the meantime, she would make him as happy as she could, and let him do the same for her.

* * *

Now that Caroline truly belonged to Seacrest Manor and vice versa, she was determined to make her mark on the small estate. She was puttering in the garden when Perriwick approached her. "Mrs. Ravenscroft," he said, "you have a visitor."

"I do?" she asked in surprise. Hardly anyone even *knew* she was Mrs. Ravenscroft. "Who?"

"A Mr. Oliver Prewitt."

She paled. "Oliver? But why . . ."

"Do you want me to send him away? Or I could have Mr. Ravenscroft deal with him, if that is preferable."

"No, no," she said quickly. She didn't want her husband seeing Oliver. Blake was likely to lose his temper, and he'd hate himself later for it. She knew how important it was to him to apprehend Oliver and his entire ring of spies. If he blew his cover now, he'd never get the chance.

"I'll see him," she said in a firm voice. She took a deep, cleansing breath and set down her work gloves. Oliver had no power over her now, and she refused to be afraid of him.

Perriwick motioned for her to follow him into the house, and they made their way to the drawing room. As she passed through the doorway, she saw Oliver's back, and her entire body tensed.

She'd almost forgotten how much she hated him.

"What do you want, Oliver?" she said in a flat voice.

He looked up at her, seven different kinds of menace lurking in his eyes. "That isn't a very affectionate greeting for your guardian."

"My *former* guardian," she corrected.

"A minor technicality," he said with a little wave of his hand.

"Get to the point, Oliver," she ground out.

"Very well." He walked slowly toward her until they were nose to nose. "You owe me," he said in a low voice.

She didn't flinch. "I owe you nothing."

They stood that way, staring each other down, until he broke away and walked to the window. "Quite a nice piece of property you have here."

Caroline suppressed the urge to scream in frustration. "Oliver," she warned, "my patience is wearing thin. If you have something to say to me, say it. Otherwise, get out."

He whirled around. "I ought to kill you," he hissed.

"You could," she said, trying not to show any reaction to his threat, "but you'd go to the gallows, and I don't think you want that."

"You've ruined everything. Everything!"

"If you mean your little plot to make me the next Prewitt," she spat out, "then yes, I have. Shame on you, Oliver."

"I gave you food. I gave you shelter. And you repaid me with the worst sort of betrayal."

"You ordered your son to rape me!"

He advanced, jabbing his stubby finger in her direction. "That wouldn't have been necessary if you'd cooperated. You always knew you were meant to marry Percy."

"I knew no such thing. And Percy didn't want the marriage any more than I did."

"Percy does what I tell him to."

"I know," she said in a disgusted voice.

"Do you have any idea the plans I had for your fortune? I owe money, Caroline. Lots of money."

She blinked in surprise. She had no idea Oliver was in debt. "That's not my problem or my fault. And you certainly lived well enough off my money while I was your ward."

He let out a bark of angry laughter. "Your money was tied up tighter than a chastity belt. I received a small quarterly allowance to cover your living expenses, but it was nothing more than a pittance."

She stared at him in shock. Oliver had always lived so well. He insisted upon the finest of everything. "Then where did all your money come from?" she asked. "The new candelabra, the fancy carriage . . . how did you pay for them?"

"That was from—" His lips pressed together in a firm and angry line. "That's none of your business."

Her eyes widened. Oliver had almost admitted to smuggling—she was sure of it. Blake would be very interested.

"The real power was to come when you married Percy," he continued. "Then I would have had control over everything."

She shook her head, stalling for time while she thought of something to say that might prompt him to incriminate himself. "I would never have done it," she finally blurted out, knowing she had to say something to keep him from growing suspicious. "I would never have married him."

"You would have done what I told you to!" he roared. "If I had gotten to you before that idiot you call your husband, I would have held my boot to the back of your head until you obeyed."

Caroline saw red. It was one thing to threaten her, but no one called her husband an idiot. "If you do not leave this instant, I will have you forcibly removed." She no longer cared if he incriminated himself or not—she just wanted him out of her house.

" 'I'll have you forcibly removed,' " he mimicked. His lips spread into a menacing grin. "Surely you can do better than that, Caroline. Or should I say Mrs. Ravenscroft? My, my, how we've come up in the world. The newspaper mentioned that your new husband is the son of Viscount Darnsby."

"There was an announcement in the newspaper?" she whispered in shock. She'd been wondering how Oliver had known where to find her.

"Don't try to act surprised, you little slut. I know you put that announcement there so I would see it. It's not as if you have any friends you'd want to notify."

"But who—" She caught her breath. Penelope. Of course. In her world, marriages were immediately announced in the newspaper. She'd probably forgotten all about the need for secrecy.

She pursed her lips and suppressed a sigh, not wanting to show any signs of weakness. Oliver shouldn't have learned of her connection to Blake until after his arrest, but there was nothing to be done about it now. "I asked you once to leave," she said, trying to be patient. "Don't make me repeat myself."

"I'm not going anywhere until I'm good and ready. You owe me, girl."

"I owe you nothing except a slap in the face. Now, leave."

He closed the remaining distance between them and grabbed her arm in a painful grasp. "I want what's mine."

She gaped at him while she tried to free herself from his grip. "What are you talking about?"

"You're going to sign half your fortune to me. As payment for my tender care in raising you to womanhood."

She laughed in his face.

"You little whore," he hissed. And then before she had any time to react, he picked up his free hand and smacked her across the face.

She jerked backward, and would have probably fallen to the ground if he weren't holding her arm so tightly. She said nothing; she didn't trust herself to speak. And her cheek stung. Oliver had been wearing a ring, and she feared she was now bleeding.

"Did you trick him into marriage?" he taunted. "Did you sleep with him?"

Fury gave her the strength to wrench her arm away, and she stumbled against a chair. "Get out of my house."

"Not until you sign this."

"I couldn't even if I wanted to," she said with a self-satisfied smirk. "When I married Mr. Ravenscroft, my fortune became his. You know the laws of England as well as I do."

Oliver started to shake with fury, and Caroline grew bold. "You're welcome to ask my husband for the money, but I warn you, he's the devil's own temper, and"—she let her eyes travel up and down Oliver's thin frame in an insulting manner—"he's quite larger than you."

Oliver seethed at her implication. "You will pay for what you've done to me." He advanced upon her again, but before his arm descended to hit her, they heard a roar from the doorway.

"What the hell is going on here?"

Caroline looked over and breathed a sigh of relief. Blake.

Oliver appeared not to know what to say, and he simply froze, his arm still raised to strike her.

"Were you planning to hit my wife?" Blake's voice was low and deadly. He sounded calm, too calm.

Oliver said nothing.

Blake's gaze zeroed in on the welt on Caroline's cheek. "Did you hit her already, Prewitt? Caroline, did he strike you?"

She nodded, mesmerized by the barely leashed fury in him.

"I see," Blake said mildly, pulling off his gloves as he walked into the room. He handed them to Caroline, who took them wordlessly.

Blake turned back to Oliver. "That, I'm afraid, was a mistake."

Oliver's eyes bugged out. It was clear he was terrified. "I beg your pardon?"

Blake shrugged. "I really hate to have to touch you, but . . ."

WHAM! Blake's fist connected with Oliver's eye socket. The older man went tumbling to the ground.

Caroline's mouth fell open. Her head swung to Blake, down to Oliver, and back to Blake. "You looked so calm."

Her husband just stared at her. "Did he hurt you?"

"Did he— No, well, yes, just a little bit." Her hand went to her cheek.

THUNK. Blake kicked Oliver in the ribs. He looked back at her. "That's for hurting my wife."

She swallowed. "It was really more the shock than anything else, Blake. Maybe you shouldn't—"

THWAK. Blake kicked Oliver in the hip. "That," he spat, "is for shocking her."

Caroline clapped her hand over her mouth to hold in nervous laughter.

"Is there anything else you need to tell me?"

She shook her head, afraid that if she opened her mouth one more time he would kill Oliver. Not that the world wouldn't be a finer place for it, but she had no wish for Blake to go to the gallows.

Blake cocked his head slightly to the side as he looked at her a little more closely. "You're bleeding," he whispered.

She lifted her hand from her cheek and looked at it. There was blood on her fingers. Not much, but enough to make her instinctively press her hand back up against the wound.

Blake pulled out a handkerchief. She reached out to take it, but he dodged her hand and instead dabbed the snowy white linen to her cheek murmuring, "Let me."

Caroline had never before had anyone to tend to her wounds, minor or otherwise, and she found his touch oddly soothing.

"I should get some water to clean this off," he said gruffly.

"I'm sure it will be fine. It's a shallow cut."

He nodded. "For a second I thought he'd scarred you. I would have killed him for that."

From the floor, Oliver emitted a groan.

Blake stared at Caroline. "If you ask me to, I will kill him."

"Oh, no, Blake. No. Not like this."

"What the hell do you mean, not like this?" Oliver snapped.

Caroline looked down. Obviously, he'd regained consciousness. Or perhaps he'd never lost it. She said, "I wouldn't mind, however, if you booted him out of the house."

Blake nodded. "Gladly." He picked Oliver up by his collar and the seat of his pants and strode out into the hall. Caroline scurried after him, wincing when Oliver bellowed, "I will summon the magistrate! See if I don't! You'll pay for this!"

"I *am* the magistrate," Blake bit out. "And if you trespass on my land again, I'll arrest you myself." With that, he tossed him out onto the front steps and slammed the door.

He turned around and regarded his wife, who was standing in the hall, staring at him open-mouthed. There was still a bit of blood on her cheek, and some on the tips of her fingers. His heart clenched. He knew she hadn't suffered a serious injury, but somehow that didn't matter. Prewitt had hurt her and he hadn't been there to prevent it.

"I'm so sorry," he said, his voice somewhere between a whisper and a murmur.

She blinked. "But why?"

"I should have been here. I should never have let you see him alone."

"But you didn't even know he was here."

"That's not the point. You are my wife. I swore to protect you."

"Blake," she said gently, "you can't save the entire world."

He stepped toward her, knowing his heart was in his eyes, but somehow not minding this weakness. "I know that. I only want to save you."

"Oh, Blake."

He gathered her into his arms and pulled her close, heedless of the blood on her cheek. "I won't fail you again," he vowed.

"You could never fail me."

He stiffened. "I failed Marabelle."

"You told me you'd finally accepted that her death wasn't your fault," she said, wiggling free.

"I did. I do." He closed his eyes for a moment. "It still haunts me. If you could have seen her . . ."

"Oh, no," she gasped. "I didn't know you were there. I didn't know you'd seen her be killed."

"I didn't," he said flatly. "I was in bed with a putrid throat. But when she didn't return on schedule, Riverdale and I went out looking for her."

"I'm so sorry."

His voice grew hollow as the memories overtook him. "There was so much blood. She'd been shot four times."

Caroline thought about how much blood had gushed from Percy's flesh wound. She couldn't even imagine how awful it must be to see a loved one fatally injured. "I wish I knew what to say, Blake. I wish there *was* something to say."

He turned to face her abruptly. "Do you hate her?"

"Marabelle?" she asked, startled.

He nodded.

"Of course not!"

"You once told me you didn't want to compete with a dead woman."

"Well, I was jealous," she said sheepishly. "I don't hate her. That would be rather narrow-minded of me, don't you think?"

He shook his head, as if to dismiss the subject. "I was just wondering. I wouldn't have been angry if you did."

"Marabelle is a part of who you are," she said. "How can I hate her when she was so important in making you the man you are today?"

He watched her face, his eyes searching for something. Caroline felt naked under his gaze. She said softly, "If it weren't for Marabelle you might not be the man I—" She swallowed, summoning her courage. "You might not be the man I love."

He stared at her for a long moment, and then took her hand. "That is the most generous emotion anyone has ever shown to me."

She stared at him through moist eyes, waiting, hoping, praying that he'd return the sentiment. He looked as if he wanted to say something important, but after a few moments he merely cleared his throat and said, "Were you working in the garden?"

She nodded, swallowing down the lump of disappointment that had just formed in her throat.

He offered her his arm. "I'll escort you back. I should like to see what you've done."

Patience, Caroline told herself. Remember, patience.

But that was far easier said than done when one was courting a broken heart.

* * *

Later that evening, Blake was sitting in the dark in his study, staring out the window.

She had said that she loved him. It was an awesome responsibility, that.

Deep down, he had known that she cared for him deeply, but it had been so long since he'd even thought about the concept of love, he hadn't thought he'd recognize it when it arose.

But it had, and he did, and he knew that Caroline's feelings were true.

"Blake?"

He looked up. Caroline was standing in the doorway, her hand raised to knock again on the doorjamb.

"Why are you sitting here in the dark?"

"I'm just thinking."

"Oh." He could tell she wanted to ask more. Instead, she smiled hesitantly and said, "Would you like me to light a candle?"

He shook his head, slowly rising to his feet. He had the oddest desire to kiss her.

It wasn't odd that he wanted to kiss her in and of itself. He always wanted to kiss her. What was odd was the intensity of the need. It was almost as if he positively, definitively *knew* that if he didn't kiss her that very minute, his life would be forever changed, and not for the better.

He had to kiss her. That was all there was to it.

He walked across the room as if in a trance. She said something to him, but he didn't hear the words. He just kept moving slowly, inexorably to her side.

Caroline's lips parted slightly in surprise. Blake was acting most oddly. It was as if his mind were somewhere else, and yet he was staring at her with the strangest intensity.

She whispered his name for what must have been the third time, but he made no response, and then he was right in front of her.

"Blake?"

He touched her cheek with a reverence that made her tremble.

"Is something wrong?"

"No," he murmured. "No."

"Then what—"

Whatever she'd meant to say was lost as he crushed her to him, his mouth capturing hers with ferocious tenderness. She felt one of his hands sink into her hair as the other roamed the length of her back before settling on the curve of her hip.

Then he moved to the small of her back, pulling her against his body until she could feel the force of his arousal. Her head lolled back as she moaned his name, and his lips moved to the line of her throat, kissing their way to the bodice of her gown.

She let out a little squeal when his hand slipped from her hip to her buttocks and squeezed, and the sound must have jolted him out of whatever spell he was under, because he suddenly froze, shook his head a little, and stepped back.

"I'm sorry," he said, blinking. "I don't know what came over me."

Her mouth fell open. "You're sorry?" He kissed her until she could barely stand and then he stopped and said he was *sorry*?

"It was the strangest thing," he said, more to himself than to her.

"I didn't think it was that strange," she muttered.

"I had to kiss you."

"That's all?" she blurted out.

He smiled slowly. "Well, at first, yes, but now . . ."

"Now what?" she demanded.

"You're an impatient wench."

She stamped her foot. "Blake, if you don't—"

"If I don't what?" he asked, his grin positively devilish.

"Don't make me say it," she muttered, turning a rather bright shade of red.

"I think we'll save that for next week," he murmured. "After all, you're still something of an innocent. But for now I think you'd better run."

"Run?"

He nodded. "Fast."

"Why?"

"You're about to find out."

She skidded toward the door. "What if I want to get caught?"

"Oh, you definitely want to get caught," he replied, advancing on her with the lithe grace of a born predator.

"Then why should I run?" she asked, breathless.

"It's really more fun that way."

"It is?"

He nodded. "Trust me."

"Hmmph. Famous last words." But even as she said that, she was already in the hall, walking backward toward the stairs with remarkable speed.

He licked his lips.

"Oh. Then I had better . . . I should . . ."

He started moving faster.

"Oh, dear." She took off at a sprint, laughing all the way up the stairs.

Blake caught up with her on the landing, heaved her over his shoulder, and carried her, unconvincing protests and all, to their bedroom.

Then he kicked the door shut and proceeded to show her why getting caught was oftentimes even more fun than the chase.

Chapter 22

con·tu·ma·cious *(adjective). Obstinately resisting authority; stubbornly perverse.*

There are times when one must act in a contumacious *manner, even if one's husband is extensively displeased.*

—From the personal dictionary of Caroline Ravenscroft

In a few short days, the honeymoon was over. It was time to capture Oliver.

Never had Blake so resented his work for the War Office. He didn't want to hunt down criminals; he wanted to walk along the beach with his wife. He didn't want to dodge bullets, he wanted to laugh as he pretended to dodge Caroline's kisses.

Most of all, he wanted to trade the prickly fear of discovery for the heady sensation of falling in love.

It felt good to finally admit it to himself. He was falling in love with his wife.

He felt as if he were going over a cliff, grinning as he watched the ground rushing to meet him. He smiled at the oddest times, laughed inappropriately, and found himself oddly desolate when he didn't know where she was. It was like being crowned king of the world, inventing a cure for cancer, and discovering one could fly—all in one day.

He had never dreamed he could be this fascinated by another human being. He loved to watch the play of emotion on her face—the soft curve of her lips when she was amused, the scrunch of her brow when she was perplexed.

He even liked to watch her when she slept, her soft brown hair spread like a fan on her pillow. Her chest rose and fell in the even rhythm of her breath, and she looked so gentle and at peace. He'd once asked her if her demons disappeared when she was asleep.

Her answer had melted his heart.

"I don't have demons any longer," she'd replied.

And Blake had realized that his demons were finally disappearing, as well. It was the laughter that was driving them out, he decided. Caroline had the most amazing ability to find humor in the most mundane of topics. He was also discovering that she prided herself on being something of a mimic. What she lacked in talent, she made up for in enthusiasm, and Blake often found himself doubled over with laughter.

She was getting ready for bed right then, humming to herself in the washing room, *her* washing room, she'd dubbed it, since she'd lived there for nearly a week. Already her feminine accouterments—not that she'd had any before Penelope had taken her shopping—were crowding his belongings, pushing his shaving kit to the side.

And Blake loved it. He loved every intrusion she'd made upon his life, from the rearrangement of his furniture to the vague scent of her that wafted through the house, catching him off guard and making him ache with wanting her.

He was already in bed that night, leaning against the pillows as he listened to her perform her ablutions. It was the thirtieth of July. Tomorrow he and James would capture Oliver Prewitt and his fellow traitors. They had planned the mission out to the last detail, but Blake was still uncomfortable. And nervous. Very, very nervous. He felt prepared for the following day's work, but there were still too many variables, too many things that could go wrong.

And never before had Blake felt he had this much to lose.

When Marabelle had been alive, they had been young and thought themselves immortal. Missions for the War Office had been great adventures. It had never occurred to them that their lives might lead to anywhere other than happily ever after.

But then Marabelle had been killed and it no longer mattered if Blake thought himself immortal or not, for he had ceased caring about his own life. He hadn't been nervous before missions because he hadn't really cared about their outcomes. Oh, he wanted to see England's traitors brought to justice, but if for some reason he didn't live to see them hang . . . Well, it was no great loss to him.

But now it was different. He cared. He wanted more than anything to make it through this mission and build his marriage with Caroline. He wanted to watch her puttering about in the rose garden, and he wanted to see her face every morning on the pillow next to his. He wanted to make love to her with wild abandon, and he wanted to touch her belly as it grew round and large with their children.

He wanted everything life had to offer. Every last bit of wonder and joy. And he was terrified, because he knew how easily it could all be snatched away.

It only took one well-aimed bullet.

Blake noticed that Caroline's humming had stopped, and he looked up toward the washing room door, which was open a few inches. He heard a bit of splashing, then a rather suspicious silence.

"Caroline?" he called.

She poked her head out, a black silk scarf wrapped over her head. "She eez not here."

Blake raised a brow. "Who are you meant to be? And what did you do with my wife?"

She smiled seductively. "I am, of course, Carlotta De Leon. And eef you don't keess me now, Senor Ravenscroft, I will have to resort to my most unpleasant tacteecs."

"I shudder to think."

She slunk onto the bed and batted her eyes at him. "Don't think. Just keess."

"Oh, but I couldn't. I am an upright, moral man. I could never stray from my marriage vows."

She puckered up. "I am sure your wife weel forgive you just this once."

"Caroline?" He shook his head. "Never. She's the devil's own temper. She quite terrifies me."

"You shouldn't speak of her in such terms."

"You're quite sympathetic for a spy."

"I am unique," she said with a shrug.

He sucked his lips in an attempt not to laugh. "Aren't you Spanish?"

She raised one arm in a salute. "Viva la Queen Isabella!"

"I see. Then why are you speaking with a French accent?"

Her face fell, and she said in a normal voice, "Was I really?"

"Yes, but it was an excellent French accent," he lied.

"I've never met a Spaniard before."

"And I've never met one who sounds quite like you."

She swatted him on the shoulder. "Actually, I've never met a Frenchman, either."

"No!"

"Don't tease. I am just trying to be entertaining."

"And succeeding handily." He took her hand and rubbed his thumb across her palm. "Caroline, I want you to know that you make me very happy."

Her eyes grew suspiciously moist. "Why does this sound like a prelude to bad news?"

"We do have some serious matters to discuss."

"This concerns tomorrow's mission to capture Oliver, doesn't it?"

He nodded. "I won't lie to you and say it won't be dangerous."

"I know," she said in a small voice.

"We had to change our plans somewhat when Prewitt discovered our marriage."

"What do you mean?"

"Moreton—he's the head of the War Office—was going to send us a dozen men as backup. Now he can't."

"Why?"

"We don't want Prewitt to grow suspicious. He'll be watching me. If twelve government officials descend upon Seacrest Manor he'll know that something is afoot."

"Why can't they just be clandestine about it?" Her voice rose in volume. "Isn't that what you're supposed to do in the War Office? Sneak about under the cover of the night?"

"Don't worry, darling. We're still getting a couple of men to support us."

"Four people are not enough! You have no idea how many men are working for Oliver."

"According to his records," he said patiently, "only four. We'll be evenly matched."

"I don't want you to be evenly matched. You have to outnumber them."

He reached out to stroke her hair, but she jerked away. "Caroline," he said, "this is the way it has to be."

"No," she said defiantly. "It's not."

Blake stared at her, a very bad feeling forming in his stomach. "What do you mean?"

"I'm going with you."

He shot upright. "The devil you are!"

She scurried off the bed and planted her hands on her hips. "How are you going to do this without me? I can identify all of the men. I know the lay of the land. You don't."

"You're not coming. And that is final."

"Blake, you're not thinking clearly."

He vaulted to his feet and loomed over her. "Don't you dare accuse me of not thinking clearly. Do you think I would willingly put you in danger? Even for a minute? For the love of God, woman, you could be killed."

"So could you," she said softly.

If he heard her, he gave no indication. "I won't go through that again," he said. "If I have to tie you to the bedposts, I will, but you're not coming anywhere near the coast tomorrow night."

"Blake, I refuse to wait here at Seacrest Manor, nibbling at my nails and wondering whether or not I still have a husband."

He raked his hand through his hair in an impatient gesture. "I thought you hated this life—the danger, the intrigue. You told me you felt like throwing up the entire time we were breaking into Prewitt Manor. Why the hell would you want to come along now?"

"I do hate it!" she burst out. "I hate it so much it eats me up inside. Do you know what worry feels like? Real worry? The kind that burns a hole through your stomach and makes you want to scream?"

He closed his eyes for a moment and said softly, "I do now."

"Then you'll understand why I can't sit here and do nothing. It doesn't matter that I hate it. It doesn't matter that I'm terrified. Don't you understand that?"

"Caroline, perhaps if you were trained by the War Office. If you knew how to shoot a gun, and—"

"I can shoot a gun. I shot Percy."

"What I'm trying to tell you is that if you come along, I won't be able to concentrate on the mission. If I'm worrying about you, I'll be more likely to slip up and get myself killed."

Caroline chewed on her lower lip. "You have a point," she said slowly.

"Good," he interrupted, his voice terse. "Then it's settled."

"No, it's not. The fact remains that I can be of help. And you might need me."

He grasped her upper arms and locked his eyes onto hers. "I need you here, Caroline. Safe and sound."

She looked up at him, and saw something in his gray eyes she'd never expected—desperation. She made her decision. "Very well," she whispered. "I'll stay. But I'm not happy about it."

Her final words were muffled as he pulled her to him in a crushing embrace. "Thank you," he murmured, and she wasn't sure if he was speaking to her or to God.

The following evening was the worst Caroline had ever known. Blake and James had left shortly after the evening meal, before the sky had even grown dark. They had claimed that they needed to assess the lay of the land. When Caroline had protested that someone would notice them, they had only laughed. Blake was known as a landowner in the district, they'd replied. Why wouldn't he be out and about with one of his cronies? The two even planned to stop at a local pub for a pint in order to further the ruse that they were merely a pair of carousing noblemen.

Caroline had to allow that their words held sense, but she couldn't shake the serpentine shiver of fear crawling in her belly. She knew that she should trust her husband and James; after all, they'd been working for the War Office for years. Surely they should know what they were doing.

But something felt wrong to her. That's all it was, a pesky feeling that simply wouldn't go away. Caroline had few memories of her mother save for their stargazing outings, but she remembered her laughing once with her husband and saying something about feminine intuition being as solid as gold.

As she stood outside Seacrest Manor, Caroline looked up at the moon and stars and said, "I truly hope you had no idea what you were talking about, Mother."

She waited for the sense of peace she usually found in the night sky, but for the first time in her life, it failed her.

"Damn," she muttered. She squeezed her eyes shut and looked up again.

Nothing. She still felt awful.

"You're reading too much into this," she told herself. "You've never had even an ounce of feminine intuition in your entire life. You don't even know if your own husband loves you. Don't you think a woman with intuition would know at least *that*?"

More than anything, she wanted to hop on a horse and ride to Blake and James's rescue. Except that they probably didn't need rescuing, and she knew that Blake would never forgive her. Trust was such a precious thing, and she didn't want to destroy theirs mere days into the marriage.

Maybe if she went down to the beach, to where she and Blake first made love. Maybe there she could find a little peace.

The sky was growing darker, but Caroline turned her back on the house and walked toward the path that led to the water. She edged through the garden and had just stepped onto the rocky trail when she heard something.

Her heart froze. "Who's there?" she demanded.

Nothing.

"You're being silly," she mumbled. "Just go to the b—"

Seemingly out of nowhere, a blinding force hit her on the back and knocked her to the ground. "Don't say a word," a voice growled in her ear.

"Oliver?" she choked out.

"I said don't talk!" His hand clamped over her mouth. Hard.

It *was* Oliver. Her mind raced. What the *hell* was he doing here?

"I'm going to ask you some questions," he said in a frighteningly even voice. "And you are going to give me some answers."

Staving off panic, she nodded.

"Who does your husband work for?"

Her eyes widened, and she was thankful that he took his time removing his hand, because she had no idea what to say. When he finally let her speak, his arm still brutally wrapped around her neck, she said, "I don't know what you're talking about."

He yanked back, so that his upper arm cut into her windpipe. "Answer me!"

"I don't know! I swear!" If she gave Blake away his entire operation would be ruined. He might forgive her, but she would never forgive herself.

Oliver abruptly changed his position so that he was twisting her arm behind her back. "I don't believe you," he growled. "You're a lot of things, most of them annoying as hell, but you're not stupid. Who does he work for?"

She chewed on her lip. Oliver wasn't going to believe that she was completely in the dark, so she said, "I don't know. Sometimes he goes out, though."

"Ah, now we're getting somewhere. Where does he go?"

"I don't know."

He pulled on her arm so hard she was sure her shoulder would come out of the socket.

"I don't know!" she shrieked. "Truly, I don't."

He spun her around. "Do you know where he is right now?"

She shook her head.

"I do."

"You do?" she choked out.

He nodded, his eyes narrowing malevolently. "Imagine my surprise when I discovered him so far afield this evening."

"I don't know what you mean."

He started dragging her toward the main road. "You will." He pulled her along until they reached a small gig parked by the side of the road. The horse was peacefully chewing on grass until Oliver kicked him in the leg.

"Oliver!" Caroline said. "I'm sure that wasn't necessary."

"Shut up." He jammed her up against the side of the gig and tied her hands together with a rough piece of rope.

Caroline looked down at her hands and noted with aggravation that he was as good at tying knots as Blake had been. She'd be lucky if any blood reached her hands. "Where are you taking me?" she demanded.

"Why, to see your dear husband."

"I told you, I don't know where he is."

"And I told you, I do."

She gulped, finding it harder and harder to keep up her bravado. "Well then, where is he?"

He shoved her up into the gig, sat down behind her, and spurred the horse into motion. "Mr. Ravenscroft is presently standing on a bluff overlooking the English Channel. He has a telescope in his hand and is accompanied by the Marquis of Riverdale and two men I do not recognize."

"Perhaps they are out on some sort of scientific expedition. My husband is a great naturalist."

"Don't insult me. He has his telescope fixed on my men."

"Your men?" she echoed.

"You thought I was just another idle lackwit latching on to your money, didn't you?"

"Well, yes," Caroline admitted before she had a chance to check her tongue.

"I had plans for your fortune, yes, and don't think I've forgiven you for your betrayal, but I've been working toward my own destiny as well."

"What do you mean?"

"Ha! Wouldn't you like to know."

She caught her breath as they rounded a corner at an unsafe speed. "It appears I'm going to know very soon, Oliver, if you insist upon abducting me this way."

He looked at her assessingly.

"Watch the road!" she shrieked, nearly losing the contents of her stomach as they careened by a tree.

Oliver yanked too hard on the reins, and the horse, already a bit peeved about having been kicked, snorted and stopped short.

Caroline was jerked forward as they halted. "I think I'm going to be sick," she mumbled.

"Don't think I'm going to clean the mess if you cast up your accounts," Oliver snapped, whacking the horse with his riding crop.

"Stop hitting that poor horse!"

He whipped his head around to face her, his eyes glittering dangerously. "May I remind you that you are tied up, and I am not?"

"Your point being?"

"I give the orders."

"Well, don't be surprised if the poor creature kicks you in the head when you're not looking."

"Don't tell me how to treat my horse," he roared, and then brought the crop down again on the animal's back. They resumed their movement down the road, and once Caroline was assured that Oliver was driving at a slower pace, she said, "You were telling me about your work."

"No," he said. "I wasn't. And shut up."

She clamped her mouth closed. Oliver wasn't going to tell her anything, and she might as well use the time to devise a plan. They were moving parallel to the coast, edging ever closer to Prewitt Hall and the cove Oliver had written about in his smuggling reports. The very cove where Blake and James were waiting.

Dear God, they were going to be ambushed.

Something was wrong. Blake felt it in his bones.

"Where is he?" he hissed.

James shook his head and pulled out his pocket watch. "I don't know. The boat arrived an hour ago. Prewitt should have been here to meet them."

Blake cursed under his breath. "Caroline told me that Prewitt is always punctual."

"Could he know that the War Office is on to him?"

"Impossible." Blake lifted his telescope to his eye and focused on the beach. A small boat had dropped anchor about twenty yards out to sea. There wasn't much of a crew—so far they had spied only two men up on the deck. One of them held a pocket watch and was checking it at frequent intervals.

James nudged him and Blake passed him the scope. "Something must have happened today," Blake said. "There is no way he could have known he'd been detected."

James just nodded as he scanned the horizon. "Unless he's dead, he'll be here. He has too much money riding on this."

"And where the hell are his other men? There are supposed to be four."

James shrugged, scope still to his eye. "Maybe they're waiting for a signal from Prewitt. He might have— Wait!"

"What?"

"Someone's coming along the road."

"Who?" Blake tried to grab the scope, but James refused to relinquish it. "It's Prewitt," he said, "coming in a gig. And he's got a female with him."

"Carlotta De Leon," Blake predicted.

James slowly lowered the scope. His face had gone utterly white. "No," he whispered, "it's Caroline."

Chapter 23

san•guine *(adjective). Hopeful or confident with reference to some particular issue.*

san•guin•ar•y *(adjective). Attended by bloodshed; characterized by slaughter.*

After this night, I shall never again confuse the words sanguine *and* sanguinary.

—From the personal dictionary of Caroline Ravenscroft

Caroline squinted at the horizon, but in the dark haze of night she could see nothing. This didn't surprise her. Blake and James would never be so stupid as to use a lantern. They were probably hidden behind a rock or shrub, using the faint moonlight to spy on the activities on the shore below.

"I don't see anything," she said to Oliver. "You must be mistaken."

He turned his head slowly to face her. "You really think I'm an idiot, don't you?"

She pondered that. "No, not an idiot. Many other things, but not an idiot."

"Your husband," he said, pointing ahead, "is hiding among those trees."

"Perhaps we ought to alert him to our presence?" she asked hopefully.

"Oh, we'll alert him. Have no fear." Oliver brought the gig to a halt with a vicious yank of the reins and pushed her out to the ground. Caroline landed hard on her side, coughing on dirt and grass. She looked up just in time to see her former guardian pull out a gun.

"Oliver . . ."

He pointed the weapon at her head.

She shut her mouth.

He jerked his head to the left. "Start walking."

"But that's the cliff."

"There's a path. Follow it."

Caroline looked down. A narrow path had been carved into the steeply sloping hill. It zigged and zagged its way down to the beach, and it didn't take much more than a brisk wind to send loose pebbles rolling down the incline. It didn't look safe, but it was considerably more appealing than a bullet from Oliver's gun. She decided to follow his orders.

"I'll need you to untie my hands," she said. "For balance."

He scowled, then acquiesced, muttering, "You're no good to me dead."

She started to breathe a sigh of relief.

"Yet."

Her stomach churned.

He finished untying her hands and pushed her toward the edge, musing aloud, "Actually, you might be most useful as a widow."

This time, her stomach heaved, but she swallowed down the bile, coughing on the acidic taste in her mouth. Her heart might be racing, she might be feeling something far beyond terror, but she had to remain strong for Blake. She stepped out onto the path and began her descent.

"Don't try any false moves," he said. "You'd be wise to remember I've a gun pointed at your back."

"I'm not likely to forget it," she bit off, poking her toe out ahead of her to feel for loose rocks. Damn, but this path was treacherous at night. She'd hiked similar paths during the day, but sunlight was a powerful ally.

He jammed the barrel of the gun against her back. "Faster."

Caroline swung her arms wildly to keep her balance. When she was satisfied that she wasn't about to tumble to her death she snapped, "I'm not going to do you a bit of good dead of a broken neck. And believe me, if I start to fall, the first thing I'm grabbing is your leg."

That shut him up, and he didn't bother her again until they were safely on the beach.

* * *

"I'm going to kill her," Blake said in a low voice.

"Beg pardon, but you'll have to save her first," James reminded him. "And you might want to save your bullets for Prewitt."

Blake shot him a look that was decidedly unamused. "I'm going to bloody well tie her to the bedpost."

"You tried that once."

Blake whirled around. "How can you stand there and make bloody jokes?" he demanded. "He has my *wife*. My wife!"

"And what, pray tell, is the usefulness of cataloguing the ways and methods of punishing her? How is *that* meant to save her?"

"I told her to stay put," Blake grumbled. "She swore she wouldn't leave Seacrest Manor."

"Perhaps she listened to you, perhaps she didn't. Either way, it doesn't make a whit of difference at this juncture."

Blake turned to his best friend, his face holding an odd combination of fear and regret. "We have to save her. I don't care if we lose Prewitt. I don't care if the entire damned mission is ruined. We—"

James laid his hand on Blake's arm. "I know."

Blake motioned for the other two War Office men to gather round and quickly explained the situation. They didn't have much time to plan. Oliver was already forcing Caroline down toward the beach. But Blake had long since learned that there was no substitute for good communication, and so they huddled together for a moment as they agreed on a strategy.

Unfortunately, that was the moment that Oliver's men decided to pounce.

* * *

Once on the beach, Caroline realized that the channel waters were not as calm as she'd thought—and it wasn't the wind that provided the turbulence. A small boat she recognized as Oliver's was moored close to shore, and the soft crunch of sand under feet soon proved that they were not alone on the beach.

"Where the bloody hell have you been?"

Caroline whirled around and blinked in surprise. The voice had sounded as if it belonged to a large, burly sort of fellow, but the man who had just stepped into a shaft of moonlight was slender and disturbingly elegant.

Oliver jerked his head toward the boat and began wading out into the water, dragging Caroline along with him. "I was unavoidably detained."

The other man perused Caroline rudely. "She's quite fetching, but hardly unavoidable."

"Not so fetching," Oliver said derisively, "but quite married to an agent of the War Office."

Caroline gasped and stumbled to her knees, soaking the length of her skirts.

Oliver let out a bark of triumphant laughter. "Merely a theory, my dear Caroline, and one you have just affirmed."

She staggered back to her feet, spluttering and swearing at herself all the while. How could she have been so stupid? She knew better than to show a reaction, but Oliver had surprised her.

"Are you an idiot?" the other man hissed. "The French are paying us enough for this shipment to set us up for life. If you've compromised our chances—"

"Shipment?" Caroline asked. She'd thought that Oliver had been carrying secret messages and documents. But the word *shipment* seemed to indicate something bigger. Could they be smuggling ammunition? Weapons? The boat didn't look big enough to be carrying something so large.

The men ignored her. "The wife of an agent," the stranger muttered. "Sweet hell, you're stupid. The last thing we need is attention from the War Office."

"We already had attention," Oliver shot back, pulling Caroline along with him into ever deeper waters. "Blake Ravenscroft and the Marquis of Riverdale are up on the bluff. They've been watching you all night. If it hadn't been for me—"

"If it hadn't been for you," the other man interrupted, yanking Caroline against him, "we would never have been detected in the first place. Ravenscroft and Riverdale certainly didn't learn of our assignation from me."

"You know my husband?" Caroline said, too surprised to even struggle.

"I know *of* him," he replied. "And by tomorrow, so will all of France."

"Dear God," she whispered. Oliver must be smuggling out a list of agents. Agents who would then be targets for assassination. Agents like Blake and James.

She thought of ten different plans all at once and dismissed them all. A scream seemed useless; if Blake was watching the beach, he'd surely already have seen her and would not need to be alerted to her presence. And attacking either Oliver or the French agent would only get her killed. The only possibility was to somehow stall for time until Blake and James arrived.

But then what would happen? They would have no element of surprise. Oliver knew they were there.

She caught her breath. Oliver seemed rather unconcerned with the War Office's presence. Without thinking, she jerked her gaze up to the clifftop, but saw nothing.

"Your husband isn't going to save you," Oliver said with cruel satisfaction. "My men are taking care of him even as we speak."

"Then why did you bring me here?" she whispered, her heart shattering within her chest. "You didn't need me."

He shrugged. "Whimsy. I wanted him to know I had you. I wanted him to see me give you to Davenport."

The man he called Davenport chuckled and pulled her closer. "She may prove entertaining."

Oliver scowled. "Before I let you make off with her—"

"I can go nowhere until the shipment arrives," Davenport bit off. "Where the hell is she?"

She? Caroline blinked and tried not to show a reaction.

"She's coming," Oliver snapped. "And how long have you known about Ravenscroft?"

"A few days. Perhaps a week. You are not my only means of transport."

"You should have told me," Oliver growled.

"You have given me no reason to trust you with anything other than the providing of a boat."

Caroline took advantage of the two men's absorption in their argument to scan the beach and cliff for any signs of action. Blake was up there fighting for his life and there wasn't a damned thing she could do about it. She had never felt so utterly hopeless in all her life. Even with her parade of horrible guardians, she'd always held on to hope that eventually her life would turn aright. But if Blake were to be killed . . .

She choked on a sob. It was too awful even to contemplate.

And then, out of the corner of her eye, she saw movement at the bottom of the path on which she'd just descended. She fought the urge to jerk her head and stare; if it was Blake or James come to rescue her, she didn't want to ruin the element of surprise.

But as the figure crept closer, Caroline realized that it was far too small to be Blake or James, or any man for that matter. In fact, it moved in a way that was decidedly female.

Her lips parted with shock. Carlotta De Leon. It had to be. The irony was astounding.

Carlotta moved closer, quietly clearing her throat once she was in earshot. Oliver and Davenport stopped arguing immediately and turned to her.

"Do you have it?" Davenport demanded.

Carlotta nodded and spoke, her voice tinged by a vague, lilting accent. "It was too dangerous to bring the list. But I have committed it to memory."

Caroline stared at the woman who was, in a way, responsible for her marriage to Blake. Carlotta was petite, with alabaster skin and black hair. Her eyes had an aged look to them, as if they belonged to someone much older.

"Who is this woman?" Carlotta asked.

"Caroline Trent," Oliver replied.

"Caroline Ravenscroft," she snapped.

"Ah, yes, Ravenscroft. How silly of me to forget that you are now a wife." Oliver pulled out his pocket watch and snapped it open. "Forgive me, now a widow."

"I'll see you in hell," she hissed.

"Of that I have no doubt, but I do believe that you will be seeing far more interesting sights with Mr. Davenport first."

Caroline completely forgot that the aforementioned Mr. Davenport was holding her arm, and she lunged at Oliver. Davenport held firm, but she managed to land one good punch against Oliver's stomach. He doubled over in pain but unfortunately didn't lose his grasp on his gun.

"My compliments," Davenport said in a low, mocking voice. "I've been wanting to do that for months."

Caroline whirled around. "Whose side are you on?"

"My own. Always." And then he lifted his arm, displaying for the first time a dark, gleaming pistol, and shot Oliver in the head.

Caroline screamed. Her body shook with recoil of the gun, and her ears buzzed and rang from the explosion. "Oh, my God," she whimpered. "Oh, my God." She had no great love for Oliver; she'd even agreed to furnish the government with information that might send him to the gallows, but this . . . this was too much. Blood on her dress and in the foamy surf, Oliver's body floating facedown in the water . . .

She wrenched herself away from Davenport and threw up. When she was able to stand again, she turned to her new captor and asked, simply, "Why?"

He shrugged. "He knew too much."

Carlotta looked at Caroline and then slowly and purposefully shifted her gaze to Davenport. "So," she said, in that delicately Spanish accent Caroline was coming to detest, "does she."

Blake's first thought upon hearing the shot was that his life was over.

His second thought was exactly the same, although not for the same reasons. As soon as he realized that he wasn't dead, and that James had managed to bring down the villain who'd been attempting to shoot him with a well-placed blow to the head, it occurred to him that the shot he'd heard had not been nearly loud enough to have been fired up on the cliff.

It had come from down on the beach, and that could mean only one thing. Caroline was dead. And his life was over.

His weapon slipped from his hands, and for a moment he was completely limp, unable to move. Out of the corner of his eye, he saw one of Prewitt's men charge toward him, and it was only at the last moment he regained enough presence of mind to whirl around and kick the man in the stomach. He went down with a grunt of pain, and Blake just stood over him, his mind still ringing with the sound of the gunshot on the beach.

Dear God, he'd never told her he loved her.

James came running to his side, a piece of rope dangling from his hands. "This is the last of them," he said, kneeling down to tie up the fallen man.

Blake said nothing.

James didn't appear to notice his friend's distress. "We've one man down, but I think he'll live. Just a knife wound in the shoulder. The bleeding is almost under control."

Blake saw her face, her laughing blue-green eyes, and the delicately arched upper lip that begged to be kissed. He could hear her voice, whispering words of love, words he'd never returned.

"Blake?"

James's voice pulled his mind out of its painful vise, and he looked down.

"We need to get going."

Blake just looked back out at the sea.

"Blake? Blake? Are you all right?" James stood and began patting his friend down, searching for injuries.

"No, I—" And then he saw it. A body floating in the surf. Blood in the water. And Caroline—alive!

Blake's mind snapped back to life. So, too, did his body. "What's the best way down?" he asked curtly. "We haven't long."

James regarded the manner in which the man and the woman holding Caroline hostage were arguing. "No," he agreed, "we don't."

Blake retrieved his weapon from the ground and turned to James and William Chartwell, the uninjured War Office man. "We need to get down as silently as possible."

"There are two paths," Chartwell said. "I surveyed the area yesterday. There is the one Prewitt used to force her to the beach, and another, but—"

"Where is it?" Blake interrupted.

"Over there," Chartwell replied with a jerk of his head, "but—"

Blake was already off and running.

"Wait!" Chartwell hissed. "This one is steep. It will be impossible at night."

Blake crouched at the head of the path and peered down, the moonlight affording him precious little illumination. Unlike the other path, this one was shielded from view by trees and shrubs. "This is our only hope of getting down undetected."

"It's suicide!" Chartwell exclaimed.

Blake whirled around. "My wife is about to be murdered." And then, without waiting to see if either of his colleagues cared to follow him, he started the slow and treacherous journey to the beach. It was agony not to be able to race headlong down the hillside. Every second was critical if he wanted to return home to Seacrest Manor with Caroline safely in his arms. But the terrain wouldn't allow anything other than the tiniest of baby steps. As it was, he had to make most of the journey sideways to keep from losing his balance.

He heard a small pebble rolling down the path and then felt it hit his ankle. The disturbance could only mean—thank God!—that James was following him. As for Chartwell, Blake didn't know the man well enough to predict what he would do, but he had enough confidence in the War Office to know that at least he would do nothing to jeopardize Caroline's rescue.

As he descended, the wind shifted and began carrying sounds from the beach. The man and the woman holding Caroline hostage were arguing. Prewitt's voice was conspicuously absent, and Blake could only assume that his was the body floating in the surf.

Then he heard a sharp cry from Caroline. Blake forced himself to calm down. She sounded more surprised than in pain, and he needed to retain a cool head if he was to make it to the bottom of the path in one piece.

He reached a small ledge and stopped to catch his breath and reassess the situation. A few seconds later, James was at his side.

"What's happening?" James asked.

"I'm not sure. She looks unharmed, but I still have no idea how we're meant to get out there and save her. Especially when they're all standing in the water."

"Can she swim?"

"Bloody hell. I have no idea."

"Well, she grew up near the coast, so we can hope. And— Good Lord!"

"What?"

James's head slowly swiveled to face him. "That's Carlotta De Leon."

"Are you sure?"

"Positive."

Blake sensed that his friend had more to say. "And . . . ?"

"And it means we're in worse trouble than we'd feared." James swallowed. "Miss De Leon's as ruthless as they come, and a fanatic to the cause. She'd shoot Caroline in the heart with one hand and use the other to flip pages in a Bible."

* * *

Caroline knew she was running out of time. Davenport had no pressing reasons to keep her alive. He clearly only intended to have what he considered a little sport with her. He probably thought it would be exciting to have his way with the wife of an agent of the crown.

Carlotta, on the other hand, was motivated by more political reasons, most of which involved the collapse of the British Empire. And it was obvious that the woman believed passionately in her cause.

Her two captors were bickering over Caroline's fate, and she had no doubt that the argument was going to escalate into a full-scale shouting match before long. She also had no doubt that Carlotta would emerge the victor. It was a simple enough outcome to predict; Davenport could always find another woman to pester. Carlotta wasn't likely to find another country she wanted to destroy.

And that meant that Caroline would end up very dead if she didn't do something soon.

She was still held firmly in Davenport's grasp, but she twisted until she was facing Carlotta, and blurted out, "They're after you already."

Carlotta froze, then turned slowly to Caroline. "What, precisely, do you mean?"

"They know you're in the country. They want to see you hang."

Carlotta laughed. "They don't even know who I am."

"Oh, yes, they do," Caroline replied, "Miss De Leon."

Carlotta's knuckles turned white around the handle of her gun. "Who are you?"

This time it was Caroline's turn to laugh. "Would

you believe I am the woman who was mistaken for you? Amusing but true."

"There is only one man who has ever seen me . . ."

"The Marquis of Riverdale," Caroline supplied. Oliver had already said his and Blake's names, so there didn't seem much need for secrecy.

"If I might interrupt . . ." came Davenport's sarcastic voice.

BANG!

The force was so great, Caroline was sure she'd been shot. But then she realized two things: she felt no pain, and Davenport's grip had gone utterly slack.

She swallowed convulsively and turned around. Two bodies were now floating in the water. "Why did you do that?"

"He bothered me."

Caroline's empty stomach churned and heaved.

"I never knew his name," Carlotta said softly.

"Who?"

"The marquis."

"Well, he certainly knows yours."

"Why do you tell me this?"

"Self-preservation, pure and simple."

"And how is this meant to save you?"

Caroline's lips curved into an enigmatic smile. "If I know this much, just think what else I could tell you."

The Spanish woman's stare was hard and steely. "If you know too much," she said with eerie softness, "then why shouldn't I kill you right now?"

Caroline fought for her composure. Her knees were trembling, and her hands were shaking, but she hoped Carlotta would just attribute that to the cold water swirling around her calves. She had no idea whether Blake was dead or alive, but either way, she had to remain strong. If he had—God forbid—been killed up on the hill, she was damned if she was going to let his life's work be completely destroyed by this tiny, dark-haired woman. She didn't care if she died in the process, but she wasn't going to let that list of War Office agents out of the country.

"I didn't say I know too much," Caroline finally said. "But I might know exactly what you need."

There was a terrifying moment of silence, and then Carlotta lifted her gun. "I'll take my chances."

In that moment Caroline realized she'd been lying to herself. She *did* care if she died. She wasn't ready yet to leave this world. She didn't want to feel the pain of a gunshot wound, to know that a bullet had torn her skin and her lifeblood was seeping out into the cold waters of the English Channel.

And God help her, she couldn't die without learning of Blake's fate.

"You can't!" she yelled. "You can't kill me."

Carlotta smiled. "Oh?"

"You're out of bullets."

"I have another gun."

"You'll never escape without me."

"Is that so?"

Caroline nodded frantically, then spied something that made her so thankful she was one inch away from committing herself to a convent just to show her gratitude.

"And why, pray tell, is that?"

"Because the boat is leaving."

Carlotta whirled around, saw Oliver's boat heading back out to open waters, and spat out a word Caroline had never before heard spoken in a female voice.

When Blake's feet hit the gravelly beach, it was all he could do not to race into the ocean and yank his wife to safety. But he'd chosen the steeper path so as not to lose the element of surprise, and he knew he had to proceed with care and caution. James landed softly next to him a moment later, and together they surveyed the scene.

Carlotta seemed to have gone positively unhinged, waving her fist and screaming curses at the receding boat, and Caroline was inching slowly backward, edging ever closer to the beach.

But just when she'd managed to go far enough so that she might possibly be able to run to safety, Carlotta whirled around and leveled her gun at Caroline's midsection.

"You're not going anywhere," she said in a deadly voice.

"Couldn't we at least get out of the water?" Caroline replied. "I can't feel my feet any longer."

Carlotta nodded curtly. "Move slowly. One false move and I'll shoot you dead. I swear I will."

"I believe you," Caroline replied, with a meaningful glance toward Davenport's body.

Slowly, without ever taking their eyes off each other, the two women moved out of the water and onto the beach.

From his hiding place behind a tree, Blake watched the entire interchange. He felt James edge closer to him, then heard his whisper in his ear.

"Wait until they get a little closer."

"For what?" Blake asked in response.

But the marquis made no reply.

Blake watched Carlotta like a hawk, waiting for the exact right moment to shoot the gun out of her hand. There was no finer shot in all of England, and Blake was confident he could do it, but not while Caroline was blocking his way.

But then, before Blake could stop him, James stepped suddenly out into the clearing, both of his hands in the air.

"Let her go," the marquis said in a low voice. "I'm the one you want."

Carlotta's head swung around. "You!"

"In the flesh."

Caroline's mouth fell open. "James?"

Carlotta's gun made an arc through the air as she changed her aim. "I have been dreaming about this day," she hissed.

James jerked his head to signal to Caroline to move out of the way. "Is that all you've been dreaming about?" he purred.

Caroline caught her breath. James sounded positively seductive. What on earth had happened between those two? And where was Blake?

"Caroline," James said in forceful tones. "Move aside. This is between Miss De Leon and me."

Caroline had no idea what he was up to, but she wasn't about to leave him to the mercy of a woman who looked as if she wanted to skin him alive. "James," she said, "maybe I—"

"*MOVE!*" he roared.

She did, and in less than a second a shot rang out. Carlotta howled in pain and surprise, and

James charged forward, pinning her to the ground. There was a scuffle, but James outweighed the tiny Spanish woman by a good six stone, and she didn't have a chance.

Caroline ran forward to help, but before she reached them, she, too, was tackled from the side.

"Blake? Oh, Blake!" She threw herself into his arms. "I thought I would never see you again."

He crushed her to him and held with all his might. "Caroline," he gasped, "when I saw . . . When I heard . . ."

"I thought you were dead. Oliver said you were dead."

Blake clutched at her, still unable to believe that she was safe. He knew he was holding her too tightly, that her tender skin would bruise from the force of it, but he couldn't let go. "Caroline," he said hoarsely, "I have to tell you—"

"I didn't leave Seacrest Manor!" she interrupted, her words coming out in a rush of air. "I swear it. I wanted to, but I didn't because I didn't want to betray your trust. But then Oliver snatched me, and—"

"I don't care." He shook his head, aware of the tears rolling down his cheeks but completely at the mercy of his emotions. "I don't care about that. I thought you were going to die, and . . ."

She whispered his name and touched his cheek, and he was undone.

"I love you, Caroline. I love you. And you were going to die, and all I could think—"

"Oh, Blake."

He held on tight to her arms, his entire body strangely off balance. "All I could think was that I would never be able to tell you, and you would never hear me say it, and—"

Caroline placed a finger against his lips. "I love you, Blake Ravenscroft."

"And I love you, Caroline Ravenscroft."

"And I don't much love Carlotta De Leon," James grunted. "So if one of you is inclined to help me, I'd like to tie her up and be done with her."

Blake broke away from his wife with a sheepish expression on his face. "Sorry, Riverdale."

Caroline followed and watched as the Spanish spy was bound and gagged. "How do you mean to get her up the hill?"

"Oh, bloody hell," James muttered. "I certainly don't want to carry her."

Blake sighed. "I suppose we could send out a boat tomorrow."

"Oh!" Caroline exclaimed. "That reminds me! I nearly forgot. I saw the people on Oliver's boat before they sailed off. It was Miles Dudley, just as we thought. I didn't recognize the other man, but I'm certain if you apprehend Mr. Dudley, he will lead you to him."

At that moment, Chartwell skidded down the hill. "What happened?" he asked.

"I'm surprised you didn't see it all from the safety of the cliff," Blake said bitterly.

But James's face lit up. "No, no, Ravenscroft, don't scold the lad. He's just in time."

Chartwell looked suspicious. "Just in time for what?"

"Why, to guard Miss De Leon. We'll send out a boat to fetch the both of you in the morning. And while you're at it, you can pull those two bodies out of the water."

Chartwell just nodded, knowing he had no choice.

Blake looked up the hill. "Damn, I'm tired."

"Oh, we don't need to go up the path," Caroline said, pointing east. "If you don't mind walking a half mile or so down the beach, the cliff disappears, and it's a relatively flat walk to the road."

"I'll take the path," James said.

"Are you certain?" she asked with a frown. "You must be terribly weary."

"Someone has to fetch the horses. You two go ahead. I'll meet you on the road." And before either of the Ravenscrofts could argue, James had taken his leave and was scrambling up the steep path.

Blake smiled and tugged on Caroline's hand. "Riverdale is a very smart man."

"Oh, really?" She tripped along behind him, leaving Chartwell to guard the prisoner. "And what prompted you to make that observation at this time?"

"I have a feeling he would be a bit uncomfortable accompanying us."

"Oh? Why?"

Blake offered her his most earnest expression. "Well, as you know, there are certain aspects of marriage that require privacy."

"I see," she said gravely.

"I might have to kiss you once or twice on the way back."

"Only twice?"

"Possibly three times."

She pretended to think about that. "I don't think three times will be nearly enough."

"Four?"

She laughed, shook her head, and ran down the beach.

"Five?" he offered, his long strides easily keeping up with her. "Six. I can promise six, and I'll try for seven . . ."

"Eight!" she yelled. "But only if you catch me."

He broke into a run and tackled her to the ground. "Caught you!"

She swallowed, and her eyes filled with sentimental tears. "Yes, you did. It's rather funny, actually."

Blake touched her cheek, smiling down at her with all the love in the world. "What?"

"Oliver set out to catch an heiress, you set out to catch a spy. And in the end . . ." Her words trailed off, and her voice choked with emotion.

"In the end?"

"In the end, I caught you."

He kissed her once, lightly. "You certainly did, my love. You certainly did."

Selections from the Personal Dictionary of Caroline Ravenscroft

July 1815
non·par·eil *(noun). A person or thing having no equal; something unique.*

A year of marriage and still I think my husband a nonpareil!

November 1815
e·da·cious *(adjective). Devoted to eating, voracious.*

I am quite hungry now that I am carrying a child,

but still I am not as edacious *as I was those days while trapped in Blake's washing room.*

May 1816
trea·tise *(noun). A book or writing which treats some particular subject.*

Blake finds so much in our two-day-old son to boast over; I anticipate a treatise *on the topic of David's intellect and charm any day now.*

January 1818
col·la·tion *(noun). A light meal or repast.*

This confinement is nothing like the last; it is a blessed day when I can even manage to partake of a cold collation.

August 1824
cur·sive *(adjective). Of writing; written with a running hand, so that the characters are rapidly formed without raising the pen, and in consequence, have their angles rounded and separate strokes formed, and at length become slanted.*

Today I tried to instruct Trent in the art of cursive *writing, but Blake intervened, stating (rather impertinently, in my opinion) that I have the handwriting of a chicken.*

June 1826
prog•e•ny *(noun). Descent, family, offspring.*
Our progeny *insist that the holes dotting the wall around Blake's dartboard were made by a wild bird somehow trapped in the house, but I find this explanation implausible.*

February 1827
eu•pho•ni•ous *(adjective). Pleasing to the ear.*

We have named her Cassandra in honor of my mother, but we both agree that the name has a most euphonious *ring to it.*

June 1827
be•a•ti•fic *(adjective). Making blessed, imparting supreme happiness.*

Perhaps I am a foolish and sentimental woman, but sometimes I pause to look around at all that is so precious to me—Blake, David, Trent, Cassandra—and I am so overcome with joy I must wear a beatific *smile on my face for days. Life, I think—I know!—is good, so very, very good.*